HIGHLAND BORN

A Scottish Medieval Romance
Highland Legion Series

By Kathryn Le Veque

KATHRYN LE VEQUE
NOVELS

Every family has legends behind it, but no family more so than the Dun Tarh clan.

Tucked deep in the Highlands of Scotland and relatives to the MacKenzie clan, the family is said to have been spawned from the lost Roman legion, the elite Ninth Hispania. For generations, the family was known for their dark men, quick to temper, fierce fighters with comely looks. They were greatly respected in the Highlands until Lares Rayan dun Tarh became the head of the family, a former priest who had fallen from grace.

Lucifer, they called him.

And his sons were known as Lucifer's Highland Legion.

Aurelius dun Tarh is the eldest son of what many consider Lares' unholy union. Highlander born but English trained because of his English mother, Aurelius is a man of two worlds. Enormous and powerful, he is the first of many handsome brothers, and it's no secret that there is probably more than one dun Tarh bastard roaming about the Highlands.

For all of his talent and power, however, Aurelius is a man of discontent. His English grandfather insists he fight in France for Edward III, so Aurelius finds himself fighting alongside men who should be his enemy, but men he nonetheless shares an alliance with.

A man of two worlds, indeed.

As a reward for his performance at the Battle of Crécy, Aurelius is presented with a bride from one of the great English warlords. The Earl of Wolsingham has no male heirs, and he wants Aurelius. Unable to protest, Aurelius finds himself betrothed to one of the richest heiresses in England… and absolutely hating it.

Valery de Leybourne, daughter of Wolsingham, doesn't like the idea of being married to a Highlander, either. A spitfire of a woman, Aurelius learns that aspect of her the hard way. He further realizes that he may very well enjoy this marriage because Valery and her spark entertains him to no end. But before the marriage can take place, an explosive family secret is revealed that might possibly ruin both families…

And it has nothing to do with Aurelius or Valery, but it could very well mean their end.

HOUSE OF DUN TARH MOTTO

Numquam vici, semper timui

Never conquered, always feared

Author's Note

This is my first official Highlander/Scottish series and, I have to say, that I'm pretty darn excited about it!

What took me so long, you ask? Nothing in particular—I simply like my English knights, but I felt a calling to head to Scotland. My fascination stems from the legendary lost legions—and there are a few—but none so famous as the Ninth Hispania. I've incorporated their mascot, the bull, into the dun Tarh's family shield. In fact, "*tarbh*" is "bull" in Gaelic and the family took that name back in the Dark Ages, but over the centuries, the spelling changed to Tarh—pronounced "Tar."

A reminder of the family's legendary origins.

Something else that is a reminder of their origins is the fact that all of the men in the family tend to have Roman names. Some have Spanish names, but most tend to be Roman as a tribute to their origins. The lost Ninth Hispania legion has been an endless source of fascination for historians down the ages because no one is really sure what happened to it. It was a big, prestigious legion that went over the Antonine Wall and then… nothing. Most historians agree that they simply assimilated into the local populations, which is probably what happened. Or it might have been alien abductions or a time warp. When speaking of the mysterious Scottish Highlands, anything is possible. (And I'm kidding about the aliens!)

So, let's talk a little about this book, because it's a big one.

The story is broken down into three parts because it's fairly complex. There are multifaceted storylines and more than one love story because the entire theme of this tale is true love. That's always the theme in my books (because I'm a romance writer!), some more strongly than others, but this one in particular is full of that theme because the emphasis is on the fact that there are many forms of true love. Man to wife, mother to child, grandparent to grandchild, friend to friend, etc.

Part of the tale involves the Battle of Crécy. We're in the mid-fourteenth century now, so we're about a hundred years, give or take, from the bulk of the de Wolfe Pack (William de Wolfe's series) and about a hundred and fifty years from the House of de Lohr (Christopher de Lohr's series). However, I have the north of England so crowded with houses and people that, inevitably, some of them are going to show up in this tale. Even though our hero is a Highlander, his lady love is not—she's English. There will be several recognizable names in this story, including a mention of Dragonblade himself—Tate de Lara.

Don't think the title is a misnomer—it implies this is a Scottish tale and the hero is, indeed, Scottish. So are more than half the characters. But the vast majority takes place in the Northern England/border area because that's where the heroine is from, and, like any good groom, Aurelius goes to her—not the other way around. She's an heiress, and he's been forced into a betrothal, as you'll see, so he goes to her great castle—and that's where the story happens and happens quickly.

And with that, let's go to our usual pronunciation guide:

Lares—LAHR-ees

Davina—Duh-VEE-nuh

Tarh—Tar (there's almost an "L" sound on the end of it, but not quite)

Leannan—a Scottish Gaelic term for sweetheart

There's a family tree and a castle floor plan on the next pages—hand-drawn by me! I don't profess to be an artist, but I sometimes draw out the castle layouts to better help me when I'm writing, so I thought I'd share the drawing with you as a peek into my process. I'm a visual thinker (and learner!), so the layouts go a long way in helping me flesh things out.

And now, let me introduce you to Aurelius and Valery. I think you're going to love them.

Happy Reading!

Dun Tarh Family Tree

*Children of Lares and Mabel**

Aurelius

Darien

Estevan "Stevan"

Lilliana

Caelus

Kaladin "Kal"

Lucan

Leandro

Cruz

Zora

- *Mabel is a descendant of Ajax de Velt through his son, Cole*

CASTLE HYDRA FLOOR PLAN

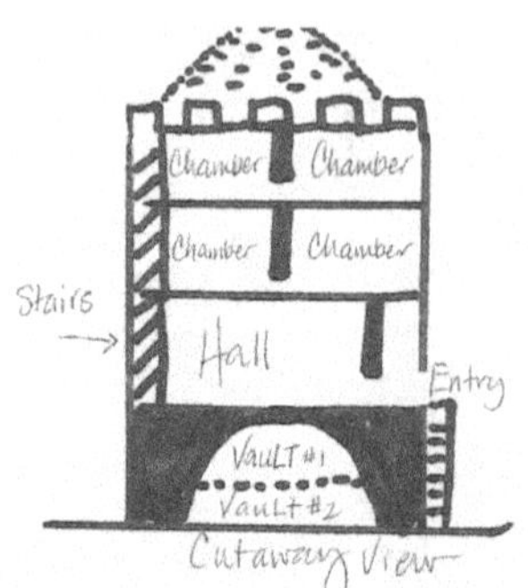

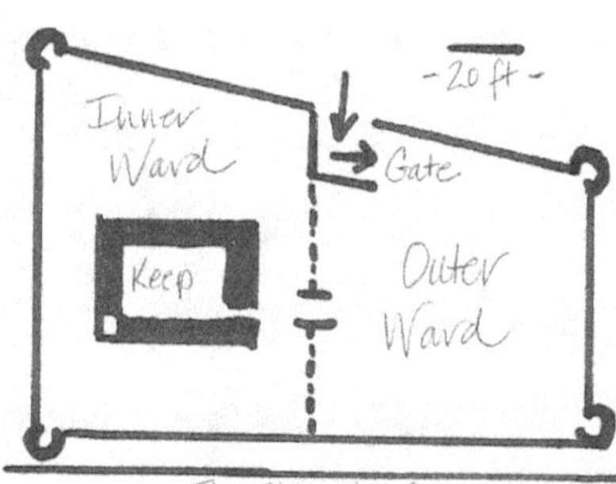

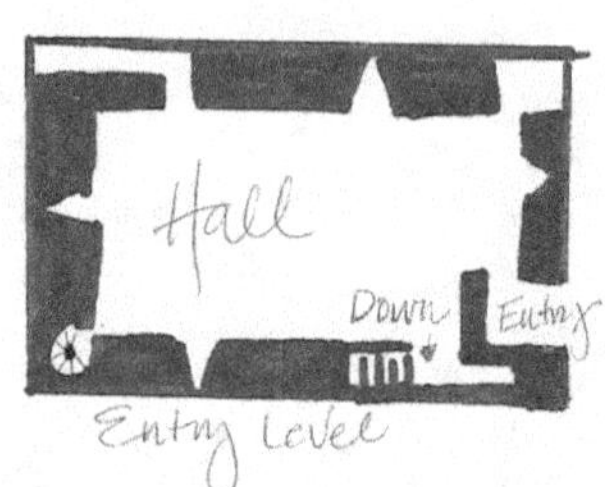

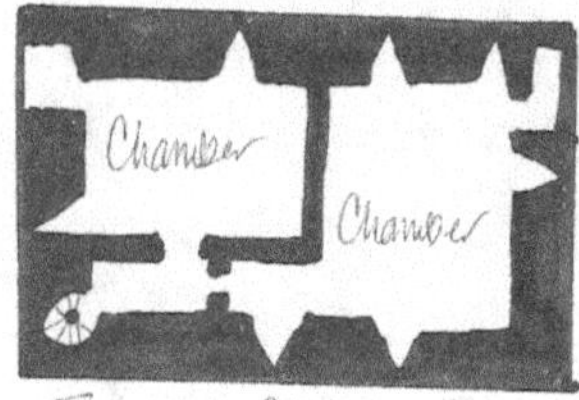

"Castle Hydra"
also Known as "The Hydra"

Lydgate Castle Floor Plan

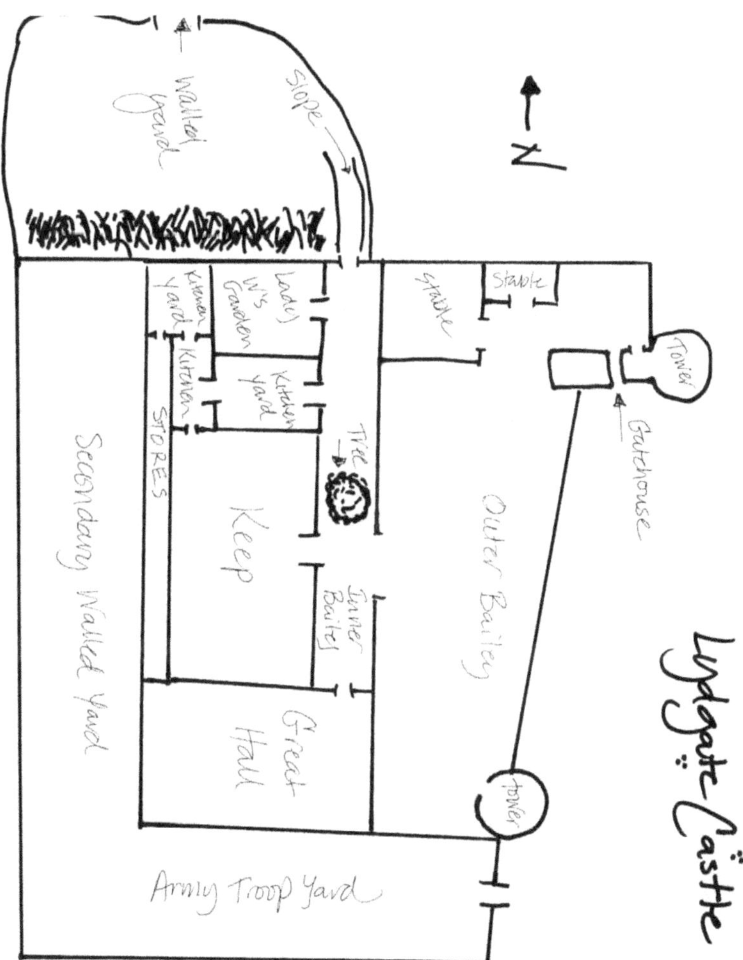

PROLOGUE

Year of Our Lord 1380
Castle Hydra, Scotland
The Highlands

IT WAS A night made of diamonds.

In the black expanse above the gray-stoned castle lit by hundreds of torches, the heavens glittered as if someone had thrown handfuls of diamonds across darkness, and even when the diamonds fell back to earth, as diamonds sometimes do, another diamond took its place. Those diamonds glowed and twinkled, bestowing the blessings of the universe upon the heads of the newlyweds at Castle Hydra.

It was rare when the place was filled with warmth and utter joy.

A place that was, quite possibly, the most cursed castle in Scotland.

But not tonight. Tonight the wine and ale flowed freely, the music filled the night, and the guests were either drunk or dancing or both. When the people of the Highlands celebrated, it was a celebration like no other.

The Hydra, as the castle was referred to, was lit up like the surface of the sun. It was the joining of two great families, even if one of the families happened to be English. Still, they were great allies to the dun Tarh family, a family that had been in possession of the Hydra for centuries. They were the Earls of Torridon, a title given to one of the dun Tarh ancestors a few generations back, a title held by Lares dun Tarh. The earldom of Torridon cut out a vast swath of land from Clan MacKenzie territories, something Clan MacKenzie accepted because Clan dun Tarh was related to them by marriage several times over. The land had come to dun Tarh through the first Earl of Torridon, who had married a Scottish clan chief's daughter.

As part of her dowry, she brought the land with her.

Lands and glens and mountains that belonged to perhaps one of the most legendary families in the Highlands, and Castle Hydra came with it. Lares, in fact, was sitting in the lord's hall, the largest chamber in the tower portion of Hydra, but still smaller than the great hall, which was filled with soldiers and Highlanders on this night. They had every right to celebrate the wedding of one of Lares' granddaughters, as part of the family, because half of the soldiers were members of the clan. Highlanders were known to breed prolifically, and someone was always someone else's cousin or brother or uncle. Therefore, this was really a family celebration, as far as Lares was concerned.

He watched with great satisfaction.

"There you are." An older woman with graying red hair and green eyes found him as he sat in a window seat of the lord's hall. She sat down next to him, handing him a cup of something warm. "I had the cook warm some wine for you, just the way you like it."

Lares smiled affectionately at his wife. "Ye do me proud,

Mabel," he said, taking the almost-hot cup from her. He hissed and set it down quickly beside him. "Good Lord, lass, do ye mean to burn my fingers off?"

She shushed him, touching the cup to see how hot it really was. "You complain like an old woman," she said. "Drink it up before one of your sons comes over here and takes it from you."

"They've been known to do that."

"Aye, they have."

"They'd take food out of my mouth and watch me starve, too."

"You've raised a selfish lot, Lares dun Tarh."

"They're yer sons, too."

"Only when they are being obedient."

He snorted before lifting the cup to his lips and drinking in the rich, spicy wine. "Ah," he said, smacking his lips. "'Tis good, it is. Ye're too good to me, Mae. I love ye for it."

Mabel fought off a grin, slapping weakly at him when he tried to pinch her thigh. "Off with you, you devil," she said. "You'll not get frisky with me."

"Ye're my wife. I can get frisky with ye whenever I want."

She shook her head. "You'll give yerself heart failure if you try," she said. "I do not think your old bones could stand the excitement."

He just laughed at her, his lovely Mabel. The woman had given birth to ten children, eight sons and two daughters, all of them having survived into adulthood. She had eight of the most powerful, strapping sons a woman could hope for. Highlanders of the most elite and worthiest kind. Considering she was only half-Scots, and from the Lowlands as well, she proved that she had just as much strength and honor in her as anyone alive. Mabel Coleby Douglas dun Tarh was a woman among women, but only a few knew just how deep that strength and honor ran.

But Lares did.

"Ye're a good lass, Mae," he said, taking her hand as he leaned into her. "I dunna know what I would have done without ye all these years."

Mabel was looking across the hall to her granddaughter and her new husband as they tried to navigate the dun Tarh mob of brothers and uncles and cousins. "You would have withered away and died," she said. "You are fortunate I have a soft spot for you."

He laid his big head on her shoulder. "More than ye know," he said, kissing her shoulder even though it was covered by her sleeve. "It does me good that we can watch Gabriela marry. That we can share this moment."

Mabel, who wasn't particularly soft or romantic in public, glanced at him. "We've watched our own children marry," she said. "Time is moving on. Now, our grandchildren are marrying, one by one. They grow up and we grow old."

He stopped leaning on her long enough to drink from his cup again. "Ye'll never be old, lass," he said. "Ye're ageless."

"I do not know what you're up to with this flattery, but my shift stays on tonight."

Lares burst out laughing, putting an arm around her and pulling her to him. She fought off a grin as her husband of many years gave her a wet kiss on the cheek, finally breaking down in a smile as he kissed her again. They looked at one another, smiling as only two people who have been in love for many years could do, when they heard a high-pitched, female voice.

"Mamie! Nonno!"

They turned to see their granddaughter, the bride, heading

in their direction. She was waving at them, finally climbing in between them to sit down on the stone bench as Lares set his cup aside and embraced her. Gabriela dun Tarh was the daughter of his eldest son, Aurelius. Dressed in a pale blue gown that had once belonged to her mother's mother, and with a wreath of flowers in her hair, she was sweet and affectionate and full of fire.

Lares adored her.

"Are ye happy, lassie?" he asked her. "Must I speak to yer groom and tell him what will happen if he mistreats ye?"

Gabriela grinned, looking very much like her grandmother in that gesture. "He knows," she said, with an accent somewhere between a Scots and an English because she'd fostered at Northwood Castle on the Scots-English border. "Da spoke to him, as did all of my brothers. Bas knows that if he so much as raises his voice to me, half of the Highlands will come down on him."

Lares approved of that greatly. He hugged her again, handing her his cup of warmed wine, which she drank from happily. She was on her third swallow when Mabel reached out and took it away.

"Enough," she said softly, watching her granddaughter wipe her mouth with the back of her hand. "You do not want to be swill-headed tonight."

Gabriela laid her head on Mabel's shoulder. "I will not be, I promise," she said. "I feel fine. I feel happy. Bas is a good man, Mamie. He comes from a very fine family."

Mabel was looking over at the corner of the hall where the groom's family was. "A very *tall* family," she said, because the raven-haired groom and the men of his family were at least a head taller than anyone else in the room. "The Pemburys have height and handsomeness to their credit. Let us hope they have honor and brains as well."

Gabriela giggled. "What a thing to say," she said. "I'll have you know that Sebastian of Pembury is a very honorable man. He's been married before, so he knows how to treat a wife. I know he's a good deal older than I am, but he's kind and handsome and I love him. We will be very happy together, you'll see."

Mabel looked at her. "I am sure you will be," she said softly. "But he has children, Gabby. He's bringing children from a dead wife into this marriage, and the best thing you can do for those children is to be kind to them. The youngest one needs a mother, but the older ones... I am certain they could use a friend. Let Bas be the parent. You will simply be someone who is good to them."

Gabriela nodded. It was no secret that Sebastian of Pembury was twenty years older than she was, a man who had lost his wife to childbirth, leaving behind an infant and four older children. He had been serving at Northwood Castle, a mighty bastion along the Scots border full of English knights. Gabriela had met him when a Northwood contingent had come to one of the dun Tarh clan's Lowland castles for a conclave. Gabriela had only been at Ashkirk Castle because she'd begged and pleaded for her father to take her with him, because she was bored to tears at the Hydra and wanted to travel. So, he'd relented. And she'd met her husband.

That was something Aurelius dun Tarh was grateful for, but he was also slightly remorseful.

He'd made it no secret that he would miss his daughter.

"I will be good to the children, I promise," Gabriela said, her manner softening. "I've had time to come to know them, and I like them already. The older children are fostering, of course, but the baby is very sweet. She's asleep upstairs, even now."

Mabel smiled. "I know," she said. "You'll be fortunate if you get her back. Nonno has taken quite a shine to her."

Hearing the name his grandchildren called him, Lares perked up. "What's this ye say?" he said. He'd been mulling over retreating to his bed, his head full of wine, but he thought on the last few words the women had spoken between them and smiled weakly. "Aye, the little one is a bonny lass. I'll hide her so ye canna leave with her."

Gabriela chuckled. "I think my husband might have something to say about that."

"He'll have to fight me for her."

Gabriela's laughter grew. "Nonno, he's much taller than you are," she said. "Have you not noticed?"

Lares winked at her. "Taller doesna mean stronger or faster," he said. "It simply means that the man will smack his head on the doorframe when leaving a room."

Before Gabriela could reply, someone shouted at Mabel, who waved and stood up. One of her sons was calling for her, so like any good mother, she would go to him. As she headed off into the crowd of merry wedding guests, Gabriela turned to Lares.

"Do you like him, Nonno?" she asked eagerly. "Bas has a quiet way about him, but he's a good man. Please say that you like him. I would be heartbroken if you did not."

Lares nodded his head, patting her hands as they wound around his elbow. "Of course I do, lass."

"Do you *really*?"

"I said I did," he said. "But I will admit that I am saddened to think of ye going to Northwood Castle. So far away."

Gabriela squeezed his arm. "Not so very far," she said. "It's not far from Lydgate Castle, where I was born. And Ashkirk is little more than a day or two away. You can visit me at Northwood when you travel to Ashkirk."

Lares shrugged. "Mayhap," he said. But his gaze grew intense. "Are ye happy, lass? That's the most important thing in the world. Are ye *happy*?"

Gabriela's expression transformed into something warm and glowing, far from the giddy girl so recently seen. "So very happy," she said softly. "I love Bas, Nonno. He loves me. I know he has children from his first wife, but I love those children, too. You will never know such happy people as Bas and me. Two people who loved each other more have never existed, except mayhap Mama and Da. Or you and Mamie. You and Mamie love each other so very much. I have always admired that."

Lares' expression seemed to soften as he reflected upon the decades of marriage to Mabel. Suddenly, he didn't seem so drunk. "Yer grandmother is more wonderful than ye know, lassie," he said softly. "She's a woman of exceptional honor and grace."

"I know she is."

His features continued to soften, his eyes taking on a distant cast. "I dunna mean to contradict ye, but ye dunna know what she is capable of," he murmured. "Ye said that two people more in love have never existed, and in a way, ye're right. But there is a kind of love that becomes more than simply the love of a man and a woman. It's a deeper love that only a few know of, something that grows from yer bones and surrounds ye like a second skin. Yer skin and the skin of yer husband or wife become part of one another. Their happiness means more to ye than yer own. I've been fortunate enough to have experienced a love like that."

Gabriela cocked her head. "A love where the happiness of your husband or wife is all that matters?" she said. "Isn't that what most married people do, anyway?"

A gleam came to his eye. "Do ye think so?"

"I would hope so."

"I can tell ye a story that would tell ye that ye're wrong. There are other forms of true love, lass."

"Then tell me, Nonno."

He did.

PART ONE

LARES

CHAPTER ONE

Year of Our Lord 1313
Mount Pleasant Castle
England/Scotland Border

THE ONLY SOUNDS were those of the bailey.

In a castle the size of Mount Pleasant, one would have thought there would have been a myriad of sounds from all over the compound. Servants, horses, dogs… even screaming children. But nothing penetrated the walls of the enormous, two-storied solar of Mount Pleasant's keep other than the muted sounds of the bailey coming in through the lancet windows.

They were, perhaps, accompanied by the sounds of his pounding heart.

He thought it was going to pound right out of his chest.

"I will admit I have been waiting for this moment, Lares." A man dressed in fine robes of silk and leather spoke quietly, sitting behind the table that Lares was standing in front of. "I have expected it every day since you arrived."

That was a whole week ago, Lares thought. Was there a slight in that comment? He wasn't sure, but it seemed to him that Ralph de Gilsland, the lord of Mount Pleasant, was laughing at him. The man wasn't exactly smiling, but his eyes were glimmering… with something.

Lares wasn't sure what it was, but he wasn't sure he liked it.

"It isna that I dinna have the courage to speak to ye, m'laird," Lares said with as much backbone as he could summon. "'Tis only that I wanted to make certain that Davina felt the same way. I wouldna offer for a woman who dinna love me in return."

"You love her, do you?"

"Aye, m'laird. And she loves me."

Ralph's gaze remained fixed on Lares for a moment before he rubbed at his forehead and averted his gaze. Aye, he'd been expecting this request. He'd been expecting it for a year. It wasn't that he didn't like the lad, for he liked him a good deal. Lares dun Tarh was from a very old and wealthy family in the Highlands, the family that had their roots far back to the Roman occupation of Britannia. It was said that Lares' family descended from a lost Roman legion who had forged their way deep into the Highlands, only to marry into the native population. Even the mascot on the dun Tarh standard was the remnant of the mascot of that lost Roman legion—a bull. That fearsome, stubborn, and powerful animal represented everything about the dun Tarh family.

Including the young man standing in front of him.

Stubborn and proud, indeed.

Lares wasn't a true Highlander in the sense that he'd spent his entire life in the Highlands, hardly venturing out of the hills. In fact, for a Highlander, he was very well traveled. Lares followed their tradition set by one of his ancestors that every eldest son of the Earls of Torridon fostered in an English household. Lares had trained in some of the finest households in Northern England, and he had also trained in the royal household of King Edward. That was also a longstanding tradition with the dun Tarh family, and at least one male, preferably the heir, was always sent into the royal household of the English king as a symbolic hostage. That was something Henry II had established with a dun Tarh ancestor long ago.

That particular tradition meant the dun Tarh heirs could be more English than Scottish.

In any case, it certainly set up the heir to a lifetime of turmoil with his siblings and other family members, because the rest of the family didn't have the same training that the heir did. It was an odd and divisive tradition, but one the House of dun Tarh kept to religiously. Lares had two younger brothers, both of them as Highland as the very earth and the very sky. Ralph knew those younger brothers, Arden and Florian, and they were a ruthless lot.

So was their father.

Julius dun Tarh, the current Earl of Torridon, had arrived with his son a week ago, feasting and reaffirming the bonds with de Gilsland. But it was for an alliance, not because he was fond of Ralph, as Julius was a man of vision and ambition. He didn't possess a warm bone in his body, a stern man that had only and always expected perfection from his sons. He, too, had trained in the royal household and also in a couple of the northern castles, homes to the allies of his clan, and he had a very English outlook on life in general.

Although his title was rooted in the Highlands, Julius didn't spend much time there, but rather at Ashkirk Castle, which wasn't far from Mount Pleasant on the English border. Julius considered himself far more of a Lowlander than a Highlander because it was at the Scots/English border where most of the action took place. He was a man with a head for politics, and he used that to his advantage, in spite of his adversarial relationship with the Lowland clans. As long as he had the support of the English and their big armies, he didn't care what his Lowland neighbors thought of him.

Ralph was well aware of this. He always thought Julius to be the rather uninteresting man, and the fact that they were allies was simply because Ralph appreciated Julius' political knowledge—and also the fact that Julius could produce a couple of thousand rabid Scotsmen on the field of battle upon request. Ralph might have appreciated Julius to that extent, but he did not want his daughter marrying into the family.

He had greater aspirations for Davina.

But Lares didn't know that. Ralph was aware that Lares had been sweet on Davina for years, but he'd only made that obvious over the past year or so, when they both became of age. Ralph suspected that Julius knew of his son's intention and, more than likely, had encouraged it because a marriage linking dun Tarh to the de Gilsland family would be quite a feather in Julius' cap. Ralph found it odd that Julius hadn't come on behalf of his son, which was the only reason he wondered if Julius knew of Lares' intention at all, but the fact remained that Lares had finally asked that fateful question.

May I seek yer daughter's hand in marriage?

Truth be told, Ralph was already feeling bad about what he had to tell the lad.

"Sit down, Lares," he said after a moment's reflection, indicating a nearby chair. "Sit down before you fall down. There's no reason to be so troubled about this. Every man must face this day at some point in his life, facing the father of the woman he wishes to marry. It is a rite of passage."

Lares smiled weakly. "It feels like an execution, m'laird."

Ralph chuckled. But, then again, Lares always did something to make him, or others, laugh. He was a tall, muscular young man, with a crown of dark, curly hair and an easy smile. He was always joking, always laughing, but beneath that exterior was an incredibly sharp mind. Men sometimes mistook his intelligence level because of his smiling manner, and that was their undoing. The easy manner was only on the surface. Beneath it, there was something dark.

That darkness also had Ralph worried.

"Not an execution," he said after a moment, reaching over to pour the man some wine because he looked like he needed it. "Simply a new experience in life. If a man lives correctly and sets his cap on the right woman, he only goes through it once."

He regretted it almost as soon as he said it, because Lares focused on the last few words. "Does that go for me also, m'laird?" he asked. "Will I only go through this once?"

Damn, Ralph thought. He hadn't wanted to get into the meat of his refusal so soon, but it seemed that they were headed in that direction. Setting the pitcher aside, he handed Lares the cup full of rich red wine.

"I like you, Lares," he said, watching Lares suck down about half of the cup in one swallow. "I like your father and I like your brothers, even if they are like a pack of wild dogs from time to time."

Lares wiped his mouth with the back of his hand, grinning. "I'll not dispute ye," he said. "I've called them worse."

Ralph snorted. "But they're excellent warriors," he said. "I'd go into a fight with them without reservation."

Lares nodded, not particularly wanting to talk about his

younger brothers. "Respectfully, m'laird, ye've not answered my question," he said. "Will ye accept my offer for Davina?"

Ralph's smile faded as he looked at the dark-eyed man. "You're a knight, Lares," he said. "You were knighted at the Lyceum, were you not?"

Lares nodded, not unaware that Ralph was still refusing to answer him. "By Thurston de Royans, m'laird," he said. "I served at the Lyceum for a few years during my training."

"And your father is a friend of de Royans?"

"Aye, m'laird."

"And your brothers are not knights?"

Lares shook his head. "Nay," he said. "It is tradition that only the eldest male be knighted. But Arden and Florian are excellent warriors, as ye say."

Ralph nodded to what he already knew before standing up and moving away from the table, clearly pondering Lares' question. His expensive slippers made soft sounds against a floor that was made from the finest pine, just as all of Mount Pleasant was made from the finest stone with the finest furnishings. De Gilsland had wealth and wasn't afraid to show it.

Lares watched closely as the man paced.

"What manner of life could you hope to give my daughter, Lares?" Ralph asked. "What could you offer her that should make you the best prospect?"

Lares stood up because he didn't want to address the man sitting down. "I will be the next Earl of Torridon," he said. "As it is, I hold the title Lord Albion. I have my own lands and I have income. But as the Earl of Torridon, Davina will be the Countess of Torridon and the mistress over the Hydra. It is the grandest in the Highlands. We have wealth and lands, and we will be very happy."

Ralph looked at him. "The Hydra *is* grand," he said quietly. "I am not disputing that. But your family's politics are… concerning, Lares."

"I understand, m'laird."

"And your brothers and their activities are concerning."

Lares had suspected that might come up. "My brothers are Highlanders to the bone, m'laird," he said. "I dunna condone what they do. I dunna participate in it. I—"

Ralph cut him off, but he wasn't cruel. Simply factual. "Your brothers have sided with the Bruce," he said. "They have created havoc for England, Lares. No doubt about it."

Lares averted his gaze. "I know, m'laird," he said. "But I dunna support their actions."

Ralph simply shook his head as if baffled by a Highlander who didn't support the Scots king. "Your father walks a precipice in his loyalties every day of his life," he said. "Everyone knows that he was educated in England and that his wife is English, yet your father is a Scottish earl. Furthermore, it is no secret that Robert de Brus rails against the Edward, and he is supported by most Scots."

"Most but not all, m'laird," Lares said quickly, nearly interrupting him. When Ralph looked at him with a regretful expression, Lares could see where this was going. There was so much conflict between the Scots and the English at this time that loyalties were being pulled apart all across the country. And that left the dun Tarh clan with some difficulties. "My family has always had loyalty to the English, from the time of Henry Curthose. We have English lands, as ye know. My father spent the majority of his youth in England even though he's a Scots nobleman, as ye've said."

"And you, Lares?" Ralph asked softly. "What of your loyalties? If you say they are with England, then you are a man without a country. The Scots will hate you for it."

Lares grunted. "They already hate me," he said. Then he chuckled ironically. "What are my loyalties? My loyalties are to a peaceful Scotland. Ye know I've been advising the Bruce on the English behavior. On the English activities. I know the English and how they think, and I've advised the Bruce on such things. But I willna take up arms against the Scots or the English, m'laird."

"Why not?"

"Because I canna take up arms against my brothers," he said. "M'laird, ye know that the dun Tarh clan and our lands are… special. My da has a big army of Highlanders, and he'll use them for the Bruce if he must. He fears that if he doesna, then the clans will turn against us and we'll lose everything. But me… I'm like my da. I've too much English in me from my years of living with them. Ye called me a man without a country. That's true, more than ye know."

Ralph was listening with sorrow because it was leading into what he had to say next. "And you want to take my daughter into that chaos?" he asked, almost gently. "Lares, she does not deserve that."

Lares stiffened. "She would be cherished, m'laird," he said. "I would protect her with my life. I swear to ye, we would be rich in love, if that counts for anything. She would be everything to me."

Ralph sighed sharply, mostly because he truly hated denying Lares. "You and I have known each other for quite some time, have we not?"

"Aye, m'laird."

"And you would expect me to be honest with you, would you not?"

"Aye, m'laird."

Ralph looked him in the eye. "Then I will tell you that I was expecting this offer from you," he said. "I know you understand that my concern is only with Davina. I must ensure her safety and happiness. Would you agree with that?"

Lares nodded, but he had a sinking feeling in the pit of his stomach. "I would, m'laird."

"And you know that I would never want to hurt you, don't you?"

Lares sighed faintly. "I could not believe ye would do it deliberately, m'laird."

"You are right," Ralph said, moving in his direction. "I would never hurt you deliberately. But what I must say will hurt you, however regrettable. Davina must be safe, and that is all I am concerned with, and you should know that I have already agreed to a betrothal with an English ally that will take her away from the borders. She will be away from the English and the Scots as they fight one another. Her future husband is an older man with great wealth and status, and she will be treated like a queen. She will be safe and happy. That is all I can wish for her, but unfortunately, that means I cannot grant your request. I am very sorry, lad."

It was a kind refusal, perhaps the kindest refusal Lares had ever heard. Ralph was a kind man, and that was evident. But Lares had suspected this would be the answer, and he was prepared. At least, as much as he could be. What he hadn't expected was that there was another betrothal for Davina, evidently already arranged. He'd never even caught wind of such a thing, not even a hint of a rumor. Truth be told, that bit of news had his belly lurching.

After a moment, he hung his head.

"Then the woman I love will marry another," he muttered, struggling with his composure. "She'll belong to another man."

Ralph felt a good deal of pity for Lares. "For her health and happiness, I think that would be best," he said. "If you think about it, Lares, I believe you would agree with me. If you truly love my daughter, then you will want her safety and happiness above your own. You will think about her before you think of yourself."

"Does Davina know?"

Ralph shook his head. "Nay," he said. "I've not yet told her because I knew she would tell you."

Lares looked at him then. "And you thought I would do something foolish, did ye?" he said. "Ye dinna trust me to do the right thing?"

He was growing agitated, and Ralph hastened to reassure him. "It is simply that it was none of your affair," he said. "Lares, the underhanded thing would have been to allow rumors to reach your ears to discourage you from the offer I knew you were going to make. But that is dishonorable. I knew you were going to ask for Davina's hand, and I wanted to tell you personally that she is betrothed to another. I wanted you to hear it from my lips."

Lares understood, sort of. But his composure continued to slip, and he raked his fingers through his dark hair. "And so I have," he said. "But it doesna change the fact that I love yer daughter and she loves me. Will ye truly give yer miserable daughter over to a man who must compete with my memory? You speak of preserving her health and happiness, but the truth is that ye simply dinna want her to marry me."

"That's not true."

"Ye're holding Davina up as the reason I should be selfless, because I should think only of her, when the truth is that ye've thought only of ye." Realizing he was about to say something he would regret, Lares turned for the solar door. "Ye speak of truth, m'laird, but ye've given me lies. I'm not as stupid as ye seem to think I am. I thank ye for yer time today, but it changes nothing. Davina loves me and I love her, and yer betrothal canna change that."

Ralph rushed after him, grabbing his arm before he could get to the door. "Lares, calm yourself," he said steadily. "I've given you the complete truth. If you were not so swept up in what you want, you would see that. You are doing exactly what you accuse me of doing—thinking only of yourself."

Lares yanked the door open in spite of Ralph having a grip on his arm. "I'm thinking that ye couldna tell me that ye dinna think I was good enough for yer daughter," he said, dark eyes flashing. "Ye painted a picture that suggested she'd be better off somewhere else. Why could ye not have simply told me ye dinna want me for her? I could have accepted that better than manipulative lies, trying to make me believe that you thought she'd be safer elsewhere and trying to coerce me into agreeing with ye. That was unkind, m'laird. I dinna deserve that."

With that, he pulled his arm from Ralph's grasp and stormed from the solar, into the keep entry, and headed out of the front door.

Ralph stood in the solar entry, watching the young man storm off, and thinking that nothing Lares had said was wrong. He knew the lad was sharp, but evidently, he was much sharper than he'd given him credit for. Ralph had, indeed, been trying to manipulate the conversation, hoping to convince Lares that everything was for Davina's benefit. He thought if he put it that way, it would mean more to Lares, but the young man saw through his scheme. Lares was smarter than that.

Ralph had the feeling this would not be the last of it.

He had to find Julius.

⁊

"LARES!"

Lares could hear his name being shouted as he marched across Mount Pleasant's bailey, a small and compact area given the size of the keep and walls. It was crammed with outbuildings and animals. He was heading for the stables, though he really didn't know why. All he knew was that he had to put distance between himself and Ralph de Gilsland. He was angry and hurt and disheartened, a bad combination where Lares was concerned.

He'd been known to act out a time or two.

"*Lares!*"

The shout came again, closer this time. He knew who it was because he recognized the voice. Coming to a halt, he turned to face Davina as she ran toward him from the kitchen hard. She was dressed in green silk, perhaps a finer fabric than she should be wearing out in the dusty bailey, but she wore it like a goddess. At least, he thought so.

His goddess.

But his no more.

"Well?" Davina said, her green eyes alight with anticipation. "What did he say?"

Lares stared at her for a moment. Those beautiful eyes and that wavy auburn hair spoke to him. He wanted to run his fingers through it, claim her as she was meant to be claimed.

Davina could be silly and petty at times, but she had a woman's soul. A good soul. The more he stared at her, the more grief he began to feel.

"He denied us," he said bluntly. Tact had never been his strong suit. "Did ye know that he already has another husband selected for ye?"

The smile vanished from Davina's face. "Another... *husband*?" she said, startled. "Where did you hear this?"

"From yer father," Lares said, jabbing a finger at the keep. "I have just come from him. Not only has he denied me, but he tells me that he has an English husband selected for ye, someone far away from the borders who will keep ye safe from the turmoil of these lands. He intends to send ye away, and I'll never see ye again."

Davina gasped, and her hands flew to her mouth. "It's not true!"

Lares sighed heavily. "I'm afraid it is."

"But he's never said a word to me!"

"For good reason. He knew ye'd tell me."

She was beginning to tear up. "But... but this is madness," she said. "I do not want another husband. I want *you*!"

"And I want ye. But yer father has other plans."

"Then what shall we do?"

She was obviously upset, and Lares moved to comfort her but thought better of it. "I dunna know," he said quietly. "I... I must think."

Davina grasped his arm. "Then you'll not give up?" she said, blinking back the tears. "You'll try again?"

"Why?" he said, and she shrank from him, fearful of his tone. He had to steady himself because he didn't want to upset her more than she already was. "He's set, Davi. His mind is made up. He must do as he feels best, but so must I."

Davina eyed him fearfully. "What does that mean?" she asked. "Please do not tell me you are going to ride from here and never return. I could not bear it if I were never to see you again."

He shook his head, shushing her, but that bright mind was working on the problem. He glanced up, toward the keep, seeing Ralph emerge and look around, clearly scouting for his daughter. Lares stepped back from her, standing a few feet away. A proper distance. When Ralph caught sight of his daughter, he didn't want the man to be concerned because Lares was standing too close.

"If I ride from here, ye're going with me," he said quietly. "Dunna turn around, but yer da is watching us. Dunna show any rage or emotion, Davi. Be calm."

She looked up at him with big eyes, wanting to turn around but fighting the urge. "Is he looking at me?"

"He is."

"What should I do?"

"Nothing," Lares said. "Davi, I've made a decision."

"What?"

"I'm leaving, and ye're going with me."

"Where are we going?"

"To the nearest church so we can be married."

Davina's features rippled with hope. "Now?"

Lares sighed again and looked around, pondering the situation. Ralph was still looking at them at a distance. He had to throw the man off his scent if he truly intended to depart with the prize.

"Lass," he said, his head turned away from her. "I'm going to make it look as if I'm angry with ye, but it's only to confuse yer da. Mayhap he willna watch ye so closely if he thinks I'm angry and want nothing to do with ye. Can ye play the part?"

Davina wasn't quite sure what he had in mind, but she nodded. "I can," she said. "What do you want me to do?"

"Weep," Lares said, turning to her and shaking a dramatic finger in her face. "Weep and carry on as if I've just told ye how disgusted I am with ye and yer da. He's watching, so make it good."

Davina did. She wailed and put her hands over her face. "Like this?" she asked, muffled.

Lares waved his hands at her in an exaggerated gesture. "Perfect," he said. "Now, listen closely. I'm going to the stable to gather my horse. While I leave, I want ye to go to the keep, but at the feast tonight, ye'll tell yer da ye dunna feel well enough to attend."

Davina shook her head dramatically, trying to play the role of an extremely upset young woman. "And I do not attend the feast?" she said. "Then what?"

Lares extended his big arms, pretending to gesture wildly. "Ye're going to make sure no one is watching ye," he said. "When it's safe, ye're to make yer way to the postern gate. I'll meet ye there. Now, wail again."

Davina did, carrying on for a moment with her hands over her face before looking at him between splayed fingers. "We'll leave when everyone is distracted with the feast?"

"We will."

He was smiling even though her hands were covering her face. "Then I'll be there," she said. "Oh, Lares… I can hardly believe it. We shall be married!"

"Wail," he commanded softly, shaking another raging hand at her and she squealed. "If yer da is to ask what I said to ye, ye must tell him that I told ye that we are finished. That I'm going away and never returning. Tell him I'm sorry I ever knew ye."

"But you aren't… are you?"

"Of course not," he said. Then he waved his hands at her in a gesture of finality. "Go inside now. I'll be waiting for ye tonight. And tell no one!"

With that, he stomped off, leaving Davina standing there with her hands over her face. Thinking she should probably run away from him to convince her father that their relationship was indeed ended, she whirled on her heel and rushed back toward the kitchen yard. There was a door that led to the lower-level kitchens there, but she could get into the keep from that door. All she could think about was this evening and how Lares would be waiting for her. She knew a church not far from Mount Pleasant where she could pay the priests to marry them. The sooner they were married, the better. Damn her father for trying to marry her to some English fool.

Davina de Gilsland was going to take charge of her own life.

Little did she know how much the situation was going to veer out of control.

CHAPTER TWO

"A *Sassenach husband*?" Julius grumbled. "Did ye have to tell him that?"

Ralph cast Julius a frustrated look but refrained from arguing with him, because he'd already done enough of that.

Julius knew why he'd done it.

He was simply being difficult.

It was midmorning on a bright, clear day. Ralph and Julius were on horseback with an escort of twenty men, some English and some Highlanders. Two scouts were spread out in front of them following the path that Lares had taken from Mount Pleasant, and, presumably, Davina with him, because no one had seen either of them since yesterday. Davina had sent word to her father the night before that she would be unable to attend the feast, and, being a sympathetic soul, Ralph had let her. He hadn't even sent anyone to check on her other than her mother, and that had been early that morning. But Davina had been missing and her bed hadn't been slept in.

That threw Ralph into a panic.

It was no great mystery where she had gone.

Or with whom.

For all of Lares' intelligence, he evidently hadn't realized, or didn't care, that the markings of his horse's hooves were unique. They'd been able to study them in the stall where his horse had been stabled the day before, and that was how they'd been able to follow the hoofprints from Mount Pleasant. They were clearly heading to Carlisle, which had the nearest church. Ralph already knew Lares' intentions. No one had to tell him, least of all the man's father, who was upset that his heir had been denied the wife he wanted, but also upset that Lares had stolen the woman he'd been denied.

Julius was a man with a dilemma.

"Let us pray he has not married her," Ralph said, shouting over the noise of the thundering horses. "If he has, there will be… trouble."

Julius looked at him sharply. "What do ye intend to do?"

Ralph wouldn't look at him. "He did not have permission," he said. "He will have married someone else's betrothed. That is thievery, dun Tarh. If he has stolen what does not belong to him, he will be punished."

Julius knew that. A man with his son's dark hair but the pale eyes of his mother, he and Lares looked a good deal alike. They had the dun Tarh male beauty. They also thought alike in many ways, but their personalities were different. Julius was older and more cunning, while Lares was younger and vivacious. But they both had an impulsive streak, something Julius had learned to control, but Lares hadn't. Not yet. But it was a streak that might cost Lares everything.

Much like Ralph, Julius could only pray they were in time to stop his foolish son from doing something ridiculously foolish that might cost him his foolish life.

Foolish, foolish, foolish!

"He's a man who knows what he wants," Julius said, making excuses. "Ye knew he'd been sweet on Davina. Ye should have seen this coming."

Ralph scowled. "Now it is my fault?" he said. "The fact that you raised a disobedient son is your fault. Do not blame me for your failure, Julius."

Those were dangerous words, but Julius knew he'd pushed the man into a corner. He was trying to cast blame, to confuse the issue so perhaps Ralph wouldn't be so hard on Lares, but the truth was that Lares was at fault. Julius was at fault. This *was* a dun Tarh problem, and there was no spin strong enough to change that.

God help him, he had to get to his son before he truly ruined everything.

"How far are we from Carlisle?" he asked, trying to shift the subject.

But Ralph was angry. He knew Julius was trying to deflect the blame, and that simply enraged him. His horse took a bad step on the road, and he held the animal firm to keep himself from falling before answering.

"Not far," he said. "My scouts are probably already there. They have orders to go straight to the cathedral and locate them."

And then what? Julius had to bite his tongue to keep from asking. *Then what will you do to Lares?* His eldest, his shining star, the only son he had who possessed half a brain and the strength to use it. What would happen to Lares if he married a woman meant for another?

God help the man.

God help them all.

CB

THE PRIESTS AT Carlisle Cathedral wouldn't even consider marrying anyone in the middle of the night.

That was what Lares had been told when he and Davina reached the cathedral, a glorious, red-stoned structure that had been standing for hundreds of years. The stone was marked and burned in places, a testament to the conflict the cathedral had seen over the years. Between the Scots and the English, the city of Carlisle, along with its castle and buildings, had always been a target.

It was a border city with a violent history.

Davina, not entirely strong and resilient, had been weary from the ride in the middle of the night to Carlisle. She was hungry and her backside hurt, and she wanted to be married quickly so they could find a tavern where she could eat and go to sleep. Never mind the fact that sleep was the last thing on Lares' mind, but he tried to be patient and understanding with her.

However, when the priests at the cathedral wouldn't entertain marrying them, no matter how much he begged or demanded, and no matter how much Davina cried, he was forced to seek shelter for the night. That was something he didn't want to do, and he considered leaving for another town to find another church that would grant his request immediately, but Davina couldn't go another mile. Therefore, he'd been forced to find a bed for her for the night.

It had been a dirty little inn tucked into the older part of Carlisle. The stones were filthy, the floor uneven, and it had a perpetual smell of mildew. Lares wanted to find other lodgings, but Davina refused. Therefore, he paid for her to stay in a tiny chamber with an old brazier in the corner and no door as he slept in the common room only a few feet away, listening to a pathetic minstrel play his out-of-tune citole all night long. It seemed to Lares that the song the man played was just for them.

I gave my heart to her. It was never mine to give again.
For the love of her, I staked my claim,
To be her shadow, evermore.

He came to hate that song.

Unfortunately, Davina had listened to it all night, too, and sang it all the way to the cathedral. He told her to shut her lips, but she wouldn't. She only smiled as he grew more annoyed.

To be her shadow, evermore...

But here they were, back at Carlisle Cathedral about two hours after sunrise because Davina wasn't an early riser. Lares was fairly certain that his father and Ralph were heading to Carlisle because, surely, it wouldn't have been difficult to follow him. If Lares had been the one doing the following, he would have determined the shape of his horse's hooves and used that to follow their trail, and he was sure his father had done that. That was a standard trick when following a man on horseback, so he suspected they'd be riding into Carlisle very shortly.

He had to hurry the marriage or all would be lost.

But Davina didn't seem to sense his urgency. She didn't have the mind of a hunter, so to her, the very fact that they had escaped Mount Pleasant seemed to be enough. She was certain her father couldn't find them, and nothing Lares said could convince her otherwise. After she rose and washed and dressed, she wanted to break her fast, but Lares put his foot down and told her she could eat all she wanted after they were married.

Truth be told, all he had to do was bed her to claim her as his wife, and he should have done that last night, but she wanted a ceremony at the door to the cathedral before he bedded her, so he acquiesced to her wants.

He was starting to wish he hadn't.

He should have gone with his instincts.

It was well into the morning when they returned to the cathedral, which was open at this hour because of the morning prayers. The faithful were wandering in and out of the side entry, which opened up into the soaring-ceilinged transept. There were enormous, red-stoned pillars throughout and a floor of hard, compact earth. For as large as it was, it was unfurnished except for the altar in the nave. When Lares spied a priest near the altar, he grabbed Davina by the hand and moved quickly in the man's direction.

The priest had a group of acolytes, evidently lads who were learning the ways of the church. They were sweeping and polishing the precious candleholders used during mass. The priest was instructing a lad how not to scratch the gold on the candlesticks as Lares approached.

"Yer grace," he said, addressing the man respectfully. "My name is Sir Lares duh Tarh. This is Lady Davina de Gilsland. We came last evening but were turned away, so we have returned this morning. We wish to be married right away."

The priest didn't seem too thrilled that he'd been interrupted during his instruction. He scratched his nose, looking Lares over before turning his gaze on Davina. He looked her over, with some disdain, before returning his focus to Lares.

"Come back later," he said.

Already, Lares was annoyed. "I will *not*," he said. "I was told that last night, so here I am. It *is* later. And we wish to be married."

The priest turned his back on him, telling one of the boys to go and find a rag, but Lares would not be ignored.

"Father," he said slowly. "I'm doing my best to be patient, but yer lack of respect isna working in yer favor. I would appreciate a measure of civility from ye, or this will not go well for any of us."

The priest caught on to his tone. With a sigh of impatience, he turned to him again, perhaps contemplating telling the couple to leave once more but thinking better of it. The Scotsman was big and clearly powerful, and the priest had no desire to have his neck snapped.

"I have duties to attend to," he said. "At this moment, that does not include your request. If you return later, I will be finished and better able to serve you."

"Forgive me, Father, but coming later is not possible. It must be now."

There was something in those words that suggested the time was now or bad things were going to happen. The priest was coming to understand that. He opened his mouth to once again tell them to come back later, but he realized a third time might provoke the Scotsman. It was with misgivings that he realized he would have to deal with him, because the man wasn't easily shooed away.

"You do not worship here," he said after a moment. "I do not recognize you."

Lares shook his head. "Nay, you wouldna," he said. "But I'm willing to pay well for a priest to say a blessing over us for our marriage. My lady wants a blessing."

The priest scratched his nose again, but the acolytes had his attention again, and he quickly instructed them, sending a couple of them away. When the children shuffled off, he turned his full attention to Lares.

"It is not as simple as wanting a blessing," he said. "What of the lady's parents? Do they approve of this marriage? Since I do not know either of you, these are questions I must ask. We do not want an irate father blaming us for a marriage he did not sanction."

Lares was rather shocked that the man seemed to know his situation exactly. But he knew that was impossible, since he didn't know either one of them, so Lares could only assume this kind of thing had happened before. This was a church, after all, and the world was full of impetuous youth.

He proceeded carefully.

"The lady doesna have parents," he said, a complete lie. "She is an orphan. Will ye marry us now?"

The priest looked straight at Davina. "Your parents are dead, my lady?"

Davina's eyes widened. "I…" she stammered, looking fearfully at Lares. "That is… aye, they are. I do not have parents."

The priest pondered that stuttering answer. He could see that he'd caught her off guard with the question, which led him to believe they were both lying. With a heavy sigh, he looked away from the pair.

"Then I must have permission from the lady's… guardian," he said. "My name is Benedict Nursia. I am not the priest in charge, but I have been here many years. The acolytes and wards are my charges. I've not conducted a marriage mass in years. I would more than likely do it wrong. Therefore, you can see that you must return and speak with Father Briant. He will know what to do."

There he was, putting them off again, and Lares was close to losing his temper. He didn't like being denied, and most especially by a priest who didn't seem to have any real sense of either urgency or compassion. The man was angry at being asked to perform a blessing and was doing everything he could to get out of it.

"How difficult is it to say a prayer for us?" he asked. "All I am asking is for you to say a prayer over us and bless our marriage. Surely you know how to pray?"

Benedict stood his ground. "I am certain I can pray better than anyone you know," he said. "But you have lied to me and the lady has lied to me, and I will not bless anyone who has told a lie to a priest. A *knowing* lie. You have committed a great sin, Scotsman."

That tipped Lares over the edge. "I willna be lectured by a man with coal where his heart should be," he growled. "It is clear ye have no understanding for our predicament. If ye did, I wouldna have to lie to you."

Benedict snorted. "So this is my fault, is it?" he said. Then he waved a hand. "Get out, the both of you. Go find someone else to marry you, because it will not be me or anyone else here. Go take your lies elsewhere."

Infuriated, Lares debated how to proceed. He could tear up the sanctuary, but that probably wouldn't get him what he wanted. He worried about the knights at Carlisle Castle, which wasn't far at all. If the priests summoned the garrison, it could go badly for him. Therefore, he had to do something non-destructive to convince the priest to at least say a blessing for them. Something that would frighten the man into it.

Something that would force him to surrender.

"Very well," Lares said, unsheathing the dagger at his side. Davina gasped, positive he was going to charge the priest with it, but instead, he pushed his way to the altar and went to his knees in front of it. "If you will not give us yer blessing, then mayhap I will summon someone who will."

With that, he rammed his dagger into the packed earth right in front of the altar and began to draw something, carving it out of the hard earth. Curious, and concerned, Davina timidly moved toward him to see what he was doing, as the priest, while greatly annoyed, nonetheless peered at what Lares was scratching on the ground. The man was drawing lines, a symbol of some kind, and he was nearly done with it when the priest realized what it was.

His eyes widened.

"*Nay!*" he shouted, rushing toward Lares. "What are you doing? Are you mad?"

Lares finished the last line on the pentangle, a star-shaped symbol related to Satan and his demons. It had been a symbol for centuries. "Ye said ye wouldna pray for us," he said, leaving his dagger in the dirt as he lifted his arms toward the altar. "I call forth Lucifer in all forms, of Asmodeus and Mammon, of the mighty Leviathan, of all demon lords to come forth and bless our marriage! Lucifer, I demand ye appear to me!"

Davina was gasping with fear as the priest rushed over and tried to rub out the pentangle, but Lares shoved him back, so forcefully that the man fell on his backside. There were a few acolytes in the sanctuary, and they began running in all directions, calling for other priests in a panic. All the while, Lares remained on his knees, his arms uplifted as he called upon the demons.

"Ye had a chance tae marry us, priest," he said, watching Benedict scramble to his feet. "Now I call forth the devil himself to bless our union. Belphegor, do ye hear my plea? God will not bless our union, so mayhap ye will!"

The priest looked properly terrified, something that filled Lares with satisfaction. He was hoping the man would beg him to stop praying to the devil and agree to give his blessing. That was the hope, anyway. Lares was rather enjoying the expression of horror on that smug priest's face. Damn the man for denying him.

He was going to pay the price.

But that satisfaction was short-lived when Lares heard Davina scream behind him. Startled, he whirled around in time to see Ralph grab his daughter as Julius charged toward Lares, reaching out to grab him by the hair.

"What in the name of all the saints are ye doing?" Julius shouted, yanking Lares to his feet. "I come in the door tae see ye summoning demons? Have ye lost what little sense ye have?"

Lares realized, very quickly, that he was in a very bad way. Ralph was already dragging Davina from the cathedral, and he tried to follow, but his father and a few other dun Tarh men held him back. He began shouting her name, and she screamed his, causing a chaotic scene. Shouts and cries echoed off the old stone walls as Benedict and his acolytes vanished in haste. The cathedral cleared out quickly as the two lovers were separated by their fathers. The last Lares saw of Davina, Ralph and another soldier had her by both arms and were dragging her out into the sunlight. Lares stood there in horror, his arm outstretched as if to grab her, as his father and others held him fast.

There was nothing more he could do.

"Da," Lares gasped, still straining against him. "Let me go! Let me go to her!"

"Never," Julius said sternly. "Lares, ye've always been stubborn and proud, but this... I dinna believe ye were capable of such things."

Lares looked at his father with tears in his eyes. "What things?" he demanded. "I want to marry her. I *will* marry her!"

Julius reached out and slapped his son across the face because he was nearly hysterical with the loss of Davina. *"Enough,"* he said. "Do ye think de Gilsland is going to allow his daughter to marry a man who was caught summoning the devil? In a church, no less? Lad, ye've been in trouble before, but not like this. Never like this. Ye'll be fortunate if the man doesna return with the local magistrate. They'll put ye in Carlisle Castle's vault and throw the key in the moat!"

Lares' left cheek was stinging from his father's blow, but it had the desired effect—he was thinking more clearly. And he was absolutely distraught with what had just happened.

"Da, I love her," he said, grasping his father desperately. "Bring her back. Tell de Gilsland to bring her back to me, please."

Julius could see that Lares was calmer, but it didn't change facts. "She's never coming back," he said, grabbing him by the arm and motioning to the men that were with him. "Come with me. We must see the priests."

Lares was bigger, and stronger, than his father, but he didn't resist as the man dragged him along. "Why?" he said. "What are ye going to do?"

Julius was beside himself. "After what I just saw, what do ye expect me to do?" he said. "Ye've always had a darkness about ye, Lares. Now I know why."

"Why?"

Julius looked at him sharply. "Because ye have a demon inside of ye," he said. "Now I know. I've seen it for myself."

Lares' brow furrowed, and he suddenly dug his heels in,

slowing his father's pace. "What have ye seen?" he said. "Da, ye saw me trying to scare the priest into marrying us. He refused to do it, so I told him I would summon the devil. I was threatening him!"

Julius didn't like that answer in the least. "Only a man possessed by a demon would do such a thing!" he said. "Either that or ye're a madman, and if ye are truly mad, then I'll take ye back tae the Hydra and chain ye tae the vault. Ye'll never see the light of day again."

Lares was starting to struggle with his father. "I am *not* mad," he said. "Da, listen to me. I dinna mean any of it. Are ye listening?"

They had reached the small doorway where Benedict and his acolytes had disappeared. Julius came to a halt and had his men kick out the back of Lares' legs so he fell to his knees, subdued by six burly Highlanders that Julian had brought with him from the Hydra. These men had known Lares most of his life, and he considered them friends, but they'd all seen him as he tried to summon Lucifer, and now they were looking back at him in various stages of shock and fear. They were confused but doing as they were ordered.

They were subduing Lares.

"Now," Julius said, his features hard as he faced his son. "I am going to find a priest, and we'll find a way to subdue this demon."

Lares shook his head. "There is *no* demon," he said, beseeching his father. "Da, *look* at me—there is no demon. I told ye why I did it. All I wanted was to marry Davina."

Julius was shaken as well as angry. He pointed toward the altar. "When I came in, I saw what ye were doing," he said. "I saw ye push the priest to the ground. I heard ye bellowing for the demon lords. I *heard* it!"

Lares was growing desperate. "I told ye why," he said. "All I wanted was—"

"Be silent," Julius said, cutting him off. "Silence yer tongue or I'll cut it out of ye. Ye've always been stubborn, but taking Davina with the intention of marrying her was beyond what I thought ye were capable of. Ye've damaged my alliance with de Gilsland at the very least, and we followed ye tae Carlisle only to find ye summoning demons. Ye've gone too far, lad. This time… ye've gone too far."

"Da, listen to me!" Lares begged. "Since when do ye not listen to me?"

"Since ye nearly ruined yerself and Lady Davina along with ye!" Julius nearly shouted. "Do ye not understand, Lares? If I dunna do something now, if I dunna put ye out of de Gilsland's reach, then there is the very real possibility that he will punish ye for stealing Davina. And if the rumors spread that ye worship Lucifer, that will be the end of ye. No marriage, no future, and no hope. Are ye comprehending what I'm telling ye?"

Lares did. It was the worst-case scenario in the situation of his own making, but he did. Slowly, he nodded. "Aye," he said. "Then ye believe me when I tell ye that I wasna summoning the devil? Not really?"

Julius wouldn't go so far as to agree. He simply shook his head. "I know what I saw," he said. "But I also know what others saw, what de Gilsland saw. I know what ye did. And I must do something about it."

"What are ye going tae do?"

Julius didn't have an answer for him, not right away. Without another word, he went through the door where he'd seen the priest go as Lares remained on his knees, held down by his father's men. Truth be told, Lares was beside himself with shock, with distress. He couldn't believe his father wasn't willing to listen to him. He also couldn't believe that his attempts to coerce the priest had blown back in his face spectacularly. He'd lost Davina, and now his father was convinced he was possessed by a demon.

It was a horrific situation, any angle he looked at it.

He'd gambled. And he'd lost.

Canon Bernard Briant, the man in charge of Carlisle Cathedral, was kind enough to listen to a panicked father who explained that he was terrified for his son's soul, that the devil surely had him within his grasp. That assertion was confirmed by Benedict, who was still shaken up by what he'd seen. Julius was convinced that the only hope for his son was to commit him to the nearest abbey, where he could live a pious life and purge any darkness from his soul.

Julius didn't mention, of course, that it was the one place Ralph de Gilsland couldn't get at his son should he and Davina's betrothed decide to punish him. Nay, he didn't mention that at all. The story of possession got him exactly what he wanted. Before the day was out, Lares was on his way to a remote abbey run by the Cistercian priests of Carlisle, and his quest to marry Lady Davina was officially ended for good.

But the legend of Lucifer's spawn, for Lares dun Tarh, was born.

CHAPTER THREE

Camerton Abbey
Two years later

PRETTY AND PERFECT, with golden-red hair and eyes of green, Lady Mabel Coleby Douglas-de Waverton peered from the window of the fortified carriage she and her mother were riding in, spying the rambling, rather large abbey in the distance. It was early morning on a fine day after weeks of rain, and the sky above the abbey was streaked with purplish, bruised clouds. Against the backdrop of the sky and the bright sunlight, it made for dramatic scenery.

"Is that it, Mama?" she asked, pointing to the monastery on the rise. "Camerton?"

Mabel's mother, Lady Irene, leaned over to see what her daughter was pointing at. "Aye," she said after a moment. "That must be the one. Your brother is somewhere in that monastery, and we must bring him home."

Mabel didn't ask why. She didn't ask questions. She knew her wayward brother, George, had ended up at the monastery because he'd been traveling far from where he'd told his parents he would be and ended up breaking a leg when his horse spooked. He'd been in a remote area of Cumbria, to the southwest of Carlisle, and he'd been taken in by the priests at Camerton Abbey. A physic had been summoned, the same physic who had sent word to Lord and Lady de Waverton on George's mishap. George, in fact, hadn't sent them word at all, and Mabel had heard her father raging about her vagabond brother with no sense of responsibility. He was so angry that he sent his wife and daughter, one hundred soldiers, and two wagons to fetch George.

And that was why they were here.

Truly, Mabel was glad for the adventure. Nothing much happened in her rather sheltered life, and her father wasn't a social man, so friends and visitors were infrequent at their home of Wigton. That was in great contrast to her brother, who loved to visit and loved to travel. George the Elder, their father, didn't even like to venture out of his home, so that was why he'd sent his wife and daughter. It hadn't been because he was too angry to come, but simply that he could not come.

But George the Elder's refusal to travel was Mabel's gain. And it was probably better for her brother, whom she loved. He was sweet and kind and thoughtful, but her father was correct— he had no sense of responsibility. He was bright, but he didn't want the stress and troubles of the lordship he would inherit someday. That meant he traveled around, visited friends and family, and spent his father's money wherever he went. George the Elder paid his son's debts begrudgingly and threatened not to pay anything more that his son incurred.

But he always did.

This was simply another one of George's follies in a long line of them.

Mabel and her mother hadn't spoken much on the journey

from Wigton to Camerton. It had been an overnight journey, and they'd spent the previous night in a tavern where everyone seemed to either be drunk or fighting. Mabel thought it was all great fun, but her mother wasn't under the same impression. In fact, it had put the woman in a sour mood, so there hadn't been much conversation in general.

As the carriage lurched over the muddy road that was more puddle than actual road, the rain began to fall again from those purple clouds. It was brief, just enough to dampen the men, who peered at the sky with discontent. The carriage hit a particularly deep rut and got stuck, but Lady de Waverton refused to get out of the carriage because it was so muddy, and she and Mabel remained in the carriage as the soldiers managed to free them from the hole.

After that, the dirty carriage lurched and bumped all the way to the abbey.

"Mama," Mabel said, a little green because of all of the swaying and violent bumps. "May I please get out and walk the rest of the way? It doesn't seem to be so muddy here at the top of the rise. All of the water seems to have run down the road."

Irene caught a glimpse of the big abbey ahead. They had already entered what looked like a small village area, with small cottages and fields of cabbages and turnips. She could see it along the side of the road along with men working them, more than likely pledges or wards of the abbey.

"I do not think so," she said, peering at the edge of the road. "It is still quite muddy."

Thinking she might become sick, Mabel hiked up her skirt to show her mother the boots she was wearing. "I am properly attired," she said, taking a deep breath. "I really must walk before I become ill."

With that, she pushed her shoulder into the door of the cab, and it swung open. She was out of the carriage before her mother could stop her. She was in a heavy wool traveling dress, one that came with breeches underneath for protection and comfort, and they were tucked into her boots. Mabel began walking, holding her skirt up to keep it out of the mud as she headed off across a field on a diagonal toward the abbey.

"Mabel!" her mother called after her. "Go straight to the abbey! Do not stray!"

There weren't many places for her to stray to. Mabel simply waved her mother off, trudging across the field, trying to shake off the motion sickness. The soldiers didn't follow her because they could see her clearly as she walked through the field of cabbages. They simply followed the carriage as Mabel crossed the field toward the abbey. Fortunately, it wasn't too terribly muddy here because it was at the top of a rise. Off to her left, a few men were working the cabbages, harvesting them because they were quite large. The wind was starting to pick up a little, blustery after the rains, and Mabel fought with her skirts to keep them from blowing around. She was paying attention to her dress, not where she was stepping, and she ended up slipping on a slick spot and going down on her arse, twisting her ankle.

"Damnation," she said.

Hand to her aching ankle, she looked off toward the road only to see that it must have angled away from the abbey before coming around again to the entry. They escort was moving away from her. Realizing there was going to be no help from her father's men, she tried to get to her feet, but her ankle hurt a great deal. Still, she managed to stand, putting most of her weight on her good ankle, as a deep voice spoke from behind.

"I saw ye fall, m'lady," he said. "Did ye hurt yerself?"

Startled, Mabel turned to see a big man with shoulder-length dark hair and dark eyes. He wasn't much older than she was, and she realized with a twinge of interest that he was quite handsome. But he was dressed in clothing better suited to a peasant and carrying a farming implement in one hand. In fact, that twinge of interest turned into one of suspicion, because he'd come up behind her and she'd never heard a sound.

That made her leery.

"If you think to assault me, know that all I have to do is scream and you'll have a hundred furious soldiers down upon you," she said. "Put the shovel down."

He did, immediately. "I dinna mean tae startle ye," he said. "'Tis only that I saw ye fall. I thought ye might need help."

She tried to take a step and almost went down again. "It would seem so," she said. "I have evidently hurt my ankle."

The man moved close to her, going to one knee as he lifted her skirt to get a look at her ankle. Before Mabel could protest, he put his big hands around her booted ankle and gave a gentle squeeze.

Mabel yelped.

"Ah," he said, peering up at her. "I think ye have, indeed. Can ye put any weight on it?"

She shook her head. "I do not think so," she said, trying to use the injured joint, but she ended up nearly tumbling onto him as she walked. "Damnation. Utter *damnation!*"

He grinned at her, a charming gesture. "I've never heard a lady use such language."

She frowned at him. "And you probably never will," she said. "Unfortunately, I have a mouth like my father, and he swears constantly."

That made his grin broaden. "'Tis nothing to be ashamed of, m'lady," he said as he stood up. "It simply means ye're passionate about the things that mean something to ye."

She eyed him, finally breaking down in a reluctant smile. "It means my mother is constantly admonishing me," she said. "She does not share your view."

His eyes were twinkling at her. "I know something about a parent not sharing a child's view," he said, his smile fading. "My father dinna share mine, either. And if it wouldna be too bold, I'll introduce myself. My name is Lares."

That was indeed a bold move, as he suggested. Introductions were made with mutual acquaintances or friends or family, but since there was no one of that position around, perhaps it wasn't bold as it was necessary, so at least they would know whom they were speaking with.

"My name is Mabel de Waverton," she said, looking him over. "You're Scots?"

"Aye."

"Are you a farmer?"

He shook his head. "Not by trade," he said. "But by circumstances."

She wasn't sure what he meant. "What circumstances?"

He gestured toward the church. "I live there," he said. "Everyone must have a task. This is mine."

She thought she understood. "Then you are a priest," she said. "Are you even allowed to speak with a woman?"

He was shaking his head before the words were out of her mouth. "I am *not* a priest," he said. "I'm a ward, although the spineless bastards would be very happy to see me take my vows."

His eyes widened when he realized he had sworn in front of

her, and she giggled. "You have a mouth like my father, too," she said.

He put up his hands in apology. "Forgive me, m'lady," he said. "But I suppose we have that in common—we speak passionately about things."

She was smiling openly at him. "I do not think that is a bad thing," she said. "More people should say what they feel. The world might be better for it."

He chuckled. "You think so, do ye?" he said. "I think if the Scots said what they thought, we'd have constant wars, all across Scotland."

She giggled again. "I suppose you are right," she said. "Isn't it men saying what they feel that starts wars in the first place?"

"That is my belief."

Distant shouting caught their attention, and they both turned to see that the de Waverton carriage had made its way to the front of the abbey. Irene had climbed out and was shouting at her daughter, waving an arm.

Mabel waved back.

"That is my mother," she said, not entirely happily. "She is waiting for me."

Lares could see that. "Have ye come on business?"

She shook her head, trying to put weight on the ankle again but faltering. He grabbed her arm so she wouldn't fall, bracing his other arm around her waist to keep her upright as she tried to walk.

"Thank you," she said in reference to his help. "To answer your question, we are not here on business. We are here to collect my brother, George. Do you know him?"

Lares held her as she took another step and ended up hopping because she couldn't put any weight on her leg. "George?"

he said curiously. "Is he a priest?"

"Nay," she said, coming to a halt because she couldn't walk any further. "He broke his leg and the priests have tended him. We've come to collect him."

That brought recognition. "Ah," he said. "*That* George. The lad in the dormitory. Aye, I've spoken to him, but he calls himself Georgie. He's quite lively, which is something that vexes the priests, I think. But I've enjoyed him."

Mabel appreciated the kind words about her brother. "He's a darling man," she said, but her smile soon faded. "I hate to trouble you, but could you tell my mother I need help? She'll send a couple of soldiers to assist me."

Lares' response was to bend over and swiftly pick her up. Abruptly aloft in the man's arms, Mabel grasped his neck for support, realizing very quickly that their faces were quite close together. Now she could see him up close, and he was a prize specimen. She had been startled by his action at first, but now that she was in his arms, something else was happening.

A sweet little flutter, deep in her belly.

She rather liked it.

"No need for the soldiers, m'lady," he said as he continued across the field. "'Tis my pleasure to help Georgie's sister, though I will admit I'm sorry ye've come to take him home. He was a bright spot in an otherwise lonely life."

"I'm sorry we must, but he should go home."

"Of course he should," Lares said. "I simply meant I'll miss speaking to him. But I suppose it doesna matter, because I'm going home as well."

"Are you?" Mabel said, trying to ignore the giddy trembling in her belly. "When do you leave?"

"Soon," Lares said. "The priests know they must release me

now that my da has died. I've been called home."

"Is that so?" Mabel said with some concern. "I'm sorry that it will be a sad homecoming for you."

They were nearing the edge of the field, and Lares could see Mabel's mother waving frantically to a few soldiers, pointing to her daughter. They started heading in their direction.

"Not a sad homecoming," he said quietly, eyeing the soldiers who were still some distance away, but by nature he had an aversion to English soldiers. "Truthfully, I'm glad to be rid of this place. I'm glad to have the opportunity to live a normal life again and not exist at this wretched purgatory."

"Has it been so awful?"

He looked to the abbey and its dark, tall walls with moss growing on the north side of the building. "Awful enough," he said. "But, then again, I will return to my family's home, which isna much better."

"Where is it?"

"Far to the north, in the Highlands," he said. "A place called Castle Hydra."

She was curious. "That's quite a name," she said. "Why is it called that?"

He shrugged. "No one really knows," he said. "It has always been called that. The home we live in has been there for hundreds of years, but before that, there was a wooden fort built by the tribes who used to inhabit the land. It sits on the edge of an inlet that leads out to sea, and my father thinks they called it the Hydra because there really was a sea serpent in the inlet in days long past. He thinks the original building on the site used to be a temple to the serpent. But who truly knows how things get their name? Men are strange creatures sometimes."

Mabel nodded. "True enough," she said. "Then your home

has been in existence for many years?"

He nodded, looking at her with those dark, twinkling eyes. "My ancestors are Romans," he said. "Ye've heard tale that the Romans once conquered the English? They tried to come to Scotland, but we ran them off or forced them to live among us. Those are my ancestors. They built the temple to the serpent. And they settled the land and married into the tribes."

She smiled faintly. "I had a tutor who spoke of the Romans and the Greeks," she said. "But I do not remember much about them."

He was forced to turn away from her so that he could watch where he was going now that they were near the end of the field. "'Tis nothing for a finely bred lass to know," he said. "The Romans were conquerors. They came to the shores of England and Scotland, back in the old days, and they forced men to serve their empire."

"Sounds fearsome."

He gave her a half-grin. "We are."

"Is that where you get your name? I've never heard it before."

He nodded. "All men in my family are given Roman or Aragon names," he said. "The Romans we descend from were men from Aragon. Therefore, our son will have a name of my choosing. Possibly after a Roman king or an Aragon prince."

Her eyes widened, and she couldn't help the snort that escaped her lips. "*Our* son?" she said. "Are we having a son together, then?"

All he did was cast her a sidelong glance, grinning, and Mabel's heart nearly beat right out of her chest. Something about that expression suggested he meant what he'd said, and, strangely, she believed him. She wasn't sure why, but she did.

Few were actually men of their word, but Mabel suspected Lares was one of them. Out in the middle of a lightly traveled area of Cumbria, working in a field of cabbages, was a man who spoke the truth.

He meant every word.

Pondering that very thing, Mabel was prevented from answering because the soldiers were upon them at this point. Her father's heavily armed men had come to collect her, and she batted them away.

"Leave me alone," she scolded them. "He's perfectly capable of helping me."

The soldiers weren't happy about it. Irene wasn't happy about it. But Mabel tightened her arms around Lares' neck and grinned at him as a gaggle of soldiers stood by, unsure what to do. By this time, there were a pair of priests who had come forth to greet the visitors, and they were all watching with various expressions of concern and outrage as Lares carried Mabel out of the field and headed toward her mother.

Lares wasn't unaware of the battery of condescending stares, either.

He knew he was going to get an earful.

"I fear our acquaintance is coming to a close, m'lady," he said, his gaze on the mother in particular. "'Twas an honor to meet ye, and I'll miss George when he leaves. Should I wish to call upon ye, where do ye live?"

Mabel looked at him. She found that she was quite sorry they would soon be parted. "Slow your walk," she said quietly. When he looked at her curiously, she smiled. "The faster you walk, the faster you must put me down."

A smile spread across his lips, and he immediately slowed. "That was a bold suggestion, m'lady."

"Then walk quickly if you do not agree."

His dark eyes studied her. "I slowed down, didn't I?"

Mabel chuckled. "You did," she said. "But my mother will be furious that I've spoken to a farmer. Look at her—she is already having fits."

"Would she have fits if ye spoke with an earl?"

Mabel wasn't sure what he meant. "Of course not," she said. "But that is different. A man of higher standing and she'd probably throw me into his arms herself."

The smile on his lips grew. "I said I wasna a priest," he said. "Nor am I a farmer, but that is my task here at Camerton. I was sent here by my da because… Well, it doesna matter why. But know that I'm not a priest nor a farmer. I was born my father's heir."

"What does that mean?"

He told her.

ↁ

"HE'S A *WHAT*?"

Irene was close to being irate as she watched the tall, handsome man in peasant clothing carry her daughter toward the abbey entry. She'd demanded to know who he was, but a few words from the priest had her turning to the man in shock.

"Say that again," she demanded. "He's the *what*?"

"He is the Earl of Torridon." The priest, a thin man with bad teeth, was looking at her rather fearfully. "That young man who has been working our fields."

Irene's mouth popped open, briefly, in astonishment. "The Earl of Torridon is working your fields?"

The priest seemed nervous as he spoke. "Lares dun Tarh has only just become the Earl of Torridon," he clarified. "We received word two days ago that his father has passed away, and Lares was his heir. He is now the earl and, as such, is preparing to return home."

Irene's astonishment took on a hint of interest. She returned her focus to the tall, dark-haired man emerging from the field of cabbages with her daughter in his arms, and she could see all manner of possibilities. Not that she wasn't selective about whom her daughter should marry, but Mabel had been difficult when it came to finding her a husband. At her age, she should be betrothed at the very least, but she wasn't. Any man that came to call upon her, either by his own initiative or by invitation, had been found wanting in Mabel's eyes. She was bright and stubborn, and had a very strong idea about the man she wished to marry.

Irene, however, wasn't so selective. If she could garner a titled lord for her daughter—an earl, no less—then she would do it. She would do what it took.

Even if the earl was Scots.

"Tell me about him," she said to the priest just as Lares and her daughter came out of the field. "Why was he here at the abbey? Does he mean to be a priest?"

The priest shook his head. "Nay, my lady," he said. "As I said, his father had him sent here after the lad was caught trying to marry a lady without permission, but also…"

He trailed off, causing Irene to look at him curiously. "Also *what?*"

The priest was hesitant as he lowered his voice. "He was sent here to save his soul," he muttered. "He was caught summoning demons, and his father sent him here to purge the demons from him. Since his arrival two years ago, he's slept little, read the Bible for hours every day, and worked the fields rigorously to purge the devil from him. God shall prevail in the end."

Irene's expression had a hint of horror to it as she listened. "Nonsense," she finally scoffed. "There are no demons in that man."

"We have worked hard to ensure that there are none, my lady."

"He looks perfectly normal to me."

"I hope so, my lady."

Irene wasn't sure what more to say to that. Her daughter and the man in question, now an earl, were coming closer, and as they drew near, Irene went out to meet them.

"What happened?" she said to her daughter. "Did you fall? You foolish child, I told you to be careful. I knew you would hurt yourself."

Mabel had little patience with her mother. "I slipped in the mud and twisted my ankle a little," she said. "But I assure you, I'm perfectly well."

"If you are well, then let me see you stand."

"I'm not that well."

Irene growled in frustration. "First your brother, now you," she said dramatically. "We are here to bring your brother home because he broke his leg, and now you are injured as well. Your father will be quite angry!"

Annoyed, Mabel squirmed with the intention of climbing out of Lares' arms, so he lowered her to the ground carefully. She stood on both feet, but the truth was that she was mostly balancing on her left foot.

"See?" she said. "I can stand. I will be completely well by the time we return home, so you needn't worry about Papa. Right now, we should be more worried about George. Have you asked to see him?"

Irene hadn't. She'd been so concerned with her headstrong daughter that the very reason they were here had completely slipped her mind.

But she wasn't going to admit that.

"Of course I have," she said, turning to the priest. "Why have you not taken me to my son yet? I demand that you take me to George immediately."

The priest had no idea what she meant, and he looked at her with surprise first and then fear. "My lady?" he stammered. "Your… your son?"

Irene threw an imperious finger toward the abbey. "I *told* you," she said, though she knew full well that she hadn't. "We've come for the young man who has broken his leg. I am Lady Irene de Waverton, and my son is inside the abbey. Take me to him immediately."

The priest darted inside with Irene following. Mabel was left standing there, or rather balancing there, as everyone seemed to be moving into the abbey. As her father's soldiers wandered back over to the escort, she looked at Lares.

"I do believe they have left us alone," she said.

The corners of his mouth twitched. "It would seem so, m'lady,"

"Would you be so kind as to help me inside?" she said. "I hate to ask, but I fear that I lied to my mother when I told her that I was well. My ankle hurts a great deal."

Lares had suspected as much. "We should tend to your ankle before it grows worse," he said. "If ye'll allow, I can help."

Mabel smiled at his kindness. "You've helped quite a lot already," she said. "But mayhap you can help me inside. I should like to see my brother."

Without a word, he bent over and picked her up again, carrying her into the dark, cool innards of Camerton. It smelled of cold earth and dust, and of the incense the priests were so fond of that came from mysterious places across the sea. While Lares was fairly certain he could become quite used to his arms around Mabel, she was thinking that she could become quite used to being carried around. By him. As he followed the voices into the dormitory where George was exclaiming his delight at seeing his mother, Mabel found her gaze lingering on Lares, only to flush and turn away when he caught her staring at him.

It was a game they played more than once. She would look, he would catch her, and before they entered the dormitory, he was looking and she caught him. Lares had gone from a simple rescue mission to a game of interest fairly quickly.

And so had Mabel.

But no more interested than Lady Irene. She didn't even care when Lares entered the dormitory carrying her daughter for a second time. Nay, she didn't mind at all because before the day was through, she'd come to know Lares dun Tarh and the tale of his remote, but evidently rich, earldom. By the next morning—for they did remain at the abbey overnight—she was to return home with two very important things: her son for one and a betrothal for the other. Lares dun Tarh had surrendered without a fight.

When their first son, Aurelius, was born a year later, it was the beginning of the legend of Lucifer's Highland Legion.

PART TWO
AURELIUS

CHAPTER FOUR

Year of Our Lord 1346
August
Crécy en Ponthieu, France

THE AIR SMELLED of death.

Everything smelled of blood and death, mud and smoke, and it filled every inch of every nostril after the battle to end all battles. It had been at Crécy that the English had defeated the French, that Edward III had crushed Philip VI, in a smug attack against the English that the French were certain they were going to win.

Instead, they'd left piles of the dead and dying.

It was nighttime now after the decisive victory. The English had formed their encampment to the north of the battlefield, east of the Maye River that ran from north to south. The deluge that had constituted much of the day had died down, leaving a sea of bloody mud in its wake. On the rise overlooking the battlefield and the town of Crécy-en-Ponthieu, the victory fires of the English burned bright into the clear night sky.

The encampment was a mixed bag of the jovial and the brutal realities of battle. The men who had survived the battle relatively unscathed were gathered around the numerous campfires, talking and drinking and showing signs of levity. But the truth was that they all had a certain glassy-eyed stare, an expression so common to men who had suffered through the rigors of battle. There was something in that hollow gaze that suggested shock and horror they would never be able to fully verbalize. It was the type of experience that men often kept buried, unable to relive the death with so many friends and colleagues.

Un jour de mort.

A day of death.

That was what the men would call the battle of Crécy in the years to come.

The English had collected into groups of allies as the evening deepened, royal knights and soldiers under Edward III and his son, Edward of Woodstock, and then men who served under the Earl of Northampton. On the extreme north of the encampment were the men under the command of the Earl of Wolsingham, a powerful man with allies from the north that included the House of de Wolfe and the House of de Nerra. Wolsingham also had an entire contingent of Highlanders from far to the north of Scotland who had been attached to the de Wolfe group. De Wolfe was the largest family in Northumbria, holding most of the major castles, with tens of thousands of men at their disposal.

Including Scots.

Even now, the leader of those Scots was heading back into the encampment. He'd been with the wounded, checking on some of his men, men who unfortunately refused to accept the fact that they had, in fact, been wounded. That was typical of the Highlanders he knew. He'd been summoned by one of the barber-surgeons attached to Wolsingham's command because the man needed to amputate the fingers of a Highlander who simply refused to let him.

That was when the man had sent for Aurelius dun Tarh.

Aurelius was the kind of man that his own men called *cumhachd sàmhach*... quiet power. It was something greatly admired by those who knew him, and he had a reputation for being a man of such quiet power that legions of Highlanders would follow him into battle with a mere wave of the hand. *Cumhachd sàmhach* was more of a trait, an inherent characteristic woven into the very fabric of a man, that couldn't be bought. It couldn't even really be taught. It was something a man had or he didn't.

And Aurelius had it.

So, he was sent for when a stubborn Highlander refused to let his smashed fingers be amputated. They were pulverized and would soon grow infected, but still, the man refused. Aurelius knew the soldier, an older man with one eye who came from Clan MacKenzie, a clan related to the dun Tarh clan, and he'd sat with him and reasoned with him as to why having only a couple of fingers on one hand was possibly better than having five. Two fingers was all a strong man would need. It had been a nearly foolish argument, but Aurelius had managed to convince the seasoned Highlander that, indeed, two fingers on one hand was all a great man needed.

The surgeon was able to do what he needed to do.

Now, Aurelius was heading back to his own campfire, passing others as he went, smiling wearily to the men who called to him by name. He was a popular figure in the force of Edward III, mostly because Aurelius and his Highlanders were always on the front lines. While the English and Welsh archers did severe damage to the calvary of the French and their allies, Aurelius and his men had gone in on foot to kill those who were wounded, to strip those who were dead, and to generally wreak havoc on anyone who had the misfortune to be on foot. They even slashed the legs of mounted men and cut a few tendons while they were at it. No one long survived against Aurelius and his marauders. They'd proven themselves more than worthy.

But now… now, it was time for a celebration.

"Aurelius!" came a shout. "What are ye doing, man? Come over here and join us!"

Aurelius could see his brother, Darien, waving him over. Darien *an geal*, or Darien the White—he was called so because of a big white streak of hair right at the top of his forehead. Aurelius had, in fact, brought four brothers with him to the field of battle—Darien, Estevan, Caelus, and Kaladin. He had eight brothers total, but his mother wouldn't let the younger boys travel so far from home, so only the older brothers were allowed to go. The youngest of the group, Kaladin, was nearly a grown man, and the truth was that his mother tried to keep him behind, but he'd snuck out and followed. He'd finally met up with his brothers and Wolsingham's group in Dover, and Aurelius knew that if he were to return home without Kaladin, his mother would probably never recover. Such was the burden of the older brother, protecting the younger—and mostly annoying—siblings. But the truth was that he didn't mind.

If his mother was his heart, his brothers were his soul.

The bond of the dun Tarh brothers was legendary.

"I'm coming," he said, wandering toward the enormous fire where they were all gathered as someone shoved a cup of wine at him. "'Tis a fine night, lads. There is much to be grateful for."

A dozen cups were lifted in agreement, men saluting Aurelius, saluting their victory. As Aurelius had said, there were many things to be grateful for. He took a seat on an upturned log next to Darien, who was already a few cups into his drink with another half-full cup in his hand. He held his cup out to Aurelius, who knocked his own cup into his brother's. Together, they drank deeply until Darien nearly fell over backward because his head was tipped back.

With a grin, Aurelius steadied him.

"Ye fought well, all of ye," he said, looking at the men gathered around the fire. "Today was the measure of a man, I must say. I've fought many battles, but I've never seen one quite like this one."

"Indeed, nor have I." A knight across the fire nodded, his features not nearly as gleeful as some of the men around them. "My family has been fighting wars for generations. I've been fighting since I could hold a sword. But this battle… this was legendary in its brutality."

Aurelius nodded to the statement of Thaddeus de Wolfe, who was sitting with his brother, Atticus, and his cousins, Rhori and Bretton, who went by Bret. Their fathers were the grandsons of the great William de Wolfe, Earl of Warenton, the man who had almost single-handedly tamed the north. The de Wolfe family had intermarried into several northern families—de Velt included—so they were distantly related to the dun Tarh clan because Aurelius' mother was a de Velt. Therefore, Aurelius and his entire family looked upon de Wolfe as cousins, and, at the moment, Aurelius was glad that the de Wolfe knights had survived, though Bret had taken a beating when he'd been unhorsed. But still, he was alive.

They were all alive.

That was what mattered.

"But ye survived," Aurelius reminded them quietly. "We all survived, which is more than I can say for the French troops."

Bret de Wolfe was standing behind his brother, a young knight with a serious air about him and his left arm secured to his body with a big linen bandage. His gaze turned toward the darkness, toward the sounds of distant agony.

"You can hear them out there, still," he muttered. "The French are trying to remove their dead, but I do not see how they possibly can. The mud… the way they were piled on one another… How do you find men who have become part of the earth like that?"

Bret, son of Ronan de Wolfe, was facing his first major battle, and it had been quite an introduction. It was true that he'd been born to battle, like all of the males of his family, but facing reivers on the Scots border and then the massive French army in bloody chaos were quite different. He'd never seen destruction like this—quite frankly, none of them really had. Not like this. Beneath the celebration for victory lay the nasty underbelly they were mostly unwilling to acknowledge except in moments like this.

There was no ignoring it.

"The story of mankind is full of battles where men become part of the earth."

Another man, a few feet away from Aurelius, spoke quietly. He was older than the rest of them, his father having been a great English mercenary back in the day. Austen de Nerra glanced up at the younger knights around him, watching their faces as they were licked by the light from the flame.

"What do you think happens when a man dies?" Austen continued. "He fades into the earth and becomes part of it. He becomes part of the food we eat and the air we breathe.

Sometimes, the earth claims her fair share of men during a battle. You think you are only fighting one enemy out there? Nay, lad. The earth is there to digest the folly of men. The mud was simply her way of doing that."

His words had the younger knights spooked and trying not to show it. In the distance, they could hear the groans of the wounded as pinpricks of light moved in the distance while the French searched for their dead and dying. No one would chase them off and no one would help them.

It was time to show mercy.

"Mud or no mud, I'm glad it is over," Aurelius said, breaking the eerie mood. He looked to Austen and his cousin, Sir Matthew Aston. "Ye performed well today, *Sassenach*. Ye showed the younger knights a thing or two out there."

Austen swallowed the drink in his mouth. "We showed them how to avoid the mud," he said, fighting off a grin at his own joke. "I think the most impressive part of the day was watching you and your Highlanders stay low beneath the cavalry and cut legs and saddle cinches. You move like a ghost, Aurelius. I know you are a trained knight, but you fight like a Highlander."

Aurelius glanced over at his brothers. "That is because I lead the finest Highlanders in all of Scotland," he said, watching his younger brothers lift their cups in agreement. "Estevan and Caelus and Kal havena seen a battle of this size before, but they performed admirably."

"Because they were scared out of their wits," Darien said, also looking at his younger brothers. He and Aurelius were a little more than a year apart in age, while Estevan, Caelus, and Kaladin were a few years younger. He pointed at Kaladin, his seventeen-year-old brother, who was bigger than almost any man there. "Kal is a baby bull. Did ye see him tucking underneath the horses of the French and ramming the horses behind the knees so they would falter?"

Aurelius snorted. "I'm surprised he could fit," he said, watching Kaladin frown. "Dunna scowl at me. We called ye a baby bull, did we not? We could have called ye a squealing piglet."

"Or a stupid whelp," Thaddeus said, smiling wearily. "I've got younger brothers of my own. Four of them, including Atticus. 'Tis an older brother's right to call the younger brothers what we want, and they can do nothing about it. Atticus, you are very much a weak little pup. What do you have to say to that?"

Atticus and Kaladin looked at each other, possibly considering protesting that particular dictum, but they both realized at the same time that any protest would not be well met, so they shrugged at each other and kept their mouths shut. That brought some laughter from the men, including Aurelius. He rather liked Thaddeus de Wolfe, a big man who looked a good deal like his father, Titus de Wolfe. Titus, and his brothers and cousins of the same generation, had been too old to come on the battle march to France, leaving the way open for the younger knights to gain experience. Perhaps Atticus and Kaladin were whelps and pups and baby bulls, but what they had done today was earn the respect of the more seasoned knights. Frankly, Aurelius was simply glad they were in one piece.

For him, that was the best possible outcome of all.

"Call them what ye will," he said after a moment. "But today, they've earned the right to sit here with us and drink to victory. And tomorrow… tomorrow we will see about heading home."

"Is it really over, Bear?" Estevan asked quietly. "Do ye think we can truly go home now?"

He'd addressed Aurelius by the family nickname that had come from Darien himself. Unable to pronounce his brother's name as a small child, Darien referred to him as "brother," which ended up sounding like "ba-bear" and, finally, just "bear." Aurelius could hear the yearning in Estevan's voice, and he had to admit that he felt the same longing for home. They'd been gone for almost a year, a very long time to be away from a family they were all close to.

It was a hunger for the Highlands that was in their very blood.

Highlands they were born to.

"I dunna know," he said honestly, looking at his brothers. "The battle seems to be over, but permission to return home must come from Wolsingham himself."

"Will you at least ask him?"

Aurelius held up a hand, quieting his brother. The lad hadn't yet learned not to speak of such things at the end of a battle. It was considered bad luck because a lot of things could happen, even after a battle was concluded, to prevent them from heading home. As he waved him off and lifted his cup with the intention of draining it, they heard a voice approach from the darkness.

"I thought I'd hear more laughter and revelry from this group."

They knew the voice, and everyone who wasn't already standing immediately rose to their feet. The entire group turned to face the Earl of Wolsingham, Adams de Leybourne, as he joined their circle.

"M'lord," Aurelius greeted him, quickly handing the earl a cup of wine provided by Austen. "Congratulations on yer brilliant victory on this day. It will be remembered for generations to come."

The men saluted him, heaping on praise, and Adams lifted a hand to both thank them and quiet them. He was good to his men, and, in turn, he was well liked and respected. When some warlords could be brutal and apathetic when it came to their armies, Adams was considered quite congenial and fair. He was a gray-haired man with a deep voice, not particularly handsome, but his wife was lovely and rich. Since he had married later in life, she was also a good deal younger than he was, but they'd been married for more than two decades and only had one child, a daughter, that no one had ever met.

Ever the gentleman, Wolsingham tended to keep his personal life, and his family, well removed from anything that had to do with warfare and his armies, but he had a reputation for being attached to his wife and daughter, and most of the seasoned knights, Aurelius included, wondered if he would want to quickly return to England now that the battle seemed to have been conclusively decided. Estevan's question about going home could quite possibly have an answer soon enough.

Wolsingham didn't keep them waiting.

"Today's battle was fought by all of us, not simply me," he said, looking to the men around him. "This group—this great group of knights—is what helped secure today's victory. I would bring particular attention to Rhori and Bret de Wolfe, along with their cousins, Thaddeus and Atticus. I've seen your fathers fight in battle, and they would have been very proud of you today."

Attention turned to the de Wolfe men, who seemed pleased

with the acknowledgement. Men began to congratulate them, speaking on de Wolfe knights of the past, but Wolsingham held up his hands for quiet.

"A moment, please," he said as the conversation abruptly died down. "I will address the army as a whole shortly, but I wanted to address this group first. I have a specific purpose in doing so. However, there is one of you, in particular, that I should like to address first."

Thaddeus, who was closest to him, cocked his head curiously. "Who, my lord?" he asked.

Wolsingham didn't answer him directly. He looked at the faces around him until he came to Aurelius. "Bear, may I speak with you privately?" he said.

Aurelius didn't hesitate. "Of course, m'laird," he said. "Shall we go to yer tent?"

Wolsingham simply shook his head, motioning for Aurelius to follow him a few feet away from the campfire, far enough so their conversation couldn't be overheard. With the sounds of muted conversation, laughter, and the cries of the wounded as a backdrop, Aurelius faced his liege.

"I am sorry if this seems mysterious," Wolsingham said, a weary smile on his lips. "But I wanted to speak to you without that group of jesters clouding the issue. I realize they are your cousins and brothers, but once they get started, it is difficult to silence them."

Aurelius fought off a grin. "That is true," he agreed. "There are times I'd like to gag the lot of them."

Wolsingham chuckled. "Well can I believe it," he said, but quickly sobered. "Bear, I wanted to applaud you on how well you fought today. It was a prideful thing for me to watch."

Wolsingham was one of the few men outside of the family

that was permitted to address Aurelius by his nickname. The dun Tarh clan had been under Wolsingham's command in various battles for the past twenty years, when Lares dun Tarh fought for the man. There was a longstanding alliance and friendship there, so Aurelius was touched by the man's words.

"Ye honor me, m'laird," he said. "I believe my men performed well, also. Even Estevan."

Wolsingham grinned. "He's very young," he said. "And very eager and very strong. If you can control that strength, I do believe you'll have a fine warrior on your hands. But that is not what I wanted to speak with you about."

Aurelius cocked his head. "Oh?"

"I intend to reward you for your performance. You have earned it."

Aurelius' eyebrows lifted. "That is kind, m'laird, but a reward is not necessary," he said. "Allowing us to return home soon would be reward enough."

Wolsingham shook his head. "It is a very special reward," he said. "I've thought long about this particular reward. You're a fine knight, Bear. You are well liked by the men. They will follow you anywhere, and that is a unique gift. I had always hoped to have a son just like you, but that was not to be. Do not misunderstand me—I am quite content with my wife and daughter. They are the sun to my moon. But a man… Well, a man wishes for a son. Your father had eight of them. I envy his good fortune when it comes to sons."

Aurelius' eyes glimmered. "I'm sure he'd sell ye my youngest brothers," he said. "Cruz is at an age where one wishes he'd been drowned at birth, and Leandro is such a wretched creature that we regularly tie him to a tree and hope wild animals will claim him."

Wolsingham chuckled. "I think your father would have something to say about that," he said. "But it is not Cruz or Leandro that I want. It is you."

"I dunna think my da will let ye buy me."

"I wasn't thinking about purchase. I was thinking about marriage."

"I'm flattered, but ye're already married, m'laird."

He'd meant it as a jest, but Wolsingham wasn't smiling. His dark eyes were intense as he fixed them on Aurelius. "I am a man without an heir, Aurelius," he said quietly. "I have an enormous empire without anyone to lead it when I am gone. I want that leader to be you."

Aurelius was coming to realize what the man was saying, and all of the humor drained from his face. "Ye… ye want me to…?"

"I have already spoken to your father," Wolsingham said quickly, as if hoping to get it out before Aurelius exploded. "A year ago, I wrote to him and proposed a betrothal between you and my daughter. He has agreed, Aurelius. Consider the betrothal a reward for your performance here at Crécy, but also because I believe you will make an astonishing and righteous Earl of Wolsingham. Most happily, for me, is that you will marry my daughter and officially become my son. God did not give me a male child of my blood, but I believe he has brought me to you. I have been wanting to tell you for months, but it never seemed the right time. But now… now, it is the right time. You are the only man worthy of my legacy and my Valery."

Aurelius was dumbfounded. "Valery?"

"My daughter, Valery."

Aurelius was staring at the man, trying not to appear too

shocked or too appalled. It was obvious that Wolsingham's offer had taken him by surprise, but he was even more surprised about his father's involvement.

"My… my father knows of this?" he managed to stammer.

Wolsingham nodded. "He knows and he approves," he said. "Lad, you'll not only be the Earl of Torridon, but the Earl of Wolsingham as well. You'll be an immensely powerful man in both Scotland and England, and your children will be those who forge nations and unite worlds. Men of your greatness should have such responsibility, Aurelius. You need not say anything about it now, because I know it is a surprise, but you can now see why I did not wish to say this in front of the men. You are betrothed to my daughter, and when we return home, we shall go to Lydgate Castle, where you can meet your future bride. Valery is a kind and intelligent woman. She is also beautiful, and I speak without bias when I say that. I swear to you that she will make you a wife worthy of the Earl of Torridon and Wolsingham."

Aurelius had no idea what to say. He felt as if he'd been kicked in the head by a horse, because he was in a daze. Nothing seemed to be clear except for one thing…

This had been planned for quite some time.

"Then I have been a betrothed man for months and ye've not bothered to tell me?" he said incredulously. "I was not even offered a say in this matter?"

Wolsingham shook his head. "That is something you must ask your father," he said. "He spoke for you, and I will not explain why because I do not know. But the fact remains that you must marry someday. I have offered you a prestigious marriage to my daughter. My grandchildren will be your children. I cannot think of a better legacy for the House of de

Leybourne or the dun Tarh clan."

Aurelius let his gaze linger on Wolsingham, decidedly un-happy. He didn't care about legacies at the moment. He didn't even care that Wolsingham was delighted. He was simply reeling with the fact that all of this had gone on and he didn't even have a voice in his own future.

"Does yer daughter know about this?" he asked.

"She does not."

"Then mayhap she doesna want an arranged marriage."

Wolsingham lifted his shoulders. "What other kind of mar-riage is there?" he said. "Lad, I know you are shocked and, quite possibly, unsure about the situation, but I assure you that this will be a good thing. Valery is obedient. As I said, she will make a fine wife. Do not insult me by suggesting otherwise."

There was a threat there, something that Aurelius should have seen coming. He'd known Adams long enough to know that the man always got what he wanted. *Always*. He was particularly good at negotiations, and Aurelius suspected that Lares might have fallen victim to some clever manipulation from an assertive earl, but that didn't matter now. It was done, and Aurelius could see that he was simply going to have to accept it.

Anything else could, indeed, be deemed an insult.

"I dunna know anything about yer daughter," he said after a moment. "No one has ever met her. I've only seen yer wife once in all the years we've been allied. Ye keep the womenfolk well away from the men ye associate with."

Wolsingham nodded. "I know," he said. "They are women. They do not need to be involved with my allies or my men, in any fashion, so they keep to their tasks and I keep to mine. I was not lying when I said that Valery was beautiful. She is quite beautiful, and I do not need some fool setting his cap for her. She's far too good for any man, but you are an exception. When you see her, you will understand why I've kept her protected. I hope you will do the same when you are her husband."

Aurelius thought that might be more manipulation, but he had to admit that it had him intrigued. *Valery de Leybourne.* He'd never even caught a glimpse of her, not a shadow. He'd never even heard rumors. This shadow of a woman, this wraith, was now his betrothed. Truthfully, he hadn't even known if she actually existed until this moment.

But she did.

And she was his.

"I would protect any woman who belonged to me," he said. "Any woman who is part of my family—my mother, my sisters, or my wife. Ye needn't worry about yer daughter, m'laird. I'm certain ye wouldna have solicited the betrothal if ye dinna trust me."

Wolsingham smiled, a gesture that conveyed the fact that he was coming to realize that Aurelius wasn't going to rip his head off after all. The Highlander had gone from shock to suspicion and now to resignation all in the matter of a few moments. He seemed to be accepting the treachery that had gone on behind his back, to force a wife upon him. But the truth was that Wolsingham had his eye on Aurelius for quite some time. This wasn't something that had simply happened. It was something that had been planned.

He wanted his daughter, and his legacy, well protected.

He'd wanted Aurelius, and he was going to have him.

"I trust you above all else," he finally said. But he wasn't going to let the conversation end without acknowledging the moment. He hoped it would make the situation more palatable in the end. "Bear, I know this is not what you expected or even hoped for. I know a marriage is not something you have probably considered at your age, but both your father and I feel this is the right thing for you and the right thing for my daughter. You must both marry, after all, and I swear to you that my daughter is not the disagreeable sort. I would not do that to you. But she is spirited. If you will only give her a chance, you might even come to like her."

Aurelius couldn't decide if the man was trying to force him to accept the idea of the betrothal or if he truly meant what he said—that Valery de Leybourne was a spirited beauty. Women like that were few and far between, but it didn't matter now.

It was done.

"I will give her the same chance that she gives me," he said honestly. "But I would ask a favor, m'laird."

"What is it?"

"That ye not tell anyone," Aurelius said, growing serious. "I will do that in my own time, and in my own way. I dunna wish for my brothers to hear it from someone else."

Wolsingham nodded. "As you wish."

With nothing more to be said, Aurelius simply nodded and turned away, heading back toward the men who were packed around the campfire. When they saw Aurelius, Darien asked him what Wolsingham had wanted, but Aurelius managed to distract him with an answer that wasn't exactly the truth, but wasn't exactly a lie, either. The truth was that he simply wasn't willing to tell his brother, or anyone, yet. He knew that such an offer from Wolsingham would provoke some envy, given that he was to be the man's son-in-law and heir. A very wealthy heir. That was his predominant thought at the moment—not the wife, but the wealth. The title. Nay, he didn't want anyone to know yet.

Not until they were headed home.

God help him, his life had just taken a turn for the unexpected.

And he wasn't sure how he felt about it.

CHAPTER FIVE

Three Months Later
Lydgate Castle, Yorkshire
Dun Tarh.

L ADY WOLSINGHAM READ the missive three times, and each time, the name written upon the parchment remained the same.

Our daughter is to marry Aurelius dun Tarh.

She could hardly believe it.

"Mama?" a young woman called, pushing through the old, creaky door without even knocking. "There you are. Did you not hear me calling?"

Lady Wolsingham hadn't. That was the truth. She'd been too busy reading the missive that had been sent ahead by her husband, the one that spoke of the victory at the Battle of Crécy and the fact that their only child was betrothed to the future Earl of Torridon. A Scotsman. More than a Scotsman, but a Highlander. Here at Lydgate Castle, they were so close to the Scots border that they were practically Scottish themselves, but not quite.

That was about to change.

"I did not hear you," Lady Wolsingham said, smiling weakly. "I… I received a missive from your father. He is on his way home. I suppose I was dreaming of the moment he would finally return. Think on it, Valery… Papa is coming *home!*"

Those were the magic words. Valery de Leybourne gasped as she rushed toward her mother, thrilled with the news. Before her mother could stop her, however, she snatched the vellum out of her mother's hands and scurried over to the window for more light so she could read the words herself. Lady Wolsingham was forced to pursue her daughter, trying to take the missive back before she read the part about the new husband that was being foisted on her. Perhaps foisted wasn't the right word, but Valery might see it that way.

Or would see it that way.

With Valery, it was difficult to know.

"Wait, my dearest," Lady Wolsingham said, pulling the missive out of her daughter's hands. "You must wait before you read your father's missive in full."

Valery was grasping for the missive even as her mother pulled it away. "But why?" she said. "I want to read of his homecoming in his own words."

Lady Wolsingham had to put out a hand to stop her daughter's grabby fingers. "*Wait,*" she said, softly but firmly. "Stop and listen to me. There is more in his missive that I do not wish for you to read. It was addressed to me, after all. You should have asked permission before taking it."

Valery gave her mother an impatient look. "When does Papa write something that I cannot read?" she said. "His library belongs to me. Every book in this castle belongs to me. Some are my very own books."

Lady Wolsingham knew that, but she shot her daughter an

impatient look of her own. "Your papa is my husband," she said. "Need I explain to you that there are times when a husband writes something personal for his wife? Not everything is meant for you, Val."

Valery understood, sort of. "Love poetry," she said, moving away from her mother and plopping in an old wooden chair with an overstuffed pillow on its seat. "The sweet strains of love and passion? Ha! Papa would sooner swallow frogs alive than write sickly-sweet love poetry."

Lady Wolsingham cast her daughter a long look before turning to reclaim her chair. "You think you know him that well, do you?" she said. "You would be wrong if that is what you think."

Valery made a face, a normal face that any child would make when thinking of passion between parents. "I do not want to know anything more," she said. "Very well, Mama. What does Papa say in his missive that I *can* hear?"

Before Lady Wolsingham could reply, the sound of grunting was heard on the landing outside of the lady's solar. It was rhythmic, but there seemed to be an echo to it. Both women knew immediately what the sound was, and Lady Wolsingham eyed the door as Valery sat forward in her chair.

"Come along, darlings," she said sweetly. "You may come in."

More grunting, which turned into honking. Two of the biggest geese in all of England waddled in through the door, heading for Valery as she held out a hand to them. They came quickly when they saw her, nibbling her fingers, waddling around the chair as she sat back and dangled her hand over the arm of the chair, petting feathery white heads as they milled around her chair.

Lady Wolsingham sighed as she turned her focus to the missive.

"You know I do not like them in my solar," she said, knowing it was futile even as she said it. "They are destructive."

Valery picked up the nearest enormous goose and put it on her lap. "I will keep them with me," she assured her mother. "They will not wander."

"They belong outside."

"Philip and Edward would be lost without me."

Lady Wolsingham shook her head in disapproval. "I thought you agreed to rename them."

Valery fought off a grin as she stroked the white back. "I *did* rename them after Papa left for France."

Lady Wolsingham looked at her irritably. "Aye, you did," she said. "You named them after the kings of France and England. Do you think that will please your father?"

Valery burst out laughing. "By calling them Philip and Edward, I can order them about," she said. "Both men are silly geese, anyway. Why not name my pets after them?"

Lady Wolsingham was not amused. "You will not call them that in front of your father."

Valery was trying not to laugh at her mother's seriousness. "I will not call them what Papa named them," she said firmly. "I will not call my babies Shite-brain and Dumb Arse."

It was Lady Wolsingham's turn to fight off a grin. "Call them Thunder and Lightning for all I care," she said, turning back to the missive. "Or go back to their original names of Sunny and Moonie. But no more Philip and Edward."

Valery simply shrugged and turned away, absently stroking the goose on her lap while her mother returned her attention to the missive she'd probably already read a half-dozen times. She knew her parents were devoted to one another, but, honestly, it had always seemed as if her father was far more devoted to her mother than the other way around. Of course, her mother showed great respect and admiration for her father, and there was affection between them, but Valery always felt as if her mother might be aloof sometimes when it came to her father. Adams de Leybourne was twenty years older than his wife, and Valery knew he'd been married once before, at a very young age, but his wife had died in childbirth. He'd been eager to remarry and found an equally eager cohort in the form of Lady Wolsingham's father, Ralph de Gilsland.

That had been many years ago.

Valery was aware that her father and mother had hardly known one another when they married. It had been hastily arranged long ago. Adams had Lydgate Castle near the Scots border, but he also had property near London that had been left to him by his mother's family. Brentford was an enormous manor house on the north side of the River Thames, a property that spread for nearly a mile along the river's edge. Her father had preferred Brentford in his younger years because it was close to London and he adored the large city, but as he grew older, he retreated more and more to Lydgate Castle or even Revelstoke Castle, a smaller castle near Middlesborough that had also belonged to his mother's family. Both Lydgate and Revelstoke mined iron, and the land was full of it, making Adams de Leybourne extremely wealthy.

But there was more. Lady Wolsingham's father was still alive, but when he passed on, his property of Mount Pleasant Castle would become a de Leybourne property purely by marriage. Ralph de Gilsland had no sons, nor had Adams de Leybourne, so two vast empires rested solely on Valery. It was her duty to marry and produce sons, or the dynasties of de Gilsland and de Leybourne might very well end or, at the very least, fade away and become part of someone else's empire.

That fact wasn't lost on Valery.

And now, her father was coming home from a long and costly campaign in France. Because her father had the money, and the army, Edward III often called upon him for his military needs, but the truth was that her father was becoming older. He shouldn't even be fighting any longer at his age, and Valery suspected her mother was going to tell him he could no longer go with his army. Widowhood wasn't something that appealed to Lady Wolsingham.

There were enough war widows in England as it was.

"What else did Papa say in his missive that you can tell me?" Valery asked, her hand on the smooth feathers of the goose's back. "That is a long missive for him to only say that he is coming home."

Lady Wolsingham was looking at the missive, her manner thoughtful. Almost… sad. She was definitely subdued, and it took her a few moments to respond.

"I know it has been some time since we last spoke on marriage for you," she said, lifting her gaze to her daughter. "We used to speak of it frequently before your father went to France."

It was a change in subject, but Valery didn't read anything into it. She simply nodded. "I know," she said. "I assume we shall speak more of it when he returns. Why do you ask?"

"I want to know how you feel about marriage. Has it changed?"

Valery set the goose to the floor when it tried to jump off her lap. "Nay," she said. "I still want to marry. I always have. I do not wish to be an old maid."

Lady Wolsingham snorted softly. "You shan't, I assure you," she said. "But will you trust your father's judgment in such matters?"

Valery shrugged. "I do," she said. "But nothing has changed in that regard. It is the same as before he left."

"And what is that?"

"That I want to have a voice in whom I marry."

"Your father has told you that he will not allow you to choose."

Valery frowned. "I do not want to choose," she said. "Not truly choose. But I do want to at least approve of whom Papa wishes for me to marry. Why are you asking me these questions?"

Lady Wolsingham looked back to the yellowed parchment in her hand. "You know that I did not choose your father," she said. "My father chose him. I did not see the wisdom of it at the time. In fact, I was quite averse. But in time, I understood his reasons. He was right, after all."

Valery watched her mother. There was a pregnant pause as she began to process what her mother was saying. The wheels of thought were turning, and now she was starting to realize that this was no random subject change. After a moment, she stood up and took a few steps in her mother's direction, pointing to the missive.

"What does Papa say about a marriage for me?" she asked quietly. "He must have said something, or you would not be trying very hard *not* to tell me."

Lady Wolsingham wouldn't look at her. "I had not planned to tell you at all," she said truthfully. "I was going to let your father tell you."

"Tell me what?"

"That he has selected a husband for you."

Valery didn't lash out in response. She didn't react angrily. No shouting, no denials. Truthfully, given the fact that she wanted to marry someday, there was no reason for her to. But she hadn't expected that her father, on a battle campaign, no less, had already chosen a husband for her. That made her suspect it was another warlord or a knight, someone her father had worked closely with. Someone he admired. Her gaze lingered on her mother for a moment before she turned away.

"Does he say who it is?" she asked.

Lady Wolsingham watched her daughter carefully. "The heir to the earldom of Torridon," she said. "He is Scots."

That brought a reaction. Valery turned to her sharply. "A Scotsman?"

"Highlander."

Valery's eyebrows lifted. "A *Highlander*?" Now she was starting to show some emotion. "He is turning Wolsingham over to a Scotsman? Why would he do such a thing?"

"He must think that it is an appropriate match or he would not have made it," Lady Wolsingham said. "The Scotsman—the Highlander—is from the dun Tarh family. That is a very old, very prestigious family in the Highlands."

Valery frowned. "How would you know that?"

Lady Wolsingham set the missive aside. "Do not forget that I grew up at Mount Pleasant, which is on the Scots border," she said. "I knew someone from the dun Tarh family long ago. Very long ago. I… I do not know what became of him, but my father was allied with the family."

Valery was still agitated about a Scotsman as a future husband, but her mother's words had her interest. "Then you know something about them," she said. "What are they like? And where is this Torridon?"

"Far to the north," Lady Wolsingham said, averting her gaze so her daughter wouldn't notice the distant glimmer in her eyes as she remembered something she'd put out of her heart and her mind long ago. "They are related to the MacKenzie clan, as I recall, but the origins of their family was rumored to have come from a lost Roman legion. The family is steeped in mystery and legend."

That was interesting to Valery. A learned woman, she knew about the Romans in Britannia and Caledonia. She'd had a tutor, a former priest, who knew all about the ancient history of England, when the Romans came. He'd been a devotee of Roman military history, among other things, something that had bored Valery but thrilled Adams. Just because he didn't have a son didn't mean his daughter couldn't learn what a son would have learned. Therefore, Valery knew more about ancient history than most young women should have.

"I suppose every family has their origins," she said, sounding as if she was torn between interest and apathy. "But there are only three things I care about."

"What is that?"

"If he is a good man and if he is educated," Valery replied. "Surely Papa knows he must be up to my standards. I cannot have a dullard for a husband."

"What is the third thing?"

"That he is handsome, of course."

Lady Wolsingham couldn't help the smile, shaking her head at her daughter's sense of priorities. "If he is a dun Tarh, then he is handsome," she said. "The family is full of men who would fit that description."

"You seem to know a good deal about them."

"Not really."

She didn't seem willing to elaborate, and Valery let the subject fade. Frankly, she was unwilling to reply more than she already had because she was already sounding superficial in her demands. He must be a good man, educated, and handsome. In her world, that was what mattered. She had seen her friends marry, and those three things were literally the only criteria they had. Sometimes young girls prioritized the frivolous over the important, and Valery tried not to be so foolish, but it was difficult. Since her family spent so much time in London, or at least they had in the past, most of her friends were well-bred women from noble families, and all that had ever been expected of them in life was to be pretty and charming and accomplished when it came to entertaining a gentleman suitor or running a household.

That was what Valery had grown up around. Because her family home of Brentford was in a section of London that had several other townhomes nearby, she had shared a nurse with other families with young girls. That was common. This had been when she was very young, and the nurse had given way to a governess, a tutor who taught the young girls to recite poetry and paint, to dance and to play an instrument, at which Valery had never been any good. Even though that sort of training ended on the cusp of womanhood, Valery's father had insisted she continue in her education, and hired a priest who taught her everything from astronomy to Roman military history.

While her friends were going to feasts and pining for men, Valery had been schooled by a man known affectionately as Trout because that was what he looked like—a fish. Trout's actual name was Father Bruno, but no one ever used it, and he didn't seem to care. Trout was serious and scholarly, but he was also strangely warm and encouraging. Valery had taken to her lessons eagerly, learning and absorbing from Trout while her mother sat in a corner and sewed. Lady Wolsingham had probably learned as much as Valery did from Trout, because she never missed a lesson. As the chaperone of her virginal daughter, she wasn't about to leave Valery alone with a man, even a priest named Trout.

But the education with Trout had made Valery a little different from her friends. She was still invited to feasts and parties, and she still saw her friends in London when she could, but she had come to the age where now she was being invited to their weddings, and all they wanted to know was when she would be married, too. Perhaps that was why she hadn't raged when her mother told her about the betrothal. Perhaps there was some relief now, in that she could tell her friends that she, too, was going to be married and would no longer be an outcast among them because she didn't have a husband yet. Truth be told, that had always bothered her a little, because her married friends had different lives than she did. They had husbands and managed their households, while Valery still lived with her parents as an unmarried, and unattached, young woman.

But that was soon to change.

Nay, she wasn't upset about it at all.

In truth, she was a little grateful.

Over in the corner, one of the geese found something to eat, or at least try to eat, and Valery was distracted from her train of thought when her mother gasped. By the time she turned around, she could see that the geese had gotten hold of some bread that had been placed on a table along with fruit and wine. They didn't want the fruit or the wine, but they certainly wanted the bread, so Valery got up to make sure they didn't make a mess. As she headed over to the geese, who were playing tug of war with the bread, there was a knock on the solar door.

"My lady?"

Sir Sterling St. John stood in the opening, addressing Lady Wolsingham. Sterling had been with the House of de Leybourne as long as Valery had been alive, a stalwart and dedicated knight who had given his life over to Adams and the de Leybourne empire. When Adams had gone to France, he'd left Sterling behind because someone needed to be in command of Lydgate, and that person was, by default, him. Though the man had missed the action over in France, he didn't particularly mind, but his son, Maxwell, had gone to France. That made Sterling a father in waiting, and perhaps a little nervous.

Lady Wolsingham answered him politely.

"What is it, Sterling?" she said, glancing up from the missive in her hands.

Sterling's weather-worn face seemed to have a hint of joy to it. "Good news, my lady," he said. "Lord Wolsingham's army has been sighted less than a day away. They should be here by morning."

That bit of news caught Valery's attention. "Papa is almost here?"

Sterling smiled at her, the young woman he very much wanted for his own son. "Aye, my lady," he said. "That means Maxwell is nearly home, too. My wife will be most grateful to see him once again."

The comment about his son was a leading one, because he'd been trying to interest Valery in Maxwell for nearly four years. Valery liked Maxwell, and he was her friend, but he was the gentle, obedient sort—and for a woman like Valery, who needed an equal partner in all things, that kind of temperament simply wouldn't do. More than that, Maxwell didn't want a wife. He preferred the company of men. But even if he was seeking a bride, he still wouldn't have been right for Valery, because as Adams had once said, a man like Maxwell would spend his life worshipping at Valery's feet, and she would spend her life bored to tears.

Lady Wolsingham knew that, and she wouldn't give Sterling the chance to engage Valery in a conversation of Maxwell's return. She'd spent the past year trying to avoid that very subject. Quickly, she stood up.

"Then we must prepare," she said. "We must ensure that we are ready to receive my husband and his army. Sterling, you will do what needs to be done to ensure the comfort and safety of the returning army. Val, come with me. We will go to the kitchens and prepare a magnificent meal for them to return home to."

When Lady Wolsingham gave orders, everyone moved. Even Valery. As Sterling headed off to prepare for his liege's arrival, and his son's, Valery followed her mother from the solar, encouraging her geese to come along. Lady Wolsingham was well on her way to the kitchens as Valery stood in the doorway, trying to coax the geese, but they ended up spilling the wine on the table in their quest to find more bread.

Scurrying back into the chamber, Valery herded the geese out as one would shepherd a gang of unruly sheep. But first, she quickly cleaned up the wine so her mother wouldn't know that Edward and Philip—or Sunny or Moonie, as they were mostly known—had left damage in their wake just as Lady Wolsingham said they would. Valery had to protect her pets at all costs, even from her unhappy mother.

But thoughts of her mother led to thoughts of her father and the betrothal he had evidently secured. As Valery followed her mother's path to the kitchens, with the geese in tow, she couldn't help but feel more and more pleased at the fact that she would, indeed, be marrying. It made her feel mature, perhaps even more womanly, to think that she, too, would have her own husband and house someday.

Even if both were from Scotland.

But that couldn't be helped. She was to be a countess, and it didn't matter if she had to marry a Scotsman in order to achieve it. That was better than any of her friends had achieved. She would be a fine lady someday, ruling over wealthy lands, having great feasts and a gaggle of children. She hoped they would be happy. But there was only one thing that concerned her.

That he had the same dreams as she did.

That he wanted a wife, too.

It was with some apprehension that she looked forward to the future.

CHAPTER SIX

VALERY WAS STILL in bed the next morning when the sentries took up the cry.

Her father's army had been sighted.

Her eyes suddenly bugged wide open and she threw back the coverlet, propelling herself out of bed and rushing, off balance, to the lancet window that overlooked part of the bailey. She couldn't see the army yet, but there was a good deal of excitement going on down below. About a hundred years ago, her great-grandfather had allowed a sycamore tree to spring up in the bailey, near the keep, and the tree was so tall now that it nearly blocked her view of the gatehouse, but not entirely. She could still see through the branches. When the colder months would come, it would lose its leaves and her view would be clearer, but at the moment, it still had its lovely autumn foliage. It was rare for castles to allow trees to spring up in the baileys because they could be used by an enemy if one breached the gatehouse, but the Lydgate sycamore was an exception.

Faunus was his name.

Valery had given the tree that name after the Roman god of forests. Faunus' yellow leaves were filling her vision, and the more she heard the sentries shout, the more excited she became. The geese, who slept in a corner of her room in their own little pen—much to her mother's dismay—were starting to rise at the sound of their mistress' excited yelp. Valery petted them both quickly and threw open the chamber door so they could waddle down to the kitchens to be fed, and so her maids could come in and clean up the animal mess from the night before. As if on cue, two maids rushed in—mother and daughter—as Valery went to her giant wardrobe and yanked open the doors.

"Your papa has come home, m'lady," the older woman said as she began to sweep up the straw that the geese had slept on. "I heard the soldiers say his army was just down the road."

"Good," Valery said, yanking out a clean shift and a lovely linen surcoat with gold silk embroidery on it in diamond-shaped patterns. "He thinks to surprise us, but *I* am going to surprise him."

The servants had a woven basket between them, using it to collect the straw, but the older woman looked at Valery curiously.

"What will you do?" she asked.

Valery grinned at the woman before dashing into a small alcove, behind a painted screen, where she stripped off her sleeping shift and began to quickly wash in the icy-cold rosewater that was there for just that purpose.

"Never you mind, Sela," she said. "Papa and I have always played that game with one another—appearing where we are least expected. Papa once leapt out of the hay loft over the stables. He startled me so badly that I struck him with a shovel."

Old Sela fought off a grin. "You two like to surprise one another," she said. "One of these days, you are going to surprise your father and his heart will seize. He'll fall over in a heap."

Valery laughed softly. "I hope not," she said. "But in the war of seeing who can startle one another more, I do believe I have the edge."

Sela and her daughter, Beryl, looked at each other and shook their heads. They continued sweeping up the straw and giving the floor underneath it a good scrub with vinegar as Valery dressed in the lovely linen garment. She scurried out from behind the painted screen, brushing her hair and pointing a finger to the ties on her back. Sela left the sweeping duties to help Valery with her fastens, making sure she was presentable to scare the life out of her father.

Valery rushed back to the alcove where her dressing things were, finishing brushing out the ends of her wavy hair and putting a gold circlet over her head to push the front of her hair back. It was a headband that kept her hair out of her eyes, a pretty piece that had yellow stones affixed to it. Giving herself one final look, and grinning at the thought of hearing her father shout when she surprised him, she dashed from her bedchamber and headed down the stairs.

By the time she reached the entry level, the servants were abuzz with the news that the army was just coming through the gates. That didn't give Valery much time. She had a plan—her father was very fond of his warhorse, a big white beast that was older than Valery was, and he always saw to the animal's comfort personally when returning from a campaign. Therefore, she was going to hide in the stables and wait for him to bring his horse around before leaping out and giving the man a shock.

Not wanting him to see her, because the keep entry was in view of the outer bailey and the incoming army, she took the small servants' stairwell down to the kitchens on the ground level. The kitchens comprised four smaller chambers, and they were running at full force on this brilliant morning. Valery was hit in the face with the heat from the ovens, which were conveniently built inside the keep and not out in the kitchen yard, as she raced through the chambers, grabbing a piece of bread as she went. The cook yelled at her, something about the porridge that was cooking, but Valery didn't stop. She continued out into the sunny kitchen yard, noting that her geese were scratching around there, chasing down bugs and other things to eat.

Blowing kisses to the geese, who were too busy scrounging around to notice her, she ran to the end of the kitchen yard, shoved all of the bread into her mouth, and entered the south side of the stables through a servants' entrance. Chewing the bread, which was difficult considering she'd stuffed it all into her mouth, she quickly mounted the ladder to the hayloft above.

And then she waited.

Her father didn't come right away. Bread chewed and swallowed, Valery lay on her belly, peering through the slats in the hayloft so she could see the main entry to the stables. She could see servants rushing around and horses being brought in, and she saw clearly when men she didn't recognize brought more horses into the corral. Since her father never let her meet any of the allied men from other armies, she had no idea who they were, but she was quite curious about them. There were two older ones and three younger ones, with the younger ones mostly tending the horses while the older ones seemed to be deep in conversation. And then she heard it.

A Scots accent.

Puzzled, and increasingly curious, she edged toward the end

of the hayloft, closer to the door. She could hear the men talking and she could see them, though mostly in profile, and at one point, they both entered the stable and lowered their voices. But they weren't low enough so that she didn't hear them.

In fact, Valery got an earful.

They were speaking of a forced marriage. They spoke of her father. They spoke of her as Wolsingham's only child. They spoke of someone named Aurelius who had been forced into a marriage he didn't want. Apparently, she was hideous because no one had ever seen her, and Aurelius was only marrying her for the wealth and title. From what the two men were saying, Aurelius was some kind of godlike hero who belonged on Mt. Olympus more than he belonged on the field of battle.

Aye, that was far more than she'd wanted to hear.

The excitement of her father returning took a dousing as Valery listened to the pair talk. It was mean and cruel and insensitive. Even if they hadn't known she was listening, if they spoke of her unfavorably in her own home, she could only imagine what was said about her on the journey home from France.

And what her betrothed—Aurelius—thought about her.

Any hope or even excitement she'd had about the marriage was crushed.

With a lump in her throat, Valery listened to the men as they finished speaking on the subject. One man, the one with the English accent, seemed to be less irate about the situation than the man with the Scots accent did. In fact, the English knight was trying to calm down the other man, who evidently had some relationship to Aurelius. Whatever the situation or relationship, the Scotsman was clearly unhappy, but the conversation eventually calmed to the point where they both seemed to agree that the marriage was a good one for Aurelius.

Aurelius.

That was the name of her soon-to-be husband.

Valery could see the men from where she was hiding, and when they wandered off, leaving the younger men behind to tend the horses, she climbed out of the loft and slipped out the way she'd come in. She no longer felt like surprising her father. In fact, she wasn't sure what she felt at the moment, knowing that her father was viewed as having forced this Aurelius person into a marriage, and she was viewed as something horrific and hidden. After having not seen her father in about a year, this was what he'd brought home with him.

Well, she didn't want any part of it.

The postern gate was off to her right, a passageway cut into the wall of Lydgate. In fact, it was two gates, one on the exterior of the wall and one on the interior, both of them wooden gates that were heavily fortified. The passageway between them, in fact, even had murder holes from the wall walk above. As Valery headed for the gate, she could hear her goose companions coming up behind her, honking loudly at the sight of her, as they usually did. She waited for them to catch up to her, and when they did, she passed through the gates with them in tow.

The postern gate dumped out into a path that led down the slope to a fortified area beyond. Lydgate was built on the rise of a hill, so Valery trudged down the hill as the geese waddled after her, out into the open area that was walled in. Sometimes, it was used for additional troops or a visiting army, where they could pitch their encampment in a walled area and be reasonably protected. There was a heavy iron portcullis with a gate cut into it that led to the wilds beyond, so she unbolted the gate and stepped through. With the geese behind her, she headed down the slope and into some trees, eventually emerging on the other side.

Before her spread a pond, created by a dammed-up brook. It was a place to swim in the summer when the temperatures became too warm, or sometimes, it was a place for her father and his men to fish. While Adams was gone, Sterling had come down to this pond often and caught fish for Lydgate's table. It was cool and gentle, with a breeze blowing through the trees and small ripples upon the clear water.

Valery took up a seat on the edge of the pond as her geese wandered into it, hunting for bugs and drinking the crystal water. When they were finished drinking and pecking around for surface insects, they began to swim out into the pond, bathing themselves.

Valery loved to watch them frolic.

In fact, watching them splash water on themselves and then shaking off the water gave her a moment's respite from what she'd just heard in the barn, but too soon those thoughts returned, stronger than before. She was trying to talk herself out of being so upset about the situation, of how she was being viewed by men who knew her betrothed, but no matter how she tried to spin it, it came back to the fact that the man she was contracted to marry felt trapped. He was only in it for the money. Valery had been viewing the betrothal as something positive, that she would finally be married like most of her friends, never dreaming that her betrothed wasn't seeing it that way. More than anything, she felt ashamed. Embarrassed and ashamed.

Perhaps she didn't want the betrothal either.

Perhaps she needed to find her father and tell him just that.

Two could play at this game.

C&

IT WAS RIDICULOUS, as far as he was concerned.

Positively ridiculous.

On a bright and windswept morning, Darien and Rhori were settling down some of the horses in the stable block of Lydgate Castle with the help of Caelus and Kaladin. It had been a relatively short ride from Darlington, where they'd spent the night before, but it had been a long ride overall from London. Interestingly enough, whilst there had been a good deal of rain in France, England seemed to be relatively dry, which meant the roads were passable and the army had made excellent time, but it had been a tense ride for Aurelius and Darien.

That was where the ridiculous part came in.

Aurelius had finally confided in his brother about the betrothal to Wolsingham's daughter, and Darien hadn't been pleased in the least. Darien, even though he was the younger brother of the two, had always been quite protective of Aurelius. He viewed Aurelius as a strong and powerful older brother, and sometimes almost godlike in a sense, and he had always felt the need to protect his brother when Aurelius clearly did not need protecting. It was something Aurelius tolerated from Darien, though sometimes it could become quite annoying.

Darien was well aware.

But that didn't stop him from being dutiful and dedicated to his older brother, and that included voicing his dissatisfaction when Aurelius told him about the betrothal. Even though both of them were in their third decade, with Aurelius having seen thirty-one years and Darien almost thirty, the subject of marriage wasn't something they discussed. Darien had no real interest in marrying so young, and, quite frankly, he enjoyed the company of different women. There was something about only one woman for a man that seemed unnatural to him, though Aurelius seemed ambivalent about that. Aurelius could attract any woman he wanted, a trait that all of the dun Tarh brothers seemed to have, but marriage wasn't something he'd ever really shown any interest in.

Until now.

Evidently, he had little choice.

As Aurelius explained it, both their father and Wolsingham had conspired to create a betrothal between him and Wolsingham's daughter. Darien was under the same impression as nearly everyone else under Wolsingham's command, and that was the fact that Wolsingham's wife and daughter were kept far from allies and soldiers alike. No one had ever even seen the daughter, and some speculated that she didn't exist, but that speculation was dashed with Aurelius' revelation. Not only did Wolsingham have a daughter, but she was to be Aurelius' wife.

For some reason, that infuriated Darien.

He didn't like the fact that his brother was being forced into something that he had no say in. He didn't like the fact that their father had seemingly gone behind Aurelius' back to secure a betrothal. But, perhaps most of all, Darien didn't like the fact that his brother would soon have a wife who would clearly take a place of importance in Aurelius' life. Darien and his brother were quite close, and Darien wasn't sure what that meant for their relationship, but he knew he didn't like it.

He was also upset that Aurelius hadn't put up more of a fight.

As he'd said, the entire thing was ridiculous.

Upon reaching Lydgate Castle, however, it began to occur to Darien why his brother hadn't put up a fight. Lydgate was absolutely magnificent, an enormous bastion north of Richmond located at the base of the Pennine mountains. In fact, the vast majority of its property encompassed those mountains, and beyond that was Carlisle and the Scots border, so there was an enormous amount of land that Aurelius would inherit when he married Wolsingham's daughter.

Aurelius had to know that.

So perhaps it was greed that convinced Aurelius to be complacent with the betrothal that was thrust upon him. To Darien, that was the only answer. He'd never known his brother to be greedy, and in a sense he did not blame him, but Darien was simply opposed to the marriage in general.

A marriage that would take his brother away from him.

Those feelings only grew more intense when the army entered Lydgate Castle, flooding into an enormous, rectangular bailey that could easily accommodate a thousand men. While Aurelius and Wolsingham began to walk about on a tour of the place, Darien was part of the contingent to help settle the men along with Wolsingham's knight, Sterling St. John. The father of Maxwell St. John, a knight who had been part of their army for the past several months, Sterling had remained behind to take command of the Wolsingham properties with Adams away. He was older, seasoned, a little crippled from years of wear and tear, but he was strong enough.

In fact, Darien knew Sterling and liked him, but now that his brother was being forced into a marriage that involved Sterling's liege, Darien wasn't quite so friendly to him. As the old knight reunited with his son in an emotional scene, Darien ignored them both and took charge of the dun Tarh Highlanders, instructing Estevan to ensure they were properly bedded down while Darien took the horses, along with his younger brothers, to the stables to ensure they were properly tended.

But much was boiling up in Darien's chest as Rhori joined him in the stables with the de Wolfe horses. Rhori had remained behind with the bulk of the de Wolfe army after Thaddeus, Atticus, and Bretton had ridden ahead, returning home with news and missives and other things for the de Wolfe warlords. De Nerra and Aston had departed for home as soon as they docked in London, so it was just Rhori at Lydgate at this time, a stopover before he continued on. The contingent that Wolsingham had taken to France was disbanding, spreading news of the king's victories.

But the fact that they were closer to home meant that Rhori's mood was good, and he chatted up a storm while Darien brooded. Seeing the rich castle wasn't sitting well with him as he checked the knees and hooves of the warhorses for any stress from the ride. Beside him, Rhori continued talking as he took care of the de Wolfe horses, and when they finally put the warhorses in the corral to eat and drink and rest, Darien began to grumble aloud.

"He doesna need or want any of this," he muttered, putting his horses into the corral as Rhori climbed over the railing to get out. "He was lured into this. Look at it. How can he resist?"

Rhori was still sitting on the top of the rail. "Who can resist?" he said. "What are you talking about?"

Darien was very aware that Aurelius hadn't told anyone about the betrothal. He led the horses to the trough and headed for the railing himself as Caelus and Kaladin came into the corral with brushes and blankets. Disgruntled, Darien leaned against the railing, watching his younger brothers work.

"Dunna mind me," he finally said. "I suppose I've heard some news that I'm not happy with."

Rhori looked at him curiously. "What news?"

Darien knew he shouldn't tell. He knew damn well he shouldn't say a word. But he couldn't help it. He was upset, and sometimes, that clouded his judgment. Crooking a finger at Rhori to follow him, he wandered back toward the stable, standing in the mouth of the structure, away from the ears of his younger brothers. Rhori joined him, now quite curious about what he had to say.

"Ye know that Wolsingham has a daughter," Darien said quietly.

Rhori nodded. "Of course," he said. "I do not know anyone who has seen the girl, but we know he has a daughter. His only child."

Darien grunted, looking out to the enormous keep that dominated the castle complex. "And ye see this place?" he said. "See how grand it is?"

"Quite grand."

"Wolsingham's daughter is an heiress. A *rich* heiress."

"And?"

Darien looked at him. "And Wolsingham and my father have forced a betrothal on Aurelius," he said. Then he waved his hand at the keep, the castle in general. "Aurelius gets all of this if he marries the lass. They forced him into it."

Rhori's eyes widened. "They *did*?" he gasped. "They gave him no choice?"

"None at all."

Rhori couldn't decide if he was horrified about that or im-pressed that Aurelius had been offered such a rich bride. "How does he feel about it?"

Darien waved him off. "He willna complain," he said. "Ye know my brother. He'll silently bear it, no matter how he feels.

He's a good soldier. He does what he's told."

"And you do not agree?"

Darien scowled. "I think it's a tragedy that he's been pushed into a marriage that he's not asked for," he said. "The only reason he hasna put up a fight is because he'll be the next Earl of Wolsingham. The man already has Torridon—he doesna need an English land. Let Wolsingham find another pasty-faced English lord for his daughter. Why does he need Aurelius?"

Rhori wasn't quite sure how to answer that. "I think if he did not want to do it, he would have said so," he said. "This is Bear's fight, Darien. Not yours. You probably should not tell anyone what you told me. It might cause… problems."

Darien knew that. He sighed sharply. "I've only told ye," he said. "But ye're not to tell anyone else. Aurelius hasn't told anyone at all, so let him decide when he wants to announce it. But I just couldna keep it to myself. My brother is being forced to marry a lass that, more than likely, no one else would want if it weren't for her money."

"Why do you say that?"

Darien looked at him as if he were daft. "Because no one has ever seen her," he said. "She's probably hideous and Wolsingham is afraid to let anyone know. Why else would he keep her hidden away?"

He had a point. Rhori scratched his head, thinking on an heiress that, indeed, had been kept hidden away, so it was possible that Darien wasn't wrong. Though it was equally possible he was.

"It is a dilemma, to be sure," he said. "But Aurelius is a prize for any woman. He brings Torridon with him, and her wealth. If you think about this then I'm sure you'll see it is a good match."

Darien rolled his eyes. "It is a good match," he said. "It is a good match on the surface. But ye know and I know that Aurelius has never had any shortage of women. Ye saw him in France—if there's a woman around, she finds him. He's had his share. He even thinks he has a bastard in Edinburgh, though he hasna told my da that. But mayhap my da already knows. My da is wise—and it's not as if he's innocent himself. He's got a reputation, too."

Rhori cracked a smile. "You mean Lucifer?" he said, chuckling. "I know the rumor. We all do. Your father is no more Lucifer than my father is."

Darien shrugged. "That's not what they say in the Highlands," he said. "My da worshipped the devil, they say. My grandfather banished him to Camerton Abbey because legend says it sits upon the gates of hell. Whilst he was there, he communed with his true father daily."

Rhori's smile grew. "I would believe that you are Satan's spawn," he said. "Aurelius, possibly. But not Lares."

"Why not?"

"Because he doesn't have the dark streak in him that you and your brothers do."

Darien's eyebrows lifted. "Then mayhap it was my mother who paired with the devil," he said. "Mayhap she's the one who birthed Satan's progeny."

Rhori snorted and slapped him on the shoulder. "Mabel is a saint," he said. "I will run you through if you say such terrible things about her."

Darien eyed him. Then he broke down into snorts of humor. "Ye only like her because she gave ye candied fruit as a child," he said. "Admit it."

"I admit it completely and fully."

"She did that with any child who visited the Hydra. That way, they'd always remember her."

"She is a very intelligent woman."

Darien continued to grin at him before finally sighing heavily and running his hand through his dark, dirty locks. "I know," he muttered, sagging back against the corral rails. "She's put up with my da and her eight ungrateful sons long enough. And as for Aurelius… I only want the best for him. It simply makes me angry that he's been forced into something he dinna ask for."

Rhori knew that. He knew that Darien was devoted to his brother. "What does he say about it?"

Darien shook his head. "Not much," he said. "What *can* he say?"

"Does he seem distressed?"

"Resigned is more like it."

Rhori folded his big arms across his chest, thinking on the situation as a whole. "Then mayhap you should be as well," he said quietly. "If he has no choice, your rage will not help him. He needs your support now. Not your anger at a situation neither one of you can change."

Darien looked at him, prepared to argue, but thought better of it. There was really nothing he could say that he hadn't already said. After a moment, he nodded.

"Ye're correct," he said, displaying some of that resignation that Aurelius had shown. "But thank ye for listening. I had a lot to say, and I dinna want to say it to Bear."

Rhori slapped him on the shoulder again. "I understand," he said. "But rather than rage about something you cannot change, mayhap you should appreciate what your brother will be acquiring. Marriage is meant for acquisition, is it not? He has done very well for himself."

With that, Rhori headed out of the stable, back to where the horses were corralled. Caelus and Kaladin were brushing the de Wolfe horses, too, and Rhori leaned against the railing and instructed them on how to treat one of the larger mounts. Then the horse kicked, Kaladin caught a hoof in the shoulder, and, as the lad went down, Darien came out of the stable. His thoughts shifted from Aurelius to Kaladin at that point because, as his mother told him and Aurelius, if one of the younger brothers came back from France in broken pieces, there would be hell to pay.

Coming from his saint of a mother, Darien believed that completely.

CHAPTER SEVEN

"… AND THAT'S why the castle is shaped the way it is," Adams was saying. "If you notice the rise it sits upon, it is long and slender. My ancestors built the castle to suit the land."

He was speaking to Aurelius as the two of them stood on the wall walk, looking at the length of the castle. Aurelius, who counted mathematics and architecture among his strengths, leaned over the wall to get a look at the base of it.

"And that is why it appears so massive when approached," he said, gesturing to the gatehouse. "'Tis a brilliant bit of planning. One looks upon the place and thinks it's positively enormous."

Adams looked around. "It is still quite large," he said. "But because of the land it is built upon, it's somewhat narrow. Long and narrow."

Aurelius understood that. "Ye had an ancestor who was most impressive in the way he thought," he said. "He used this rock to his advantage."

"Indeed, he did."

"Has the castle seen much action?"

Adams nodded. "To the northwest is Carlisle and Scotland,"

he said. "There is one main road that leads through the mountains to Carlisle, and the Scots have been known to take it. There's also a nasty bishop in Spennymoor who likes to raid villages from time to time, so the villagers come to us for protection."

Aurelius looked at him curiously. "Ye have a prince of the church violating his flock?"

Adams snorted. "If it were only that simple," he said. "This prince of the church had his position purchased for him by his father, a very powerful French *duc*. The bishop is French, and he views the English as nothing more than vermin. Unfortunately, he also has a French army given to him by his father, and there have been times when he's harassed us. He's done it to Bowes Castle, too, but will not go as far as Richmond. He'd rather give Bowes and I trouble."

Aurelius shook his head at the thought of a petulant bishop. "I canna say I'm looking forward to meeting such a man."

Adams grinned. "Hopefully, you will not," he said. "But now that we are on the subject of meetings, I would like you to meet my daughter. Shall we go to the keep?"

Aurelius scratched his head. "I'd rather we waited," he said. "Can we not meet tonight? I assume we shall feast?"

"We shall," Adams said, but he was frowning. "Why should you not wish to meet her now?"

Aurelius lifted his arms. "Because I've not bathed in weeks, and I'm sure I look as if half the dust on the roads between London and Lydgate are covering me," he said. "I'd rather wait until this evening, after I've cleaned up."

Adams nodded. "If you wish," he said. "I can have a bath sent to you."

"Or ye can tell me where the nearest lake is."

Adams chuckled. "You'd rather swim in cold water than bathe in a proper tub?"

Aurelius frowned. "A tub is for women," he said. "I've been washing myself in the water as God intended since I was a wee bairn. Where can I bathe?"

Adams pointed in a northwesterly direction. "If you go through the kitchen yards, there is a postern gate," he said. "Keep walking. You'll run into a pond."

Aurelius nodded his thanks, heading for the tower with the stairwell. "I willna be long," he said. "Where can we pitch our shelters?"

"You do not wish to stay in the keep?"

Aurelius glanced at it as he reached the stairwell. "Are your womenfolk in the keep?"

"Naturally."

"Then I'll stay with my men."

"As you wish."

With that, he headed down the narrow spiral stairs that took him from the wall walk down to the long, rectangular bailey below. It was full of men at this point, and he could see Darien as he organized the men they'd brought with them. He went to his brother, mentioning the area where they were to set up their encampment, but he also asked where he had put his saddlebags. Darien motioned to one of two wagons the Highlanders had brought with them, so Aurelius went over to the small wagons that had been built from heavy pieces of wood to form a solid, sturdy conveyance. They could carry anything over any terrain. He had to dig around a little to find his saddlebags, but once he located them, he dipped into one of them until he located his soap.

Aurelius may have been accustomed to washing in what he

termed "God's bathtubs," which were really just lakes or ponds or even streams, but he wasn't so much of a barbarian that he didn't use soap to ensure that every time he did bathe, he actually emerged clean. To him, there was something confining about a bathtub that he didn't particularly like. It was unnatural for a man to bathe in a tub when God himself had created such beautiful natural bathtubs. He liked bathing beneath the sky because it made him feel at peace and at one with nature. For a man who had spent his life warring one way or the other, peace was hard to come by.

He relished it.

After pulling forth a white, lumpy bar of soap that was made with olive oil from Aragon and smelled of rosemary and lavender, he also grabbed a clean tunic and a clean pair of leather breeches and headed in the direction that Adams had indicated. The breeches weren't typical of the Scots, but he preferred them to the long tunics and trappings that they usually wore. That was the English-trained knight in him, requiring something to cover his legs. He felt more comfortable that way. Not strangely, his brothers had picked up on the habit, too, and tended to wear breeches as well.

Something decidedly different from the usual Highlander.

Passing through the bailey with clothes in one hand and soap in the other, he found himself looking around at the castle. He'd seen it from the wall, but now he was down in the thick of it, noting the soaring keep, which seemed to have a separate bailey all its own. They were in what seemed to be the outer bailey, a place that was vaster than he'd given it credit for. He could see a small stone building at one end of it, more than likely some type of a hall, but closer to the keep was the great hall, long and slender just like the shape of the bailey.

Somewhere in between the keep and the great hall were the stables and kitchens. They were at the northernmost area of the castle, and he passed by the stables, noting that the corral had several dun Tarh horses in it. He could see his younger brothers brushing some of the animals, while still other horses already had blankets across their backs. He lifted a hand to his brothers as he passed from the stables and into the kitchen yard, which was quite cluttered.

The kitchen yard had several outbuildings in it, including a buttery and a smokehouse. Most castles didn't have an entire building dedicated to smoking meats, but Lydgate evidently did. He could see the wood piled next to it and holes in the roof for the smoke to escape. He suspected that because Lydgate bordered a mountain range that was covered in forests, that there was no shortage of game. He imagined that the smokehouse was kept quite busy year round, which was good for him when he became lord of Lydgate, because he rather liked smoked meats.

Another feature for a castle he was coming to appreciate.

Crossing the somewhat dusty and cluttered kitchen yard, Aurelius could see the postern gate ahead. There were two gates built into the thickness of the wall, and both were unlocked, which was normal at most castles during the day because those wishing to conduct business with the kitchens would enter through the postern gates rather than the gatehouse. Passing through the gates, he started down the slope that led down to a grassy, walled area. He was taken with dramatic scenery on this side of the castle with the mountains as a backdrop.

Beyond that was Scotland.

Aurelius hadn't been this close to Scotland in over a year, and he had to admit that he was feeling some longing for the land of his birth. He missed his parents and his sisters, but mostly, he simply missed his home. All of it seemed so far away as he gazed at the mountains covered with a dark matting of trees. Where he came from in the Highlands, there were enormous mountains, usually dark and desolate unless it was springtime and they were covered with carpets of purple heather. France had been muddy and wet and sometimes hot, but always miserable, and to him the land didn't have nearly the charm that Scotland had.

Wherever he went, the Highlands always called him back home.

And here he was, in England, and so close to the Scottish border that he could almost smell it. He could smell the moors after a rain or the flowers when they bloomed in the spring. He could see the brilliant blue sky as it touched the mountains, as if they were always in competition for who was the most beautiful. He could hear the water from the brook as it trickled through the rocks on its way to the sea, and he could see the dust of the roads as he walked upon them, watching his feet as they left imprints upon the land he so loved.

Not to get too poetic, but that was the way he thought whenever he envisioned his home. There was something lyrical about the land that always brought out his poet's heart. Not that he was much of a poet, frankly, because the truth was that he was terrible when it came to putting his feelings into words, but it was enough that he could feel them in his heart. Sometimes, during the long years that he had been away from his home, that was all he had to carry with him.

With thoughts of Scotland on his mind, Aurelius made his way across the walled area and saw that there was a portcullis cut into the stone. It was more of a gate in that sense, but he walked through it and immediately he could see a pond ahead of him. In fact, it was quite a lovely pond, surrounded by trees and grass, and already he could feel that cold water washing over his body. His very *weary* body. He had been riding hard and fast since they left Crécy, and it would feel good to relax, even if it was with English water.

His pace picked up the closer he drew. When he came to about ten feet from the water's edge, he briefly stopped to drop his clean clothes to the ground, but then he kept going. With every step he took, he loosened or removed something from his body, and by the time he hit the water, all that was left were his breeches, and those came off very quickly. Soap in hand, he dived into the icy pond.

Bliss!

It was a silent, cold world that he found himself in, and he lingered in it for just a few moments. There was no sound, no fighting, no travel, and nothing to distract him. Simply cold and silence. But he had to breathe, so he surfaced. With soap in one hand, he began to lather up his head, scrubbing the dark hair that he'd inherited from his father. It was brown, but a very dark brown with a hint of auburn in the sunlight. He scrubbed and rubbed until he could scrub no more, and then he went under again, rinsing out his hair until the strands came clean of the slimy soap.

It was then that he realized he had company.

Two very big geese were swimming alongside him, eyeing him curiously. They were mostly white, with gray and white wings and big orange beaks. He treaded water for a moment, wondering where they came from and why he hadn't seen them until now, but he continued swimming after a moment, heading out into deeper water. There was a dam at the western edge of the pond, and he moved in that direction.

The geese followed.

It didn't matter where he went. He'd go under the water and come up only to find the geese closer than they had been before. As he neared the dam, he went deep under, looking up at the geese as they swam above him. He tried to get away from them, but the moment he came up for air, they spied him and quickly moved in his direction. He swam left; they moved left. He swam right and they moved right. All the while, they were inching closer and closer. Snorting at the nosy intruders, he was considering getting out of the pond altogether when he heard a voice behind him.

"They think you have something to eat."

Startled, he turned to see a woman sitting on the shore. She had been hidden from his view when he entered the water by a copse of trees. He wouldn't have even noticed her unless she spoke, so now he found himself looking at a woman from a distance.

A young woman.

"I have nothing to eat," he said. "Clearly, nothing at all."

She cocked her head. "You're Scots."

"Was it my French accent that gave me away?"

He was jesting. He thought he heard her snort, but he was too far away to really see her face or much about her other than the color of her hair—honey blonde—and the shape of her as she sat there.

"I think it was most definitely your French accent," she said. "Where did you come from?"

He gestured toward the castle. "Lydgate."

"I live at Lydgate. You do not live there."

"I dinna say I lived there," he said. "Ye asked me where I

came from, and that is where I came from. I just arrived with Wolsingham's army."

She nodded but didn't say anything for a moment, and he began to inch closer to her as the geese came up behind him. When he saw the birds flanking him, he wondered if he was about to have his eyes pecked out by hungry geese.

"If ye know these beasties, will ye send them away?" he said. "I'm at a disadvantage in the water like this."

She seemed to be pondering his request, or so he thought, until she spoke. "Who are you?" she asked.

He was moving closer to her, trying to get away from the geese. "My name is Aurelius dun Tarh," he said. "Who are ye?"

She sat up a little straighter, seemingly studying him. There was a great pause before she answered.

"So it *is* you," she muttered. "You're the one marrying Wolsingham's daughter."

He'd come close enough that he could touch the bottom, so he stood up, the water level still at his shoulders as he looked at her more closely now. She was an exquisite creature with lush blonde hair, pulled back with some sort of bejeweled circlet, revealing a beautiful oval face with a firm jaw, prominent cheekbones, and full lips. Her eyes were big and lovely, too, but he couldn't see the color. Surprisingly, he had to admit that this was more than likely the most beautiful English lass he'd ever lain eyes on. Out here in the middle of the wilds of the north of England, he found a maiden that no one else could compare to.

And then something Adams said came back to him.

I was not lying when I said that Valery was quite beautiful.

He began to grow suspicious.

"What would ye know about a marriage involving Wolsingham's daughter?" he asked.

She sat forward, her hair spilling over one shoulder in a waterfall of glorious waves. "I told you that I live at Lydgate."

"Lots of people live at Lydgate, I would wager. It doesna mean they know about a betrothal."

She conceded the point. "True."

"I gave ye my name. It would be polite to give me yers."

She averted her gaze, brushing the grass off her skirt. "Surely you know who I am," she said. "Imagine the most hideous creature at Lydgate and that would be me. The awful monster who has somehow trapped Aurelius dun Tarh into marriage."

Suspicions confirmed, it became clear to him, very quickly, who she was. "Trapped me into...?" he repeated, bewildered. "Who said anything about being trapped?"

Her eyes widened. "Ha!" she said sharply. "Do you deny this?"

"I dunna know what to confirm or deny, to be perfectly honest."

That wasn't what she wanted to hear. "Until I was told about the betrothal, I did not even know you existed," she said. "If you've gone around telling your men that I somehow forced this betrothal, then you could not possibly be more wrong."

Her indignant stance was gaining steam. "Lady Valery, I've said nothing of the kind."

He acknowledged her name, and evidently, that meant the battle lines were drawn. He knew her and she knew him, and she was going to take him to task.

"Haven't you?" she said angrily as she leapt to her feet. "I am your worst nightmare, so take a good look, Scotsman. It shall be your last, because when I am finished telling my father what your men said about me, you will be lucky if he doesn't run you out of Lydgate with a knife at your back."

She started to storm off, and he hastened after her. "Wait, m'lady, please," he said, sloshing through the water as he followed. "Will ye please tell me what happened?"

She whistled to the geese, who had been following Aurelius. "Surely you know," she said. "I heard your men in the stables talking about it."

He shook his wet head. "Talking about *what*?" he said. "I wasna there. Will ye tell me what ye heard? And from whom?"

She stopped, fists on her hips as he came to waist-deep water. "How can you ask me that?" she said. "They were only repeating what they'd heard—from you."

"M'lady, I swear to ye, I never slandered ye. I swear this upon my oath."

She scowled. "What oath?"

"I'm a knight."

Her scowl deepened. "You are Scots."

He nodded patiently. "I am a Scots knight," he said. "I fostered at Berwick Castle and at Winchester Castle. I was knighted by the Earl of Warenton, so I *have* taken an oath of chivalry."

Her scowl left her, replaced by an expression of confusion. "Warenton?" she repeated. "De Wolfe?"

"Aye."

That almost seemed to change her mind about him. *Almost*. But not quite. All it managed to do was calm her down, just a little, but she was still rightfully enraged.

"Very well," she said impatiently. "You want to know what I heard, and I will tell you. I was in the stables when I heard a man who sounded very much like you speaking to an English knight and telling him that Aurelius was pushed into a marriage by his father and my father, and that you were resigned to marry a pasty-faced English wench because you would inherit greatly when you did. He said you hadn't argued the betrothal because you were a good soldier and you did what you were told."

Aurelius knew those words. He'd heard them from Darien before. With a grunt of deep regret, and also of great anger, he closed his eyes briefly as she relayed words that he knew damn well his brother had spoken. Darien had been opposed to the union from the start, as if it was his very own marriage, and now Darien's big mouth had gotten him into trouble with the very woman he was supposed to marry. He was going to throttle his brother the next time he saw him.

But first, he had to try to salvage the situation.

"M'lady," he said steadily. "Please believe me when I tell ye that I never said such words. What ye heard was my brother… He thinks that he is defending me, but I never asked him to. And I never said such things."

She wasn't in a forgiving mood. He could just see by the expression on her face. The geese had come out of the water and were starting to mill around her, but he was still there, waist-deep, unable and unwilling to go any further, because they really *would* have a problem if he did. He wasn't about to show his naked arse to the woman, at least not until after they were married, and then he hoped to show it to her often.

That was, if they even made it to the marriage.

At this point, it didn't look good.

"My father does not know what I have heard," she said. "If you cannot control the mouth of your own brother, then I have doubts about your ability to command Wolsingham. Mayhap you can explain that to him."

"I would rather explain it to ye."

"I do not want to hear it."

"Why? Because I might be telling the truth and ye canna admit it?"

She looked at him coldly. "That is a rude thing to say."

He figured he had nothing to lose at this point. She believed what she believed, and he could see that there was no changing her mind.

Unless he did something drastic.

He came out of the water.

"Mayhap it is rude," he said, rising from the pond like Venus rising from the waves. "But I am the man ye are to marry, according to yer father and mine. I had nothing to do with it either. I am simply doing as I am told. I never once protested. Now, if ye think ye can find someone better than me—a man who would never lie to ye, who would always treat ye with respect, and who would hold ye on cold nights with the body that stands before ye—then go tell yer father yer version of the truth. I willna stop ye. But ye should get a look at what ye're going to be missing."

Aurelius stood in front of her, as naked as the day he was born, and watched her reaction closely.

It wasn't long in coming.

Surprisingly, she didn't run. And never once did she look below his chest, which both insulted and impressed him. She met his gaze steadily before looking at his neck, his shoulders, and then back to his eyes. Aurelius kept waiting for her to take a good look at his manhood, which, by all accounts, was quite impressive, but she never did.

She kept her eyes on his.

"Are you attempting to seduce me?" she finally asked.

The rage was gone from her voice, which was a good sign.

But she didn't seem the least bit impressed by his muscular frame, enormous arms, slim waist, and the family jewels. Aurelius was now leaning toward being quite insulted by her lack of response to his male beauty.

"If I was trying to seduce ye, ye'd know it," he said. "I'm simply being honest with ye. I'm showing ye what will soon be yers."

"You act as if I'm inspecting a stallion."

"There is one thing a stallion and I have in common."

"What's that?"

"If ye look below my waist, ye'll see it."

She nodded as if he'd just said something interesting. Not alluring, or shocking, or outright bawdy, but interesting. As if they were speaking about the damn weather. Was it possible the woman was actually blind and simply couldn't see him for what he was? This woman of uncanny beauty had the power to *resist* him?

He was flabbergasted.

As Aurelius stood there and wondered what his next move should be, Valery leaned down to the geese still milling around her feet.

"Babies," she said sweetly. "My babies? *Bite!*"

That seemed to be some magical word that those two feathered pests understood. She said it again—*bite!*—and pointed at Aurelius. Suddenly, the geese were running toward him, honking and hissing, and he turned on his heel and dived right back into the pond, swimming as fast as he could away from the geese who were now entering the water. Given that he was swimming for his life, he didn't see Valery as she stood there and giggled, watching him outswim the geese, who were determined to bite him.

He deserved it, as far as she was concerned.

Aurelius was well out in the pond when she turned around, preparing to head back to the castle, and saw his clothes on the ground. A trail of them led to a pile that looked clean enough. She hadn't seen him enter the pond from where she was sitting, which was why she hadn't known he was nude until he got into waist-deep water, and then she suspected as much. When he'd come out of the pond… Well, it had taken everything in her not to look down *there*.

But she'd wanted to.

That saucy, cheeky Scotsman.

Bending over, she picked up his clothes. All of them. With a piercing whistle, she called the geese away from him as he swam at the other end of the pond, and she headed back toward the castle with all of his clothing in her arms.

Every last stitch.

And that was the way she left her future husband.

CHAPTER EIGHT

D ARIEN HAD A black eye.

Truthfully, he wasn't all that surprised that he had one. He assumed, at some point, that his brother would hear what he had said about his future marriage and confront him. What he hadn't expected was that his brother would do it naked.

Darien was with the Highlanders in the field adjacent to Lydgate Castle, the one that was surrounded by walls, as they set up their encampment on the soft, damp grass. Everything was proceeding efficiently until Aurelius appeared. His appearance in and of itself wasn't unusual, but his state of dress was. The man was as naked as the day he was born, using a small branch that had a heavy smattering of leaves on it to preserve his modesty. He didn't even care that his backside was completely exposed. He only seemed concerned with covering up his manhood, as he probably should have been, and he'd come through the small opening in the wall and headed straight for his brother when he caught sight of him.

After that, Darien ended up on his backside.

With a stinging left eye, he picked himself up and demanded to know why his brother had hit him, even though he could already guess. Aurelius was absolutely livid, shouting at his brother in front of their men, raking him up one side and down the other. For a man who didn't normally raise his voice, not even in the heat of battle, it was quite rare to see Aurelius shouting. But by the time he was finished, everyone understood why, and Darien was humiliated.

Not that he didn't deserve it.

When Aurelius was finished ripping on his brother, he dropped the branch and proceeded to parade, nude, over to the provisions wagon where his possessions were. Considering the lady had taken all of his clothing with her, he had nothing left, so he stole his brother's clothing. It was Darien's best clothing, leather breeches and a linen tunic, so Aurelius looked rather primped and polished once he'd put everything on, and he dared Darien to say anything about it. But Darien didn't. He knew he'd been wrong. Rhori had tried to warn him, but he'd run off at the mouth anyway. Now, Aurelius knew.

Everyone knew.

Darien wondered who else knew.

More of Wolsingham's troops began to flood into the walled area where the dun Tarh men had set up camp, mostly troops that had been on loan from allies. Now that Adams was home, he would send the troops back and compensate those who had given him the men with money, or more men, or even livestock, depending on what had been agreed upon. As the day lagged and sunset approached, the grassy area was filling up and the gate in the wall, the one that led to the pond, was closed up for the night. Campfires sprang up as night descended, staving off the darkness as the structure of Lydgate began to glow from fires spread out all over the compound. The smell of smoke grew heavy in the cooling evening air.

And Darien watched it all, nursing a bruised ego and a swollen eye. Aurelius had retreated to his tent, and he remained there even now as Darien oversaw the operations. Estevan and Caelus and Kaladin had returned from the stables some time ago and were working alongside the men to secure tents and make sure there was food to eat and wine to drink, provisions they had purchased in France before they departed for home.

Over his shoulder, Darien could hear Caelus and Kaladin squabbling about something and Estevan's slow, steady voice trying to shut them up. But the younger brothers wouldn't be put off, so Estevan slapped Caelus on the side of the head simply because he was frustrated. Giving up on the pair, he left them to their argument and approached Darien.

"The whelps want to know when they are returning home," he said. "Caelus says he's going to walk home if we dunna send him back to Mam, and soon."

Darien turned to Estevan, looking at Caelus and Kaladin over his shoulder and watching the boys pretend they weren't interested in their older brothers' conversation.

"I suppose I understand the impatience," Darien said. "But the truth is that I dunna know. This betrothal was not expected, so I dunna know if Bear intends to keep us here with him for a time or if he intends to send us all home."

"Shall I ask him?"

Darien shook his head. "I will," he said. "Meanwhile, I suspect he will expect all of us to attend tonight's feast in Lydgate's hall, so make those two piglets wash and change into cleaner clothing. We dunna want Aurelius erupting if we bring mud babies into the hall."

"Not to mention Mam erupting if she finds out we let filthy

lads into the hall of an ally."

"Precisely," Darien said. "See to it."

Estevan turned back to his bickering younger brothers as Darien turned for Aurelius' tent. Pausing a moment to timidly touch his left eye and hope Aurelius didn't throw another punch at his face, he stepped inside.

"Bear," he said quietly. "Do ye expect all of us to attend ye in the hall tonight?"

Aurelius was seated on a portable chair, bent over a traveling table. He'd placed his writing kit upon it and was scratching something out on a yellowed piece of vellum by the light of a single taper.

"Aye," he said, not looking up. "On the morrow, I want ye to send a messenger to the Hydra. Da doesna know I've accepted the betrothal and that we're here at Lydgate Castle for the wedding, so send a messenger with all due haste."

"I will," Darien said, peering at what his brother was writing. "What are ye telling him?"

Aurelius dipped his quill in the ink, tapped off the excess, and continued to write. "That I've accepted the betrothal to Wolsingham's heiress, as he intended, and that ye tried to ruin it," he said frankly. Then he paused and looked at his brother. "Dunna think I've forgiven ye. I've never known ye to be petty or stupid, Darien, but ye proved to be both today."

Darien sighed heavily. "I said that I was sorry," he said. "I dunna know what more ye want me to do. Sometimes I say things and then they canna be unsaid. Ye know that about me."

Aurelius grunted. "Ye're going to speak with my future wife," he said, returning to the vellum. "Ye're going to tell her that I said none of the things ye created in yer mind. Those were all yer own stupid opinions. Not mine."

Darien knew he didn't have a choice, but he wholeheartedly didn't want to confess his sins to a woman he'd never even met. "If ye make me do that, she'll think we're a family of birds," he said, wriggling his fingers at his head. "Silly, flighty birds with sand for brains."

"Ye're the only bird I see."

"She'll think we're all mad!"

Aurelius looked at him again. "'Tis better than her thinking I've been lamenting this betrothal and telling everyone that a hideous creature trapped me into marriage," he said. "If ye speak to her tonight, I'll not tell Da what ye've done."

That was a bargain Darien couldn't refuse. He didn't want to be on his father's bad side. "Very well," he said begrudgingly. "When do ye want me to do it?"

"As soon as ye're introduced, ye'll ask for a private word with her," Aurelius said. "Sit at the end of a feasting table and speak with her, only make sure it is a conversation with just the two of ye. Apologize for what ye said and assure her I never said such things. And when ye're done with her, ye can apologize to her father. He's the one I worry over."

Darien watched him for a moment, seeing the way he seemed quite determined to right whatever situation was between him and his betrothed. To Darien, it didn't seem a normal concern after a misunderstanding. There was more behind it. After a moment, he frowned.

"Why are ye so concerned over this?" he asked seriously. "This is a woman ye've never even met before. Why do ye care what she thinks?"

Aurelius paused. "Ye've not seen this woman."

The way he said it made the inference obvious, and he instantly had Darien's attention. "What about her?" he said.

"She's not a hideous creature?"

Aurelius shook his head firmly. "The lass is an angel."

"Beautiful?

"I've never seen finer."

"And ye want to marry her because she's beautiful?"

"That's as good a reason as any."

Now Aurelius' attitude was starting to make some sense. "And ye want me to tell her ye never said a word against her because ye dunna want a beautiful woman to get away," Darien said. "Ye want me to smooth the way."

Aurelius looked him in the eye. "I want ye to repair what ye've tried to ruin," he said. "Her reaction to me was yer fault, Darien. Ye and yer flapping lips."

Darien put up his hands in surrender because he didn't want to get into it again with his brother. They'd already had words, and flying fists, on the subject.

"Very well," Darien said to placate him. "I'll speak with her tonight."

"See that ye do," Aurelius said, returning his attention to his missive. "And once ye have, ye'll apologize to her father. I dunna care what excuse ye make up for yer behavior—tell him yer fatigue has infected yer brain. Do what ye must. But ye'll make up for what ye said or I'll send ye back to Da, and he can decide what's to be done with ye."

There was a threat in that, one Darien was unwilling to tempt, so he simply nodded his head. "I'll do everything I can," he said. "But if they dunna accept my apology, I dunna know what more I can do. Ye'll have to take yer pound of flesh then."

"I willna. Da will."

"So ye've said."

With that, Aurelius turned back for his missive, and Darien

quit the tent. He struggled not to feel insulted or ashamed by what Aurelius had said, but it was difficult. He was a man with considerable pride. He knew what he'd said was wrong, but there was part of him that stood by it. Aurelius *had* been forced into a marriage. That wasn't a lie. But Aurelius had accepted it with much more grace than Darien had.

And it wasn't even his marriage.

With a heavy sigh, Darien focused on what he needed to do that evening—apologize to the woman who was about to ruin Aurelius' life. Or maybe he wouldn't do it at all. But then again… he didn't want another black eye. Therefore, if the opportunity presented itself, he'd do it.

And hate every bloody minute of it.

℈

SHE WAS READY for him.

Valery had been given most of the afternoon to think about that saucy, cheeky Highlander, and she had a plan in mind. He deserved to be punished for his behavior, in her opinion, and she was going to show him what kind of a woman he was to marry. She'd already made up her mind that she *would* marry him. She would have the most handsome husband out of all of her friends, and that was something she simply couldn't pass up. Even if he did speak like a Scots and probably had the intelligence of a goat, that didn't matter. Once she saw him, nothing really mattered.

She wanted him.

For an entirely self-serving reason.

Did she believe him when he told her that he hadn't said those terrible things about her? Truthfully, she did. There was something sincere about the man. Even after he told her he had been knighted by the Earl of Warenton himself, she believed everything he told her. He just didn't seem like the lying kind, but, then again, she didn't know the man. He could be a very smooth prevaricator for all she knew.

But something in those intense eyes told her otherwise.

All she could think about, all afternoon, was Aurelius dun Tarh. She didn't even know where to start when describing the man—he had pale eyes, though she wasn't sure what color they were. They looked like the color of the sea on a warm summer's day. He had a granite-square jaw, straight nose, and full lips embraced by the scrub of a beard. His hair was quite dark, shoulder length, so barbaric looking but also quite alluring.

But that body…

She'd really only seen him from the waist up. Once he'd come out of the water, she had refused to look below his chest. She knew he wanted her to, but she wasn't going to do what he wanted her to. The man had a thick neck, impossibly broad shoulders, enormous arms, and a powerful chest covered by a faint matting of dark hair. Beyond that… she didn't know, but she was certain the rest of him was as titillating. Even to think on it made her face hot.

Damn that cheeky Scotsman!

Therefore, she dressed very carefully for the evening's feast. She knew her parents would want her to look her very best, so she donned a white silk gown with silver thread woven throughout, a gown that embraced her curvy figure. She was a maiden, of course, but Valery wasn't one to shy away from anything that had to do with men or marriage or the relations between men and women. She had plenty of married friends who were more than willing to describe sexual intercourse and how pleasurable it was after the initial loss of one's virginity.

Valery had always wondered what it would feel like, to have a man's body in hers. It seemed strange and alien, but clearly, men and women had been doing such things since the beginning of time.

She, too, would do it eventually.

With Aurelius.

She had to fan herself again at the very thought.

Beryl, the servant girl, helped her dress and helped her with her hair, which was left long and flowing but pulled away from her face with a silver circlet. The gown had somewhat of a plunging neckline, displaying the swell of her breasts, and she wore a silver cross with rubies as an adornment. In fact, she wore silver everywhere—ears, wrists, and fingers. It wasn't as flashy as gold, nor as precious, but she looked like a silver goddess.

That was her intention.

As the day gave way to evening and the fires were lit all around Lydgate, her mother came to see her to ensure that she was properly dressed for the meal. Lady Wolsingham seemed oddly subdued, and Valery attributed it to the fact that her daughter was about to meet her betrothed. Her mother tended to be quiet anyway, so Valery didn't give it much thought as the woman left her with a kiss and headed down to the kitchens to ensure the meal would be ready soon. That left Valery mostly alone, putting on the finishing touches for the evening, which included rose-scented perfume and one very large thorn.

The latter was meant for her future husband.

Smelling like a floral garden, looking like an angel, and wielding a nasty thorn she'd taken off one of the vines in the walled garden her mother kept, Valery finally made her way down to the great hall. The inner bailey of Lydgate, where

Faunus the Tree lived out its life, was rather small and tightly packed, with the great hall being built along the north side. It was built against the keep, and they shared a common wall, making the hall long and slender, but still large enough to hold hundreds of people.

By the time she entered the warm, fragrant hall, it was about half-full of men who had just returned from France. Valery had come in through a servants' entrance, not the main one, because her father always admonished her against entering in full view of men with nothing but lust on their minds. That was his version, anyway. She knew it was to keep her away from his men, and it was something they'd been doing since she'd been a young girl. She could sit at the end of the hall, on the dais with her mother, but they never mingled with the rank and file. It simply wasn't done. More often than not, they didn't eat in the hall.

Her father was already at the dais when she entered, and he embraced her sweetly. Valery almost said something about planning to surprise him in the stable, but she refrained. She didn't want to explain what had really gone on in the stable, so she omitted the situation altogether. But Adams was more than happy to see his only child and hugged her tightly, so tightly that she finally had to push him away.

"Papa, I love you, but if you squeeze me any harder, you are going to ruin my dress," she said, gently pulling away. "We have missed you very much. How was your time spent in France?"

Adams pulled her down into the chair next to him, clinging to her hands. "It was long and cold and bloody," he said. "But I am home, and I do not wish to speak on the horrors of war. I want to know how you and your mother have been. Have you been well? Have you been happy?"

Valery smiled at her eager father. "We have been both," she said. "Truly, nothing remarkable has happened. We have lived here as we always do, but I did go to Amelia de Hetton's wedding a few months ago. She married a de Lumley. You remember Alphonso de Lumley?"

Adams nodded. "I do, indeed," he said. "The man has a fleet of ships that go all along the eastern coast."

"He's a pirate."

"So some say, but a rich pirate. She married well."

"It seems that I am to be married well, too."

Adams' warm expression faltered. He'd known they would speak on the subject, but he was hoping it wouldn't be so soon. He wanted to hear about her life over the past year first, to reacquaint himself with the daughter he'd left behind. But he couldn't avoid her statement.

He averted his gaze.

"It is true," he said quietly, caressing her hands with his own. "Your mother told you?"

Valery nodded. "She did," she said. "I hear he's a Scotsman."

Adams bobbed his head faintly. "He is," he said, lifting his eyes to hers. "I wanted to introduce you when we arrived, but he insisted on bathing first. He should be here momentarily."

"Tell me what kind of man he is."

It was an expected question. In fact, Valery had decided early on that she was going to pretend that she'd never heard the terrible words spoken against her, and she'd never met Aurelius dun Tarh. It might give her a little leverage over the man if he knew she had withheld something that could potentially get him into a good deal of trouble—that he'd stood in front of her naked and that his brother had said terrible things about her. It wasn't that she was being manipulative or sneaky. It was simply that such power, over a man she didn't even know, would be a good thing because she was proceeding into unknown territory.

It was always good to have a little ammunition.

"He is a magnificent warrior," Adams said, cutting into her train of thought. "Every man in the army respects him greatly. Aurelius dun Tarh is fearless, brave, and talented. He can read an enemy's mind, and he knows how to deal with subversion and surprise tactics."

Valery frowned. "That's the kind of warrior he is," she said. "But what kind of *man* is he? Is he kind? Is he eccentric? What is he *like*, Papa?"

Adams shrugged. "He is stoic for a Highlander," he said. "He rarely raises his voice, even in battle. He had his share of camp women following him about, but… Forgive me. I should not have said that. He may have had women pining after him, but I never heard of him taking one to his bed. God's Bones… I more than likely should not have said that, either. Forgive me, Val. That was not what I intended to say about him."

Valery was listening with amusement. "You needn't be ashamed," she said. "You are not speaking to a child. I know the ways of men and women."

Adams grunted, letting go of her hands so he could collect his cup of wine. "It is all of that reading you do," he said. "I do not know why I permitted such things."

Valery started to laugh. "Because reading is as natural as breathing to me," she said, reaching to collect her own wine. "You could not stop me."

"I could have!"

"How?"

Adams sputtered. "I... I cannot think now, but I could have," he said, watching his daughter laugh. "I could have gouged your eyes out."

She winced. "Too painful," she said. "And gory. Speaking of books, I must tell you of a book I found in Newcastle."

"When did you go to Newcastle?"

"When Mama wanted to find some new fabric for dresses she wanted to have made," Valery said before sipping at her wine. "There was an apothecary's shop there, and it had things I've never seen before. Magical things from far away. It also had some very old books, and the man sold them all to me."

"All of them?"

Valery nodded. "Indeed," she said. "Two are written in a language I do not understand. When I asked the priest what it was, he told me that it was written by demons. But the other two books are written in Latin."

"What kind of books are they?"

A smile played on her lips as she sat back against her chair. "One is a book on ancient poetry," she said. "It is very beautiful, written by some Roman philosopher. But the other book is called *The Golden Ass*. It is an ancient tale of a Roman boy named Lucius."

"Oh?" Adams said, only truly half interested because books bored him. He lifted his cup to his lips. "What is it about?"

Valery was still trying not to grin at him. "Lucius' adventures," she said. "He's turned into a donkey by an evil witch. He even beds a woman while he is in the form of a donkey."

Adams spat out the wine in his mouth, spraying it all over the table at his daughter's shocking statement. As Valery laughed uproariously, Adams wiped his mouth with the back of his hand as he looked at his daughter in horror.

"Is that what you have been doing in my absence?" he said, aghast. "Reading about things so unseemly that not even noblemen will speak of them? Valery, how could you do such a thing?"

She waved her father off. "Do not be troubled, Papa, truly," she said. "It is only a book. And I do not speak to anyone of it, so the secret is safe. But it was quite an adventure Lucius had."

Adams was still disgusted by it all. "Not another word, Valery," he said. "You will never speak of that again lest you greatly embarrass me and bring shame to this family."

Valery thought he was overreacting, but she didn't argue with him. She didn't want to fight with him on his first night back. "As you wish," she said. "Now, tell me—when am I to meet my future husband?"

She was diverting the subject, but Adams was still lingering over a donkey having relations with a woman. "As I told you, he shall be here this evening," he said. "And, for pity's sake, do not bring up this horrible book you have read. He will think you a deviant."

If you only knew how the Scotsman appeared nude to me, she thought.

Maybe there was a bit of deviant on both sides.

But she fell silent, drinking her wine and watching the hall fill with men as Sterling came to the dais to speak with Adams. He'd already spent most of the afternoon with the man, even though the knight had wanted to spend it with his son but, like a good soldier, he gave his liege his full attention. Maxwell, in fact, was dead asleep in the quarters he shared with his parents, a small cottage in the outer bailey where the lad had practically grown up. Sterling's wife, thrilled to have her son home, begged his father to simply let him sleep, so Maxwell was passed out while others gathered for the feast.

Valery wondered if Sterling knew about her betrothal yet. If he didn't, he soon would, and she knew that would make him very unhappy. As the knight and her father huddled in their own private conversation, Valery casually rose from the chair she was sitting in and moved to the one next to it. She assumed her father would like to have her betrothed sit next to him, so she was already clearing the way.

While her father wasn't watching, however, she removed the thorn from the small silver purse on her wrist and worked it into the cushion of the chair. Each chair at the dais had a cushion at the insistence of her mother, so she rammed the thorn up through the bottom of the cushion and wedged it in good. All the Highlander had to do was sit down and he'd end up with a thorn in his backside. Perhaps he'd think twice before exposing himself to her like he had earlier in the day.

At least until they were married.

Until then, however, he deserved to be punished.

As Valery gleefully anticipated the moment when Aurelius dun Tarh would find himself with a thorn in his arse, Lady Wolsingham joined the dais after having made sure the meal was well in hand. She arrived with Sterling's wife at her side because Lady St. John, Cedrica, was also Lady Wolsingham's lady-in-waiting. The thin, dark-haired woman had managed to pull herself away from her sleeping son to tend to her lady, and soon, everyone was taking their seats. Sterling sat on the other side of Valery, wondering aloud why she'd left the seat next to Adams empty, but Valery didn't reply. Her attention was on the hall entry.

The Highlanders had arrived.

There were five of them, entering with other English

knights, but the Scots in particular pushed through the crowd and headed for the dais. Though Valery was quite ready to play her joke on Aurelius, the sight of the man, fully clothed, momentarily stumped her. He was clad in leather breeches and a pale linen tunic that was a shade too small and showed off his impressive muscles, and she found herself looking at perhaps the most handsome man she'd ever seen. Witnessing him wet in the pond hadn't done him justice. Now that he was dried and combed and shaved, she could see just what a specimen he was.

And he wouldn't even look at her.

"M'laird," he said as he came to the dais, focused on Adams. "I've brought my brothers with me. I hope that doesna displease ye."

Adams shook his head as he stood up, extending a hand to Valery. "Of course not," he said. "The dun Tarh brothers have earned a place at my table. But I should like to introduce you to my daughter, Lady Valery. I know you have been eager to meet her. Valery, this is Aurelius dun Tarh."

At that moment, he turned to look at Valery, who had risen to her feet and saw, quite obviously, when his gaze raked down her body. The silver dress drew his eyes like a moth to flame. But then his eyes returned to hers, his gaze as intense as it was when he'd stood naked in front of her. There was something searing about the man's eyes, something that threatened to melt her, but Valery stood her ground.

Barely, but she did.

"My lord," she said evenly. "It is an honor to finally meet you."

That gave Aurelius pause. She could tell that he was confused by her words—but she could also tell when he quickly realized she hadn't told her father about their earlier meeting. If she had, she would have said so, quite obviously. And Adams probably would not have been so hospitable toward him.

That knowledge seemed to bring some relief to his features.

"The honor is mine, m'lady," he said, bowing elegantly. "Yer father told me that ye were quite beautiful. He dinna exaggerate."

Valery smiled modestly. "You flatter me, my lord."

"I never say anything I dunna mean, m'lady."

"Come and sit," Adams said quickly, indicating the empty chair next to him. "Sit between my daughter and I so that we may become better acquainted."

The moment was upon her. That enormous thorn poking up through the cushion was about to ram itself right into his tender buttocks when he sat down. Valery waited with great anticipation as Aurelius came around the table, making his way to the chair Adams had indicated. She even smiled pleasantly at him when their eyes met, and he smiled back, enough to show her the big dimples in each cheek. The man was possibly more handsome when he smiled. Adams even pulled out the chair for him so he could take his seat more comfortably, and Valery remained on her feet, watching his face, as he sank down into the chair.

The reaction wasn't long in coming.

Aurelius' smile vanished and his eyes closed for a brief, sharp moment before reopening slowly. But he didn't move. He didn't jump up or yelp. He simply sat there and took it. But his gaze moved to Valery. Somehow, he knew she had done something. When she smiled knowingly, his suspicions were confirmed.

She'd gored him.

"I am honored to be at yer table, m'laird," Aurelius said,

sounding as normal as he possibly could. "I believe ye've hosted my father before. He spoke of yer impressive hall and fine food."

Adams had no idea that the man was in such pain or that his daughter was surprised by Aurelius' lack of reaction. Pleased at his guest's kind words, Adams began waving the servants forward with food and drink.

"Your father has been a guest in my hall more than once," he said. "Lucifer can eat more than any sane man I've ever seen."

Lucifer.

The mention of the name brought a smile to Aurelius' lips, even if he was struggling with a spear to his buttocks. "Ye're one of the only ones he permits to call him that to his face," he said.

"Call him what?"

"That old and dark name."

Adams knew what he meant. A jesting glance told Aurelius that very thing. *Lucifer* was a name that Lares dun Tarh had been called since the days of his marriage to Lady Mabel. It was common for allies and enemies alike to refer to him as such. It was more of an affectionate nickname, something men like Adams used as a term of endearment. Aurelius was well aware that men believed his father was a fallen priest, a man who had been caught worshipping the great fallen angel of Lucifer himself, and Lares had never made an effort to clear up that rumor because he felt that the mystery of it all created stronger allegiances and more fearful enemies.

There was a benefit to men thinking he was akin to the devil.

"Mayhap it is old and dark," Adams said after a moment. "But your father is old and dark, so it suits him."

Aurelius grinned. "He is, indeed," he said. Then he sat back, trying to take the weight off the thorn in his right buttock, as he looked to the woman on his right. "I'm sure that old and dark man will be quite eager to make Lady Valery's acquaintance, as I certainly was. M'lady, I'm quite shocked that tales of your beauty are not on every man's lips from London to Edinburgh. A woman like you should be legendary."

Valery had been listening to the conversation between her father and Aurelius, stumped because her betrothed seemed not to mind that he had a thorn up his ass. She was torn between confusion and frustration that her prank hadn't brought more of a reaction from him.

Perhaps he needed a little prodding.

"There are many beautiful women in England," she said. "But there are many thorns among the roses, as well. I'm sure you would know more than I would about the *thorns*, my lord."

The inference was obvious, at least to Aurelius. Now he knew what was drawing blood on his backside.

Thinly, he smiled.

"When a man finds true beauty, the thorns dunna matter," he said evenly. "In fact, I've not yet met yer mother, but I dunna need to be introduced to know she is, in fact, yer mother. I can see that ye get yer beauty from her."

That compliment changed Valery's expression somewhat as she glanced past her father to where her mother was sitting. "That is a kind observation," she said. "And I agree with you. My mother is very beautiful."

"Will ye introduce me, m'lady?"

That drew Valery and Adams' attention off him and onto Lady Wolsingham, on the other side of her husband. But Aurelius had asked Valery that question with a purpose. The very second she stood up to go to her mother, presumably to introduce the woman to her future husband, Aurelius leaned off the thorn, putting his hand down to the seat to feel a very sturdy, very sharp thorn. It was moving slightly and he grabbed it, giving it a good yank and loosening it but unable to pull it free. By this time, Valery was with her mother and Adams was introducing the woman to Aurelius, who abruptly stood up and lifted his cup to her.

"Lady Wolsingham," he said. "May I toast a truly lovely lady?"

It was very flattering. Valery had her hands on her mother's shoulders, and Adams lifted his cup to his wife, encouraging the entire table to do so. All of the attention was on Lady Wolsingham, and as the compliments were raining down on a woman who didn't seem particularly happy at the attention, Aurelius set his cup down and reached down to adjust the cushion he'd been sitting on. To anyone looking, it was a natural action. He was simply fluffing it. But what he'd really done was give another good yank and pull the thorn free of the cushion itself.

The tables were about to turn.

Politely, he fluffed Lady Valery's cushion, secretly embedding the thorn into it. He was swift, and his back was to Valery and her father so that even if they looked at him, they couldn't see what he was doing. As he put the cushion down, thorn pointed up, Valery came away from her mother.

Aurelius sat down quickly in his own chair.

"That was kind of you to speak so generously about my mother," she said. "She told me that she knew a dun Tarh, once. She was raised on the borders."

Aurelius was calm and collected, giving her no hint of what awaited her, as she moved to take her seat. "I dinna know that," he said, watching the woman perch her bottom right over the seat. "I look forward to speaking with her about it. Mayhap she knew a cousin or even an uncle."

Valery's buttocks came down on the seat, and, before she could reply to his statement, she screeched and bolted off the chair. The entire dais turned to her in surprise, and nearly half the hall as well, at least those closest to the dais. Valery's gaze was on Aurelius accusingly, but when she realized everyone was looking at her, she smiled weakly and calmly picked up the cushion.

"My apologies," she said, calming those who looked concerned. "I… I sat down too hard and pinched my skin. There is no trouble."

Everyone turned back to their meal and conversations, but Valery discreetly threw the cushion on the floor. Short of inspecting it, which she didn't want to do, there wasn't much else to be done if she didn't want to sit on the thorn again. The thorn that Aurelius had somehow put in her chair.

Truth be told, she was impressed at his cleverness.

Slowly, she sat down and collected her wine.

"That was unnecessary, Highlander," she said quietly, not looking at him.

Aurelius, too, was looking at his cup and not at her. "I dunna know what ye mean."

"I'm quite sure that you do," she said. "But remember one thing."

"What is that?"

"No one rejoices in revenge more than a woman."

He fought off a grin, falling silent as a servant brought trenchers, first for Valery and then for him. When the servant wandered away, he sat forward and focused on his meal.

"Then the thorn was revenge, was it?" he muttered. "Next time, use a method of revenge that one canna use against ye."

"You deserved that thorn."

"Did I?"

"You are fortunate that I told my father nothing of what you did today."

"For that, I am grateful."

"Then why did you put the thorn back in my chair?"

He did look at her then. "To remind ye that anything ye can do, I can do better."

She sat forward, her gaze fixed on him. "That sounds like a challenge."

The corners of his mouth twitched with a smile as he turned back to his food. "Not at all," he said. "It simply means that ye may have had yer way with others, but ye'll not have yer way with me. I'll match ye sin for sin and then some. Therefore, it would be best if we try to get on with one another. 'Tis what yer father wants. 'Tis what I want, too."

Valery watched him pick up a knife and stab a big hunk of beef. It was steaming and succulent. Thinking on what he said, she turned to her own food, even if her attention was mostly on him.

Now he had her curiosity.

"Then you are agreeable to this betrothal?" she asked. Before he could answer, she continued as if the question had been stupid. "Of course you are. Why wouldn't you be? You will inherit Wolsingham. It is a great fortress. Of course you would be agreeable."

His mouth was full as he spoke. "Lady, there is no richness or inheritance in all the world that could convince me to take it if the price to pay was too high," he said. When she looked puzzled, he clarified. "What I mean is that there are no riches that could attract me if the price to pay for it was marrying someone who wasna worth the price."

"And I am worth the price?"

He smiled then, still chewing. "I have a feeling ye're worth the price and then some," he said. "Any lady who would try to teach me a lesson by running off with my clothes and then put thorns in my cushion to put me in my place must surely be worth a great deal."

He swallowed and grinned, which made her want to grin, too. "That is ridiculous," she said, though she was smiling. "How can you even know that?"

He tapped his head. "Because it shows me that ye're intelligent, conniving, and have spirit," he said. "I like those qualities in a lass."

"God's Bones, *why*?"

"Because ye'll let no man get the best of ye. Am I wrong?"

He was smiling so openly at her that Valery could do nothing more than shake her head. "You are not wrong," she said, realizing her stomach quivering with a giddy feeling because of the way he was grinning at her. "I'm no one to be trifled with."

He cocked a dark eyebrow. "I've come to realize that," he said, someone ironically. "Now that we know where we stand, tell me what ye're passionate about. Singing? Horses? Gardens?"

"Do you truly wish to know?"

"I wouldna asked if I dinna."

She appeared thoughtful, as if debating what to tell him. Debating just how much she should reveal herself to him. But she finally relented. "Books," she said simply. "I like to read books."

He looked at her, surprised. "Is that so?" he said. "What do ye like to read?"

She shrugged. "Anything," she said. "I was telling my father earlier that I purchased new books while he was away. Well, they're new to me, but they are very old books."

"What kind of books?"

"A book of Roman poetry," she said. "Another is an ancient Roman tale of a boy who was transformed into an ass by an evil witch, but I promised my father that I would not speak of it."

"Why not?"

"Because it is a very naughty book."

He had more food in his mouth but swallowed before continuing. "I'm intrigued," he said. "Will ye not tell me about the story?"

"Do you like to read?"

"I do."

Somehow, those two words caused most of the animosity to drain out of Valery right then and there. The man liked to read. She'd met so many that didn't or thought it was a fool's hobby. Even her father's knight, Sterling, didn't like to read or write. He had a scribe, a former priest, do all of his missives and accounting. That wasn't unusual for knights who were more focused on warfare and command than on scholarly skills that some considered weak, but Aurelius didn't seem to share that opinion.

The first strains of genuine interest in the man began to clutch at her.

"Do you truly?" she asked.

He nodded. "I never say anything I dunna mean."

"But what do you like to read?"

He was well into his meal, wiping his mouth with the back of his hand as he thought on her question. "When I was young, there was a priest in the village who taught me to read from the Bible," he said. "That was the first thing I ever read, but when I went to foster, I discovered the skalds."

Valery knew exactly what he was talking about. "Northmen poets?"

He nodded. "I fostered at Berwick Castle," he said. "A great-great-grandfather of a former lord of Berwick was a Northman prince, so the books of skalds were at Berwick. Have ye ever read one?"

Valery shook her head. "I have not," she said. "I've never had the opportunity."

He took a gulp of wine before continuing. "Do ye know anything about Northman poetry?"

"Not too much. Only that it comes from their god, Odin."

Aurelius held up a finger. "True," he said. "But there is a legend behind it."

"What legend?"

"That Odin had to change himself into a great eagle to steal the mead of poetry, a drink that was brewed from the blood of the god Kvasir," he said. "All great skalds must drink of the mead in order to write their fine poetry."

Without even realizing it, Aurelius had Valery completely captivated. He was communicating with her on her level, on something that was dear to her heart. She was leaning closer to him, interested in every word.

"I have heard that," she said seriously. "Not all of it, but I have heard of the mead of poetry."

Aurelius looked away from her long enough to take another bite. "From what I was taught, skalds were almost like priests," he said, returning his attention to that enraptured face. "They worked their entire lives on their talent, but it wasna as if they were making up beautiful prose or creating tales. Skalds almost always spoke of events or heroic deeds. They tell the tales of their people. There is one verse that I can remember where the skald speaks of bloodied shields and stained spears, and leaving the dead for the wolves. When the skald speaks of things like that... I understand."

He seemed to lose some of his humor a little, and Valery thought she knew why. "Do you speak of the battles in France?" she asked quietly. "Where you just came from?"

"That, and others."

"May I ask you a question?"

He looked at her then. "Ye may always ask me a question, m'lady," he said, his voice tinged with softness. "I'd not deny ye anything. I hope to prove that to ye."

There was something seductive in that statement, a tone that Valery was unfamiliar with. Looking at Aurelius as he spoke softly to her made the uneasiness in her belly feel like a runaway wagon. Everything was rolling and quivering.

She cleared her throat quietly, feeling the least bit unsteady.

"Was... was it terrible in France?" she asked. "I could ask my father, but he seems happy to be home. I do not want to dampen his joy. But I thought you might tell me what it was like."

He'd opened his mouth to reply when Adams suddenly turned to the two of them, putting a hand on Aurelius' shoulder. "Bear," he said, completely interrupting their conversation. "I forgot to tell you that I sent a missive off to your father this afternoon. I have invited your mother and father to Lydgate for the wedding. Of course, we will not hear anything from them for quite some time because it will take the messenger many days to reach the Hydra, but I am hoping to see your mother and father by the time we celebrate the Festival of Christ. We could arrange the marriage when they arrive, if you are agreeable to such a thing."

Aurelius didn't know what to say. Although he'd just shared a pleasant conversation with Valery, it had been a short one. He still wasn't sure if their introduction or early relationship was even on good terms. He was quite agreeable to a wedding because even in the short time he'd known her, he realized there was something about Valery that he found quite attractive, but he had no idea what she was feeling.

That was key.

Therefore, he did the only thing he could—he deferred to the lady.

"I will be agreeable to whatever Lady Valery wishes," he said. "We've only just met one another. Mayhap we should have more time to become acquainted before we speak of wedding dates."

"The Festival of Christ is agreeable to me, Papa," Valery said before Aurelius was even finished speaking. "I see no reason not to set a date."

Aurelius tried not to look too terribly pleased at her sudden approval. That wasn't the same lady who put a thorn in his chair and then threatened him with the glee of revenge. Frankly, he was surprised. Surprised and perhaps even a bit confused.

… or even suspicious.

In any case, he simply nodded in agreement as Adams appeared very pleased. He was also a little drunk, having imbibed two cups of his good wine in short order. Standing up, he shouted for silence in the hall before proceeding to announce the betrothal between his daughter and Aurelius dun Tarh.

The men in the hall went mad with approval, shouting

congratulations to Aurelius. Since many of them had never seen Valery, and all of them knew Aurelius, the congratulations went to Aurelius and to Adams as if they were the happy couple. Even when Aurelius turned to Valery and extended his hand to her, pulling her to her feet, the congratulatory shouts were still aimed at him. Valery was an afterthought.

But not to him.

Aurelius didn't realize how pleased he would feel with such an announcement. Across the table and down several seats, he could see Darien, Estevan, Caelus, and Kaladin. They were all clapping, too—only, in their case, with a little less enthusiasm. Caelus and Kaladin appeared positively bewildered. But Aurelius was fixed on Darien, pleased that his brother's big mouth hadn't ruined a moment that would propel him into his future.

His destiny.

But he wouldn't have it were it not for Valery. When he turned to tell her so, he was faced with an empty chair and no lady. Even Lady Wolsingham was missing, and Aurelius never saw her leave. Something told him that the absence of his betrothed was not a good thing, not even when Adams invited him to sit and celebrate with drink. All of the dun Tarh brothers joined in, as well as the de Wolfe and de Nerra men, all of them celebrating Aurelius' good fortune.

Am I worth the price?

Valery had asked him that question, and he had assured her that she was very much worth the price. But he realized, as the men in the hall congratulated him, that he hadn't shown her how worthy she was. He'd let himself be overwhelmed with men who only wanted to commend him on his good fortune.

With a woman like Valery, he could only imagine how she

might hold that against him.

He had to prove to her that she was, indeed, worth the price.

CHAPTER NINE

"MY LORD, MAY I have a word?"

Sterling was standing at the entry to Adams' solar at dawn. Adams had been up for an hour or two, ever since a groom summoned him because his favorite horse, the one he'd ridden all the way back from France, seemed to have turned up with a fever of unknown origin. Sterling had been on the wall at the changing of the guards, spying his liege as the man moved around in the stables, but the truth was that he'd been up all night.

He had something to say to Adams de Leybourne.

And Adams knew it. After the betrothal announcement last night, he was surprised it had taken Sterling this long to approach him. He'd just entered the foyer of the keep, removing his cloak as Sterling stood stiffly by the solar door. Pushing through the heavy oak panel, which was already open, Adams tossed the cloak onto the nearest stool as he made his way to the hearth.

"Was it a quiet night, Sterling?" he asked, trying to pretend like he didn't know why Sterling had come. "I would assume most nights have been quiet since I've been away?"

Sterling had followed him inside the solar, shutting the door quietly behind him. "There was no trouble, if that is what you mean, my lord," he said. "But Bowes saw some action about three months ago."

Adams had made it to his table, the one that generations of his family had conducted business on. "What kind of action?" he asked.

"Spennymoor, my lord," Sterling said. "The usual harassment, only this time it was regarding sheep. He accused de Royans of Bowes Castle of thievery when it came to a flock of sheep."

Adams snorted softly. "De Royans is no more a thief than I am," he said, refamiliarizing himself with the maps and documents on his desk, which hadn't been touched since his departure. "Was there any resolution?"

"De Royans rode for Spennymoor the next day and burned it to the ground."

Adams' head shot up, and he looked at Sterling in surprise. "Destroyed the bishop?"

"As de Royans put it, he put forth his hand to smite the bishop from the earth."

Adams grinned. "Well done to de Royans," he said with approval. "But surely there must be some reprisal?"

Sterling shrugged. "Not yet, but de Royans asked for your support should the French *duc* send troops to Bowes."

"De Royans has our support, without question."

"That is what I told him, my lord."

Adams nodded and refocused on his papers, sitting heavily on the chair that was next to the table. He was preoccupied with everything he was seeing, knowing he had to reacquaint himself with much.

"I asked to have my saddlebags brought in," he said. "Have you seen them?"

Sterling nodded, pointing to a chair near the heart. "Over there, my lord," he said. "As you requested."

"Good," Adams said. "Please bring them to me."

Sterling collected the saddlebags, bringing them over to the table and setting them down carefully as Adams went to open them. Sterling watched the man as he rummaged around. His expression, usually one of eager obedience when Adams was present, was unnaturally hard. For certain, there was much on his mind.

There had been ever since the betrothal announcement last night.

"I wanted to ask you how my son performed on campaign, my lord," he said. "Did Maxwell live up to your expectations?"

Adams was pulling forth small scrolls, rolled vellum with muster sheets and other accounting. "Maxwell is a good lad," he said. "He performed well for the most part."

Sterling's brow furrowed. "There were times when he was lacking, my lord?"

Adams shrugged. "He is young."

"Would you please tell me how he failed to perform?" Sterling persisted. "If he has shamed the family name, then I have a right to know."

Adams looked at him then. "Nothing so dramatic," he assured him. "But there were two times, specifically, he refused to wait for a command to proceed. Knights at his age always think they know everything, and Max is no exception. He will outgrow such urges if they do not kill him first."

Sterling digested the comment, but his expression had cooled. He suspected there was an insult in what Adams had said, and he didn't take that well, not when he and his father before him had served the earldom of Wolsingham flawlessly for many years. He had intended that such service would pave the way for Maxwell's marriage to the Wolsingham heiress, but as of last night, he knew that was not to be—and he could not help the rage, the disappointment, building in his heart.

"I suppose that gives me the answer I have been seeking, then," he said quietly.

Adams unrolled one of the vellum scrolls, peering at it. "Your answer for what?"

"Why you betrothed Lady Valery to someone other than my son."

Adams paused to look at him. The subject had finally come up, and he wouldn't pretend he didn't know what Sterling meant. Setting the scroll down, he leaned back in his seat, regarding the father of a fine young knight.

Just not fine enough for his daughter.

"Sterling," he said quietly. "I know you have long had ambition to wed Maxwell to my daughter, but you also know that never, at any time, did I give you any hope that such an arrangement would take place."

That was true, but it didn't stop Sterling from feeling affronted. "Nor did you give me any clear answer that it was not to be, my lord," he said. "You never told me that Maxwell was not a prime candidate."

Adams could hear a rebuke in that statement. "What makes you think that he was ever a prime candidate?" he said, feeling annoyed. "Furthermore, Maxwell has never, at any time, shown the least bit of interest in Valery—or any other woman, for that matter."

Sterling stiffened. "I see no need to insult my son, my lord."

Adams rolled his eyes and stood up. "Sterling, I have spent a solid year in France with your son," he said. "Max is bright and ambitious. He is skilled and well educated. But we must face facts, my friend. He is not interested in women. A marriage between Valery and Maxwell, even if I had a mind to do it, would only make them both miserable."

Sterling's fair features were beginning to turn red with anger. "You said it yourself," he said. "He is young. He will soon realize that he must marry a woman, and whatever he has done in the past, and with whom, will fade from memory. The follies of youth."

Adams could see how upset Sterling was becoming with the conversation, but facts were facts. All of Lydgate knew that Maxwell St. John had had a male lover since he was about eighteen years of age, a fellow knight who had been sent away at Sterling's request.

But that hadn't stopped true love.

"Sterling, I am going to tell you something," Adams said. "I know you do not wish to hear it, but I am going to tell you anyway. You requested that Gaspard de Jourdain be sent from Lydgate because you did not want your son having a close male friend. A man with whom he shared everything. Because of your service to Lydgate, I granted your request and sent Gaspard to Northwood Castle. You are aware that Northwood Castle sent men with me into France, are you not? Gaspard was in command of the Northwood contingent. Max and Gaspard have spent an entire year together, and I've never seen your son happier."

Sterling's jaw was twitching furiously at the news. "And you allowed this?" he hissed. "Knowing how I felt about… about Gaspard, you allowed him to serve with my son?"

Adams shrugged. "Gaspard is an excellent knight," he said. "Max is an excellent knight, and I was heading into combat. I am not going to send a skilled warrior away because you want me to. Sterling, you must face the fact that your son loves a man. I have told you this before, and it is unfair of you to pretend that love does not exist."

Sterling's lip flickered into a snarl. "You will not tell me how I should feel or not feel," he growled. "Whatever my son seems to think is right and worthy is not something I wish for him."

"I do not think that is fair."

"Had you betrothed him to Valery, he would have forgotten about Gaspard!"

"Raise your voice to me again and I will send you away from Lydgate permanently."

The tension in the solar was thick enough to cut. Adams had been calm for the most part, but now Sterling's anger was rousing his own. But Sterling knew he'd crossed the line, so he struggled to calm down. Given the subject, it was difficult, and the fact that Maxwell and his friend Gaspard had just spent an entire year together ate at him. Clawed at him.

He thought he'd ended that relationship.

Gaspard and Maxwell had fostered together and were the best of friends until they grew older and stronger feelings developed. The truth was that Sterling liked Gaspard a great deal. He always had. Gaspard had been like another son to him—until the rumors reached his ears that Maxwell and Gaspard were more than friends. Sterling had refused to believe it until he caught a glimpse of the truth one day when neither Maxwell nor Gaspard knew he was around. A beautiful, tender kiss, from lover to lover, was something Sterling had witnessed in the stables one morning.

Gaspard had been gone the next day.

But the memory of that kiss still lingered.

"Forgive me, my lord," Sterling finally said. "I am emotional where my son is concerned."

Adams knew that. "I understand," he said. "But I, too, have a child. I want the best for her, just as you want the best for Maxwell. Ultimately, I want her to be happy. I should think you would want the same for Maxwell, and in his case, marrying him to a woman—any woman—will make him miserable. I cannot believe that is what you truly want."

Sterling sighed heavily. "I want him to have what all men have," he said. "A wife, children, property, and prestige. I want him to have a destiny."

"Mayhap Max has different ideas about his destiny."

"That is not for him to choose."

Adams grunted. "I cannot say that you are wrong because I have chosen my daughter's destiny," he said. "But that was never going to be with Maxwell, Sterling. I am sorry if that disappoints you."

Sterling's rage had cooled into something that weakened him. Drained him. It made him feel lethargic. All he could think about was his talented son with no future. No wife, no children to carry on his name.

"Is one's happiness worth the loss of a legacy?" he muttered. "It is not that I do not want my son to be happy. I do. But I want him to have a legacy. That is something all men deserve."

"Then mayhap that is something you must speak to Maxwell about," Adams said. "I cannot answer for him. But from one father to another… Let your son choose what makes him happy. If you do not, he will grow to hate you for it."

Sterling glanced at him. "Did you let Valery choose?"

Adams shook his head. "She is a woman," he said. "Women are not expected to choose their own happiness. But I chose someone I felt would give her the best opportunity for a lifetime of it."

"Dun Tarh?"

"I think so. I hope so."

Sterling didn't have much to say after that. He simply nodded his head, resigned to what had happened. He felt so incredibly desolate—for the loss of a bride for his son, but also for the realization that the relationship he'd tried to prevent had not been prevented at all.

More than likely, it had thrived.

At that moment, he felt as if he'd lost everything.

Mayhap it would have been better had Maxwell died in France.

As Sterling lost himself in horrible thoughts, Adams spoke quietly.

"I have decided to have a feast in celebration of Valery's betrothal," he said. "I know you do not want to hear it, nor do you wish to celebrate it, but as my knight, you must find the courage to do both. I shall write the necessary missives today to local allies and friends alike and invite them to feast in honor of Valery and Aurelius' betrothal. You will ensure that the invitations are delivered."

It was like another stab to the gut for Sterling. Duty above all, no matter how he personally felt. That had always been his mantra, but, at the moment, he'd never felt less like performing his duties.

Yet he had no choice.

"As you wish, my lord," he said with quiet resignation. "How many will there be?"

"At least twelve families locally."

"Then I will make sure the messengers are prepared."

With that, he silently quit the chamber. Adams watched him go, knowing he was hurt and thinking on a father who had always had great ambition for his son and a son who didn't conform to the rules that men lived by. For Adams, he didn't care who a man loved so long as his character was good, but there was a reason for that. He had a younger brother, now a priest, who had also favored men, and their father's answer was to commit him to a life of piety.

Adams had always pitied his brother because of it.

In any case, it was a world where most men were judged by their actions and appetites—and in Maxwell's case, anyone who served with him knew he only had eyes for one person. Adams had never seen him judged, not by the dun Tarhs or the de Wolfes or the de Nerras, or any other allies who happened to know the truth. They, too, judged Maxwell on his merits, not his preferences. But Adams knew that Maxwell wouldn't find that kind of tolerance everywhere.

He'd seen it before.

It could ruin a man.

With thoughts of Sterling and Maxwell on his mind, Adams returned to his table and the accounting he now had to go through for a tally of his expenditures in France, in both lives and money. But he couldn't seem to forget his conversation with Sterling. However, he knew one thing for certain.

It wouldn't be the last time that subject came up.

For Maxwell's sake, he was sorry.

CHAPTER TEN

AMELIA DE HETTON'S laughter always sounded like scream-ing for some reason. Even a giggle sounded like a howl. That was what woke Valery up on the morning after the announcement of her betrothal.

Amelia's screaming.

It was right in her ear because Amelia had flopped on her bed to wake her up. What she really did was nearly startle Valery right out of her skin. Suddenly, Amelia was on the bed with her, hugging her and laughing in her ear, and Valery was so surprised that she ended up falling out of bed.

That made Amelia laugh even harder.

"You silly goose!" she cried. "Get off the floor! I've come to see you!"

Valery picked herself up, rubbing her eyes as she looked at Amelia spread across her bed.

"God's Bones, Amelia," she said. "What are you doing here?"

Amelia was dressed in her finest traveling clothes—silks and ribbons and furs. She sat up on the bed, smoothing out the rabbit trim of her sleeves.

"I'm going to visit my husband in Liverpool," she said. "He has been there for the past two months, tending to his ill mother and leaving me at home. Can you imagine? Leaving his new wife at *home*."

Valery frowned. "That is positively beastly," she said. "How could he do such a thing?"

Amelia threw up her hands. "That is what I said to myself," she said. "How could he do such a thing? So I have spent my time punishing him."

Yawning, Valery sat on the bed next to her. "Punishing him?" she said. "How?"

Amelia batted her eyes devilishly. "How do you think?" she said. "I've invited his friends over to sup, and I've flirted with them. I've gone into the village, to the tavern, and I've flirted with every man worth my attention."

Valery stopped yawning and frowned. "Why would you do that?"

"Because the rumors will reach his ears, silly," Amelia declared. "Then he will know it is not safe to leave me alone. He will never do it again!"

Valery looked at her friend in disbelief as the woman stood up and went to pet the geese. She was one of the only people whom the geese allowed near. As she crooned to the fowl and fed them bits of stale bread off the table, Valery was trying to overcome her shock at what Amelia was telling her. Not only had the woman visited unexpectedly, but she was evidently engaged in something unsavory.

"God's Bones," she muttered, wiping a hand over her face. "At least let me wake up a little and get dressed before you tell me of your life since I last saw you. You seemed so happy at your wedding."

She was up, staggering over to the alcove where she kept her toiletry things, as Amelia continued to pet the geese.

"There is nothing more to tell," Amelia said. "You know everything that has happened. Alphonso and I were married all of four weeks before he received word of his mother's ill health and off he went."

Valery was at her wardrobe, selecting her clothing for the day. "But I do not understand," she said. "Why would he not take you with him?"

Amelia shrugged. "His mother did not want him to marry, you know," she said. "It was his father's doing."

"But Alphonso had seen almost forty-five years!"

"I know," Amelia said. "That does not mean he is old. It means he is experienced."

"Experienced in what?"

Amelia looked at her in surprise before breaking down in giggles. "Just what you would expect him to be experienced in," she said. "I've not seen you since my wedding night. Do you remember we used to speak of what our husbands would be like and how it would feel?"

Valery was behind the painted screen now, pulling off her sleeping shift. "Of course I do," she said. "I remember everything we would speak of. You and me and Elyse and Alisabeth. Do you remember how Elyse thought a woman became with child by having a man spit in her mouth?"

They both burst into laughter. "She learned quickly that is not how it happens," Amelia said. "She has three children now."

"That is a lot of spitting."

More laughter. Valery began splashing rosewater on her, washing off the sleep on her face and body.

"Speaking of marriage," she said, having some good news of

her own. "Have you seen my mother yet?"

Finished with the geese, Amelia began looking around for food or drink. "Not yet," she said. "Have your servants not brought you food yet?"

Valery dried off her face. "How could they?" she said. "You woke me before they did. You probably broke through the gatehouse, charged your way into the keep, and kicked my door down. Who let you in, anyway?"

Amelia smirked as she went to the chamber door, opening it and calling for food. There were always servants lurking nearby, especially Sela and Beryl, who hated to let Valery out of their sight. Confident her request was heard, Amelia shut the door and headed over to Valery's wardrobe.

"The gatehouse guards recognized me," she said. "I can convince them to do anything for me, and you know it. I did not see Sterling, though I saw many standards and men that I did not recognize once my escort entered the bailey. Who are all of the men?"

Finished drying her face, neck, and torso, Valery pulled a soft shift over her head. "Papa returned from France yesterday," she said. "He brought about a thousand men with him, including an entire band of Highlanders."

Amelia's brow furrowed, though Valery couldn't see it. "I did not know your father was allied with Highlanders," she said. "Alphonso does not have good things to say about them. Nor did my father."

"What do you think of them?"

"I do not care. A man is a man."

"Then know that I am betrothed to one of them. Papa announced it last night."

That seemed to change Amelia's opinion of Highlanders

immediately, because she let out a squeal. "You are to be married?" she cried happily, rushing behind the painted screen to hug her friend. "Val, I'm so very happy for you! Tell me all about him! Have you met him yet? What does he look like?"

Valery laughed at Amelia's eagerness. "Aye, I've met him," she said. "Now that you are here, you shall meet him too."

"What does he look like? Is he handsome?"

Valery pulled the dress over her head and stepped out from behind the panel so Amelia could help her secure the garment. "I do not mean to insult Alphonso, or Elyse's husband or Alisabeth's husband, but I shall have the most handsome husband of all of you," she said. "He is… Well, I've never seen a more handsome man."

The humor left Amelia's face as she looked at Valery in surprise. "Truly?"

Valery nodded. "You will see for yourself."

She pointed to the back of her dress, and Amelia went to lace her up the back. "Tell me," she demanded. "I want to know *now!*"

Valery fought off a grin as Amelia laced the garment up the back, very tightly and roughly, as if to punish her for having a handsome betrothed. "He's tall," she said, grunting as Amelia yanked. "Very tall. And he's young."

Amelia stopped lacing and suddenly stood in front of Valery, looking as if she wanted to cry. "He's not an older warlord?"

"Nay."

"But your father knows so many."

"I know."

"But I was certain it would be one of those old bores!"

Valery jabbed a thumb at the half-done laces. "Finish and

I'll tell you the rest," she said. As Amelia went back to finishing the lacing with her mouth molded into a deep grimace, Valery continued. "His name is Aurelius dun Tarh, and his father is the Earl of Torridon. Aurelius is his father's heir, so not only will I be the Countess of Wolsingham someday, I'll also be the Countess of Torridon."

The more Valery talked, the more unhappy Amelia became until she finally laced up the last of the garment and tied it so tightly that she nearly broke the ties themselves.

"That's just not fair," she said, pouting. "You were already going to be a countess, and now you shall have two earldoms? I do not even have one."

Valery shot her a long look. "If you tell me that you are jealous, I will give you a smack," she said. "You have great wealth and power, Amelia. How can you begrudge me the same thing?"

Amelia sighed sharply. "I did not mean it the way it sounded," she said. "I simply meant… Oh, Val, I've been so unhappy. Marriage is nothing as I'd hoped, and I feel so alone. My husband spends more time with his mother than he does with me, and I have no one at all. Wealth and power do not warm my bed."

The tone of the conversation grew serious as Valery went to her friend, looking into the woman's face and seeing her distress.

"I am sorry to hear this," she said softly. "Have you truly been so terribly alone?"

Amelia nodded. "Why do you think I came here?" she said. "Traveling to see my husband was just an excuse. I have not seen you in so long, and I've missed you. I need someone to talk to. I thought I married someone to talk to. But his mother calls and he flies to her side. What can I do?"

Valery could see that the marriage between Amelia and Alphonso had some cracks in it. She found herself looking at a disillusioned woman, surprisingly so. She was concerned to realize that the marital situation wasn't all joy and laughter.

"But when you were married, there seemed to be happiness on both sides," she said, taking Amelia's hand. "At least, Alphonso seemed happy. He seemed very attentive."

Amelia was close to weeping. "He was," she said. "He was up until the time his mother summoned him. I asked him not to go, but he said that she was old and would die soon and he needed to be with her. She cannot die soon enough for me."

Valery shushed her softly. "You do not want to wish such terrible things," she said, squeezing her hand. "Everything will be well again, you'll see. Alphonso shall return to you and you shall have all of his attention. I know he was mad about you. Everyone could see it."

Amelia took some comfort from her friend's words. "I know," she said. "But that all changed when his mother snapped her fingers."

"Mayhap he loves his mother and is sad that she is ill."

Amelia didn't want to address what was more than likely a valid point. She was still wallowing in self-pity and trying to justify her trip to Liverpool. Therefore, she simply shrugged and tugged Valery over to her dressing table where combs and ribbons and pins were strewn.

"Sit down," she told Valery, pushing her into the chair. "Let me fashion your hair beautifully so that your Highland husband will see how fortunate he is."

Valery let the woman push her around. That was usual when it came to Amelia. It was clear she didn't want to discuss the subject of her absent husband further than they already had, so Valery simply sat still while Amelia began to brush her hair. She was quiet and depressed, characteristics completely foreign to Amelia. That told Valery the situation must be dire, indeed. Amelia was lonely, flirting with men she invited into her husband's home, hoping it would get back to him so he would return to her.

Or denounce her for being a whore.

Such a scenario wasn't out of the realm of possibility. Valery thought Amelia was asking for trouble with her behavior, but she didn't say so. She simply sat there while Amelia worked on her hair, braiding it, wrapping it around her head, and creating a masterpiece. Amelia had always been good at that sort of thing.

But as Valery sat and watched, listening to Amelia as she began to talk about the down-and-dirty details of being bedded by her husband—which only turned out to be thrice in the entire time they'd been married—her thoughts wandered to the Highlander she was betrothed to. Yesterday had been a rude introduction, to be sure, but they'd managed to have a some-what decent conversation at sup—before the announcement of the betrothal and the shouts of congratulations, which weren't meant for her. Only for him.

It reminded her of Amelia's husband, who would rather spend time with his mother than his wife.

Was that the kind of life she was in for? A man who took all of the glory himself, with none left for her? Was she doomed to a marriage with a man whom she didn't know, from a culture she didn't understand? God, she hoped not. She really hoped not. She didn't want to end up like Amelia, lonely and engaging in questionable tactics to get her husband's attention. Well, she wouldn't stand for it.

Perhaps she'd better make that clear to Aurelius dun Tarh.

CHAPTER ELEVEN

H E LOOKED JUST like him.
Lares.

It was true that, over the years, Davina had thought on Lares occasionally and wondered if he was at least content with the way his life had gone. Not happy, because she knew he'd never be happy in an abbey, but she hoped that he was at least content. Perhaps he'd even come to terms with his life. Perhaps he'd found a skill he was particularly good at, and he'd used that skill for the abbey, working hard and living a productive life. Even if he was a monk.

But, clearly, that had not happened.

Lares had married.

Evidence of that marriage had been sitting at her dinner table last night—five dun Tarh brothers, all of them looking like Lares to some degree. She could hardly believe it. But the features were unmistakable, just as she had remembered him. The eldest, in particular, had a flowing mane that looked very much like his father's, while the second eldest had a big white patch of hair over his forehead, stark against his dark hair. She'd been introduced to the five dun Tarh brothers but was told there were eight total, plus two sisters.

Lares had ten children.

That was a far cry from being a monk.

Odd how Davina hadn't known about her husband's alliance with the dun Tarh clan, but not so odd considering she never paid any attention to his affairs and deliberately kept away from his men or allies. As it had been explained to her last night, the dun Tarh clan came through Castle Questing, the House of de Wolfe, because de Wolfe was allied with—and kin to—the House of de Velt. Evidently, Lares had married a de Velt woman, so the family tree of an old and distinguished English house branched off into one of Scotland's oldest and most legendary families. Adams had told her all of it when the feast was over and everyone had gone to bed. Then he'd gone to sleep next to her, snoring long into the night as she lay there and pondered the news.

The sons of the man she'd once been madly in love with.

And her daughter was to marry the eldest one.

There was incredible irony in that realization.

The autumn day after the feast dawned bright and pleasant, and Davina took her sewing down into the garden to sit in the sunlight, as she often did on pleasant days. There was a small, walled garden on the north side of the castle, one exclusively for her use, and she retreated to it to ponder thoughts of Lares dun Tarh and the fact that he'd peripherally entered her life once again. As she sat on a wooden bench with her needlework laid out beside her on the seat, she wondered how to tell Adams that she knew Aurelius' father. Clearly, she would see Lares when their children were married, so she wondered if it would be better if she told Adams that she'd known the man many years ago and be honest about it.

Well… perhaps not completely honest.

She wouldn't mention that terrible day at Carlisle Cathedral when it all ended.

Adams didn't need to know that Lares was the man she had been torn from when her father pledged her to the Wolsingham heir. She'd met Adams immediately after the situation with Lares, and he'd known there had been an "undesirable suitor," courtesy of her father, but nothing beyond that. He'd never asked her, she'd never told him all of it, and for all of these years, it simply wasn't something they'd ever spoken of.

But now… now she had to face it.

Davina wasn't even certain if, after all these years, it mattered anymore. She and Adams had lived a good life together, and they had learned to enjoy one another's company. He wasn't the love of her life, but he was a good man. There had never been once, in all that time, that the mysterious "undesirable" suitor ever came up. Truthfully, that was the only secret Davina had ever kept from her husband, and she really didn't consider it a secret as much as it was simply something in her past that didn't matter any longer.

But that could all change if Lares was suddenly back in her life, even if it was as the father of her daughter's husband. Frankly, Davina found it quite shocking that Lares had married at all, because the last time she saw him, he had been surrounded by Highlanders and his own father, who had been determined to punish him. She thought back to that violent, terrible day. It was something she'd had to push out of her mind long ago, because too many reflections had driven her to the brink of madness when she thought on Lares' fate. She simply had to forget about him.

And she had, until now.

Now there was Aurelius.

As handsome as Lares had been, his son had a reflection of his father's beauty and then some. All of the dun Tarh lads had that male beauty that was rare and startling. Tonight would be another feast with them, and perhaps she'd have the opportunity to speak with one or more of them, but the thought of holding a conversation with Lares' sons did strange things to her heart. She wondered if it was going to hurt to speak to men that should have been hers and Lares. She wondered if old feelings would resurface.

God, she hoped not.

She wondered if she'd be strong enough to handle them.

Overhead, birds flew by, brushing the flowers in the garden, looking for a morning meal. Davina's attention moved to the birds, to her flowers, to the small trees in her garden. She didn't tend them personally, as many fine women did, but rather let the servants do it. She simply enjoyed her garden. There was something magical about it, and she found satisfaction with the beauty without having to get her hands dirty. As she leaned over to inspect a rose that was just beginning to bloom, she caught movement over by the garden gate. A shadow appeared, and as she watched, that shadow became a man.

The very man she'd been pondering.

Aurelius dun Tarh had made an appearance.

☙

"An escort arrived this morning," Estevan said. "Do ye know who it is?"

He was speaking to anyone who could answer him, but mostly he was looking at Aurelius and Darien. In the main tent belonging to dun Tarh, his older brothers were breaking their fast around a small, portable table that had seen better days. They had watered ale, bread and cheese, and a big hunk of cold meat they'd procured from the kitchens of Lydgate. The younger men hadn't eaten yet because they had duties to attend to, so Aurelius and Darien were making sure they ate almost everything. It wasn't unusual for them to just leave scraps for their brothers.

Such was the privilege of the older, bigger brothers.

It taught the younger men self-reliance.

"I dunna know," Darien said, chewing. "But they came early. I saw them when I went to the kitchen for the meat."

Estevan pulled a stool up to the table. "Do ye want to know what *I* heard?"

Aurelius eyed him but didn't respond. He was too busy eating bread and cheese. But Darien wasn't too busy.

He glanced at his brother.

"What did ye hear, little man?" he asked.

Estevan hated it when they called him that. He hadn't reached his growth spurt yet and was, indeed, shorter than his brothers. Unhappily so.

And they never let him forget it.

"I heard it was an old friend who is trying to lure Lady Valery into traveling with her," he said. "This lady evidently has a husband who has a brother who has been trying to woo Lady Valery."

Aurelius' head jerked in Estevan's direction. "Is that so?" he said, suddenly interested in what Estevan had to say. "And ye know this for certain?"

Estevan shook his head. "Of course not," he said. "But that's what some of the men have been saying."

Aurelius was immediately in a foul mood. He was already

feeling uncertain because of the way his conversation ended with Valery the night before, and now she had a friend who had come, possibly to lure her into the clutches of another man. Aurelius had an ironclad betrothal with the woman, so it wasn't as if he had a chance of losing her, at least legally and morally. But he didn't know her, and he didn't know her past, or her thoughts or feelings, and that was where he was uncertain.

He was in uncharted territory.

"Get out," he growled to Estevan. "Go about your business. And if ye hear any more foolish stories, come and tell me right away."

Estevan wasn't pleased at being sent away, but he did as he was told. Once he was clear of the tent, Aurelius stood up and went over to his saddlebags.

"Another man already, is there?" he rumbled. "We'll see about that."

Darien watched his brother rummage through his bags. "They're just rumors," he said. "I wouldna worry over them."

Aurelius paused to look at him. "That's where ye'd be mistaken," he said. "I know nothing about this woman other than what her father had told me. I dunna know what's in her heart. I dunna even know if she has someone she's fond of. Her father was gone an entire year and he betrothed her, not knowing how she even felt about it. What if there *is* someone else?"

"Did ye ask her?"

Aurelius scowled. "Of course I dinna *ask* her," he said. "I've only just met the lass, and I'm supposed to ask her if she fancies someone else?"

"Do ye want *me* to ask her?"

Aurelius rolled his eyes and turned back to his saddlebags, pulling out a comb. "Nay," he said flatly. "That is the last thing I want. I dunna need yer meddling, Darien. Ye've caused enough trouble already."

Darien scratched his head and looked away. "I told ye I was sorry," he said. "I'll not say it again."

"I'm not asking ye to. I'm simply telling ye the situation."

Darien wasn't going to stand by and be scolded for a second day. He stood up, yawning. "Then I'll leave ye to yer worrying and go about my business," he said. "De Wolfe is leaving today, I think. I'll go see if Rhori and the others need help."

"Good."

Darien headed to the tent opening, but paused before stepping through. He glanced at his brother, who was combing his long, dark hair, trying to work through a knot. It wasn't like Aurelius to comb his hair unless there was some special occasion, so that told Darien his brother was more invested in the situation than he let on. Yesterday, there had been something superficial to the betrothal, the initial meeting and announcement. But now, a day later, reality was settling. Aurelius was to have a wife, and that was the truth of it.

Hesitantly, Darien spoke.

"Much like Estevan, I heard something last night that ye might want to be aware of," he said. "There was a table of soldiers next to us, and they were talking. Mayhap ye've already heard it."

Aurelius was combing furiously at a tangle. "I willna know until ye tell me."

Darien was still hesitant, given the trouble he had indeed caused, but he decided to come out with it. "It seems that Maxwell's father has been pushing for a betrothal between his son and Lady Valery," he said. "Ye *know* Maxwell, Bear."

Aurelius' irritation faded as he looked at his brother. "St.

John?”

"Aye."

Aurelius thought about that a moment before returning to the tangle in his hair that he'd nearly combed out. "Of course I know him," he said quietly. "We've spent the better part of a year fighting alongside the man. And… and his father wanted *him* for the lady?"

"That's what I heard."

Aurelius finally combed through the tangle. He was quiet a moment as he deliberated that bit of news before finally speaking. "Either his father doesna know his own son or he's blind to the man," he muttered. "St. John and de Jourdain aren't meant to be separated. They'll grow old together."

"I know," Darien said. "Surely the man's father must know that his son will never marry a woman."

"Mayhap he hopes time will change him."

"I just thought ye should know what the men were saying."

Finished with his hair, Aurelius tossed the comb aside. "Even Wolsingham must know that such a match isna possible," he said. "If he was going to make a match between his daughter and St. John, he would have already done so."

"Probably."

Aurelius scratched his head, thinking of the powerful knight with a powerful sword who only had eyes for another knight. After a moment, he shook his head.

"Pity," he muttered. "'Tis a pity that St. John… Well, 'tis a pity."

"What do ye mean?"

Aurelius shrugged. "I was thinking that it is a pity that St. John canna marry a person of his choosing," he said. "He calls de Jourdain his best friend, and that's all he'll ever be able to call him. St. John is a good man, Darien. I suppose I meant that I find it a pity when a man like that canna be happy on his own terms."

"And a pity when a father canna accept a son as he is."

"Mayhap he's simply afraid for him," Aurelius said. "Men like St. John and de Jourdain can be punished. Ye know that."

Darien did, in fact, know that. He'd been around men and armies long enough to know that there were men who loved other men, as a man loved a woman, but those men kept to the shadows because of the potential punishment should their tastes be brought into the forefront. It was something others were aware of, but it was never openly spoken of. In fact, Darien and Aurelius had served with Maxwell and Gaspard for an entire year, and they'd never spoken of what was clearly a strong attraction between them. But the truth was that in their younger years, they'd had a kinsman who preferred the company of men. He'd been a bright lad, generous and kind, and one night, he'd simply disappeared. No one had ever seen him again, and no one knew what happened, but the clan elders admonished those who asked questions.

Put him from yer minds, lad. 'Tis safer that way.

That was something they never spoke of, either.

Therefore, there was a natural sense of protectiveness and apprehension when it came to Maxwell St. John. Perhaps there was something in what Aurelius said—that the man's father was more concerned for his son's safety than anything else.

That wasn't an unreasonable fear.

With lingering thoughts of Maxwell, Darien continued to stand at the tent opening as Aurelius moved to join him, both of them looking out over the bright morning, with trees in the distance turning colors as the weather grew colder.

"Where are ye going now?" Darien said, pushing Maxwell from his thoughts. "Mayhap to find a certain young lass?"

Aurelius cast him a long look. "Would ye think otherwise?"

"I wouldna. Ye dunna comb yer hair for no reason."

Aurelius lifted up the dark ends. "How does it look?"

"Like ye're wearing a dead cat on yer head."

Aurelius scowled at his brother. "Opinions like that are why no one likes ye."

Darien fought off a grin. "Then why'd ye ask?"

Aurelius sighed heavily, looking out to the wall and the dramatic landscape beyond. "I've not had a good start with the woman I'm to marry, and I intend to rectify the situation," he said. "I'll do it today."

"Ye dunna want company?" Darien asked.

"Nay," Aurelius nearly barked. He stepped out of the tent opening and waved a hand at his brother. "Go find the de Wolfe cubs and help them prepare for their journey. Leave me to my own affairs."

Darien did grin then, watching his brother head out of their encampment. But his smile soon faded at his knowing that Aurelius did have a job ahead of him. Lady Valery was a beautiful lass, no doubt, and Aurelius seemed keen to make the situation work. Whatever that would take.

And it would. When Aurelius wanted something, he usually got it.

But in this case… he was in for an uphill battle.

CHAPTER TWELVE

AURELIUS HAD TAKEN the wrong gate.

Coming into the castle proper, he thought he'd turned into the kitchen yard, but he was actually in a small, walled garden. A woman was seated upon a wooden bench, sewing something that was quite elaborate, and she seemed startled to see him. Aurelius immediately recognized Lady Wolsingham.

"M'lady," he said, coming to an immediate halt. "Forgive me. I thought this was the kitchen yard."

Lady Wolsingham was on her feet, sewing still in her hands as she faced him. "The gates are next to one another," she said. "It is an easy mistake if you are unfamiliar with Lydgate."

Aurelius looked up, at the top of the wall, at the keep that soared four or five stories behind it. "I hope to become familiar with it very quickly, m'lady," he said. "Again, forgive me for disturbing ye. I'll leave ye to yer solitude."

He started to back out, but Lady Wolsingham stopped him. "Wait," she said. "Please… do not go. We were introduced briefly last night, but I did not have the opportunity to be mannerly. You are most welcome here, my lord. Is there a proper title that we should use when addressing you?"

Aurelius was standing in the opening, his hand on the iron gate. "The courtesy title for the heir to the Earl of Torridon is Lord Albion," he said. "The title belongs to me."

Lady Wolsingham nodded respectfully. "Then you shall be addressed as Lord Albion," she said. "I hope your stay at Lydgate has been pleasant so far."

Aurelius nodded. "Very pleasant, m'lady," he said. "Lydgate is a grand place."

Lady Wolsingham smiled faintly, lifting her head to look at the great walls as much as her tight wimple would allow. "I was quite intimidated when I first came here," she said. "I grew up at a great border castle, but when I married my husband, we lived in London in the early years. We did not truly come here until much later."

"I will admit that the only time I've been to London is to pass through it," Aurelius said. "I should like to go someday to visit. I hear there are many sights to see."

Lady Wolsingham nodded. "Quite a few," she said. Then she paused and indicated the bench she was sitting on. "Would you like to sit for a moment, Lord Albion?"

Aurelius hadn't been called by his actual title in years, but the English were quite formal about such things, he knew. And he was quite agreeable to sit and talk with Lady Wolsingham, his betrothed's mother.

Perhaps she might give him a little insight into the woman he was to marry.

"Thank ye, m'lady," he said, coming in and taking a seat at one end of the bench while she sat on the other. Her elaborate sewing was between them, and he picked up one end of it so he wouldn't sit on it, handing it back to her. "Ye have a great talent for sewing."

Lady Wolsingham smiled appreciatively. "You are very kind," she said. "Do you appreciate such skill?"

He nodded. "My mother has great talent, too," he said. "It's not usual for a great lady to sew clothing, but she likes to do it. She makes clothing for my sisters."

"Oh?" Lady Wolsingham seemed very interested. "How clever she must be."

"She is, m'lady."

"Where is your mother from?"

He grinned. "England," he said. "She married a man who couldna be more Scots if he tried. The greatest Scots married the greatest Englishwoman."

"And they had ten children."

He snorted softly. "They were prolific together, 'tis true."

"Where was your mother born?"

"Pelinom Castle, m'lady," Aurelius said. "It is—"

"North of the River Tweed," Lady Wolsingham said, finishing for him. "Your mother is a de Velt?"

He nodded. "She is, m'lady," he said. "Do ye know Pelinom, then?"

"I know it well," Lady Wolsingham said. "I, too, was born and raised at a border castle."

"Where were ye born?"

"Mount Pleasant Castle," she said. "Have you heard of it?"

Aurelius nodded immediately. "Aye," he said. "My family owns Ashkirk Castle, which isna far from it. Do ye know it?"

"I do," Lady Wolsingham said. Then she smiled weakly. "It seems that we know the same castles in the same area. How remarkable."

Aurelius returned her smile, displaying his big white teeth. The man had a smile that could light up a room. "I've never been to Mount Pleasant, though my father says we were once allied with de Gilsland," he said. "There was a falling out years ago, though I dunna know what it was. But I am certain ye and I will have no falling out, Lady Wolsingham?"

She shook her head firmly. "We will not, Lord Albion," she said. "I will make sure of it. But it is good to talk to someone who knows of the same places I do."

Aurelius was warming to the conversation because Lady Wolsingham was welcoming and kind. He appreciated that, given the surprising nature of his betrothal to her daughter. She seemed genuinely curious about him. But that brought a subject to mind that he was most interested in…

Her daughter.

"I would be happy to talk about the borders and the places we might both remember," he said, his smile fading. "But I was wondering, m'lady—if it wouldna be too much trouble—if I might ask ye about yer daughter."

A gleam came to Lady Wolsingham's eye as she looked at him. "Of course you may ask," she said. "I cannot promise you that I will answer every question, but I will answer what I can."

He knew what she meant. As Valery's mother, her loyalty was to her daughter. He smiled sheepishly.

"I understand completely," he said. "I suppose what I wanted to know was if I had offended her last night. If I did, then I'd like to know how I should ask forgiveness. Is yer daughter the forgiving kind? Or should I bring her a gift as a token of sincerity?"

Lady Wolsingham was trying very hard not to grin at a man who seemed clearly nervous when discussing a woman he didn't know, but perhaps very much wanted to know. It was endearing, really.

"You sound like a husband already," she quipped softly.

Aurelius' eyes widened. "Do I?" he said. "I dunna mean to. What I mean is… God's Teeth, I dunna know *what* I mean. I only meant to ask if she was offended last evening when the men were congratulating me on the betrothal. They dinna congratulate her."

Lady Wolsingham's expression was sympathetic. "You are astonishingly thoughtful, my lord," she said. "I do not think I've ever heard a man apologize for what a lady might or might not be feeling."

He averted his gaze, now somewhat embarrassed. "I have a mother who insists that I am polite toward women," he said. "She doesna allow any of her sons to be disrespectful."

"She sounds like an extraordinary woman," Lady Wolsingham said quietly. "I… I do hope your mother and father plan to come for the wedding. I should like to meet your mother."

He looked at her then. "If ye were born at Mount Pleasant, mayhap ye already do," he said. "She spent time there, in her youth. Her name is Mabel Douglas. Her mother was a de Velt, her father from the Douglas of Galloway."

Lady Wolsingham seemed to think on that. "I do not recall knowing her," she said. "I spent my youth fostering at Prudhoe and Lincoln Castle. I was gone for many years."

"Then she'll be happy to know ye when she comes for the wedding," he said. "If I know my mother, and I do, she'll be on the road south the very day she receives Wolsingham's announcement. Nothing can keep her away."

Lady Wolsingham smiled. "I shall consider it an honor to meet her," she said, sounding particularly soft and sincere. "She seems to have raised a good son."

Aurelius chuckled. "I was her first," he said. "I do believe she made all of her mistakes and triumphs on me before she raised the rest of the brood. But I will confess I'm very much my da's lad. He's the one person I canna do without."

Lady Wolsingham's smile faded as she looked to the sewing in her hand, folding it up and collecting her things. "Speaking of the one person you cannot do without," she said. "Unless you have any further questions, mayhap we should go in search of my daughter? I've not seen her yet this morning, but that is not unusual. I am going to confess something to you that I probably should not, but she is not an early riser."

Aurelius glanced up at the keep as if to see the very subject of their conversation. "She had a visitor this morning," he said. "I was told a friend had arrived to see her, so surely she must be awake now."

"Oh?" Lady Wolsingham said curiously. "Who has come?"

"Ye dinna see an escort in the bailey when ye came into the garden?"

Lady Wolsingham shook her head. "I came through the kitchen yard and avoided the bailey," she said. "No one told me that we had a visitor."

Aurelius gestured in the direction of the bailey. "I was only told it was a friend, but I dunna know who it is," he said. "Would ye like to find out?"

"I would."

"Then let me help ye."

Aurelius stood up and held out his hands so he could help her with the long piece of sewing she had, which was more like a tapestry than a simple piece. He picked it up, being polite, and when Lady Wolsingham realized what he was doing, she looked at him with genuine appreciation.

"You are very kind to assist me," she said, putting the last of her thread in a basket and standing up. For a moment, she simply looked at him, her green eyes glimmering before she spoke again. "Lord Albion, I feel as if we have become friends in this short time."

"I hope so, m'lady."

"May I be so bold as to give you some advice?"

"I would appreciate anything ye can tell me, Lady Wolsingham."

She was careful with her words. "My daughter," she began. "She was our only child, and my husband was not a disciplinarian. She has been raised to believe she can learn anything, do anything, and say anything. She is highly educated, and there are times when she believes she knows best. She has many friends that she has had since childhood, silly girls with silly dreams, who might have made her feel… unusual because of it. Most women do not read Homer or Ovid. My advice to you would be to accept her for who she is."

"And who is that, m'lady?"

A smile tugged at Lady Wolsingham's mouth. "A young woman who would rather read a book than dance, or tend an injured horse than sing," she said. "I believe my daughter is a woman of substance, Lord Albion. She is much more than the foolish women who pine for men and care only for wealth and appearance because, deep down, she wants to be accepted and appreciated. If she ever shows apathy or disinterest, it is because doing so protects those tender feelings. She has a tender heart. Do you understand what I am trying to tell you?"

Aurelius had been listening carefully. This was the most he'd been told about his future wife since he'd been informed of the betrothal, and he absorbed it eagerly. "I think so," he said. "She is not the usual flighty lass."

Lady Wolsingham laughed softly. "Nay, she is not," she said. "Treat her with respect and she will never leave your side. This I swear."

Aurelius liked hearing that. In fact, he needed to hear it. It wasn't that he was looking for a wife to worship him. He'd had women worship him, and he grew bored very quickly. What he wanted was a woman who could match his wits, a woman with a bright mind and a good spirit to match. Beyond that, he wasn't sure what more he wanted, but he knew one thing— Lady Wolsingham's words had given him hope that Lady Valery wasn't simply another beautiful face. Was he to be so fortunate, purely by happenstance, that he'd found a woman who had much more?

He had all the hope in the world that it was true.

"Thank ye," he said sincerely. "If she returns the respect I give her, I'll never leave her side either."

Lady Wolsingham nodded, appreciating his response, but also knowing there was nothing more she could say on the subject. *Should* say on it. Aurelius was going to have to learn about Valery on his own and not from her mother's perspective.

She'd done all she could.

"Shall we go into the keep, then?" Lady Wolsingham said, gesturing toward the stone edifice. "If you wait in the solar, I'll make sure Valery comes to you. You can ask her yourself if you offended her last night."

Aurelius grinned, still holding her sewing as she began to walk out of the garden. He felt good about the conversation, and he rather liked Lady Wolsingham. As she'd said, they'd become friends. He truly felt that way because the truth was that she reminded him of his own mother, though Mabel wasn't as gentle as Lady Wolsingham seemed to be. Mabel was no-nonsense, while Lady Wolsingham seemed to be more of a soft touch. Aurelius rather liked that in a future mother-in-law.

The inner bailey was bustling at this hour as they came out of the garden and headed toward the keep, but as they drew closer to it, two young women appeared and Aurelius recognized one of them. At least, he thought he did, but she didn't look anything like she had the previous night. Valery looked quite… different.

It was all he could do not to burst out laughing at the sight of her.

CHAPTER THIRTEEN

I T WAS A monstrosity.

God help her, it was.

Amelia had outdone herself on the hairstyle she'd created on her friend, and it was horrific. When Valery found herself looking at the style in the mirror, that was the only way to describe it. Amelia had always been so good with hair that seeing what she'd done took Valery's breath away, and not in a good way. Then it occurred to her that Amelia had perhaps done it intentionally. It was clear she'd been jealous that Valery was betrothed to a younger, more handsome man. Perhaps this was Amelia's way of making Valery look less attractive to her attractive suitor.

And Valery had fallen for it.

She tried to unwind some of the elaborate braiding, but Amelia insisted that this was the latest fashion and was quite lovely. Valery pointed out that Amelia wasn't wearing her hair in such a fashion, to which Amelia explained that it was impossible for her to do such a hairstyle on herself. Amelia coaxed her out of her chamber because she wanted to meet Aurelius, and, suddenly, they were out of the keep when Valery didn't want to go anywhere with her hair so elaborate. She paused just as they quit the keep and turned to go back inside, but Amelia insisted she looked lovely. In fact, she had her by the arm by now, dragging her.

And then the worst happened.

Who should be approaching but Lady Wolsingham and Aurelius, both of them looking at Valery with great curiosity. Amelia had a malicious grin on her face as she looked between Valery and her mother and then finally to Aurelius, whose square jaw was set and his expression emotionless. He was looking at Valery without any reaction at all, but all Valery wanted to do was turn and run inside. Amelia, however, waved to Lady Wolsingham in a most obvious manner.

"Lady Wolsingham!" she cried. "How delightful to see you! I hope you do not mind that I have come for a visit!"

Lady Wolsingham wasn't looking at Amelia. She was looking at her daughter's hair. She knew that Valery would never have dressed her hair in such a fashion, so she could only assume it was Amelia's doing. Silly, petty Amelia. Who would probably like nothing better than to embarrass Valery, her smarter and prettier friend.

It wouldn't be the first time.

"Nay, I do not mind," Lady Wolsingham said, looking at her daughter. "Valery… are you well, child? Did you sleep well?"

"Doesn't she look beautiful?" Amelia said gleefully, yanking Valery closer to her mother and the tall, handsome man at Lady Wolsingham's side. "Her hair is the latest fashion. I did it myself, so that she would look beautiful for her betrothed. She told me that she is to be married."

She was looking straight at Aurelius as she spoke, batting

her eyelashes in a flirtatious fashion. That told Lady Wolsingham everything she needed to know. Perhaps she had displayed gentleness with Aurelius only moments earlier, but that gentleness fled in the face of Amelia's blatant attempts at sabotage.

She'd never liked Amelia much anyway.

"*You* did this?" Lady Wolsingham said to Amelia. "You made her hair like… like *this*?"

Amelia was grinning, clinging companionably to Valery's arm, but there was a very snide hint to her manner. "Everyone is wearing their hair like this in London," she said. "My maid told me so."

Smack!

Lady Wolsingham's hand flew straight into Amelia's backside.

"You dare to come to my home and make a fool of my daughter?" she said. The smacking hand slapped Amelia's buttocks again. "You vicious cat! You did this on purpose to shame her!"

Amelia screamed, putting her hand over her buttocks because Lady Wolsingham struck her again. As Amelia took off on a run with Lady Wolsingham charging after her, Aurelius watched it all with a great deal of surprise and amusement. Amused that the gentle woman he'd just been speaking with evidently had a fiery side. He was about to say something to Valery, but she was fleeing back into the keep.

He went in pursuit.

"M'lady?" he called, hearing her run up the stairs. "M'lady, wait!"

He could hear sniffling and running feet. Making the split-second decision to follow, he took the stairs two at a time, following the sounds of distress, and ended up running straight into Valery's bedchamber as she tried to hide from him. Realizing he was in a maiden's bower, he rushed back to the door and remained there, unwilling to go any further. But he could hear her sniffling behind a painted screen, and somewhere in the chamber, he could hear the sounds of geese.

Those damnable geese were around.

"M'lady, truly, 'tis not so terrible," he said, looking around her chamber and trying to see where the geese were. "Ye needn't hide. I promise… truly, it's not so terrible."

"You do not have to pretend, my lord," she said, weeping softly. "I told her I did not like it, but she… Oh, I should *not* have gone outside. I should have made her brush it out. I am very sorry you had to see it."

Aurelius could hear the hurt in her voice. "Ye have nothing to apologize for," he said, somewhat gently. "I am happy to see ye, no matter what yer hair looks like."

It was sort of a compliment, and Valery sniffled, trying to regain her composure. "You are kind to say so," she said. "If you will allow me to make myself presentable, I would be delighted to speak to you downstairs."

"Would ye let me remain outside yer door? We can talk through the open panel."

"Why would you want to do that?"

"Because I've waited all morning to speak to ye," he said quietly. "Please dunna send me away. I promise I'll not look inside yer chamber whilst ye comb yer hair."

Valery fell silent for a few moments, thinking on his offer. It had been kindly presented, trying to convince her that the rat's nest on her head made no difference. Perhaps to him it didn't, but to her, it did. Still, he was trying his best to convince her otherwise.

She could feel herself relenting.

"You really should not be here, you know," she said.

She sounded more in control of herself, and he smiled faintly. "I know," he said. "But ye and I must build trust between us at some point. We can start now. I promise to stay right on this landing and not look into yer chamber. In fact, I'll stay right on the top step. We can converse while ye fix yer hair."

She fell silent again. Aurelius was still standing in the doorway, knowing she was considering his words, hoping she might agree to them. When she didn't answer quickly enough, he stepped out onto the landing.

"See?" he said. "I'll stand right here. I canna see ye, so ye can come out from behind the panel. Moreover, if ye dunna like my behavior, ye can send yer guards to bite me."

He meant the geese, but he hoped she wouldn't take him up on that. After a moment, he could hear soft footsteps inside the chamber as she moved around. She hadn't sent him away, which was a good sign, and nor had she ordered the geese to charge him, so he waited patiently while she pulled herself together. He felt that this was a somewhat important moment, because if she sent him away, then he knew he had an uphill battle in trying to establish a relationship between them. A surprise betrothal, especially when it wasn't wanted, could turn her against him.

But if she didn't send him away…

"I saw you with my mother," she finally said. "Did you require her assistance with something?"

"Nay," Aurelius said. "I was coming to find ye and happened to see her in her garden."

"Why did you go to her garden?"

"I dinna do it intentionally. I got lost."

"Ah," Valery said. "It is easy to do here. There are many doors in many walls."

"Seems like a labyrinth."

"It is, in a way," she said. Then she grunted, as if something had hurt her. "God's Bones, what did she do to me?"

"M'lady?"

More grunting and hissing. Aurelius leaned toward the door and called again.

"M'lady, is something amiss?"

He could hear her sigh heavily. "I do not know what she has done to my hair," she said, sounding as if she was verging on tears again. "She put in pins and ribbons and braids, and I cannot seem to find a way to unwind it. Do you see any servants that can assist me?"

Aurelius looked down the stairwell and even poked his head into an empty chamber. "Nay, m'lady," he finally called to her. "I dunna see anyone. May I be of assistance?"

"Not unless you know anything about hair."

"I do, in fact. I combed an enormous tangle out of my own hair this morning."

"I do not think that is the same."

"Won't you let me try?"

She gasped. "Are you *mad*?" she said, sniffling. Then she grunted again. "I do not think I will ever get this out."

Aurelius stopped asking if he could assist her. He simply went into the chamber, where she was seated at a table that had a big, polished bronze mirror propped on it. When Valery saw him, she gasped and tried to run away again, but he grabbed her by the arm and pushed her back onto the stool she'd been sitting on. The geese, now near the window, began to honk and hiss at him, but he braved the threat.

He had a point to make.

"I know I promised to stay outside, but ye're clearly in distress," he said, trying to get a look at her hair even as she put her hands over it to hide from him. He peeled one hand off only to have it replaced by another. "If ye'll only let me get a look, I promise I'll untangle ye. Or would ye rather stay like this while I go hunt for a servant?"

He pushed her hands out of the way, and she ended up covering her face in embarrassment. "I want you to go away," she said firmly. "I do not want you to see me like this."

He dropped his hands and stepped back, realizing he'd overstepped himself. Now she was doing what he'd hoped she wouldn't—she was sending him away. He was disappointed to realize it was his own fault.

"If that is yer wish," he said. "I will find a servant to help ye. I'm sorry if I embarrassed ye."

She still had her hands over her face. "Please go."

Saddened, Aurelius didn't push. He simply retreated to the door. But something made him pause, looking over at the woman with the bird's nest on her head as she sat there with her hands over her face in shame.

"Before I go, I want ye to know something," he said softly. "I've been many places in my life. I've known many people and I've seen many women. That makes me an expert, I suppose, so I can say without a doubt that ye'd be the most beautiful woman in England no matter what yer hair looks like. I dunna care that yer friend put it in a bunch on yer head. I was glad to see *ye* this morning, not yer hair. I didn't even notice it. All I noticed was ye."

With that, he turned away and headed toward the stairs.

He'd put his foot on the first step when he heard her calling to him.

"Wait," she said. "Come back."

He did, trying not to appear too eager. He only stood in the doorway, looking at her as her hands came away from her face and she turned to him.

For a moment, she simply looked at him, studying him, unsure what to say. He wasn't entirely sure why she'd called him back if she was only going to stare at him, but he had hope that there was something brewing in that sharp mind.

Treat her with respect and she'll never leave your side.

There were many ways to show respect.

Perhaps he needed to take the first step.

"I swear to ye that all I want to do is help," he said softly. "If yer friend did this to ye simply to shame ye, ye can tell her that it dinna work. Ye're still beautiful, and nothing she can do will change that."

As he watched, she sighed faintly, perhaps with some resignation, and turned back toward the mirror. "Be cautious removing the pins," she said. "It feels as if she's wound them into my hair."

Fighting off a smile, Aurelius came back into the chamber and walked up behind her, his eyes meeting hers in the mirror before he glanced over at the geese, who seemed to be settling back down by the window. At least they weren't hissing at him. Confident they'd stay away, at least for the moment, he looked down at the blonde mass on the top of her head, inspecting it carefully before he spied a hairpin and removed it. It pulled some hair, but not too badly.

One out, an unknown number to go.

Truthfully, Aurelius had never been so careful about anything in his life. The iron pins really were jammed into the mass of hair, and, more than once, Valery put her hands up to hold her hair steady while he pulled.

It was an odd bonding experience, but a powerful one.

Bonding over something… personal.

"You've done this before," Valery finally said.

He was focused on a pin at the back of her head. "Nay, I've not," he said. "This is the first. The question is, will it be the last?"

Valery's lips twitched with a smile. "Probably not," she said. "If you're any good at this, I shall make you fashion my hair every day."

He snorted, grinning. "It is too much work," he said, glancing at her in the mirror to see that she, too, was smiling. "How do women do this every day? I'm exhausted, and I'm not even finished yet."

Valery chuckled, displaying a smile he'd not yet seen and found utterly enchanting. "We do it because society tells us that we must be beautiful for men," she said. "We must be well groomed and pleasing."

"And that means taking great lengths with one's hair?"

"Of course," she said, sighing with relief when he took out the last pin and the braids started falling away. "You'd not like it much if every woman had an unbrushed mass of hair. We'd look like Christ after he'd been out in the wilderness for forty days."

He laughed softly, pulling on ribbons that were now easily coming out. "I hardly comb my hair, and I've never had any trouble attracting women," he said. "But I will admit that for ye, I did comb it."

"The big tangle you boasted about earlier?"

"The same."

"Child's play," she scoffed, though there was humor to it. "Now that you've seen what a woman's hair can look like, you can see that we have it much worse."

He handed her two ribbons he'd pulled free. "I would agree with that," he said. "And I'm sorry."

"About what?"

"That foolish men make ye feel as if ye must beautify yerself in elaborate ways."

"And you do not think so?"

"As I said, ye'd be beautiful no matter what ye did."

He could see her smiling in the reflection of the bronze mirror, flattered by his words. It was about time she was, because he wasn't usually such a flatterer—but with Valery, it seemed to come so easily.

"Do you know what I think?" she said after a moment.

"I'd like to."

She snorted at his cheeky reply before continuing. "I think that you must say such things because we are betrothed," she said, turning around and gazing up at him as he stood behind her. "Let us be clear, Highlander. I do not need to be flattered. I would prefer the truth above all else. Empty compliments mean nothing to me. Do you understand?"

He looked down at her, at that exquisite face, so flawless and lovely, but also hard and determined.

"I understand," he said quietly. "But let us be clear on something else. I never say anything I dunna mean. Ever. I will tell ye the truth, always, even if it isna something ye want to hear. I wouldna be showing ye any respect if I dinna, and above all, the woman I marry will have my respect unless she does something to destroy it. Do *ye* understand?"

She was still looking up at him, now nodding her head. "I do," she said. "I appreciate your candor."

"And I yers."

Lowering her gaze, Valery turned back around, facing the mirror as he resumed releasing her braids from the ribbons. She was watching him in the mirror, how carefully he was handing her hair.

This man she was to marry.

Truthfully, she hadn't been sure about his being in her chamber and handling her hair until this very moment. He seemed sincere enough, and he'd said all of the right things, but gazing into his eyes as he pledged to always tell her the truth was a pivotal moment for her. Perhaps he didn't sound like she did when he spoke, or perhaps he didn't share the same culture or family or friends with her, but Valery knew sincerity when she saw it. She knew honesty. At least, she hoped she did.

She believed him.

"Was it terrible in France?" she asked. When he looked at her, surprised, she lifted her shoulders. "That was my question to you last night before my father interrupted us. If you do not want to answer my question, simply say so. I have heard that men who have suffered through battle do not like to discuss it."

He appeared thoughtful as he refocused on her hair. "There is nothing I willna discuss with ye if yer question is sincere," he said. "But it is not something ye'll understand."

One of the blonde braids had fallen over her shoulder, and she picked it up, unweaving the strands. "Mayhap not," she said. "But I do understand a little."

"From wielding a sword?"

He had a smirk on his lips, teasing her, and she didn't take offense. She didn't sense that he was trying to offend her. "Nay," she said. "My father has a collection of rare books, and several of those books speak of war. There is one in particular, copied from a manuscript of a Roman general, that speaks of the horror of war."

"So ye've learned of war through books?"

"How else am I to learn?"

He removed the final ribbon that had been laced through her hair, handing it over to her as she set it on the table in front of her. But he didn't stop there. She had a head full of braids, and he took one, unweaving the strands just as she was doing.

"Have ye never been part of a siege here at home?" he asked.

She shook her head. "Not really," she said. "We've had some trouble here and there, but nothing lasting. Sometimes the Scots come through the mountains and try to steal our sheep, but they've never made it back into Scotland with them. My father's men make quick work of them. When you are lord of Lydgate, will you make short work of your countrymen? Or will you let them take the sheep?"

Aurelius could have taken offense at that question, but he didn't because it was not an unreasonable one. He was Scots, and for all she knew, that was where his loyalties lay. He would forgive his countrymen anything. But that wasn't the case, and he needed to make that clear.

"Let me ask ye a question, m'lady," he said. "If some English women were to break into Lydgate and steal your possessions, would you let them do it or would you stop them?"

"I would stop them, of course. They are my belongings."

"And I will stop the Scots for exactly the same reason."

She smiled faintly, catching his eye in the mirror. "I simply wanted to know."

He smiled in return, but he was mostly focused on the braid

in his hand. "I know," he said. "Ye and I have much to learn about one another. I want to make sure you know everything so ye dunna think ye're to marry a man who would be disloyal to the English side of his family. Any man who tries to steal from me, or hurt me or my family, no matter if he is Scots or English or anything else, becomes my enemy."

That satisfied Valery for the most part. "And that is good, but you still have not told me about France."

They'd veered back to the subject of the French battles, and his smile faded. "Why do ye want to know?"

"Because I want to understand."

"Understand what?"

She thought on that for a moment. "Hardship," she said. "I want to know what you have experienced and I have not. I read a great deal about battle, but what I read is poetic. There is truth to it, but no substance."

He understood, sort of. "Then you seek substance?"

"I will always seek substance, not the paltry picture men will paint for their women."

My daughter is a woman of substance.

That was what Lady Wolsingham had told him. Valery was curious, always seeking to learn, which he found fascinating. That wasn't an attitude that most women he knew possessed. He could see that she wasn't simply being nosy. She truly wanted to know.

Perhaps if he told her the truth, she might understand what, exactly, she was asking.

"Very well," he said after a moment. "If ye want to know, I'll tell ye. I'll tell ye of a day of fighting that was unlike any I've ever seen. It was raining, and the field was so muddy that the horses were up to their knees in it. Men who fell would drown in the mud. They called it the Bloody Meadow."

Valery was working another braid, unraveling it, but her fingers slowed. "That's a terrible thing," she said. "Where was this?"

"Crécy.

"And many men died?"

He, too, had another braid in his hand, unwinding it but also feeling the silkiness of the strands. Since he'd started this endeavor, he hadn't taken the time to feel the texture of her hair, but now he was. He was being secretive and greedy about it, running the hair between his fingers and resisting the urge to lift it to his nostrils.

This woman he was going to marry.

A woman he was quickly becoming enamored with.

"Many died," he confirmed quietly. "It was midday on the field of battle when I found a lad who had been wounded, and I carried him away to be tended. As I headed back into the fighting, a man walked toward me. An English soldier. He had taken an ax to the face, and the ax was still there. The blade had carved into his jaw, from his ear, down the left side of his face, and it was partially embedded in his neck. How he was still alive was a mystery, but he came toward me, staggering, and I steadied him. His tongue had been partially severed and his jaw was hanging from his face, but he managed to tell me that his name was Radegund, and he spoke of his wife and daughters. He wanted to make sure they knew that he had fought bravely. I assured him that they would. Then he continued walking toward the rear of the battlelines, where the surgeons undoubtedly couldna save him. There was no way for him to survive. That is the battle ye are asking about, m'lady, and if no man wishes to speak of it, that is why. We witnessed courage ye couldna possibly comprehend."

By the time he was finished, Valery's expression was one of horror. She stopped unwinding her hair and turned to look at him. "My God," she whispered. "The poor man."

Because she'd turned around, she'd pulled her hair from his fingers. Rather than stand there without anything to do, he moved away from her, finding a chair next to the table and sitting upon it.

"Aye," he agreed softly as he looked her in the eye. "A poor man who was so brave and so terribly injured, but still, he thought only of his family. Not of himself, but of those he would leave behind. Still, he did his duty."

He left Valery with a disturbing mental image. She lingered on it, finishing the braid that was in her hand until her entire head was finally loose and free of Amelia's crippling hairstyle. Collecting a horsehair brush, she began to smooth out the strands.

"Your fame is well known wherever men journey," she murmured.

He had been watching her brush her hair, and was now looking at her with a gleam in his eye. "I know that," he said. "I've heard it before."

"It is from *Beowulf*," she said. "You have now told me of the heroism of Radegund, however cruel and stark it was. He has been well remembered. When I tell that story to someone else, he will be remembered yet again. Is that not what Hrothgar meant when speaking of heroism to Beowulf?"

"That is exactly what he meant," Aurelius said. He sat back in the chair, his gaze surprisingly warm. "When ye told me that ye wanted to know about France, I told ye the story of Radegund so you would know the horrors of what ye are asking. But ye've reminded me that stories of heroism are what keep the memories of those men alive."

Valery turned to look at him. "I wanted to know so that I could understand what my father had been through," she said. "And you… I do not know you, but when we speak as we are, I am coming to know you little by little. I want to understand what you have been through, too. I believe that will help me understand the kind of man you are."

He grinned. "And what do ye know so far?"

With a smile on her lips, she turned back to her mirror. "That you are cheeky and bold," she said, casting him a side-eye. "What more should I know?"

He laughed low in his throat. "I would say that is sufficient for now," he said. "If ye know anything more about me, it will take the mystery out of our relationship. And I like to keep a bit of mystery."

She was trying not to laugh. "Is that so?" she said. "And what have you learned about me? I'm not so mysterious."

He shook his head, his laughter fading. "I've learned that ye have geese who can attack on command," he said, nodding his head toward the geese who were basking in rays of sunlight streaming in through the window. "But I have also learned that ye're a woman of substance. And I look forward to learning much, much more."

Valery couldn't help the blush that crept onto her face. "You're being cheeky again."

"Not nearly as cheeky as I'm going to be, lass."

She looked at him then, realizing the blush was growing worse. "For a man sitting in the chamber of a maiden, that is terribly bold talk," she said. "I should demand you leave this instant."

He shrugged, a lazy smile on his lips. "Yer wish is my command," he said. "If ye want me to go, I will. I'll not argue with ye."

"If you do not stop being cheeky, I will indeed ask you to leave."

"Do ye *want* me to behave, then?"

The way he asked her made her laugh. She couldn't help it and she couldn't stop it. It was a naughty thing to say, and they both knew it, but she started laughing, and he laughed right along with her. They laughed and laughed until the tears came, and then they laughed some more. Valery couldn't remember the last time she'd laughed so hard and so long, and she really didn't even know why.

Nor did Aurelius.

Needless to say, she never answered his question.

CHAPTER FOURTEEN

A MELIA WAS HAVING a difficult time sitting down.

After Lady Wolsingham was finished with her that morning, her backside was stinging and she'd received a scolding, the likes of which she hadn't received since she'd been a child. But Lady Wolsingham didn't hold back, and, truthfully, Amelia knew she deserved it. She'd done everything Lady Wolsingham said she did.

It was time for the evening meal, and the great hall of Lydgate was full of men. Smoke sputtered from the enormous hearth, rising to the ceiling as conversation and music flowed. A man with a citole, a single traveling minstrel, was sitting next to the hearth, and he was trying to sing above the buzz of conversation, but it was difficult. The hall was loud this night. Amelia was relegated to the end of the dais, mostly sitting by herself, but across from her sat four young men she didn't know until Lady Wolsingham introduced them.

These are the dun Tarh brothers, Amelia. Behave yourself.

Suddenly, the visit to Lydgate wasn't so fun after all.

The three weren't of any interest to her because they were a little too young for her taste, even if they were older than she was, but there was a big, strong, young Highlander with a patch of white in his dark hair sitting directly across from her who was probably ten years older than she was. He was quite handsome, she thought.

Maybe this visit would be salvageable after all.

"Were you in France with Lord Wolsingham too?" she asked, raising her voice to be heard over the noise.

The man was eating heartily of his meal of mutton and gravy, but he was polite. "Aye, m'lady," he said. "I was fighting in France, too, and my name is Darien. I heard Lady Wolsingham call ye Amelia."

"That is my name," she said. "Amelia de Hetton. Lady Valery and I have been friends since we were infants."

"It's good to have friends from long ago."

"I think so."

There was a lull in the conversation as Darien looked to Estevan because the man was muttering in his ear, but Amelia didn't take kindly to having his attention diverted.

"How long will you be remaining at Lydgate, my lord?" she asked, rather loudly. "They usually have a big hunt closer to the Epiphany. My father used to hunt with them, and he always had great fun."

Darien looked at her. "It has been a long time since I have hunted," he said. "I would probably spear one of my brothers accidentally."

"I'm sure that's not true."

He shrugged. "And I'm equally sure that it is," he said. "Do ye hunt, m'lady?"

Amelia shook her head. "I do not," she said. "No one has ever taken the time to teach me."

It was a leading statement, as she'd intended it to be, but

Darien was prevented from answering by a big body suddenly in their midst. A man with big arms and a handsome face approached Darien, holding out a hand to him in greeting, and Darien rose to accept it.

"Ah, Max," he said. "I dinna see ye last night or today. Where have ye been?"

Maxwell St. John had made an appearance. A fair man with curly blond hair and a handsome face, he looked like the depictions of the archangels. There was something pure and shining about him, and quite likable. He smiled broadly at Darien's question.

"You'll not believe it," he said. "I fell asleep yesterday when we returned home, and I only awoke this afternoon. My mother thought I was dead."

He chuckled as Darien grinned. "I will admit that I slept like the dead last night also," he said. "I slept better than I've slept in an entire year."

The smile faded from Maxwell's face. "Completely understandable," he said. Then he indicated the table. "May I sit?"

Darien nodded, pointing to the seat at the end of the table, which meant he would be between Darien and Amelia. Perhaps that was on purpose, since Darien didn't have much interest in Amelia, but she seemed to have a great deal in him. Maxwell took the seat, noticing Amelia and politely acknowledging her.

"My lady," he said, though his tone wasn't nearly as friendly as it had been with Darien. "I heard you arrived today."

Amelia was grossly unhappy to see Maxwell, who was interrupting her conversation with Darien. She'd tried to charm him years ago, but he'd had no interest in her. She'd taken offense at that, of course, and there had been animosity between them ever since, though it was more on her side than on his. Maxwell simply didn't care about the small-minded lass who had been Valery's friend since childhood. In fact, no one at Lydgate much liked Amelia except Valery, and even that was a mystery. But Valery was, if nothing else, loyal—even when the person she was loyal to wasn't worth it.

"Greetings, Maxwell," Amelia said with equal coldness. "I see that you have returned from France."

"God has spared me."

"I am certain your father is delighted."

It was the extent of their conversation. Maxwell returned his attention to Darien, and when Amelia saw that she was soon to be cut out, she spoke quickly.

"Darien and I were just speaking of the hunt that Lord Wolsingham has every year around this time," she said. "I was telling him I do not know how to hunt because no one has ever taught me."

Darien caught Maxwell's rather droll expression before answering. "Surely yer father has taught ye something," he said. "Or yer husband?"

"Alas, there is no husband to teach me," Amelia said, looking rather coy. "But a teacher does not have to be a husband or a father or even a brother. I'm sure you've learned much in the Highlands when it comes to hunting. Mayhap you will be kind enough to teach me."

Darien glanced again at Maxwell, who discreetly rolled his eyes at Amelia's boldness. That told Darien that Amelia was perhaps quite friendly to every man. Not just him.

He forced a smile.

"If I have time during my stay here, mayhap I shall," he said. "But I must defer to whatever my brother has planned for me. He is marrying Lady Valery, after all. Lydgate will be his one day. He may have duties in mind for me."

That wasn't the answer Amelia wanted. She was smiling at him, but it turned into something of a grimace. "And Lady Valery is my dear friend," she said. "I am certain she would be disappointed to hear that her betrothed's brother would not assist a woman who asked for his help, don't you think?"

There was a threat in that statement. Darien had no idea how they even got there, but he didn't like being threatened. Especially not by a lady who, thus far, hadn't proven to be a charming or even remotely entertaining dinner companion. He'd opened his mouth to reply when a cheer rose up among the men and they all turned to see Lord Wolsingham entering the hall along with Aurelius. Men were trying to talk to Wolsingham, and to Aurelius, as they headed toward the dais, but everyone saw quite clearly when Aurelius abruptly came to a halt and headed back to the entry door because Valery was just coming through.

He waited for her so that they could walk to the dais together.

Now the evening was about to get interesting.

ᙣ

WHEN THE HALL was full, Valery rarely came in through the main entry.

But Aurelius had insisted, and her father hadn't fought him on it, so here she was, emerging into a hall full of the men her father had always kept her from. Aurelius had waited for her in a gentlemanly gesture, one that Valery appreciated, but she wasn't used to the crowded hall, so she ended up on Aurelius' left side, the one closer to the wall and away from the clamoring men. Aurelius stayed right by her side even though he was speaking to the men as he walked along, but she simply wanted to get to the dais, so he stopped talking and escorted her straight to the table where her parents were waiting. So were Amelia, Maxwell, Sterling, and the dun Tarh brothers. Aurelius waited until Valery sat down before taking his own seat between Valery and her father. Once they were seated, the servants began to emerge with the food.

And there was food aplenty.

The music struck back up, as did the hum of conversation. Valery, who had essentially spent the morning talking to Aurelius and coming to know him, was on the side of the table with Amelia, Maxwell, Darien, and the rest of the dun Tarh lads. She hadn't seen Amelia since the hairstyle incident, and now she faced the woman with her hair softly curled, perhaps a little frizzy from the braids, but nonetheless more of her natural style.

Amelia shifted her chair more in Valery's direction.

"Where did you disappear to?" she asked. "I've not seen you since this morning."

That was a deliberate move on Valery's part. She had come to the conclusion that Amelia had indeed been trying to shame her with that ridiculous hairstyle. She'd known the woman her entire life and seen her do such things to other women. Amelia was a bully disguised in silks, and everyone knew it. Valery had remained friends with her throughout the years because they'd known the same people and fostered together. There was a time when Amelia had been a comfort to her in those years away from home, and that was why they remained friends. But after this morning's debacle, Valery was starting to rethink that friendship, as difficult as it was for her to let something of length and substance go. The truth was that she didn't want to take the chance that Amelia might try something like that again. After the time she'd spent with Aurelius that day, she didn't want the man's opinion turned against her.

Something had happened that afternoon.

He'd been attentive and interested. They'd laughed at silly things. That was something Valery had never experienced before. He'd spoken a little about his brothers, the younger ones in particular, mischievous scamps who would fart in the faces of sleeping siblings and then hide and giggle at the reactions. He told the story of Darien trapping a younger brother, Cruz, in a coverlet that he had farted in and then laughing when the boy coughed and cried so much that he vomited. That had brought their mother's wrath, unfortunately, but that afternoon, Valery had had a taste of the antics of eight brothers.

It was glorious, farts and all.

After her hair was back to normal, with his considerable help, and they sat talking in her chamber with the door wide open for propriety's sake, Lady Wolsingham had joined them in the early afternoon, and Aurelius had reluctantly taken his leave, but the conversation still lingered. It was all Valery could think about. She'd dressed carefully for sup in a blue silk surcoat with a voluminous white silk shift underneath, hoping a pleasant presentation would make up for the hair debacle earlier in the day. But he never seemed to care about her hair. As he'd told her, he'd only noticed *her*.

She was coming to believe him.

When it was finally time for the evening's feast, Valery was certain she'd never looked forward to a meal more in her entire life. Her mother had already gone to the hall, as was usual, so she accompanied her father and Aurelius into the hall. As Aurelius was caught up in polite conversation with Adams,

Valery found herself facing the woman who had tried to embarrass her. Perhaps she might have let it go in the past, but not tonight.

She wasn't in a forgiving mood.

"I was busy returning my hair to its normal state after your creation nearly ruined it," she said after a moment. "How long must you stay, Amelia?"

Amelia was a little taken aback at the tone. That wasn't something she usually heard from Valery. Although she knew very well why, and Valery wasn't wrong in her reaction to a ridiculous hairstyle that had been more of a setup than an actual prank, Amelia wasn't in the habit of confessing her sins. She simply pretended none of it had happened.

"I was hoping to stay a few days, at least," she said, collecting her wine. "There's far more entertainment here. Isn't your father due to have his annual hunt soon?"

Valery looked over Amelia's head to Maxwell, who lifted an unhappy eyebrow. Valery knew that Maxwell and Amelia didn't get along, mostly because he'd spurned her advances a few years ago, and now Valery was starting to understand the man's dislike for her. Somehow, in the matter of a day, Valery had developed a dislike for her also.

It was a visit no longer welcome.

"That will not be for a few weeks yet," she said, turning for her own wine. "Surely you must get to your husband and his mother soon. That *is* where you were going, isn't it?"

Amelia looked stricken at the comment, revealing something she'd tried to keep hidden from Darien, but before she could reply, Darien spoke up.

"Then ye *are* married," he said, shaking his head. "Ye dinna make that clear. Nay, lady, I'll not teach ye to hunt. I'll not be a teacher to another man's wife. If ye want to learn to hunt, ye must ask yer husband."

Amelia was positively aghast at his insinuation, right as it was. "I meant nothing untoward when I asked you to teach me," she said defensively. "If you thought so, then it is your own lewd mind that created that inference. You did not get that from me."

Darien was unable to answer before Maxwell leapt to his defense. "That's not true," he said. "I heard you clearly. You were flirting with the man, and when he asked you if you had a husband, you did not answer him directly. So you *are* married now? I had not heard that, but for shame, Amelia. That is not how a married woman behaves."

Amelia was most definitely on the defensive now as her sins were put on parade. "And how would you know?" she snarled. "What do you know about women, Maxwell St. John? I notice that *you're* not married yet."

Maxwell snorted. "Just because I rebuffed your attempts at seduction does not mean I do not know about women," he said. "It simply means I do not want to know about *you*."

Amelia shrieked, deeply insulted, and turned to Valery. "Are you going to let a mere knight speak to me like that?" she demanded. "Tell your father that he has said terrible things to me. I want him punished!"

"I've seen cows with better manners than her," Darien muttered to Maxwell from across the table, loud enough for Amelia to hear. "She tried to seduce ye, too?"

"She did."

"God was on yer side when ye refused her, lad."

"God had nothing to do with it. It was pure aversion and nothing more."

As Darien nodded fervently, Amelia shrieked again, and Valery put up a hand to prevent the woman from starting a brawl.

"Be silent," she hissed at Amelia. "I will not have you disrupting my father's table."

"But—!"

Valery wouldn't let the woman talk. "You came to Lydgate uninvited," she pointed out. "You came and created your usual chaos, so I would say that you have overstayed your welcome. Go back to your chamber and be gone in the morning. Your presence is no longer welcome, Amelia. I mean it."

Amelia could not believe what she was hearing. "Why should you say such terrible things to me?" she half hissed, half cried. "You are mean. And nasty. I'm going to tell your mother!"

She started to get up, but Valery was faster. She ended up yanking Amelia right out of her chair and then began to drag her in the direction of Lady Wolsingham, who was seated on the other side of her husband.

"Mama?" Valery called out. "Mama, Amelia thinks that I am mean and nasty because she was scolded for lying to Sir Aurelius' brother about being married. Now she wants to complain about it."

Lady Wolsingham was on her feet. "Is that so?" she said. "Please, dear Amelia. Do complain. I would like to hear it."

Amelia was afraid of Lady Wolsingham. After the spanking she'd endured earlier in the day, she could see that she was on the verge of another. Pulling her arm free of Valery's grip, she began to back away.

"I... I had no complaint, my lady," she said. "But I do want to thank you for your hospitality. I... I must be on my way in the morning."

She was nearly to the end of the dais by now, nearly tripping on the step that led to the floor of the great hall. As she hastened to turn away, Maxwell picked up a piece of bread and threw it at her discreetly. Darien saw him and did the same thing, hitting her in the side of the head. More bread was flying at Amelia as she made haste to leave the hall. It was Estevan, who had heard all of the conversations, who finally picked up a boiled turnip from his trencher, mushy and wet, and threw it right into her back. It stuck as she screeched.

Half of the hall erupted in laughter.

Even Valery was laughing as she watched her former friend try to remove the turnip from between her shoulder blades. Lady Wolsingham, a smile playing on her lips, began to follow Amelia simply to make sure the woman made it back to her chamber as she'd indicated.

"I'll see to her," she told her daughter as she walked past. "Return to your guests, my love. You needn't worry over Amelia de Hetton any longer. I will make sure she is gone in the morning—for good."

Grinning, Valery watched her mother wander after Amelia, who was scurrying away at the sight of the countess following her. As she went back to her chair, she felt strong, warm fingers wrapping around her left hand. Surprised, she looked up to see Aurelius smiling at her.

"Well done, m'lady," he said in a voice that sent a chill up her spine. "No one rejoices in revenge more than a woman."

Valery's smile was back when she heard her own words coming out of his mouth. "You remembered."

"I remember everything."

"Then remember that it is a mantra I live by."

He chuckled softly, lifting her hand to his lips for a gentle kiss that did not go unnoticed by those at their end of the table. But it startled Valery so much that she very nearly missed the chair when she tried to sit down.

But startled in the best way possible.

"Careful," Aurelius said, grabbing her with both hands so she wouldn't fall off the chair. "I dinna mean to distract ye. Only congratulate ye."

Valery had to grab for the seat to ensure she was actually sitting in it, because she couldn't seem to take her eyes off Aurelius. He put a cup of wine in front of her, which she accepted gratefully. She still wasn't over her embarrassment of nearly falling off the chair, however.

Nor was she over his kiss to her hand.

"Truly, my lord," she said before sipping at the wine and eyeing him. "You must show more control. Kissing my hand for all to see is quite… improper."

Aurelius' expression was warm. "It was nothing more than a gesture of appreciation," he said. "But I willna do it again if it disturbs ye."

She took another sip of wine, only it was more like a gulp to ease her rattled nerves. "I did not say it disturbed me," she said. "But mayhap you should simply show more control until we are married."

His eyebrows flew up. "I must restrain myself until then?" he asked, incredulous. Then he shook his head and sat back in his chair. "Ye ask too much, m'lady. A glorious creature like ye and I'm not allowed to show my appreciation?"

Valery's cheeks turned a flaming red. She took another drink of wine, tongue-tied, and Aurelius noticed. When their eyes met, all she could do was grin and look away. He leaned in her direction and lowered his voice.

"Must I really wait?" he said, smiling. "Please tell me that ye dinna mean it. I swear to ye, I cannot wait that long. Such a lovely hand deserves to be kissed, and kissed often."

Valery turned her head away from him, smiling bashfully. "You forget yourself, my lord."

Aurelius leaned closer. "I've not forgotten myself," he said, lowering his voice even more. "I've never been more truthful in my life. But if ye dunna want me to, then I willna. I'll do whatever ye wish."

Valery was swept away by his gentle flirting, something she wasn't adept at. It wasn't that she hadn't had many suitors—it was simply that the ones she did have had been sent away by her mother over the past year because her father had been absent. That didn't leave much opportunity for courtship or flirting, even as her friends married and she remained a maiden. Before that, her father hadn't been keen on anyone courting his only child, so she'd buried herself in her books.

But now… now she had a suitor who was quite charming.

Of course she didn't want him to stop.

"I simply said you must control yourself," she said. "That means being… discreet."

He smiled broadly, big dimples in each cheek and those big white teeth on display. "Thank ye, m'lady," he said. "I promise I will be much more discreet from now on. But may I ask a favor of ye?"

"What is it?"

"Will ye at least call me Aurelius when we are speaking in private?" he said. "I would like to think we're moving past the formalities. I'd like it very much if ye would."

She looked at him, realizing he was quite close to her. God, he was so big and handsome, with a manliness that seemed to overwhelm her in a way she didn't understand. It was the smell and the warmth of him, the gleam in his eye when he looked at her. He made her heart race and her palms sweat, and she loved every minute of it. Like now. She was flushed and giddy, but it was the best feeling in the world, as far as she was concerned.

It was difficult not to become upswept in it.

"If you wish," she said. "You may address me as Valery if you wish, as long as Papa does not hear us. He might not want us to be so familiar with one another so soon."

"Valery," he said, low and sweet as he rolled it off his tongue. "I've never heard a more beautiful name."

She was back to flushing again, laughing softly. "You flatter me too much," she insisted weakly. "Not everything about me is beautiful."

He frowned. "How do ye know?" he said. "I see nothing but beauty when I look at ye. I would hope ye'd want yer future husband to see just that."

She shrugged in agreement. "That is true," she said. "I would hope my future husband would find something agreeable about me."

He rolled his eyes and sat back in his chair. "Agreeable?" he said. "Lass, there isn't anything about ye that is not completely and utterly agreeable. And if there is, I look forward to finding out what it is, because from where I'm sitting, ye're as close to perfect as I've ever seen."

Flattered to the point of feeling lightheaded, Valery had to look away or risk making a fool of herself. Her entire body was giddy with delight. She happened to catch Maxwell's gaze as he sat at the end of the table, and he smiled at her, nodding his head with approval. He'd heard nearly everything, no matter how Aurelius had tried to keep his voice down, and he liked what he'd heard.

Valery smiled timidly in return.

"I apologize that I've not had the opportunity to properly greet you, my lady," Maxwell said. "It seems that I've done nothing but sleep since I returned. My father thinks I've grown lazy since I've been away."

"Ye've not grown lazy," Aurelius replied. "Ye can tell yer father for me. I spent the past year eating and sleeping and fighting alongside ye, Max, and ye're the most un-lazy person I've ever known."

Maxwell's attention shifted from Valery to Aurelius. "You honor me," he said, lifting his cup. "May that be the finest thing said about any man, especially you."

Aurelius lifted his cup in Maxwell's direction. "I'll drink to that," he said before taking a big swallow and smacking his lips. But his focus remained on Maxwell. "We've seen quite a bit together, haven't we?"

Maxwell's smile faded. "We have," he said. "But your hero-ism at Crécy is something I shall never forget."

That had Valery's attention. "What heroism?" she asked, looking at Aurelius. "What did you do?"

Maxwell knew that Aurelius would downplay whatever happened, so he hastened to answer her. "You may not know this, Val, but you are to marry a man of greatness," he said. "Never mind the fact that when Aurelius dun Tarh gives a command, all men follow. Nay, that has nothing to do with it. He is not a man to sit back and let others suffer. He is a man that will suffer along with them."

Valery's gaze was still lingering on Aurelius even as she continued to speak to Maxwell. "Tell me," she said.

Maxwell lifted his cup for more wine as a serving wench with a pitcher walked by. "There are too many incidents to list, but I can tell you one for certain," he said, making sure the wench filled his cup to the rim. "Keep in mind that he was not mounted in the heat of the fighting on that muddy, bloody meadow. He was on foot. I saw him carrying out lads who had fallen, men who could not get to safety, but Aurelius took them away from the fighting only to return and continue to fight. But there was a man who had taken a sword across his belly. I was fighting off two Frenchmen or I would have helped him, but Aurelius saw him and went to his aid. Unfortunately, the man was nearly cut in half. Moving him would have killed him instantly. I watched as Aurelius knelt beside him, holding his hand and fighting off anyone who came close. He stayed with the man until he passed before carrying him away so his body would not be swallowed by the mud. That, my lady, is heroic."

Valery was still looking at Maxwell as he finished speaking, thinking on what Aurelius had told her earlier about the man with the ax to his face. Clearly, many terrible things had happened at the Battle of Crécy, and he'd only told her about one. Now she was hearing about another. Things that no man would say about himself.

That gave her some insight into the character of the man she was to marry.

It was a way for her to understand, and relate, to him.

"You stayed with him so he would not be alone," she said, looking at Aurelius. "That is astonishingly brave."

Aurelius wasn't happy that Maxwell had brought up that particularly difficult moment in his life, but it was out in the open now. It wasn't as if he could tell Maxwell to take it back and the very idea would be erased. He held her gaze for a moment before looking to his wine.

"He was an old man who had fought for my father, long ago," he said. "He was big and gruff and bad-tempered, but he could swing a mace like no one ye have ever seen. We needed him. He was the first man into battle and the last one out. I dunna know how he fell, only that he did, and I saw him as he lay in the mud, trying to get up, but… everything was cut. He could not move."

"I saw him."

From across the table, the youngest dun Tarh lad, Kaladin, spoke up. His dark eyes were aglow at the memory of what they were speaking of, because he'd been there. The younger dun Tarh men, as squires for the fully fledged knights, stayed on the peripheral of the battle and dragged the wounded out if they could, so Kaladin and Caelus had seen everything from the bloody, messy meadow. All eyes turned to Kaladin, and he shoved Caelus away when the man tried to quiet him.

"I saw it," he insisted, looking at Aurelius and Maxwell and even Valery. "He was lying on his back and his guts were hanging out. They were spilling out and he was trying to put them back in so he could get up and walk away, but he couldna do it. Bear found him and sat with him, telling him he was very brave and that he had already won the battle for the English. The man was still trying to fight because men were fighting all around him."

Valery was somewhat taken aback at the stark image the young man was painting, but something else the lad had said stuck with her. "He called you Bear," she said. "I heard someone else refer to you by that term. What does it mean?"

Aurelius was trying to push the memory of that gory old man out of his thoughts, and her question caught him off guard. "It is a name Darien gave me when we were young," he said. "He couldna say 'brother' very well—it came out as 'bro-bear.' Bear is what the family calls me."

Valery understood. She thought it was rather sweet. But her thoughts drifted back to what Kaladin had said. "What you did for the man," she said. "That must have been very dangerous. Very noble, but very dangerous."

So much for trying to forget about the old Highlander. Now those images were back. Valery was praising him for his noble actions and bravery, making it sound as if he were an avenging angel and single-handedly fighting off the French. But it was so much more than that. Dangerous was where it began—deadly was where it ended. Truthfully, he was surprised he hadn't been cut down with all of the swords around him as he knelt in the mud beside the old man and held his hand until he stopped breathing.

"I wasna the brave one," he finally said. "The brave one was the old man who died in the mud. They were all brave, those men who fought and died in that muck. 'Twas not a dignified way for a man to die."

Valery could see that he wasn't comfortable with the subject, so she didn't press him. She'd already done that in the morning, when they spoke of the battles in France, but this situation was something he didn't have any fondness remembering.

"I'm glad Kaladin told me," she said quietly, for his benefit. "We are remembering the old man well this evening. That is never a bad thing, is it?"

He smiled weakly. "Nay," he said. "But I'd rather speak on other things."

"As you wish," she said, allowing him to change the subject, even if his heroism was something she was interested in. "Was there something specific you wished to speak on?"

That was a good question for Aurelius, because there was something that had been on his mind since he left her with her mother earlier that day. They'd spoken about many things, but nothing too deep or serious. That was intentional on his part. It all went back to what he'd been thinking yesterday, about the fact that Adams hadn't seen his daughter in a year, and many things could happen in a year, including a young lady with a suitor on her mind. She hadn't brought it up, nor had he even caught rumor of any suitors for Lady Valery except for what Estevan had told him, but the more he came to know her, the more he felt that he truly *needed* to know. Not that he thought her attention was elsewhere, but it was better to be certain. He'd been charming and kind, but if a woman's heart was wrapped up in someone else's arms, it would be a difficult road ahead for him. He was nearly to the point of no return with her, as quickly as that had come, and he didn't want any obstacles now that his focus was on her.

Now that he could see her as his destiny.

Simply to clear the air, he felt that he had to ask.

"There *is* something I'd like to speak on," he said. "I feel that I should before we go any further."

"Further with what?"

He gestured to the two of them. "With us," he said. "Yer father wants us to become acquainted, and we are. I suspect he'd be quite happy if we find each other agreeable."

She grunted softly. "He'd be bloody thrilled if we actually liked one another."

Aurelius chuckled. "I'm sure he would," he said. "And if I may say so, I do like ye. I've not found anything about ye that I dunna like. But the truth is that ye dinna know me until yesterday, and for a woman as beautiful as ye are, surely ye had other suitors before me. What I want to say is that if I've disrupted something, some*one* that ye wanted, ye have my apologies. The betrothal was between my da and yer da, and I dinna know of it myself until a short time ago."

Her smile faded as she listened to him. "Then you're unhappy with it?"

He shook his head quickly. "I am happy," he said. "*Very* happy. But ye may not feel the same way."

"And you are concerned for my feelings?"

"I will always be concerned for yer feelings."

Valery gazed at him a moment, wondering if the man was simply too good to be true. He was brave, heroic, and not self-absorbed? She found that astonishing. But he was asking her personal questions now, trying to come to know her and the situation he now found himself involved in, and she could understand that. That cheeky, saucy Scotsman she'd met only yesterday had suddenly become a very real part of what was now her life. He was her betrothed, to be her husband, and she felt shockingly comfortable with the situation.

That was, in large part, Aurelius' doing.

"I am happy with it also," she finally said. "And nay, there is no suitor that I am pining for. I've never really had one, to be truthful. But you, on the other hand..."

He frowned. "Me *what*?"

"You said you had no trouble attracting women," she said. "You told me that this morning. Is there a special lass in Scotland that I am stealing you from?"

He smiled, a reluctant gesture. "Nay," he said. "There have been a few that have tried to pull me into marriage, and I could have married if I'd wanted to, but somehow, they didn't seem right. Not that the lasses were lacking, but it was more a feeling I had. That they weren't right for me."

"And you do not have that same feeling when you look at me?"

He thought on that briefly before shaking his head. "Nay," he said. "I canna explain it, but I dunna have the same feeling, and I've known you for far less a time than I've known other women. You intrigue me, lady. And I'm not often intrigued."

She fought off a grin. "We cannot build a marriage on intrigue."

He lifted his eyebrows. "I hope we build it on respect and laughter and the trust I'm trying to build," he said. "But I needed to know if there were any… obstacles."

"There are none."

He beamed. "Can I kiss yer hand again?"

She looked around nervously. "Nay," she said. "You must wait until it is appropriate."

"When will that be?"

Valery opened her mouth to reply, but her father suddenly stood up and began shouting for silence. Seeing this, both Aurelius and Maxwell stood up, shouting as well. Between the three of them, they silenced an entire hall full of men very quickly, enough so that Adams was able to be heard from one end to the other.

"Good men," he said. "As I announced last night, my daughter will soon marry Aurelius dun Tarh."

Cheers and whistles went up all around, but Adams held up his hands for silence before continuing.

"Aye, it is quite exciting," he said. "I agree with your enthusiasm. In fact, it is my privilege to introduce Aurelius to my local allies, so we will be having a great feast to celebrate the betrothal next month. We shall hunt and drink and feast for days. For those of you who are here as part of the contingent I brought home from France, I hope you will return home to your lords and tell them of this great feast. They are all invited, of course. I would have every neighbor and close ally celebrate this great event on the seventh of next month. That is a special day because it is my daughter's day of birth. A fitting celebration for my lovely Valery."

The men roared as all attention turned to the lady in blue on the dais. Valery was so unused to attention from men in the hall that she was quite embarrassed by it, shaking her head when her father told her to stand for the applause. She refused, trying to shrink away from the attention. Aurelius, seeing how uncomfortable she was, stood up in her stead.

"On behalf of my future wife, I thank ye for yer kind attention," he said. "Although she's too much of a lady to speak to the likes of ye, know that she is appreciative."

The men roared with laughter and went back to their drink as both Aurelius and Adams sat down. Adams leaned in Valery's direction.

"You have my permission to say a polite word to the men, Val," he said. "They were simply showing their happiness for yer betrothal."

Valery rolled her eyes. "Papa, how could you embarrass me like that?" she said. "I would sooner jump off the wall and into the moat than speak to a hall full of your men. Aurelius, thank you for stepping in to save me. I am very grateful."

As Aurelius smiled at her, Adams interrupted the moment. "I realize I've kept you away from my army for most of your life, but in moments like this, you have my permission to acknowledge their praise."

Valery frowned and stood up. "I do not want to acknowledge their praise," she said. "I want to go to bed."

Adams wasn't sure why she was so irritated, but he waved her off. He had drink and food to keep him busy. But Aurelius didn't, and he stood up next to her.

"May I escort ye to the keep?" he asked. "Ye might need protection from this rabid crowd."

But Valery shook her head. "No need," she said. "I will go in through the kitchens. I will be quite safe."

"I would like to escort ye, very much."

She looked at him, realizing he simply wanted to be with her. Possibly be alone with her. Here in the hall, they were surrounded by men, but if he escorted her outside… alone… Well, the very thought made her heart race. A smile spread over her lips.

"Very well," she said. "But nothing inappropriate."

"Not even a kiss to yer hand?"

"You'd better not try."

He nodded, grinning, as she wagged a finger at him. When she moved away from the dais, he tried not to look too eager as he followed. A little subtlety was good, especially when the woman's father was around. Aurelius was thinking of that lovely little bailey that surrounded the keep, the one with the big tree that hid most of the bailey from the prying eyes of those on the wall. A lovely little bailey where he might sneak in more than a kiss to the hand. Even though she told him not to try.

He could hope, anyway.

But little did he know that wasn't what lay in store for them in that lovely little bailey.

CHAPTER FIFTEEN

THEY'D PICKED UP a tail.

Aurelius and Valery were only halfway out of the hall when Aurelius realized it. Maxwell was behind them, following them all the way outside, across the big bailey, and then the smaller inner bailey. When they came to the enormous tree, Aurelius stopped and turned to Maxwell.

"I dunna need any help, laddie," he said, a glimmer of humor in his eye. "If ye think to protect the lady's honor, I assure ye that no one can protect it better than I."

Maxwell was fighting off a grin. "Do not be ridiculous," he said. "Don't you know I did this so Wolsingham wouldn't be suspicious?"

"Suspicious of what?"

"Of whatever you intend to do."

"That is *our* business."

Maxwell looked at Valery over Aurelius' shoulder. "I suppose it is," he said. "Valery, dearest, if you need me, just scream. I'll come running."

With that, he winked at Aurelius and headed out of the smaller bailey, leaving Aurelius shaking his head and Valery giggling.

"I have missed him," she said. "I'd forgotten how much."

Aurelius looked at her. "He's a good man," he said. "Annoying, but a good man."

Her gaze lingered on him for a moment. "You *do* know that he is no competition," she said. "What we were discussing earlier about suitors… Maxwell's father wanted me for his son, but my father did not. Maxwell is like my brother. And I do not think he shall ever marry."

Aurelius moved toward her in the moonlight. "I served with him for a year," he said quietly. "I think I know the man fairly well."

Valery didn't elaborate on that conversation. She didn't know Aurelius well enough to do that, to be completely honest about Maxwell, but she suspected Aurelius already knew. If he did, there was nothing more to say. But if he didn't, she didn't feel comfortable being the one to tell him. Being protective of Maxwell, someone she'd known her entire life, she would never betray him so.

"His parents missed him terribly while he was away," she said, turning for the bench that had been built underneath the tree. "Have you met his father, Sterling?"

Aurelius nodded. "Briefly," he said. "We were introduced last night. I noticed he dinna eat with us tonight."

Valery gestured to the wall. "He has been known to take the night watch," she said. "Also… I suspect he was not happy with the betrothal announcement. He had high hopes for Maxwell and me."

"Sometimes things dunna always go as we hope."

"True," she said. "But sometimes things happen that you never even hoped for."

He smiled at her in the darkness. "Those are the best things of all."

"Do you think so?"

"I do."

Valery was quite sure they were speaking of the same thing—their betrothal—and she was struggling not to get caught up in the magic of it all. Life wasn't magic, and nor were relationships. Having never been courted, and never having even been fond of a man in a romantic sense, this was all new to her, and as levelheaded as she was, it was difficult not to become enamored with all of it.

Enamored with Aurelius.

But there was something inherently terrifying in that.

"Do you truly think this will work?" she finally asked. "Aurelius, let us speak plainly. Our worlds are so different. Until yesterday, we did not know one another, and now we speak of battle and books as if it is the most natural of things. We pretend that everything is well and good and these will be days of sunshine and roses for us. But is that really true?"

He averted his gaze in a pensive gesture, moving to the bench that was lodged beneath the sycamore. Sitting down, he finally looked up at her.

"Who's to say?" he said. "Life has no promises, Valery. If ye are looking for promises and certainty, then yer first lesson will be that there is no such thing. Life will be what we make of it."

"But what do you *want* to make of it?"

He shrugged. "I would imagine I want what you want," he said. "I must marry. So must you. It would be good to marry someone we can speak to of books and battles, and other things. It would be good to learn to laugh with someone who finds a cheeky bastard hilarious. I know I'm a cheeky bastard, but I'm *yer* cheeky bastard, according to yer father and mine."

She smiled faintly. "I know," she said. "But this all seems so sudden, doesn't it? Yesterday, I was sending my geese to bite you, and today… we are laughing together."

"What are ye afraid of?"

Valery thought hard on that question. She went to sit on the bench next to him, a foot or so away, pondering the answers she might give. But she could only come up with one.

"I'm afraid of disappointment," she said honestly. "I'm afraid of loss."

"Losing me?"

She half nodded, half shrugged. "In a sense," she said. "I am not the easiest person to get along with. I'm opinionated and stubborn. I'm always right about things. I do not capitulate easily. That could be very tiresome for you."

He chuckled. "I like a challenge."

"I could prove to be a big one."

He cocked his head thoughtfully. "I'm not the easiest to get on with either," he said. "Ye canna always be right because *I'm* always right. I'm the next Earl of Torridon, with a long legacy behind me that gives me the confidence to know there is nothing I canna do if I put my mind to it. I've got seven brothers and two sisters, all of whom will marry, and I will be the head of our family. That is a big responsibility. Now, I will also be the Earl of Wolsingham, a Highland-born English earl. The enormity of what I am facing is quite real. I couldna do it if I dinna have a partner in it who could be as strong as I was in all things. Mayhap I've only known ye a day, Valery de Leybourne, but I know good character when I see it. I see it in ye."

"And you are sure of this?"

He grinned. "Ye're asking about certainty again."

She looked away. "I know," she said. "But this world we are facing is quite new to me. Until yesterday, I was simply the daughter of an earl. There were no immediate expectations upon me. But now…"

"Now there is the expectation of two earldoms upon ye."

"Exactly."

"What if there wasn't?"

"What do you mean?"

"Just that," he said, leaning forward so he could see her face more clearly in the darkness. "What if I had no earldom and you were the daughter of a simple knight? What if it were just the two of us, facing a betrothal? Two simple people whose fathers decided we should marry. Would ye still go through with it, knowing ye'd be getting nothing out of the marriage but me?"

Valery considered the question. She thought about the laughter they'd shared, the conversations that led her to believe he was more than a warrior, more than a Highlander. He had intelligence not readily seen in men these days. He also had a sense of humor that was both endearing and naughty. There were many things about Aurelius dun Tarh she found intriguing and attractive, more than any man she'd ever met.

A smile tugged at her lips.

"I suspect you would be quite enough," she said after a moment. "More than enough, actually."

He smiled broadly and reached out to take her hand. "I'll tell ye a secret," he said. "The first five minutes I knew ye, I knew I wanted to marry ye. Had we not already been betrothed, I would have begged yer father for an agreement."

His big, calloused hand was searing against her flesh, and Valery's heart began to race again. "Even after I sent the geese to bite you?"

"Even after," he confirmed softly. "By the way—where are those two feathered monsters?"

She laughed softly. "Asleep in my chamber," she said. "They have a bed in a cozy corner."

His eyebrows lifted. "And they do this every night?"

"Aye."

He scratched his head with his free hand. "Do ye mean I, too, must sleep with the beasties after we're married?"

She tried not to grin at the horror in his voice. "They're really quite sweet when you get to know them," she said. "They've been with me since I was a small girl. When I went to foster, my mother tended to them, but when I returned, they came to me as if I'd never been away. They are my pets."

He could see that he was defeated. "Very well," he said with resignation. "As long as they dunna try to bite me in my own bedchamber, I'll live alongside them. But ye should know that I dunna share very well."

"Share what?"

"*Ye.*"

The flush was back to her cheeks as she turned away bashfully, and he lifted her hand to gently kiss it. That brought giggles, which made him laugh. Soon, they were laughing at each other in a most delightful way. It was a sweet moment, one of hope and discovery, but they were rudely interrupted by a shadow in the darkness.

"How sweet. How touching."

It was a male voice, back near the corner of the keep, and Aurelius was instantly on his feet, pulling Valery behind him.

"Show yerself," he said steadily.

The figure moved. It had been blending in with the shadows

of the tree branches, and was now moving in their direction. As it came closer, Valery recognized the figure. She'd been seeing it every day for many years, and she came out from behind Aurelius when she realized who it was.

"Sterling," she said, sighing with relief. "You startled us."

Sterling came into the light, illuminated by the moon and the torches on the inner wall. The lighting was faint, but it was enough to show his face. Both Valery and Aurelius quickly realized that he didn't look like himself.

Something was off.

"Sterling?" Valery said curiously. "What is the matter?"

He was looking at her, his focus seemingly dazed. The night breeze shifted, and suddenly, they could smell alcohol. Alcohol and piss.

He was drunk.

Very drunk.

Valery looked at Aurelius with concern, but he was fixed on Sterling, who was clad in mail with weapons at his side, including a broadsword.

The man was armed.

"M'lord," Aurelius said evenly. "Is there something ye need? Something I can help ye with?"

Sterling shook his head slowly, nearly throwing himself off balance as he did so. "Nay," he said. "I just wanted to see the man who has taken my son's wife. I wanted to look you in the eye and ask you why you feel you are so much better than Maxwell. He's an English knight, after all. One of the best. What makes you better than he?"

"I am not better than Maxwell," Aurelius said. "I served with the man for the past year. He's an excellent knight, and I consider him a friend."

"Then why did Wolsingham pick *you*?"

"Ye would have to ask him."

"I did," Sterling spat, growing agitated. "He gave me lies. Lies and disloyalty. I've served the man for many years, as my father served his father. And what do I get for that loyalty? My son is denied his right. His *right!*"

"I am not Maxwell's right," Valery said, putting herself in front of Aurelius because she was afraid Sterling might actually attack the man. "Go home, Sterling. You're drunk. Go home and I will not tell my father about this… this encounter."

Sterling looked down at her, torn between obeying her and defying her. He took a step back, unsteadily.

"*Why?*" he said, suddenly begging her. "Why could you not have stood up for Maxwell? Why could you not have told your father that he should be your husband?"

"I told you to go home," Valery said in a steely voice. "I will forgive you because you are drunk, but any further conversation and I might not be so forgiving."

Sterling drew in a long, deep breath through his nose and took another step back, and then another. What he was doing wasn't clear—either he was trying to regain his composure or he was gearing up for an attack. Valery could feel Aurelius trying to gently pull her behind him, but she wasn't moving.

She went on the offensive.

"Sterling, I am sorry you are disappointed," she said sternly. "But you know I had nothing to do with my father's decision. He made the decision he felt best for Wolsingham, not the decision he felt best for you or for Maxwell. You are my father's knight. You are not a member of the family. You cannot expect that in matters such as this, my father would marry me to your son, who has nothing to bring to a marriage. He has no land, no title. I am the daughter of an earl—I must marry someone of my station, and that is not Maxwell. I know you understand that, but you've created this world in which you've been slandered, and there is simply no truth to it. You've made it all up in your mind. Now… *go* to bed."

Sterling didn't like the truth. He knew she was right, but he didn't like it. Any of it. He jabbed a weaving finger at her.

"This is *your* fault," he said. "You could have shown interest in Maxwell. If you had, your father would not have denied you."

Valery eyed the man because he seemed to be quite unsteady on his feet. "Maxwell is my friend and I adore him, but as my husband, we would have made each other miserable," she said. "Why do you try to force Maxwell to be something he is not? That is not fair to him."

"You will not tell me about my son!" Sterling boomed. "Speak another word and I will cut your tongue out, you harlot!"

"Get out of my sight," Aurelius growled, suddenly in front of Valery and advancing on Sterling. "Another word to her and she'll not be the one who's cut. Get away from me, old man. I've had enough of ye."

Seeing Aurelius advance had Sterling unsheathing his broadsword. Valery screamed and jumped out of the way as he swung it at Aurelius, who somehow managed to dodge it. He was running at Sterling, grabbing the man's wrist as he held his broadsword and squeezing until Sterling cried out in pain. Valery screamed again as the broadsword clattered to the ground, but suddenly, Sterling produced a dagger. Valery could see it flashing in the darkness.

"I will… kill you!" Sterling grunted as he struggled with Aurelius. "You filthy… beastly… Scotsman! I will kill you! I will kill you both!"

The dagger flashed again as Aurelius and Sterling were in a life-or-death battle. Valery was terrified, but she gathered her wits enough to run forward and grab the broadsword that had fallen to the ground. She pulled it away as Sterling screamed threats and obscenities at Aurelius, who wasn't attacking the man as much as he was simply trying to prevent Sterling from attacking him. As the struggle ensued in the small bailey, another figure darted in from the outer bailey.

Maxwell had returned.

He had been almost to the great hall when he'd heard Valery's distant scream. That had brought him running all the way back to the inner bailey, where he was faced with a most unexpected sight.

His father and Aurelius were in a struggle.

"Papa!" he gasped. "Papa, stop this! Aurelius, stop fighting!"

"Your father threatened to cut me!" Valery shouted, wanting Maxwell to know that Aurelius was not at fault. "He has daggers and he is trying to kill Aurelius!"

Horrified, Maxwell watched the struggle. "Papa, *stop!*" he begged. "Drop your weapon! *Please!*"

Sterling wasn't listening. He was in a fight for his life. Unable to stay out of it, Maxwell came up behind his father and grabbed him, trying to keep his arms and hands away from Aurelius. Thinking he was being attacked from behind, Sterling panicked and slashed his son's hand, drawing streams of blood, but Maxwell didn't falter. He begged his father to stop fighting, but Sterling wasn't listening. He slashed again at Aurelius, who grabbed his wrist to deflect the dagger. But Sterling went mad, panicking because he was being trapped by two men. He began to kick and twist, trying to turn his body sideways. Anything to break free.

But it was to no avail. He was being held fast. That terrified him, and, in his terror, he twisted hard enough that he accidentally deflected the dagger aiming for Aurelius straight into his own chest instead.

Immediately, the man collapsed.

"Oh, God," Maxwell said, lowering his father to the ground. "Oh, God… Papa, *nay!*"

Aurelius was helping him lower Sterling, shocked and dismayed over what had happened. "I was trying to disarm him," he said, breathless from the fight. "I was trying to force him to drop the weapon, but he wouldna do it."

Maxwell was beside himself. "Why?" he pleaded, almost in tears. "Why did he do this? Why did he go on the attack?"

Valery was kneeling beside Sterling, greatly concerned. "He is drunk," she said, trying to be of some comfort to Maxwell. "He was not himself. This was not your father, Max. It was the wine that made him behave this way."

"It should have been… *you,*" Sterling said, spitting up blood as he grabbed at his son's hand. "You should be Valery's husband, not this… this Scots dog. *Not him!*"

With that brief, horrific speech, Maxwell understood everything. He'd not spoken to his father about the betrothal since his return, but he knew the man would not have taken it well. Now, he knew just how badly that was.

He could hardly believe what he was hearing.

"My God," he breathed. "You did *not* do this, Papa. Tell me you did not challenge Aurelius."

Sterling coughed, and blood sprayed on Valery's neck and chest, on Aurelius' arm, and splattered onto Maxwell's face. "It should have been… you," he said, more blood spilling out of his mouth. "A man must have… have a legacy. This was yours. She was yours! I was trying to make them both understand that all of this belongs to *you*!"

Aurelius gently pulled Valery out of the way, as he was far more experienced in tending battle wounds, and she was blocking him. Valery stood up and moved aside, her hands over her mouth, watching with complete devastation as a man's life drained away.

"I was never meant for Valery, Papa," Maxwell said, tears finding their way onto his cheeks. "You *know* this. You hoped and dreamed, but it was not to be."

Sterling looked up at his boy, grasping at him. "But why?" he said, sounding as if he were begging. "What did I do wrong that we should not share the same dream? How did I fail you?"

Maxwell broke down. "You did not fail me, Papa," he said. "It was nothing you did. I am my own man. I am who I am. God made me the way I am."

"But I must have failed you."

"All you did was love me. You wanted the best for me. I understand that."

Sterling grabbed hold of his son's hand as Aurelius continued to peel back layers of mail and fabric, trying to see how deeply the dirk was buried. But Maxwell only had eyes for his father as the man squeezed his hand weakly.

"If I have failed you, I am sorry," Sterling whispered, coughing again and gurgling up blood. "I only wanted happiness for you. I want you to have more than I did."

Maxwell put his free hand on his father's forehead. "Forgive me that I want my own happiness and not the happiness you think I should have," he murmured. "I hope you will accept that, even if it is not what you wanted for me."

By this time, men were starting to spill into the inner bailey. Valery's screams and the sounds of a struggle had drawn them. Someone had gone on the run for Adams, but mostly the men were gathered around, looking at Sterling with a dagger in his chest while his son comforted him and Aurelius tried to tend the wound. Valery knelt down next to Aurelius.

"What can I do?" she asked, her voice trembling. "Do you need rags or hot water or something?"

Aurelius had his hand on the dagger, but he turned to Valery, whose face was very close to his.

"If I remove this, he will bleed to death in front of us," he whispered. "There is nothing to be done. Let Maxwell and his father have their moment, for there is nothing left to do."

She looked at him in horror. "You… you cannot help him?"

"He is beyond help, lass. I am sorry."

Valery nodded, but her lower lip was trembling. As Aurelius watched, her face crumpled and she looked away, weeping softly. He reached out to comfort her, putting a gentle hand on her blonde head as she put her hands over her face and wept. He'd seen so much death over the past year that he was numb to it, but she wasn't. In front of him, a man was losing his father, and it was his fault, even if it had been in self-defense.

He wasn't immune to the suffering he'd caused, inadvertent though it may have been. He remembered Maxwell speaking on his father, a dedicated and resolute man who was very firm in his principles. It must have, indeed, been devastating for him to lose out on what he felt was his son's destiny. He was willing to fight and kill for it in the end. To Aurelius, that only made Sterling a man of strong beliefs, not a drunk who had picked a futile fight.

Sterling St. John was a warrior who deserved a warrior's

end.

"Behold, I see those I love, and my relatives who have died before me," Aurelius murmured, his gaze on Sterling. "I see my father seated in the golden halls with an empty seat beside him. I see the greatest warriors who have ever lived, surrounding my father, calling to me."

Maxwell heard him. He looked at Aurelius, tears all over his face, but he knew what the man was saying. It was a warrior's prayer, long repeated, long told, something that every warrior deserved when the veil of life was about to close over him forever. His eyes met Aurelius', and the Highlander nodded briefly, as if to encourage him to pray along with him.

As heartbreaking as it was, Maxwell did.

"Death is not the end, but the beginning, for a true warrior never dies," he said in unison with Aurelius. As they spoke, others around them joined in. "He takes his place of greatness among those who are worthy. Mourn not the glorious dead but rejoice in their legacy. They wait for me, not in this life, but in the next, where their legends shall live forever."

Just as they finished, Sterling gave one final cough and fell still. Aurelius knew he was dead even if Maxwell didn't want to acknowledge it. Silently, Aurelius removed the dagger in Sterling's chest, and, as he'd predicted, blood spilled out, all down the man. Valery, at Sterling's feet, was still weeping softly when Aurelius put his hand on Maxwell's shoulder.

"Yer voice was the last he heard in this life," he murmured. "If I had a son, that is what I would want. To hear my son's voice at the last. Ye gave him a great honor, Max. Ye transitioned him from this life to the next with the honor he deserved. That is a great ending for any man."

Maxwell was still holding his father's hand. "God," he muttered. "Is it true? Is this really the end? I only just came home from battle. I'd not even had the chance to really speak with my father yet. And now this?"

Aurelius wasn't sure what to say to the man. He removed his hand but remained next to him as Maxwell reconciled himself to the horrible events of the night. They were all struggling for composure when Adams suddenly came into the small bailey. He pushed men out of the way until he came to the terrible scene, and even then, all he could do was stand there and gasp.

"*What* is this?" he demanded, pointing frantically to Sterling. "What happened?"

"He tried to attack me, Papa," Valery said, sniffling as she stood up and faced her father. "He was drunk, and he blamed me for the betrothal to Aurelius. He blamed you. He said it should have been Maxwell, and he was angry."

Even beneath the silver moonlight, Adams went ashen. "He said that?" he said. "My God... He confronted you about it?"

"He did."

"Is *that* what this is all about?"

Valery nodded. "He told me that he was going to cut my tongue out, and Aurelius defended me," she said, wiping at her eyes. "Aurelius was unarmed, Papa. Sterling used his broadsword, and when Aurelius disarmed him, he unsheathed a dagger. He was accidentally stabbed in the ensuing fight."

Adams couldn't believe what he was hearing. He put a hand over his mouth in astonishment, looking down at Aurelius and Maxwell, who were kneeling down by Sterling's body. The more he looked, the more astonished he became.

"Oh... God," he finally mumbled. "Nay... oh, *nay*, I cannot believe he would do this. Why would he do such a thing? Has the man gone mad?"

"Nay," Aurelius said. "Not mad. He was drunk. Sometimes men do things they wouldna normally do when there is drink in their veins. He was very angry about the betrothal."

"It's true," Maxwell said, choked with emotion. "He was furious about it."

Although no one was blaming him, at least not openly, Adams could feel the distinct creep of guilt. He had made the decision for the betrothal, after all. But if he had to do it over again, he would still make the same decision. Nothing would change. Clearly, Sterling had not accepted that decision. But to attack Valery because of it was beyond Adams' comprehension.

"Maxwell," he said, watching Maxwell lift his tear-stained face. "You understand why I did not betroth you to my daughter. You *know*."

Maxwell nodded. "I do," he said. "This is not your fault, my lord. My father wanted things that can never be."

That seemed to give Adams some peace. "And I am sorry for you, lad," he said. "But your father loved you. He loved you very much."

"I know, my lord."

Adams hesitated to say anything more. This simply wasn't the time or the place, at least for more personal things, but there were a few items that needed to be addressed immediately now that Sterling was lying dead.

Business, to a certain extent, had to go on.

"Have some men help you take your father to the vault," he said quietly. "Wrap him tightly, and we will store him there until you speak to your mother and decide what's to be done with him."

Maxwell nodded wearily. "Aye, my lord."

"And you," Adams said, looking him in the eye. "You are now my commander, Max. I am sorry to demand this of you so soon, but with your father gone, the duty now falls on you. Do you understand?"

"I do, my lord."

"You will have a great legacy here if you want it. I believe your father would want it, too."

Maxwell could only nod. All he could really think of was his father lying dead at his feet and not some legacy post that he and his father and grandfather had held. He didn't care, honestly, but he had a duty to fulfill at the moment.

A duty to his father.

As he motioned for some men to help him lift his father, Aurelius came up on the other side. He put his big arms underneath Sterling, but before he lifted, he looked up at Maxwell.

"I'll understand if ye dunna want me to help ye," he said. "But I'd like to just the same."

Maxwell's eyes were full of grief. "It was not your fault," he said softly. "It could just as easily be you lying here. You are not to blame."

"May… may I help, too?"

Valery asked the question softly, crouching down at Sterling's head, her eyes red-rimmed from weeping. Maxwell didn't have the heart to deny her, so he instructed her to put her hands under Sterling's head. When the other men were in position, they all lifted on Maxwell's command, including Valery. She only had Sterling's head, but she took very good care of it. She held it firmly, gazing at the man who, only minutes earlier, had been alive and well. A man she'd grown up knowing as a kind, dutiful man who was devoted to his family.

It was strange, really.

She'd asked Aurelius about the battles in France. She'd asked if they'd been bad, wanting to understand what her father and Aurelius had faced. Perhaps she wanted to feel closer to them, to see life through their eyes. She'd learned quickly that they'd faced death. Men like Radegund with the ax in his face, and the unnamed Highlander who'd had his guts cut out. At the moment, she was facing death, too. Now, she had an inkling of what they'd all dealt with, but more than that, she watched how Maxwell handled his father's body.

The two had a complex relationship and always had, but at the moment, none of that mattered. The only thing that was apparent to Valery was how much Maxwell loved his father. Love, true love, took many forms, and what she witnessed was the true love between a son and his father, even in the moment of death. *Especially* in the moment of death.

Valery de Leybourne grew up that night, just a little.

And Aurelius had the privilege to watch it.

PART THREE
VALERY, DAVINA, AND MABEL

CHAPTER SIXTEEN

Six weeks later

THEY WERE MOVING with stealth.

On a secret mission, Valery was following Maxwell, but she wasn't quite sure where they were going. All she knew was that he had come to her whilst she was in the small bailey with her geese, back to their original names of Sunny and Moonie, and he'd put his fingers to his lips to silently beckon her.

She'd followed.

They left the small bailey, beneath the branches of Faunus the Tree that were nearly empty of leaves at this time of year, and through the servants' gate into the kitchen yard. Beyond that was the walled area where the dun Tarh men had set up their encampment, and they were still there, so she followed Maxwell through that open field. He'd even reached back to grab her hand, running with her all the way across the winter-dead grass and through the small gate that opened out into the pond.

That was where Aurelius was waiting.

Maxwell ran her right up to Aurelius, practically flinging

her into the man's arms. But the truth was that he didn't have to do much flinging because at that point, Valery was running faster than he was. She saw Aurelius and flew to the man, leaping into his arms and nearly toppling him.

They'd finally come together.

"There," Maxwell said, panting from having run so fast. "Keep her here. I'll be back later to fetch her."

Aurelius and Valery were already deep into a series of passionate kisses, but Aurelius pulled away long enough to address Maxwell.

"Not too soon," he said. "I've not seen her since last night, so give me time."

Valery clamped her mouth over his, suckling his lips. "Give *us* time," she said between heated kisses. "If my father comes looking for me, tell him you've not seen me."

Maxwell frowned. "He'll know I've seen you," he said, gesturing to the enormous castle behind him. "Hundreds of men just saw us together, Val. He'll *know*."

Valery turned to look at him with Aurelius kissing any bit of flesh his lips could come into contact with. "Then if that is the case, come fetch me," she said. "We'll be here, out of sight."

Maxwell shook his head at the pair of lovers. "You had better name your firstborn after me for this," he said. "I am risking everything so you two can be alone."

"Thank you, Max," Valery said as Aurelius suckled on her ear. "I love you for it."

He grunted. "If you hear a loud whistle, that means danger approaches," he said. "Do you understand me?"

Aurelius and Valery were locking lips again, lost in one another, and Maxwell rolled his eyes, grinning as he walked away. He had become a close and good friend to Aurelius, going so far as to sneak Valery to him these days. The death of Sterling was in the past, something that had, strangely, bonded the men more closely than they ever had been before. There was understanding there, and there was, above all, trust. With the wedding drawing closer, and the celebratory feast just a few days away, Adams was keeping a very tight rein on his daughter, who had fallen madly in love with her betrothed.

And he'd fallen madly in love with her.

Even now, she was in his arms, her legs wrapped around his narrow waist as he carried her into the trees clustered around the pond. This had been their secret meeting place for the past few weeks, ever since Adams decided that it was solely up to him to preserve his daughter's purity until her wedding. He loved Aurelius like a son, but he could see the passion brewing between the pair, and he wanted his daughter to go to her marital bed a virgin. He felt strongly about it, perhaps fearful that if Aurelius took her innocence before they were legally wed, it might change his opinion of her. Perhaps he would feel there was no mystery left.

Adams seemed intent on preserving it.

But the reality was that Valery and Aurelius had done nearly everything but engage in the act of intercourse. Valery was an eager student, and Aurelius was more than happy to teach her how to pleasure a man. He, in turn, had shown her his skill in pleasuring a woman, so moments like this were very precious to them. Full of love and discovery.

Finally, alone.

Aurelius had an old horse blanket already spread out amongst the trees.

Valery immediately pulled him down onto it, climbing on top of him, fully clothed, and leaning over him for a moment simply to gaze into his handsome face. She stroked his cheeks, his hair, as she studied him.

"You've not fallen in love with someone else since the last I saw you, have you?" she asked.

He pretended to think. "Only two or three women," he said. "Nothing to worry over."

"*Just* two or three?"

"That was all I could work in between last night's feast and this morning."

"You're becoming lazy in your old age."

He laughed, low in his throat. "Lazy for want of ye, lass," he purred, pulling her down to his mouth. "Only for ye."

His lips slanted over hers, and Valery gave in to his strength, his heat. In little time, she was on her back, and he untied the top of her garment, for she was wearing things these days that could be easily removed. When her breasts sprang free, he feasted, suckling her nipples as she sighed and groaned. That only fed his lust, and he tossed up her skirts, sliding his fingers between her legs. Gently, he inserted them into her tender body as he nursed her breasts.

With the top of her garment wide open and her skirts pushed up around her waist, Valery was lost in a haze of passion. Aurelius suckled her and fondled her until he could stand it no longer, and then, he put his face between her legs and pleasured her with his tongue. Valery was quick to climax when he did that to her, but today, she didn't have the patience for it. She grabbed hold of his dark hair and pulled his head up.

"Not today," she said, panting as she looked at the man between her legs. "Today, we are going to do something different."

"What?

"Today, I want all of you."

He smiled seductively. "And I'd like nothing better," he said. "But ye made yer father a promise."

She sighed sharply. "And how is he to know if I break that promise?" she asked. "Are you going to tell him?"

"Of course not."

Her hands in his hair loosened, and she began to caress his face. "Aurelius, we are to be married before the end of the year," she said. "Sooner if we can, but I do not want to wait until my wedding night to know all of you. You were my husband the moment we were betrothed. You became my dearest love shortly thereafter. We've been teasing and toying with one another ever since. I want to know you as my husband. What is the difference if we do it now or when we are married? We shall do it every night for the rest of my life if I want to. Don't *you*?"

She was breaking him down, which wasn't hard to do. Did he want to bed her, as a husband bedded a wife? Of course he did. He couldn't remember when he didn't. But he was trying to obey Adams' wishes, which was a silly thing to do in hindsight. He'd never loved anyone or anything more in his entire life than he loved Valery. She was his all for living, everything he had ever wished for.

Did he want to feel his body in hers?

God, he did.

So very much.

"Are ye sure?" he said after a moment. "Because once we do it, I canna take it back."

Valery sat up so quickly that she smacked him on the side of the head with her right thigh when he didn't move quickly enough.

"Of course I am," she said, rising to her knees as she ripped her surcoat over her head. "I would never want to take back something of such beauty. Something that makes me yours for all eternity."

As he watched, she tossed the surcoat aside and pulled her shift over her head too. Very quickly, she was nude in front of him, and Aurelius didn't hesitate. That was all the coaxing he needed. He was already intimately acquainted with a body he couldn't live without, so this moment was something he'd dreamed about. He was ready for it. Therefore, he yanked off his own tunic and stood up to remove his breeches. His manhood, nearly fully aroused, sprang free. He barely had his boots and breeches off his feet before Valery grasped his manroot with her hot little hands. Her mouth went over him, as he'd taught her, and he was very nearly lost.

"Wait," he whispered tightly. "If ye do that, we'll not get any further. Take yer hands off. *Off.*"

Disappointed, she did, watching him toss his clothing aside. Then he fell to his knees, pushing her onto her back, and his big body covered hers.

After that, passion consumed them.

They didn't usually remove all of their clothing in encounters like this, so this was something new and exciting. Valery relished the feel of his big, heavy body on top of her, instinctively opening her legs for him. Aurelius feasted on her breasts, her neck, her mouth, before putting his hand between their bodies. Valery could feel him touching her, rubbing the head of his enormous phallus against her virginal opening.

"I've hoped to prepare ye for this moment," he murmured, looking deeply into her eyes. "It'll be more than ye could have imagined. For us both, I think. Just know… know that I love ye with all that I am, Valery. What we do now demonstrates that love. *My* love. For the rest of time, I'll love ye and no other, I swear it."

Valery wrapped her arms around his neck, kissing his mouth with her soft lips. "And I'll love you and no other," she whispered. "Give me all of you, Aurelius. Make me your wife, my dearest love, in every sense."

He didn't keep her waiting. The foreplay had made her hot and slick, and even though she was a virgin, he'd been preparing her for this moment with his fingers. He'd spent weeks acquainting her with the feel of a man inside her. Therefore, when he finally slid into her, there was no pain. Simply pleasure. It only took him two thrusts to seat himself fully, and all Valery could do was lie there and gasp. Her legs wrapped around his hips and her pelvis arched up to him—her body responding to the primal mating ritual.

He was lost.

Aurelius kept his thrusts gentle at first, keeping in mind that she was new to this, but her gasps and groans broke his concentration. He realized very quickly that she had the ability to arouse him like no one else ever had. Her soft breasts against his bare chest ignited his entire body with lust. He gathered her against him, thrusting harder, trying to be careful about her newness. The last thing he wanted to do was frighten her. He wanted her to love this as much as he, and by the sounds she was making, he suspected she was. Her legs were still wrapped around his hips, holding him fast, but he unwrapped them and raised himself, holding her legs open as he continued to pound into her sweet and submissive body.

He wanted to watch her as he made love to her.

God, what a sight.

Valery had a sensuous figure. Her breasts were full, the

nipples hard, and her long torso was slender. She had rounded hips that drew his lust, made him imagine the children she would bear from them. *His* children. He'd had women before, many times, but he'd used the age-old trick of removing himself just before he climaxed to prevent any bastards. But with Valery, he had no intention of pulling out.

He wanted to spill himself into her.

He wanted to brand her with his seed.

Valery, however, was already so aroused that she cried out with her first true womanly climax before he could slow his pace and perhaps extend her pleasure. But it didn't matter. He was rapidly approaching his own release, as much as he wanted this moment to last forever. He was so aroused by Valery that he lowered himself onto her again and slanted his mouth over hers, kissing her deeply as he spilled himself into her.

And even then, he didn't slow down. He continued to thrust, feeling what he'd put into her. Feeling her body against his, surrounding him, giving him a home he'd never had before. Giving him a woman that belonged only to him.

With her, he was home.

"How do ye feel?" he asked softly, his face in the side of her head. "Did I hurt ye?"

Valery shifted slightly, putting her hands between their bodies, feeling his semi-flaccid member as it remained half buried in her. "I feel… I don't know," she said. "I feel warm. I feel loved. I feel as if this moment is the most important moment of my life. It belongs only to you and to me. This is *our* moment, Aurelius."

He closed his eyes, feeling her gentle hands on his tender member. "It is," he whispered, kissing her forehead. "Ye belong to me as no one else ever has."

She was still stroking him, touching her body as well, feeling where they had joined, but that wasn't unusual with her. Valery was, if nothing else, curious about everything. Sometimes she had an almost analytical, detached manner about it, but he knew it was because she was quite brilliant and wanted to learn about everything. Even the mating between men and women.

"I *am* yours," she murmured, removing her hands but reaching around his hips to grab both buttocks as he remained buried in her. "Can we do it again?"

He laughed softly. "I'd be happy to, but ye must give me time to recover a little," he said. "It takes a man a bit of time to build up again."

Valery nodded thoughtfully at that, but when he tried to withdraw, she wouldn't let him. She kept her hands on his buttocks and her pelvis smashed against his.

"Not yet," she begged softly. "I've waited my entire life for this moment. Do not end it yet."

He kissed her, sweetly at first, but the passion that was so easily ignited between them roared to life, and in a short amount of time, he was thrusting into her again, grinding his pelvis against hers, taking his time with her. There was no frenzied thrusting this time, simply a slow and purposeful movement that had Valery climaxing again very shortly. He was about to pick up the pace because he could feel himself building to another release when she suddenly reached between their bodies to touch him. That was all it took for him to release himself so hard that he bit his own lip.

Valery's hands were all over his buttocks and in between their bodies, touching his male member, feeling him as his climax died down. It was the most wildly intimate thing he'd ever experienced. Putting a hand on her left breast, he'd moved to fondle her gently, to work them both through the powerful passion they were feeling, when a distant whistle suddenly pierced the air.

If you hear a loud whistle, that means danger approaches.

Aurelius was on his feet before he took another breath.

"Quickly," he said, tossing her the shift. "Get dressed, *mo leannan*. Hurry!"

Mo leannan. It meant "my sweetheart." Dazed from their encounter but not senseless, Valery yanked on her shift, followed by the surcoat. Aurelius already had his breeches on, followed by the tunic, and he was yanking his boots on even as he headed for the trees. Valery didn't say a word—she simply motioned for him to hide, and he blew her a kiss as he ran into the bramble. As he disappeared, Valery quickly smoothed her hair, slipped on her shoes, and plopped down on the horse blanket. She looked around to make sure there were no signs that Aurelius had been there, and, satisfied, she picked up a handful of sticks lying on the ground. The pond wasn't too far away, so she started tossing the sticks into the pond as if wiling away the day. It was all quite casual.

Until Adams appeared.

The man was huffing and puffing. It was clear he'd run down to the pond, or at least went as quickly as he was capable of running, fully expecting to find his daughter and her betrothed in an indelicate situation.

But he only found his daughter.

"What are you doing out here?" he demanded. "And where is Aurelius?"

Valery looked puzzled. "I do not know," she said. "Where is he supposed to be?"

Adams scowled. "Max was seen running out here with you,"

he said. "I can only assume he was bringing you to Aurelius, whom no one has seen in a while. And do not tell me that you've been out here with Shite-brain and Dumb-arse, because they are in the kitchen yard. I have seen them. Well? What have you to say to that?"

"What do you want me to say?"

"Are you going to tell me that you've not been with Aurelius?"

Valery frowned and stood up, brushing the dried grass off her rumpled skirt. "If you recall, you forbade us from being alone until we were married," she said. "Didn't you?"

Adams put his hand on his hips. "I did," he said. "Proprieties must be observed, but you do not seem to realize that."

Valery sighed heavily. "Papa," she said. "We are in love. Why are you trying to keep two people who love one another, and are soon to be married, from spending time alone? I do not understand you. Don't you want grandchildren?"

Adams nearly choked on the bawdy suggestion. "*After* you are married, of course I do."

"I want to be married to him now," she said. "We are having the great feast in a few days. Let that be a wedding celebration and not simply a celebration of the betrothal."

Adams' harsh stance eased a little. "We are not certain when Aurelius' parents will arrive," he said. "We received word from them more than two weeks ago that they were coming south, but it could be another week or two. It is winter. The weather might not be in their favor."

"Yet you are having a betrothal feast without them."

"That was planned when I returned from France to introduce Aurelius to our allies."

"But you have waited more than a month before having it."

Adams sighed faintly. "You know that was because of Sterling's death," he said. "I did not feel it appropriate to have a celebration so soon afterward."

Valery took some pity on him. "I know," she said. "But you are trying to control things now that do not need to be controlled."

"What do you mean?"

She went to him, wrapping her hands around his elbow in an affectionate gesture. "I mean you and Aurelius' father created our betrothal," she said quietly. "You hoped that we would at least tolerate one another, but instead, we have fallen in love. Now you are trying to keep us apart. You *wanted* us to be together, didn't you?"

He was stoic. "I want you to be a pure bride," he said. "If you are not, then I have failed as a father to protect you."

Valery laughed softly. "Papa, I have fallen in love with the most amazing man," she said. "You do not need to protect me from him. He will take care of me, and love me, for the rest of my life. Isn't that what you hoped for?"

He was trying not to look at her, knowing she had a point, but he couldn't quite manage it. "Of course it is," he said. "But I'm still your father. I still have a right to protect you. Even from your amorous betrothed."

Valery continued to smile at him. "But you do not need to," she said. "More than likely, he needs to be protected from me. I will surely lure him to his doom."

Adams was struggling not to chuckle, shaking his head at his naughty daughter. "Enough with that," he said. "But I am not immune to being in love with someone and wanting to be with her."

"You and Mama?"

"Nay, me and the Virgin Mary. Of course me and your mother."

Valery burst out laughing. "Papa, you are a fool," she said. "But you are my fool, and I love you dearly. Will you *please* let Aurelius and I spend some time together, alone? *Please*?"

Adams cast her a long look. "I suppose that if I do not, you will sneak out here to the pond."

"That would be a fair assumption."

He shook his head in defeat and looked away. "I do not have a choice in this, do I?"

"You do not."

He grunted unhappily. "Very well," he said. "If it means that much to you."

"It does," she said, standing on tiptoes to kiss his cheek. "It truly does. Thank you very much."

Adams felt as if he'd been manipulated, but he really didn't mind. He was glad that his daughter had found love. He was glad that everything was working out as he'd hoped and that Wolsingham had a future. His ancestral home and title would continue to live on through his daughter.

Aye, there was much to be grateful for.

"Aurelius?" he suddenly shouted into the trees. "Did you hear that? I will permit you and my daughter to be alone from time to time!"

"But not too much," Valery quipped, grinning when he looked at her.

"But not too much!" Adams shouted.

Valery started laughing, which finally broke him down. He laughed too, feeling happy that his daughter was happy. That she would marry the man she loved and they would be happy together. Truly, it was all he ever wanted.

With Valery on his arm, Adams headed back to Lydgate.

CHAPTER SEVENTEEN

Three days.

IN THREE DAYS, the celebratory feast for the betrothal of Valery de Leybourne, daughter of the Earl of Wolsingham, and Aurelius dun Tarh, son of the Earl of Torridon, would begin. No one knew when it would end.

That was the truth.

Much had happened in the days leading up to the feast. It all started when a few family groups began to show up, all of them revolving around one castle or another. It was as if the allied castles of the north had opened their gates and spilled forth hundreds of people, all of them heading straight for Lydgate and a celebration that was costing Adams a great deal of money. He'd had some time to stockpile barrels of wine and ale, and two days before the feast, he'd taken a group of people out hunting to procure meat.

Valery had been with the hunting party.

Aurelius and Darien had also gone, along with Estevan, Caelus, and Kaladin, Adams, Maxwell, and about twenty soldiers. It had been a brisk day as the first day of winter closed in, and breath hung in the air all day long. The first kill had been by Valery, who brought down a three-point buck with tremendous skill as Aurelius and her father carefully advised her. She had a steady hand and a dead eye. Down the animal went, and Valery was congratulated by all.

Especially Aurelius.

He couldn't have been prouder of her. He'd been part of numerous hunting parties over the years, and there had been a few where women had come along to clean and prepare the kill, but he'd never been part of a hunting party where a woman actually did the hunting.

He found he rather liked it when that woman was Valery.

He was falling more in love with her by the day.

The hunting party had been out from dawn to dusk, and Valery had proven her ability to ride at length and shoot with a bow and arrow, and she wasn't afraid to collect her kill. Of course, she couldn't move the buck, but her kind and considerate betrothed did it for her, along with his brothers. Even Darien was starting to see what caliber of woman his brother was to marry and, reluctantly, admitted his initial thoughts of her trapping him into a terrible marriage were incorrect. Like everyone else, Darien could see how completely enamored Aurelius was with Valery.

And for good reason.

In truth, the past several weeks since the arrival home from France had been quite pleasant for everyone, the death of Sterling notwithstanding. The incident had only slightly marred what was essentially a positive situation with Aurelius and Valery's betrothal, and that was because Adams himself spread the rumor that Sterling had been protecting Valery from an assassin who killed him and then slipped off into the night, never to be seen again. No one questioned the earl, and life moved on with Sterling having died a hero.

And that was the way Adams and Aurelius and Valery wanted it.

But the hunt was a major event in the days leading up to their celebratory feast, and all of Lydgate was preparing for the onslaught of guests from Berwick, Bowes, Kyloe, Alnwick, Richmond, and Carlisle Castles. Those were the primary castles, and the primary lords, that Adams wanted to introduce Aurelius to, so everything at Lydgate was bustling as the hunting party brought back three bucks, two doe, and a plethora of smaller birds and mammals. Servants worked into the night cleaning the carcasses and hanging them in the smokehouse, which was working to capacity.

Aurelius loved the smell of the smoking meat.

The Earl of Carlisle, Tate de Lara, was one of the first arrivals. The silver and blue de Lara pendant announced the man the day after the hunting party, and Adams went out to meet him. Tate was the bastard son of Edward I, a man who had forged his own path and was an icon in England as a whole. Kings could tear each other up and the nobility of England could go to war against one another, but one word from Tate de Lara was all it usually took for men to stand down and listen. For the man they called Dragonblade, all of England would take note.

Aurelius was quite happy to meet him.

After Carlisle arrived came Richmond Castle. In fact, on the third day after the hunt, Valery awoke to more guests crowding into Lydgate's vast bailey. Beryl and Sela had pulled her out of bed, preparing her toilette for the day, as she stumbled over to the window to watch the parade down below. Banners were flying, armies were setting up encampments in the walled grounds, and she even caught a glimpse of her father down below as he welcomed yet another favored ally.

Finally, the event they'd been waiting for was happening.

The day had arrived.

"This is so exciting," Valery said, yawning. "Who else has arrived this morning? Do we know?"

Sela was warming water over the fire as the geese rose from their nest over near the hearth and began to waddle toward the open chamber door. With Sunny and Moonie heading out to conduct their geese business for the day, Beryl began sweeping up the straw they'd been lying on.

"Bamburgh has arrived," Sela said, trying not to burn herself as she shifted the coals around. "That is the House of Herringthorpe. Carlisle, Richmond, and Northwood are here. Did you know your father invited the Earl of Teviot from Northwood Castle?"

Valery yawned again. "Nay," she said. "He did not tell me whom he invited, but he told Aurelius. Where *is* Aurelius?"

Sela finally had the wood where she wanted it, and a steady flame continued to heat up the big iron pot of water. "I've not seen him," she said, brushing off her hands as she stood up. "Mayhap he's in the smokehouse again?"

Valery giggled. It was well known that Aurelius couldn't keep out of the smokehouse with all of that lovely meat smoking in it. "He came to me last night smelling like a wildfire," she said. "It was even in his hair."

Sela chuckled as she began to pull out brushes and a comb. "The man likes his smoked meat," she said. "And what of his brothers? I hear they do, too."

Valery moved away from the window, going to sit down so Sela could start on her hair. She'd rolled it up the previous night in bits of rag so that this morning, she would have a head full of lovely curls. Sela began to unwind her hair from the pieces of rag as Valery used a small iron instrument to clean out her nails.

"I think we are going to have to go hunt again if we can't keep those five out of the smokehouse," she said, inspecting her nails. "Honestly, I've not spent a lot of time around the brothers because Aurelius occupies most of my waking hours, but they all seem quite likable. Even Darien seems nice enough, surprisingly."

Sela looked over at her. "Did you not like him, m'lady?"

Valery thought back to the day Aurelius and his brothers had arrived and she heard Darien talking about her in the stable. It seemed like a lifetime ago.

"It does not matter any longer," she said, willing to let bygones be bygones. "It's strange, really. I never had any siblings. Now, I am to have nine."

Sela nodded. "Your father seems to like to have them around," she said, handing the hair rags to Beryl once she unrolled them. "But I suppose any man likes to have mischievous boys around to remind him of his days as a boy."

Valery glanced at her in the reflection of the bronze mirror. "Why would you say that?"

"Because those are days of no responsibility and only play."

Valery nodded and went back to her nails. "That is true," she said. "I'm sure Papa wishes I would have a dozen boys, all of them to carry on Wolsingham, if not in name, then in spirit."

Sela began to brush out the curls. "Do you think you will live in Scotland, then?" she asked. "Will you raise your children in the Highlands?"

Valery shrugged. "I do not know yet," she said. "I've never

even seen Castle Hydra, but Aurelius is the heir. That is his seat. But Lydgate will also be his seat, as the Earl of Wolsingham."

"Have you not discussed it?"

Valery shook her head. "Nay," she said. "But it is of little matter. I do not feel strongly one way or the other. Whatever Aurelius prefers will be agreeable with me."

Sela watched that warm, giddy expression wash over Valery's face, the same expression that occurred every time she spoke of Aurelius. Beryl saw it too, and snickered softly as she went to put away the strips of rag that had been rolled up in Valery's hair.

"Of course it will, m'lady," Sela said, vigorously brushing out some of the tighter curls and shaping them around her hand. "Sir Aurelius is a good man. A handsome man. And he'll make you a wonderful husband. In fact, everything is ready for the celebration. The hall is prepared. The kitchens are ready. The servants even have clean tunics that Lady Wolsingham provided for them."

"Except for the sick," Beryl said quietly. "The cook has a few sick servants, and it has been a great deal of work for her to prepare the meals without them."

Sela brushed her off. "Pah," she said. "It is nothing. I saw two of them working in the kitchens this morning, preparing food, so there is no sickness."

Valery had looked up from her nails, listening to Beryl and Sela speak of ill servants. "You are certain the cook has enough help?" she asked.

Sela nodded. "If she doesn't, you know she will not keep it to herself," she said. "Have no worry, m'lady. Lydgate is running at full measure for your celebration."

Satisfied, Valery returned to cleaning her nails, but she'd

hardly made a move before her chamber door was flying open and Aurelius stood in the open panel.

"Val!" he gasped, holding up a piece of vellum. "What do ye suppose I have in my hand?"

Valery had no idea. Fortunately, she was clad in a heavy sleeping shift, so she was at least somewhat presentable as he burst into the chamber, but that didn't ease her irritation at him.

"Did you lose a hand?" she demanded.

He stopped in his excitement and frowned. "Clearly, I have not," he said, holding up both hands. "Why do ye ask?"

"Because I thought you must have, since you did not knock," she scolded. "You're fortunate that I am adequately dressed."

That was Sela and Beryl's cue to depart, and quickly, for Lady Valery was quick to temper, and they didn't want to be witness to a verbal beating for the poor, sweet Highlander.

Even if he did deserve it.

Sela had Beryl by the hand, pulling her from the chamber and slipping behind Aurelius so they could make it out the door. Once clear of the chamber, they shut the panel quietly and headed to the small chamber across the hall where things such as coverlets and brooms were kept. Beryl had the hair rags in her hands, and she began to put them in a basket on the floor.

"We'll wait here," Sela whispered loudly. Then she leaned her head in the direction of Valery's chamber. "I do not hear any shouting. Hopefully there will be no shouting, not today."

Beryl shook her head. "You needn't worry so," she said. "Sir Aurelius is going to have to learn how to deal with his own wife. He'd better learn now."

"True," Sela said. But then she frowned. "Speaking of his wife, why did you mention the sick kitchen servants? There was no need."

Beryl looked at her mother with exasperation. "Mama, several are sick and one died early this morning," she said. "I heard someone say it was the blue death."

Sela sighed heavily. "Pah," she scoffed. "Even if it is, Lady Wolsingham will know what to do about it. She will not let it affect the celebration or the guests. It is only a few servants, after all."

She seemed dismissive of Beryl's concerns, so Beryl simply stopped talking about it. The servants in the kitchens and stables often came down with ailments that quickly passed, and rarely was it transmitted to the house servants or the soldiers or even the family, because the kitchen and stable servants had duties that mostly kept them isolated from everyone. Therefore, her mother was probably right. There was nothing to worry about.

At least, Beryl hoped not.

CB

"WHY DID THOSE two run off so quickly?" Aurelius wanted to know, pointing to the shut door. "Every time I come around, they flee as if the devil has just made an appearance."

"The devil has," Valery said, grinning. "You frighten people, my darling. Does that not make you proud and happy?"

She was jesting with him, and he rolled his eyes, grinning, but that didn't stop his excitement. He'd burst into his betrothed's chamber for a reason, and he held up that reason again.

He shook the vellum.

"This is from my da," he said. "They have just crossed over into England. My mother wanted to stop and see her kin at Wigton Castle, so they will be delayed a day or two, but we should be seeing them before the end of the week."

Valery stood up and took the vellum from him, reading his father's words for herself. "How lovely," she said, feeling his excitement. "I'm terribly excited to meet them."

He pulled her into an embrace, gazing down into that lovely face he'd come to cherish. "And I'm terribly excited for them to meet ye as well," he said. "I know they'll love ye."

"I hope so," Valery said. "I have a gift for your mother, but what do you think I should give your father? I still cannot decide. My mother and I made him a cap for when the weather turns colder, but I think that may not be grand enough. I feel as if I must make a larger gesture."

Aurelius grinned, kissing her soundly. "My da's greatest gift will be for ye to love me," he said. "That is all he'll care about. And if ye decide to give him the cap, he'll love that too."

Valery handed him the vellum and returned to her table, sitting down as she picked up her hairbrush. "My mother and I have made your mother that lovely robe," she said. "You know the one? My mother had already started making it, but I helped her finish it with some of the pelts from the recent hunt. But I'm concerned because your mother is such a talented seamstress. It may not be fine enough for her."

He shook his head at her. "Ye worry too much, love," he said. "She will love anything ye give her because she knows ye made it yerself. It will mean a great deal to her."

Valery was having a rare moment of self-doubt. "Do you really think so?"

"I do."

Slowly, she began to brush her hair again, the mass of blonde curls that Sela had tried to tame. "I hope you are correct," she said. "I truly do. I do so want to make a good impression on her."

Aurelius wasn't sure he could say any more to her that might give her confidence that other assurances hadn't. He went to her, bending over her and kissing her on the top of her head as she continued to brush her hair. Then he lifted the vellum again, reading his father's words, before the chamber door opened and Lady Wolsingham stood in the opening.

Her eyebrows lifted.

"What's this?" she demanded lightly. "I find you two alone in Valery's chamber? How very shocking."

Aurelius grinned at the woman and went to her, putting his hands on her shoulders and planting a chaste kiss on her forehead. He truly adored his future mother-in-law, a woman who had been so kind to him in the beginning and who continued to be kind and understanding.

"I swear to ye that nothing untoward has happened," he said. "I was simply telling Val that my father has sent a missive. They should be here by the end of the week."

Lady Wolsingham's features lit up. "Is that so?" she said. "How lovely to hear. I will house them in the keep, of course. They can have the rooms on the entry level, near the solar. Or do you think they would rather be on the top floor? There are a lot of stairs to climb, but the chambers are larger."

Aurelius found it amusing that Lady Wolsingham turned into the same bundle of nerves that Valery did when discussing his parents.

"I think they'll be happy wherever ye house them," he said. "Truly, they'll not care a bit. My parents aren't picky people, I swear it."

Lady Wolsingham wasn't quite willing to take his word for it. "Nevertheless, they shall be treated impeccably," she said. "Now, I can see that my daughter is not dressed yet, so you will go to the great hall, where Adams is breaking his fast with some of his guests. I know he would like to introduce you to them, so go down and join them whilst I help my daughter dress."

Aurelius did as he was told. He kissed Valery politely on the head and kissed Lady Wolsingham on the cheek, quite wholesomely, before winking at them both as he quit the chamber. While Valery smirked, Lady Wolsingham went to shut the door behind him and bolt it.

"He is a cheeky rascal," she said with feigned disapproval. "Whatever do you see in him, I wonder?"

Valery laughed softly. "Everything," she said. "I see everything in him. Don't you?"

Lady Wolsingham nodded. "Indeed, I do," she said. "He is very much like his fath… Well, very much like a cheeky Scots. Now, what did you plan to wear today? Let us make it something fine and lovely. You will have a hall of guests by this evening."

Valery paused in her hair brushing and looked at her mother. "Wait a moment," she said. "What were you going to say just now? About Aurelius?"

Lady Wolsingham was moving to her daughter's wardrobe. "I do not recall," she said. "What was I going to say?"

Valery watched her mother open the doors to the large wardrobe and start fishing around. "It sounded as if you were going to say that Aurelius was very much like his father," she said. "Is that what you were going to say?"

Lady Wolsingham faltered. She stood at the wardrobe,

looking up at the things that were hanging on pegs. She started to shake her head as she reached for an amber-colored silk, but she paused again.

Valery saw her take a deep breath.

"I think you must have imagined it," she said.

Valery was coming to suspect that her mother wasn't being truthful. "Nay, I did not," she said. "I did not imagine that you were about to say that Aurelius was like his father. Why would you assume that? Do you know his father and have neglected to tell us?"

"Don't be ridiculous."

"I am certainly not being ridiculous," Valery said. "Did you know his father? You were raised on the border, and the dun Tarh clan has a garrison on the border. It's possible you knew him in your youth."

Lady Wolsingham didn't reply. She was still fingering the garments that were hanging on pegs, and as Valery watched, the woman's shoulders slumped.

"I was not going to say anything," she said softly. "It is not even worth mentioning, truly."

"Then you *did* know him?"

Lady Wolsingham nodded. "A very long time ago," she said. "So long ago that I've not even told your father. I doubt Lares dun Tarh would even recognize me."

Valery's eyes widened. "Truly?" she said. "But why haven't you told me before? Why didn't you tell Aurelius?"

Lady Wolsingham waved her off. "Because it was so insignificant," she said. "It was not worth mentioning, truly. It was so long ago."

Valery shrugged. "But that would still be a lovely recollection, even if it is from childhood," she said, turning back to her mirror. "Did you know him from your time at Mount Pleasant?"

"Aye," Lady Wolsingham said, removing the amber silk and the matching shift. "Ashkirk Castle was an ally at that time."

She brought the dress over to the bed and laid it out alongside the fine shift as Valery continued to brush out the tight curls.

"Do you remember much about him?" Valery asked. "How well did you know him?"

Lady Wolsingham faltered again. At least, she fell silent enough that Valery paused in her brushing to look at her. "What is wrong?" she asked her mother. "Did you know him well?"

Lady Wolsingham remained silent. She looked over the amber silk surcoat, picking at imaginary threads, before finally speaking.

"If I tell you the story, you must swear to me that you will never repeat it," she said. "Not to Aurelius and not to your father. Not to anyone. Can you swear this to me?"

Valery stood up from her table. Her mother sounded… odd. Very odd. Valery truly had no idea why until she went to the bed and saw her mother with tears in her eyes. Concerned, she sat down on the bed and took her mother's hand.

"Of course I will not repeat it," she said softly. "I will take it to the grave. But what is your story?"

Lady Wolsingham blinked quickly as if to compose herself. Then she looked at her daughter before letting out a hiss. "I have never repeated this to anyone," she said. "For years, I've put Lares dun Tarh out of my mind. I hadn't thought of him until your father sent that missive saying that he'd betrothed you to Aurelius dun Tarh. I did not know it was Lares' son until

I saw him. Then… then I knew. He looked just like him."

Valery was listening intently. "But what do you know about Lares?"

"I know that the last time I saw him, he was being taken away by his father and several men," Lady Wolsingham said. "The last I heard, he had been forcibly committed to an abbey in some remote area of Scotland. I had no idea he had somehow been released and married."

Valery looked at her in surprise. "He was a priest?" she said. "Aurelius never told me that."

Lady Wolsingham shook her head. "It is possible he does not know," she said. "That is why you must not repeat this story, Valery. I may know things that Lares has chosen to keep buried. You must never tell Aurelius what I tell you."

"I will not, I swear it," Valery said, taking her mother's hand. "But is that all there is to it? That you knew him and he was committed to an abbey?"

Lady Wolsingham looked at her hesitantly. "Nay," she said. "Lares and I were madly in love with one another. As much as you love Aurelius, that is how much I loved Lares. We wanted to be married, but my father denied us. Imagine if you were unable to marry Aurelius, Valery. Imagine that pain you would feel. It would be horrible."

Valery was looking at her mother in shock. "Positively wretched," she said, squeezing her hand. "But why did Grandfather deny you?"

Lady Wolsingham closed her eyes as she returned to that terrible day. "I've not thought of this in so long," she whispered. "It is so painful to remember, but Lares and I decided we would not obey my father. We fled, with my father and his father in pursuit. Julius dun Tarh and Ralph de Gilsland tracked us all the way to Carlisle Cathedral, but the priest would not marry us. Lares was a passionate man back then, Valery. Passionate and reckless. He told the priest that he would pray to the devil if the priest would not marry us, but unfortunately, our fathers heard his threat. That is why he was sent to an abbey and I was taken away and given over to Adams de Leybourne. Adams had just lost his wife in childbirth and was eager to wed again, so my father paid him an enormous dowry and we were married."

Valery's mouth was hanging open in response to the tragic tale. "Oh… Mama," she gasped. "You and Lares were separated so cruelly?"

Lady Wolsingham had to take a deep breath. "We were," she said. "We were so in love with one another… I surely thought my life was over. I prayed for death. But death did not come. Your father did. And my father never told him about Lares, for obvious reasons. No man wants to marry a woman who has run off with another man. I vowed never to tell him, either, but now Lares is coming to Lydgate and I had to tell someone of my past with him. I feel as if I will burst if I do not. It is a secret too heavy to bear."

Had Valery not loved Aurelius as she did, her mother's story might not have had such an impact. But she did love Aurelius, desperately, and she couldn't imagine being separated from him. She put her arms around her mother and hugged her tightly.

"I'm so sorry, Mama," she murmured. "I'm so sorry you were denied your love."

Lady Wolsingham sighed heavily. "I was denied," she muttered. "It left a wound, one that gradually healed, but I fear Lares' appearance may weaken it."

Valery released her mother, looking the woman in the face.

"It will not weaken," she said. "You will not weaken. You and Papa have had a good marriage, and from what Aurelius has said, his parents have had a good marriage as well. Do… do you love Papa as you loved Lares?"

Lady Wolsingham hesitated for a moment before finally shaking her head. "Nay," she murmured. "Your father is a good man. He has been a good husband. But the kind of love I felt for Lares… That is a love a woman only feels once in her lifetime. He was *my* once in a lifetime."

"Do you still feel it?"

"Nay," she said. "It was part of the wound I spoke of. It healed long ago. It is not meant to be reclaimed, but rather left to memory."

Valery nodded in understanding. "When Lord and Lady Torridon arrive, you will greet them both pleasantly and kindly," she said. "Will you acknowledge that you recognize Lares?"

Lady Wolsingham shrugged. "I think that I should," she said. "But only to him. We knew each other long ago, and that is where our association will stay. There is nothing left of it."

Valery took her mother's hands again, looking at her strained features. She could see how difficult it had been for her mother to tell her the truth, and she was sympathetic. But it also broke her heart to know that her mother had loved so deeply and was denied.

She felt that to her bones.

"Thank you," she said softly. "For telling me the story. I'm very glad you did. And it will stay with me, and only me, forever."

Lady Wolsingham forced a smile, touching her daughter's cheek. "I am glad I told you," she said. "Now, mayhap, you understand a bit of your mother's past. I knew love, a true love, once. And now you know the same. Know how precious it is, Val. What you and Aurelius have is very, very precious. It was not meant to last for Lares and me, but it *will* last for you and Aurelius."

Valery smiled at her mother, knowing that it must have been difficult for her to say such a thing. Somehow, she was seeing her mother through new eyes now—a woman who had been forced into a marriage with a man she didn't love, but a woman who had remained faithful in spite of it. Now, she was greatly in support of her daughter loving the son of the man she couldn't have.

True love took many forms.

This was one of them.

"Thank you, Mama," Valery whispered, leaning forward to kiss her on the cheek. "I will remember that forever."

Lady Wolsingham kissed her only child in return, giving her a squeeze before pulling her off the bed and helping her dress for the day. Guests were arriving, guests who would want to greet the bride, so Lady Wolsingham was determined to make her daughter shine as she had never shone before. She was going to marry a dun Tarh, something that had been denied to Davina de Gilsland long ago.

But it truly didn't matter to Davina.

Valery would be happy, and that was all she was concerned with.

Finally happy.

CHAPTER EIGHTEEN

H E WAS DARK and suave and handsome, with sharp cheekbones and a trim beard. Gaspard de Jordain had ridden escort for the Earl of Teviot from Northwood Castle, a man by the name of John de Longley. John was a pleasant red-haired man who had married well, and he'd had six daughters before finally having a son. The lad was fostering at Bamburgh Castle, but one would have thought he was the Christ child from the way de Longley spoke of him.

And Gaspard listened to it all.

He'd gone to serve de Longley when Sterling St. John had asked Wolsingham to find another position for him. Gaspard had never regretted the reasons behind his dismissal, but he'd regretted being stationed far from the man who was closest to his heart. He'd come to Lydgate hoping to catch a glimpse of Maxwell, but he got much more than that. Maxwell had greeted him at the gate like the long-lost friend he was, reaching out a hand to welcome him but going no further than that. Gaspard was greeted by other soldiers at the gatehouse, men who knew him and liked him, so he felt as if he was coming home in so many ways.

And this evening, he found himself feasting with Maxwell and a few other knights.

It was like a dream come true.

He *was* home.

"Honestly, I never thought I would see the day when Lady Valery would marry," he said to the knights at his end of the table. "I thought she was too good for any man until I met Aurelius dun Tarh. It is a fine match."

The knights at the table just below the dais were from several allied houses, men who had served and fought together for many years. Rhori de Wolfe had returned, representing the House of de Wolfe as a whole, and Welton de Royans had brought the contingent from Bowes Castle. Richmond, which was a royal outpost at this time, had sent Devin de Nerra as a royal representative in the north, while the Earl of Carlisle had brought his premier knight, Alex Summerlin. Grandson of the man Edward I used to call "the Legend," Alex was big and blond and was a master with a broadsword. He'd also served in France and was at the Battle of Crécy. It was, therefore, a tightly knit group that looked to the dais, where Aurelius was seated with a beautiful woman resplendent in amber silk.

"I've never even seen Wolsingham's daughter before," Welton said. "I've fought in many skirmishes for the man, and I've been a guest at Lydgate several times, but I've never seen her."

"He kept her hidden, and for good reason," Gaspard said. "You know he never let his womenfolk near the soldiers or allies."

"True," Welton said, his gaze on the dais. "But seeing her now, I do not blame him. A woman like this is not meant for the masses. She's exquisite."

"Aurelius thinks so," Maxwell said, his eyes twinkling at the happy couple. "I am pleased to say that are mad for one another. It's rare when a betrothal turns out to be a love match."

"Is it truly?" Gaspard said. "I find that astonishing."

Maxwell looked at him. "Why?"

Gaspard shrugged. "Because I know them both," he said. "Do not forget that I served Wolsingham for a few years. Even if Wolsingham wouldn't allow his daughter around his army, he would allow her around the knights, so I know her. She is stubborn, educated, and always, inevitably, correct about any given situation. And so is Aurelius. I would think they would kill one another."

Maxwell grinned. "Untrue," he said. "Aurelius worships her, and I find that quite charming."

"Well," Rhori said, lifting the cup to his lips. "I wish them well. I truly do. Aurelius deserves some happiness."

"He's a worthy man," Alex said. "Where is Darien, by the way? I was hoping to see him."

Maxwell craned his neck back, looking to one of the tables at the base of the dais, across from them. "Over there," he said. "He's with Carlisle. See him? Teviot is with him also."

They could see Darien with the earls, but the younger brothers were nowhere to be found in this gathering of important men. Alex, too, craned his neck to see Darien amongst the warlords, deep into their wine and conversation.

"Ah," Alex finally said. "There he is. Has he been here since the return from France?"

Maxwell nodded. "Aurelius sent some of his foot soldiers back to the Highlands, but kept his brothers here," he said. "He told me that his mother and father are due here in a day or two. Lares dun Tarh is about to make an appearance, lads."

They all knew what that meant. The legendary Highland

earl, the one who probably single-handedly gave the dun Tarh clan most of its mysterious reputation, was due any day. There wasn't one of them who didn't have a healthy respect for the Earl of Torridon, descendant of Romans, supporter of the English wars, and conjurer of demons. So it was said, anyway. It was Devin de Nerra who finally lifted his cup in tribute.

"Lucifer appears," he said. "I've always wanted to see what the devil's spawn looks like."

"He's just a man," Alex said frankly. "I do not give those legends any credence."

Devin looked at him. "You do not believe that Lares dun Tarh is the spawn of the devil?" he said. "You do not believe that he was caught summoning the devil those years ago and then sent to Camerton Abbey in penitence, an abbey that is said to sit upon one of the seven gates of hell? You do not think that is something of a coincidence? That may be your downfall, lad."

The others started chuckling at de Nerra, who was a big man with dark eyes and a brooding manner. He could make anything sound frightening. But Alex shook his head at him.

"I do not believe any of it," he said flatly. "Unless the man walks in here smelling of brimstone and sporting cloven hooves, everything they say about him is rubbish. If you really want to know, ask Aurelius. But that would make him the son of the devil, and you might not like his answer, so be careful if you do."

More laughter as it turned against Devin. He brushed them all off, picking up a pitcher in the center of the table and topping off Alex and Welton's cups. When he came to Rhori, however, he noticed that the man was leaning on the table, his head in his hand.

"What's the matter with you?" he said, pouring more drink

into his cup. "You have been quiet all evening. Do you not believe in the devil's spawn either?"

Rhori grunted. "I do *not*," he said. "But I am weary, I suppose. I do not feel much like eating."

"Then drink," Devin said. "You do not need to eat with such quality drink."

Rhori smiled weakly and took a long drink of wine. Gaspard, sitting next to him, peered more closely at him.

"You were well this morning when we arrived," he said. "But you do not look particularly well now."

Rhori made a face at him. "Always a man with kind words," he said sarcastically. But then he burped loudly and stood up. "I hate to disappoint you, lads, but I think I am going to find my bed. I'm feeling my age tonight."

Gaspard snorted. "You are the youngest one here."

Rhori waved them off, wandering away from the table as the others watched him go. Gaspard's gaze lingered on him before he shook his head and turned back to his drink.

"He ate like a horse this morning when we arrived," he said. But he pushed any lingering concern aside and reached into his purse, pulling forth a silk sack that produced a pair of dice. "Who wants to play a game of Hazard? Let me see your coin."

That wasn't an uncommon game with them, and was a chance to win some money and have a good time, so they began pulling out their purses as the men around them noticed what they were doing and wanted to join in. All but Maxwell. He didn't want to play, and stood up from the table, preparing to make his rounds through the hall. When Gaspard saw this, he handed the dice and control of the game over to Devin, who took it with gusto. As Devin began issuing the rules to those who wanted to play, Gaspard stood up and went to Maxwell before the man could get away from the table.

"Since when do you not play dice?" Gaspard said, a smile on his lips. "I was hoping to win money from you tonight."

Maxwell grinned. "Mayhap later," he said. "I still have duties, even at the feast. Lydgate is my command now, and all of this is my responsibility."

Gaspard's smile faded. "I know," he said. "I heard about your father. I wanted to write to you and tell you how sorry I was, but… I did not. Forgive me."

Maxwell made sure they were a couple of feet apart, nothing too close, nothing suggestive. He reverted to the behavior they'd always had when they served together. Nothing that would suggest they were anything other than friends and colleagues.

Nothing that suggested there was love involved.

"There is nothing to forgive," he said quietly. "He always thought you were a fine knight, Gaspard. In spite of everything, he never spoke ill of you. I hope you know that."

Gaspard nodded. "I would like to think so," he said. "Your father was always kind to me. I admired him."

Maxwell smiled weakly. "And that is a fine thing to be said about any man."

Gaspard smiled in return, but it was brief in case anyone was watching them. "What now?" he said. "I don't suppose…"

"Suppose what?"

Gaspard was hesitant to continue, but he did. "As much as I like Northwood Castle, it is not my home," he said. "Do you think Wolsingham will let me return to Lydgate? With your father gone…"

Maxwell understood what he was trying to say. Without Sterling, there was no longer any reason for Gaspard to stay away. He'd only been sent away because Sterling requested it, and now that barrier was removed.

And Maxwell had been highly aware of that for some time now.

"I have been thinking the same thing," he finally said. "But I fear that asking Wolsingham so soon after my father's death might make it look as if I'm being an opportunist. Let a proper amount of time pass before I bring it up with him. It will seem more respectful that way."

Gaspard nodded, but he was disappointed. "I understand," he said. "I do not wish to be disrespectful to your father's memory."

"I know," Maxwell said. "Nor do I. But it would be good to serve together again."

"Agreed," Gaspard said, but he wouldn't say anything more on that. In fact, he thought it best to change the subject before they ventured into a more sentimental conversation. "How is your mother?"

Maxwell looked to the dais where his mother was sitting with Lady Wolsingham. "I think she would like it if you were to greet her," he said. "She was always very fond of you."

Gaspard looked to the dais too, seeing Lady St. John as she sat quietly next to Lady Wolsingham. Conversation was going on all around her, but she didn't seem to be participating much. She simply sat there, looking quite alone.

"I adore your mother, you know that," Gaspard said. "But she does not look as if she is ready for a great feast so soon after your father's passing."

Maxwell shook his head. "She is not," he said. "She loved my father a great deal. She has taken his death hard."

"Then I will go and speak to her."

"Good," Maxwell said. "And when you are done, you can

join me for my rounds."

Gaspard nodded and took a step in the direction of the dais before pausing. He looked at Maxwell, a hint of warmth in his eyes.

"I have missed you," he muttered. "You are in my thoughts every day, you know."

Maxwell smiled faintly. "As you are in mine."

And with that, they parted. There was nothing more to say, or nothing they should say in a room full of men who didn't understand the love they had for one another. They were friends, and brothers, but more than even that. There was nothing that could separate them permanently—not fathers, nor a society that frowned upon the feelings they harbored. They could have been kept apart for fifty years, but upon seeing one another after those years, it would be as if they'd never been separated.

Bonds like that weren't made to be broken.

Even Valery knew that.

She'd been watching Maxwell and Gaspard from a distance. To the casual observer, they were simply having a conversation, but she knew it was more than a conversation to them. They'd been separated ever since they returned from France, so it surely must have been exciting to see one another again. She only knew how she would feel if she'd been separated from Aurelius for that length of time. Now that she understood what it was to love someone, it made Maxwell and Gaspard's situation all the more tragic.

Sitting next to Aurelius, she slipped her hand into his.

He'd been speaking with Adams and the lord of Bamburgh Castle, Asher Herringthorpe. It had been a lively conversation because Herringthorpe was a lively man, a great orator, and he made men laugh readily. He was also quite handsome, and kept trying to convince Aurelius to surrender Valery. Had he not been so charming about it, and clearly not serious, Aurelius might have had to gut the man, but instead, he laughed right along with him as Valery flushed modestly. But now, with her hand in his, Aurelius turned his attention to her.

"Are ye enjoying yerself, *leannan*?" he asked. "'Tis a lively gathering."

She nodded, cozying up to him. "It seems like a dream," she said. "I've never had a celebration like this, just for me. If it is a dream, may I never wake up."

He grinned. "Nor I," he said. "I'm excited for my da and mam to arrive. I've not seen them in over a year."

"That's a very long time," Valery agreed. Her gaze moved to Darien seated with a pair of earls. "Darien seems to be enjoying himself. But where are the younger brothers?"

"Asleep, I think," Aurelius said. "Darien said they weren't feeling well, so he told them to go to bed."

"All three of them?"

"From what he said."

"How old are those three?"

"Old enough to fight battles and swing swords. Estevan is especially good at it."

"Yet they go to bed when they are told?"

Aurelius chuckled at her. "Of course they do," he said. "They are following orders."

"I suppose," Valery said. Then something down the cluttered table caught her attention. "Look—there's my mother. She's coming this way."

Lady Wolsingham was walking along the dais, behind the diners, heading in her daughter's direction. Aurelius stood up when she came near, reaching out a hand to politely help her as she maneuvered behind the chairs. She took his hand gratefully, smiling at him before turning her focus to her daughter.

"Lady St. John has Gaspard to keep her company," she said. "I am going to retire for the night."

Valery stood up also. "Why?" she said. "The night is still young."

Lady Wolsingham smiled weakly. "I am feeling a little tired this evening," she said. "My belly feels unwell, so I am going to go to bed. But you must stay and make sure our guests are entertained. Will you do that?"

Valery nodded. "Of course," she said. "Are you sure you are well enough to make it to your chamber? Aurelius can escort you."

Lady Wolsingham shot her a long look. "And take him away from you?" she said. "I would not dare. You two remain here, alongside Adams, and ensure that everyone is entertained. I will see you in the morning."

Valery kissed her mother on the cheek and the woman continued on, departing the great hall through the servants' entrance. Aurelius was already sitting down, but Valery remained on her feet, her gaze lingering on the door her mother had just disappeared through.

Aurelius tugged gently on her.

"Sit down," he said. "Would ye like more wine?"

Valery sat, but she was still preoccupied. "You said your younger brothers didn't feel well?" she asked.

He nodded, reaching for the pitcher on the table. "You know how lads are," he said. "They are ill one night and perfectly well in the morning."

"And now my mother feels ill."

"What of it?"

She looked at him. "This morning, Beryl mentioned that some of the servants had been ill," she said. "Do you think there is something contagious around?"

Aurelius shrugged. "That happens all the time in a place like this," he said. "People contract illnesses all the time, but it runs its course."

She conceded the point. "That is true," she said, reaching for her wine. "But I will still look in on my mother later. And you should look in on your brothers."

"If ye wish."

Satisfied, Valery turned to her drink and to the food that had been placed before her—luscious chunks of beef and carrots in a thick gravy that she sopped up with bread that Aurelius cut for her. There were also platters filled with smoked venison and wild pheasant. Tate de Lara joined those at the dais, and between him and Herringthorpe, the conversation was quite lively. Mostly, they discussed politics, but de Lara had several children, and he would always veer the subject back to them, which Valery thought was rather sweet. She wondered if Aurelius would be that kind of father, sitting at a table of warlords and making sure he told them stories about his children.

If they had any.

She certainly hoped they did.

Once her belly was full and she sat back in her chair, satisfied, and Aurelius engaged in conversation with men who were to be his allies, Valery found herself watching Lady St. John, as she and Gaspard were deep in conversation. Gaspard was holding her hand, and it was clear that she was upset, still grieving the loss of her husband, and it was difficult for Valery to not feel some guilt over that. It wasn't as if she'd had a hand in Sterling's death, but that wasn't the point. She had been involved, even if she had been innocent. She found it difficult to look at Lady St. John because all she could see was agony over the death of someone she loved.

Clearly, that was the worst death of all.

It gave her a good deal to think on.

As Valery sat and contemplated life and death, the evening continued flawlessly. Men drank and ate, sang, played games, and generally enjoyed themselves. It was truly an evening to remember, and she was looking forward to the next few evenings with more feasting and more stories. She wanted her betrothal celebration to be something she would remember for the rest of her life as something lovely and exciting, as any young woman would wish for, and it truly was. She went to bed that night with a smile on her face, thinking of Aurelius and how proud and handsome he looked.

The man she was to marry.

As she told him, it all felt like a dream.

By morning, however, that dream had turned into a nightmare.

CHAPTER NINETEEN

"WHO ELSE IS down?"

It was early on the morning after the celebratory feast, a cold morning with mist clinging to the ground and the smell of smoke heavy in the air. The question had come from Aurelius, standing in Adams' solar, and Maxwell had an entire list of people who were suffering the same terrible stomach and bowel issues. It had started the night before with only a few people, so it went mostly unnoticed, but a couple of hours before dawn, it hit many other guests, nobles and soldiers alike, including Lord and Lady Wolsingham. Now, as the sun rose, Lydgate was a castle with a very big problem.

It was clear that something very bad was spreading.

"In addition to Lord and Lady Wolsingham, all four of your brothers are ill," Maxwell said, telling Aurelius what he already knew. "The Earl of Carlisle is showing symptoms, as well as Rhori and Gaspard. There are also countless soldiers who are ill, and about half of Lydgate's servants."

"What of the other knights?"

"De Nerra, de Royans, and Summerlin are all well enough," Maxwell said. "In fact, de Nerra and de Royans departed this morning before dawn. They wanted to get away from whatever is happening, and I cannot say I blame them. Summerlin wants to stay, but de Lara has told him to take the army back to Carlisle for the same reason. He is departing as we speak."

Aurelius had been up most of the night, as had Maxwell, assessing the growing problem. He absorbed Maxwell's report, contemplating the developing situation as he turned to the lancet windows that overlooked the bailey. It was strangely quiet out there this morning, in direct contrast to yesterday morning. Yesterday, the bailey had been full of people preparing for a celebration.

Today, there was tense silence.

"Valery mentioned last night that some servants had been ill over the past few days," he finally said. "She even wondered if something contagious was happening, but I assured her that it was nothing terrible. How wrong I was."

"What do you mean?"

Aurelius sighed wearily. "We found out early this morning that two servants had died and no one bothered to tell Lady Wolsingham," he said. "The servants were so consumed with preparing for the celebration that they were afraid to tell her."

Maxwell nodded faintly, regret in his manner. "I know," he said. "I heard."

Aurelius shook his head with exasperation. "Did ye know that the cook forced some of the sick servants to work in the kitchens?" he said. "Touching the food that went to the guests. That is why we have so many sick right now. That damnable fool of a woman may have condemned us all."

Maxwell knew the old cook. He had for many years. She was a tough old bird, and sickness, to her, was not real. She accused her ill workers of lying and being lazy. He could well understand how the woman forced sick servants back to work, neglecting to tell Lady Wolsingham what was going on because she didn't want to disrupt the celebration.

And now, they were seeing the results of that behavior.

The illness was spreading.

"I am certain the cook is regretting that decision bitterly this morning," Maxwell said. "But the fact of the matter is that we now have many who are down with what some believe to be the blue death. If that is really true, then we have a very big problem, Bear. The blue death *will* kill."

Aurelius hated hearing that, but he had to face facts. With Adams down, he'd been forced to take charge, and he intended to do a damn good job of it. He took to command easily as it was, but now, he had to think bigger. He was no longer commanding a Highland regiment. He was in command of an English castle—a very big English castle that was facing a serious problem.

He had some decisions to make.

"Then we must ensure no one else becomes ill," he finally said. "I would suggest ye tell our remaining guests not to leave. Whatever this is, we dunna want it spreading when they flee home."

"Agreed."

"Tell them to keep to their encampments, not to come into the castle, but not to leave."

"I will."

"Do we have any local physics to call upon?"

Maxwell nodded. "Aye," he said. "There are physics in Willington and Durham."

"What about the physic we took with us to France?"

"Old Myron?" Maxwell said. "If you recall, we picked him

up in London. When we returned home, he went back to London. I could send for him, of course, but it would take weeks."

Aurelius shook his head. "No time," he said. "Send for Willington and Durham. We need someone to tell us what we're facing. We need help."

"I'll send for them immediately."

Aurelius turned away from the window and looked at him. "Valery is tending to her parents," he said quietly. "Wolsingham was quite unwell this morning, but Lady Wolsingham seems to be not as severe. How is Gaspard?"

Maxwell smiled weakly. "He has my mother to tend to him, and he'll want for nothing, I assure you," he said. "But if I may make a suggestion, we should put all of the sick in the great hall, where they can be more easily tended. I do not mean Lord and Lady Wolsingham, of course, but everyone else should be moved. Those of us doing the tending will not be spread so thin if they are all in one place. And someone should be in charge."

Aurelius ran his fingers through his dark hair in a pensive gesture. "I will ask Valery," he said. "She seems the logical choice."

"My thoughts also, but my mother is quite knowledgeable as well."

"Then put her in charge now," Aurelius said, thinking it was a better idea. "I fear that Valery is consumed with her parents at the moment, so yer mother may be better able to organize the sick more quickly."

Maxwell nodded. "I'll go to her now," he said. "Is there anything else?"

Aurelius drew in a long, deep breath. "Aye," he said. "Send for a priest."

Maxwell seemed to sober, thinking he meant for those who might perish. "I will do it right away," he said. "It will be a comfort to those who are feeling… poorly."

Aurelius shook his head. "Nay," he muttered. "Not for that. To marry Valery and me."

Maxwell's brow furrowed. "*Now?*"

"Now," Aurelius confirmed. "We're to be married anyway, and quite honestly, I dunna want to wait any longer. We are facing something potentially deadly, and I want to face it with her as my wife. We will face it together, come what may."

Maxwell understood. Uncertain times were ahead, and Aurelius wanted something he'd been very much looking forward to. He wanted Valery as his wife. He wanted that comfort and confidence.

"Very well," Maxwell said quietly. "I will send for the priest and the physics. Then I will be in the hall, should you need me."

Aurelius nodded. "Thanks to ye, Max," he said. "I appreciate yer help."

"You shall have it."

"How are *ye* feeling?"

"Quite well."

"Good. Off with ye."

Aurelius followed him out of the solar, only he headed for the floors above while Maxwell headed out into the misty morning. The keep was cold and damp at this early hour, and as he mounted the stairs to the third floor, he caught sight of Sela, the servant, as she rushed into Valery's chamber on the second floor. He'd heard that her daughter, Beryl, was one of the sick. By the time he reached the third floor, where Lord and Lady Wolsingham's chamber was, he could hear the soft buzz of conversation coming from their large, comfortable bower.

Making his way to the door, he stood in the opening and knocked softly on the doorjamb.

Lady Wolsingham was wrapped up in a robe, sitting by the fire, while Adams was flat on his back in the enormous, carved bed. Sunny and Moonie were on either side of him, taking up his bed, while Valery was bent over her father, offering him a cup of something. When Aurelius knocked, everyone in the chamber looked to the door and Adams started to wave him over.

"Come!" he said, sounding weak but loud. "Come in, lad. Tell me what is happening. My daughter will not let me get out of bed!"

He sounded agitated, and Aurelius came into the chamber, eyeing Valery, who simply rolled her eyes at her petulant father. But he managed to smile at her as she walked past him.

She pinched him on the arse.

"I've come with a report, m'laird," he said, grunting at her sharp but affectionate pinch. "It seems that several people have come down with the same ailment. Max is sending for physics from Willington and Durham, and we are instructing the guests to stay in their encampment and not leave. We dunna want this spreading."

"Nay," Adams said, pushing the geese aside as he tried to sit up. "This is a terrible, terrible thing. For it to happen at my daughter's celebration is unforgivable. I must apologize to my friends and allies for exposing them to an illness."

Sunny and Moonie didn't take kindly to being shoved around, so they plopped off the bed and waddled underneath it as Aurelius approached the end of the bedframe. Adams looked terribly pale to him, and his lips were bluish, indicative of the severity of whatever had him in its grip.

The man simply didn't look good.

"If ye will allow me to speak to them, I'll do it on yer be-half," Aurelius said. "Carlisle seems to be the only warlord who may have contracted the illness. I'll go and see him this morning."

Adams nodded, but he was weary and listless. "And my men?" he said. "Who has come down with this terrible affliction?"

"About half yer army," Aurelius said. "Max is well, but Gaspard has come down with it. So have all my brothers and Rhori de Wolfe."

Adams looked at him with concern. "Not your dear broth-ers!" he gasped. "Aurelius, I am so sorry, lad. And your father is due soon!"

Aurelius moved closer to the man. "My father thought they would arrive by the end of the week," he said. "That is only in a day or two, so with yer permission, I'd like to ride north. I want to intercept my father before he arrives. Obviously, I dunna want my parents to come down with this illness."

"Of course not," Adams said, waving him onward. "Go. Go now. Tell them not to come."

"And what of the rest of Lydgate?" Lady Wolsingham asked from her position near the heart. "Aurelius, what of the kitchens and the hall? I've given orders to destroy all of the food in the kitchen and to wash everything down. Have they done that yet?"

Aurelius turned to her. "I dunna know, m'lady, but I shall find out," he said. "Maxwell and I have decided to move the sick into the great hall, with yer permission. It will be easier to tend them if they are all together."

Lady Wolsingham was pale this morning, her dark blonde

hair free of its wimple and braided down her back. "A wise decision," she said. "How is Lady St. John?"

"Well, m'lady," he said. "She will help us move the sick into the hall. I will leave Valery here to tend the two of ye."

Lady Wolsingham shook her head and wearily stood up. "I can do that with the help of Sela," she said quietly. Then she looked at her daughter. "You are needed elsewhere, my dear. Take care of our people and our guests. I will tend your father."

Valery frowned. "But you are ill, too," she said. "I must help you."

Lady Wolsingham waved her off. "You can come to me when you have the time," she said. "But I feel your duty is with our friends and allies. They will need your help. You may return to us when you have the time."

Valery was uncertain. She didn't want to leave her parents, but her mother seemed certain that she could handle both herself and her husband, who was appearing increasingly pale. After a moment, Valery looked to Aurelius to see what he thought of her mother's directive, and he simply shrugged.

"If yer mother feels she can tend yer father, then mayhap ye should listen to her," he said softly. "We have many sick and not many to skillfully tend them."

"Like Aurelius' brothers," Lady Wolsingham said. "Go to his brothers, Valery. See what you can do for them."

Valery didn't have much choice with her mother practically pushing her out of the door. She had a damp cloth in her hand, and, with a sigh, she handed it over to her mother.

"Very well," she said. "I will see what I can do. But I am coming back."

Lady Wolsingham nodded patiently. "I know."

"You must rest, too."

"I will, I promise."

"Shall I take Sunny and Moonie with me?"

Lady Wolsingham looked at the pair, now settled under the bed. "Leave them," she said. "If they want to depart, they will."

After that, there wasn't much to say. Valery went over to the doorway and called to Sela, who appeared after a few moments. Her hands were full of rags and other things, and Valery explained that she was to remain in the keep and help her parents. Confident that her mother and father would be well tended, Valery looked to Aurelius.

"Take me to your brothers, then," she said. "I will do what I can for them."

Aurelius smiled, holding out an elbow to her, which she took gratefully. He leaned down, kissing her on the forehead.

"I'm so very sorry that yer celebration has taken such a turn," he murmured, kissing her forehead again. "Ye deserved so much better."

She smiled at him. The man was so sweet to her, always concerned for her. It was something she never knew she was missing in her life, but now it was something she was so very grateful for. It was something that made her know she could never live without him.

"There will be other celebrations," she said. "At the moment, I'm more concerned for my parents and the other people who are ill. Are your brothers terribly bad?"

He shook his head. "I'm not sure," he said. "I dunna think so. Caelus and Kaladin dunna seem to be too terrible, but Darien seems to have been hit worse than the rest."

"Then let us go to them right away."

Aurelius took her to her chamber first so she could collect her cloak against the damp morning. They continued out of the keep and out into the mist, but Valery could feel the change in the air just as Aurelius had. The day before had been full of excitement and celebration, and now everything seemed tense and still. The only sound she could hear were the soldiers on the wall, going about their duties in the murky soup. No chatter, no song.

Just… quiet.

"It seems so… cold out here," she said, taking Aurelius' hand as they headed toward the dun Tarh encampment. "Cold and damp. We should move your brothers into the keep. It will be better for them there."

Aurelius led her through the gate in the wall with the dun Tarh encampment down the incline. "We can move them into the great hall," he said. "There's no need to move them to private chambers."

"They're your brothers," Valery pointed out. "You are the next lord of Lydgate, so they enjoy special privileges. There are two small chambers near the solar on the entry level. We can put them there."

He knew better than to argue with her once her mind was set. "If ye dunna think it would be too much trouble."

"Don't be silly. Of course it will not. I will tend to them myself."

He squeezed her hand as they headed down the slope, finally entering the cluster of dun Tarh tents. It was quiet here, too, with a smoldering cooking fire struggling against the mist. Aurelius took her to a large tent, and before they even entered, they could hear the younger men shouting. Aurelius came through the opening, watching Estevan and Caelus arguing as Kaladin sat up on his pallet and wiped away tears as fast as they would fall.

"What is going on here?" Aurelius demanded. "Kal, why are ye weeping?"

"Because he's sick and hungry and Estevan willna let him eat," Caelus said, frowning. "We want some bread, and he will not let us have anything."

Valery looked at Aurelius, and the two of them passed expressions of both concern and sympathy. Valery turned to the younger brothers, who were really young men. Even the youngest one, Kaladin, was just a year or two younger than she was, but she got the sense that there was some immaturity with them, especially with Aurelius and Darien ordering them around. Even though they'd just come back from a year at battle, they still needed to grow up a little.

"A physic will be coming soon," she said as Kaladin quickly wiped his tears, embarrassed that he'd been caught. "I do not want to give you something to eat that may upset your belly, at least until the physic says so. But I will bring you something to drink. That will help."

Kaladin couldn't even answer her, so ashamed was he, and Caelus simply shrugged. Both of the younger brothers had dark circles around their eyes, and the entire tent smelled of sewage. Valery noticed that their pallets were stained and the place just seemed generally dank and dirty. But she didn't comment, instead moving to Darien, who was on his back as Aurelius stood over him. Valery gazed down at the man, who seemed unusually pale.

"I hear that you're not feeling well," she said. "What are your symptoms?"

Darien let out a long, heavy sigh. "Everything I ate last night has come out of me, one way or the other," he said. "It started early this morning."

Valery put a hand on his forehead. "No fever," she said. "It seems that you have what everyone else has."

"So I've been told."

"We are going to move you and your brothers into the keep," she said, smiling kindly at him. "It will be warmer there, and I can tend to your needs better."

Darien was gazing up at her with big, dark eyes. "*You* will be tending me?"

"Why not?"

Darien didn't seem to have an answer. In fact, he seemed indecisive. "Are… are ye sure ye want to?"

Valery frowned. "Why wouldn't I?" she said. "You are soon to be my family, Darien. Of course I will tend you."

She moved to pull his blanket down, but he grabbed her hand quickly. Valery thought he didn't want her moving his cover, but he simply held her hand still as he looked up at her. There was something working behind those dark eyes on this brother with the white patch of hair at the front of his head. Darien was the firebrand, the destroyer. He was unafraid to do or say what needed to be done or said.

But he appeared anything but unafraid at the moment.

"If I die, I want ye to know something," he said, his voice quiet. "When ye and my brother were first betrothed, I said… I thought… things I shouldna have. I want ye to know… I was wrong, Valery. Ye've been good for my brother. He loves ye, and that must make ye a worthy woman, indeed. I'm sorry said otherwise."

It was the apology he was supposed to have made at the first feast he attended at Lydgate but never had the chance. Valery wasn't aware of that, of course, but she well remembered what she'd heard when her father's army first returned from France.

Perhaps Darien was aware that she'd known, or perhaps he could only really guess at it, but he was an intelligent man. Surely he knew that something would have gotten back to her. Castles with close-knit groups could spread rumors like wildfire. With a twinkle in her eye, she put her free hand on his forehead.

"There is an old saying," she said. "No one rejoices in revenge more than a woman. I should punch you in the nose for everything you have said, but I will not. That is one revenge I would not rejoice in. I think, given the situation, I would have drawn the same conclusions you did. And for a short time, I did. But something unfriendly has turned into something quite friendly. Don't you think so?"

A smile tugged at Darien's pale lips. "I do."

"So do I," Valery said. "And I think we are truly family now, the good and the bad of it. Agreed?"

"Agreed."

With a wink, she removed her hand from his forehead and looked him in the eye. "Now," she said. "Because we're practically family, I'm going to be perfectly honest with you. It might be a good idea for you and your brothers to bathe so that when you come into the keep, you will be more… comfortable."

Darien wasn't following her. "Why?"

"Because ye smell like shite," Aurelius said bluntly. He'd been listening to his brother's apology and Valery's reply with a heart full of joy, but he wouldn't show it. He never wanted Darien to know that *he'd* so easily forgive him, so his manner turned sharp. "All of ye smell like it. This entire tent smells of it. Ye've been living like animals out here, and it shows. Ye're not going to take that smell with ye into the keep, where decent folk live, so get out to the pond and wash off that smell and any shite ye might have on ye. Even if this illness is loosening yer bowels, ye dunna have to wear yer own shite."

He was pointing out toward the pond, which was quite cold this morning. As Darien looked miserable at the mere suggestion, Aurelius went over to his possessions and pulled out a bar of lumpy white soap. He went back to Darien, shoved it into his hand, and then tugged the man into a sitting position. Very slowly, Darien rose, but he was unsteady. Even Valery could see that. She went over to Aurelius and lowered her voice.

"Mayhap you should go and help them bathe," she said. "Darien does not look well at all. You do not want him drowning."

Aurelius shook his head. "Nay, I dunna," he said, looking at Estevan, Caelus, and Kaladin as they picked themselves up slowly. "This whole lot might drown if I'm not there to watch out for them."

Valery patted his arm in agreement. "Go with them," she said. "I will return to the keep and make sure those rooms are prepared for them. And I'll see about having something for them to drink when they arrive. That is important."

He looked at her curiously. "Why?"

She moved for the tent opening to get out of the way of the hunched-over brothers. "Because when I was younger, I had something that caused everything in my body to come out from the top and from the bottom," she said, trying to be discreet as she gestured. "A physic from Auckland told my mother that whenever that sort of thing happens, the liquid in a body must be replaced or the person will suffer greatly. He gave me very salty ale and salty broth to drink, and it helped a great deal. In fact, that's what I was giving my parents—watered, salty ale. That is what I will give your brothers."

He grasped her hand, lifting it for a gentle kiss. "They are very fortunate to have ye to tend them," he said. "I know my mother will be very grateful."

Valery toyed with his fingers. "Are you really going to ride off to find them?"

Aurelius looked at Estevan helping Darien walk. "I am," he said. "I must. But meanwhile, we must take care of this lot."

Valery let go of his hand and stepped out of the tent. "Bring them into the keep once they've washed off," she said. "I shall be ready for them."

He called to her before she could get away. "What about yer mother's instructions about cleaning the kitchen?"

"I will make sure it is done."

With that, she headed off, back into the mist, as Aurelius helped his walking wounded brothers over to the pond, where icy water awaited them. But there was little choice—the illness had them soiled, and Valery wanted them clean before they came into the keep, probably for their own health as well as to reduce the smell, and that was exactly what he would ensure.

As his brothers leapt into the pond, hooting at the shock of the cold water, Aurelius found himself following them in. As he'd told Valery, he wanted to make sure no one drowned and everyone soaped up, but there was also concern there. He'd spent the entire year protecting his younger brothers, making sure no harm befell them, and he wasn't about to relinquish control to an illness that seemed to be taking hold. They may be his annoying brothers, but they were *his*.

And he loved them.

As always, Aurelius dun Tarh would take control.

CB

THE KITCHENS HAD been scoured.

The cook, who was also ill thanks to her bad decisions, was unable to complete Lady Wolsingham's instructions, so the only two kitchen servants remaining had carried them out. All of the bread and meat and vegetables that had been served at the feast had been piled into the kitchen and either burned or buried, and the kitchens themselves had been scrubbed with vinegar made from apples because it was all they had. Floors, tables, pots—everything had been cleaned, rinsed with hot water, and cleaned again.

Valery could smell the vinegar before she entered the kitchen, and when she finally did, the smell was overwhelming. The two women who had done the cleaning were fearful that they hadn't done enough, but Valery assured them that they had done a fine job with it. But the fact that they'd thrown out most of the prepared food meant they had to start from the beginning.

There were sick people to feed.

Valery instructed the two servants to make an enormous pot of broth and another pot of gruel, something she also remembered that the physic from Auckland had given her. The servants, fortunately, knew how to cook, so they took bones and meat from several chickens that had been killed the day before and put those into a pot along with carrots, onions, and garlic. After filling the pot with water, they set it to boiling over the hearth while a second pot was prepared with cracked wheat and water. Valery instructed them to make both concoctions very salty.

The wheels were in motion.

With food being prepared, which was going to take a few hours at the very least, Valery also had the servants prepare boiled water with fruit juice and fruit rind in it, along with breaking out fresh casks of ale, which would be cut with the boiled water. While that was being done, Valery went in search of servants who were still well enough to help her with the beds for Aurelius' brothers. She found three women who were trying to go about their usual duties of sweeping and tending the keep and had them prepare the rooms for the brothers. Satisfied that everything was proceeding as planned, she was headed for the stairs with the intention of checking on her parents when she heard someone call her name.

Maxwell was standing in the keep entry.

"Max?" she said, veering away from the stairs and heading toward him. "Aurelius gave a report to my father a short time ago. I was just going to see to him again. Is there anything new I should tell him?"

Maxwell shook his head. "Nay," he said, his manner bordering on impatient. "Where is Aurelius?"

Valery gestured toward the north. "He is with his brothers," she said. "Why? Is something amiss?"

Maxwell sighed sharply. "Not exactly," he said. "But some of the guests departed against my orders. I was unable to stop them."

Valery frowned. "Why should you stop them?"

"In case they are ill so they do not spread it wherever they go."

"I see," she said. "Do we know if they were ill?"

Maxwell shook his head in disgust. "I think a few were," he said. "Richmond, Bowes, and a few others have already gone, and I knew that, but they had no one that was ill. Bamburgh also departed, and I take no issue with them, but some of the smaller houses with ill soldiers left even after I told them not to.

Northwood and Carlisle are the only ones left."

"What of the physics you have sent for?"

"They will not arrive for some time," Maxwell said. "We will have to do our best until they come."

Valery nodded, seeing that they would be on their own until help arrived. "Not to worry," she said. "The kitchens have been cleaned out of anything that might have made people ill, and I had them prepare broth and gruel for the sick. We can hold fast until the physics arrive, I think."

Maxwell looked at her. The Valery he knew before the advent of Aurelius dun Tarh had been a bright and concerned young lady, but there had almost been something cold about her. Analytical. She had compassion, but it hadn't been readily evident. There was something about finding love that had softened her usually rigid edges. He could see it now.

He could see a grown-up woman before him.

She would make a fine countess someday.

"I think we can hold fast, too," he said, a twinkle in his eye. "I think that you'll make sure of it, no matter what."

Valery caught the twinkle and fought off a grin. This was the Maxwell she'd known all her life, the one so ready to both tease her and praise her. He was the closest thing she'd ever had to a brother.

"I shall do my best," she said. "But I will need your help."

"You have it, my lady," Maxwell said. "You will always have it."

Her smile broke through. "I know," she said. "And we are better for it. Max... I want to say something to you. I want to say that I hope you remain here forever. I know your father and grandfather did, but it never seemed as if your heart was here. If I can convince Papa to let Gaspard return, will you remain forever? I do want you to be happy here."

Her concern touched him. She knew that his situation wasn't easy, that turmoil and loneliness seemed to settle on him more than most. But he also knew that she had always supported him, even when Gaspard was sent away. It had been Valery who went to Sterling to plead for leniency. Sterling hadn't been swayed by her, but at least she had tried. That was something Maxwell would never forget.

"I have never been unhappy here," he said. "I intend to make it my legacy, as my father wished. At least I can do something he wanted me to do."

Valery's smile faded because she knew what he meant. Sterling's ghost had been heavy upon in him the weeks since his father's death. Maxwell had been questioning everything—his life, his loves, his father's wants—so she hesitated to speak openly of it. But she wanted him to know how she felt.

"You can do something for your father by remaining," she said quietly. "But having Gaspard serve with you… That is something for yourself. I am certain Papa will allow him to come back. He has sorely missed Gaspard's sword. He's told me so."

The conversation was turning serious, skirting that subject that no one spoke of. But Maxwell had something to say about it.

"I want you to know something, Valery," he said. "Your father has never been unkind to me when it came to Gaspard. In fact, I know he tried to ease my father's stance on at least one occasion, because I heard him. When my father asked that Gaspard be sent away, I stood outside your father's solar as he told my father that he felt he was being needlessly cruel. Your father is a man with a great capacity to understand."

"Do you know why?" Valery asked softly.

Maxwell shook his head. "Nay," he said. "Why?"

Valery reflected on her father and his younger brother. "Because Papa's only brother had the same preference that you do," she said. "My grandfather's answer was to commit him to an abbey, to save his immortal soul. He became a priest, an Augustinian hermit, so he spent his days in solitude and prayer. No contact with the world and hardly any contact with his fellow monks. My father loved his brother and felt this was a terrible fate for him. That is why my father has been understanding of you and Gaspard. Because of a long-dead uncle I never met."

Maxwell seemed subdued at the revelation. "I did not know," he said. "How very tragic for your uncle. I am sorry for him."

Valery shrugged. "It is not something my father ever speaks of," she said. "Please do not bring it up to him, because it remains a painful thing. But now you know."

Maxwell nodded, pondering the hermit uncle and a lifetime of loneliness. "I suppose that I am fortunate my father did not consign me to the same fate," he said. "In any case, your father's generosity toward me is something I shall never forget. Why would I ever want to serve anyone else?"

Valery put her hand on his arm, squeezing him in encouragement, in support. "I am glad to hear that," she said. "I know that Aurelius thinks very highly of you and Gaspard. You make an elite pair of knights that we are proud to have."

Maxwell smiled, modest though it might be, and removed her hand from his arm. "Stop being so sentimental," he teased. "And do not touch me. Your future husband might see, and he will try to cut me in half."

Valery laughed. "I sincerely doubt that," she said. "But I must see to my parents now, and I'm sure you have tasks to attend to."

Maxwell gestured toward the gatehouse. "I do," he said. "I must send riders out to stop any guests who have not yet reached Lydgate. They must be turned away. I will also wait for the physics and the priest."

"A priest?" Valery said. "That is an excellent suggestion. He will be a comfort for the ill."

Maxwell eyed her strangely, realizing she didn't know that Aurelius had asked for the priest so they could be married. He didn't want to spoil the surprise, so he passed over her comment and pointed to the stairs.

"Go and tell your father that we have things well in hand," he said. "I will send word with the physics arrive."

Nodding, Valery headed up the stairs while Maxwell quit the keep. She hustled her way up three flights of stairs, coming to the landing outside her parents' chamber door just as Sela was emerging. When the old woman saw Valery, she pointed frantically inside the chamber.

"M'lady," she gasped. "You'd better hurry."

Seized with concern, Valery rushed into the chamber only to be confronted with a nightmare.

The day, for her, had just grown exponentially worse.

CHAPTER TWENTY

"**W**HERE ARE WE?"

The question came from a woman riding comfortably on a fat white mare, a mare she'd ridden all the way from the Highlands and into the north of England. Normally, she would have taken the fortified carriage her husband had made for her many years ago when the children were younger and she liked to travel to her family home of Mount Pleasant in the Lowlands of Scotland, but the carriage was very heavy, and with the roads being compromised by the winter season, it would only slow them down to travel in a conveyance like that.

So they were on horseback.

All of them.

Mabel de Waverton dun Tarh wasn't used to riding so much. She hadn't done it in years, but she still managed to make it down from the Highlands and into her beloved England without a hitch. Although the landscape in the Lowlands of Scotland and the landscape of Northern England was the same, the feel was different for her.

She was home.

She'd actually been home for a few days. A brief visit to her home of Wigton Castle had introduced her younger children to her brother, George, who had a wife and four sons who were exactly as he'd been in his youth. Too much money, too much drink—the de Waverton lads had quite the reputation. George told her all about it on the night they'd spent at Wigton. But in the morning, they had to continue south, and it was with sadness that Mabel bade her brother farewell.

Onward they went.

Zora, Cruz, Leandro, and Lucan were the younger siblings that had accompanied their parents south to their eldest brother's wedding. The only dun Tarh sibling who didn't come was Lilliana, because she was already married and had a home of her own. Mabel and Lares were determined to bring their entire brood together for the sake of Aurelius' wedding, a betrothal that Lares had never told his wife of because he honestly wasn't sure it would ever take place, so the missive announcing Aurelius' marriage to the Earl of Wolsingham's daughter had come as a complete surprise.

Mabel had brained her husband with a heavy cushion when she found out.

So, with fifty Highlanders, they headed south. About ten of them were from Aurelius' group, men who had spent a year in France, but men that Aurelius had sent north after the stopover at Lydgate Castle. Lares and Mabel had run into the men heading north, and a small contingent broke off to escort them back south. Since they had already been to Lydgate, they knew the route.

Lares let them lead the way.

Now, they were in a small village north of Lydgate. According to the men who had already been to Lydgate, the castle was about half-day's ride to the south. The village was hardly anything more than cottages and a well, but there was a small tavern on the south end of the main road that provided food and rented chambers. It had a painted pig over the doorway, indicating that it was a public house. They had started traveling before dawn on this day, so Lares called a halt when the tavern came into view.

"Down with ye," Lares said, motioning to his wife and children. "Everyone down. We'll stop here and eat something."

Mabel dismounted stiffly. "You did not answer me," she said. "Where are we?"

Lares took her hand to help her off the saddle. "I'm not certain," he said, looking around. "Some tiny Sassenach village full of tiny Sassenachs."

He said it with disdain, and Mabel struggled not to smile. "You forget that you're married to a Sassenach," she said. "These are my countrymen."

He frowned. "Are ye a Sassenach?" he said, eyeing her. "Ye dinna tell me that before we married."

"Didn't I?" she said, removing her hand from his so she could straighten her traveling dress. "I was certain that I did."

"Ye dinna."

"That is your misfortune."

He tried to kiss her, but she pushed him away by the face. He laughed, as he always did with Mabel. Their entire marriage had been full of such laughter and teasing, and it was something he treasured. He knew that he was a fortunate man.

Running into her in that field all those years ago was the best thing that ever happened.

Off to their right, the children began to gather. Leandro was the eldest of the group, a strong lad who was already taller than his father, with dark blond hair he kept short. He was a natural leader, much like Aurelius, even at his young age. Next to him was Lucan, barely a man, with his long, reddish-blond hair and a quick wit. The youngest son was Cruz, with curly, flaming-red locks and the temperament to match. He was only a couple of years older than Zora, the youngest dun Tarh child at nine years of age. She was a beautiful child with dark hair and was tough as nails.

It was Zora who took charge of the group.

"Are we going inside, Da?" she asked. "I'm hungry."

Lares simply nodded and pointed to the door. Zora, her cloak wrapped around her, charged forward with her brothers in tow. The tavern door opened, and they could hear Zora announcing that she was hungry and demanding they bring her food. Lares shook his head, snorting at the boldness of his youngest child, while Mabel collected herself.

"I shall go in with them," she said. "I could use something to eat as well."

"Go," Lares said. "I'll join ye soon. I want to see the horses watered first."

Mabel acknowledged her husband and followed her children into the tavern, where Zora was making more demands of the tavernkeeper. Lares could still hear her voice, and he grinned because the lass would have made a spectacular warrior had she been born a male. But she was female, though a powerful one. Truth be told, it was going to be difficult to marry her off, because not many husbands would tolerate a lass so bold. Secretly, he hoped she would stay with him forever and spend the rest of her life bossing his men around.

His baby.

"M'laird?"

Lares was addressed by one of the men who had gone to

France. An older man who carried the lines of a hard life on his face, he was nonetheless strong and resilient. He approached Lares as some of the other men collected the horses and began to lead them across the road to the livery on the other side.

"Make sure the horses are properly tended," Lares said, pointing to the herd. "If Lydgate is as close as ye say it is, then we can spend an hour or two here and still make it to the castle by nightfall."

But the soldier shook his head. "Nay, m'laird," he said. "That is what I have come to tell you. I just saw a few soldiers from Lydgate on the edge of town. They're riding out to tell everyone that there is disease at Lydgate. We are not to go to the castle."

Lares' expression darkened. "What do ye mean?" he said. "We've come hundreds of miles for this. I'll not stay away from Aurelius' wedding."

The soldier was firm. "The Lydgate soldiers said that the celebration started last night and by morning, more than half the guests were ill," he said. "He said that some had even died. Ye dunna want to take yer wife and children into a castle that is stricken with a plague, do ye?"

Lares was growing increasingly upset. "God's Bones," he muttered, realizing the news was serious, indeed. "Is it true?"

"It seems to be, m'laird."

"And they've come to tell everyone to stay away?"

"That's what they said, m'laird."

Lares thought on that a moment, understanding that something very bad was at the end of his journey. Frankly, he was shocked.

"Then what does this mean?" he said, though it was a rhetorical question. "What does this mean for the wedding? And my lads… Aurelius is there. So are Darien and Estevan and Caelus and Kaladin. My *sons* are all there. I will *not* stay away."

The old soldier could see that Lares would not be kept away. He knew better than to fight him on it. "Then mayhap only ye should go," he said. "Leave the family here, and ye go and find out what ye can. I'll go with ye."

That was something Lares could agree with. He didn't like the sound of a castle full of sickness, but he liked it even less that five of sons were part of it. No directive, no matter how severe, was going to keep him from his sons.

"I willna go in," he said. "But I will go to the gates. I'll demand to speak with Aurelius. He can tell me what is happening."

"That is wise, m'laird," the soldier said. Then the man eyed the tavern because they were still hearing Zora's voice inside. "Are ye going to tell Lady Torridon what has happened?"

Lares half shrugged, half nodded. "I must, I suppose," he said. "Otherwise, she'll wonder why I'm going to the castle without her."

The soldier nodded. "I'll gather a fresh horse from the livery," he said. "I'll be ready after ye've told Lady Torridon."

There was a sense of urgency in the air, something that hadn't been there before. As the man split off, shouting to a few other soldiers to accompany him, Lares squared his shoulders and headed into the tavern. Truthfully, he felt a little dazed by what he'd just been told. But he had to get to the bottom of what was happening at Lydgate, especially since some of his sons were at the castle. It was confusing and disturbing.

Once inside the dark, low-ceilinged tavern, he spied his family in the corner, by a window. As he approached the table, Zora was telling the tavernkeep that they wanted a lot of food.

Lares grabbed the man by the shoulder and told him to bring enough food to sufficiently fill up four children and one adult. As the man scurried away, happy not to have to listen to a nine-year-old's demands, Lares reached down and grasped Mabel by the elbow.

"I must speak with ye," he said quietly.

Without hesitation, Mabel stood up, admonishing Zora to behave herself, and followed her husband back outside. The mist from the morning had lifted, leaving everything damp, but clouds were beginning to gather overhead. There was rain on the wind.

"I do hope it does not rain until we reach Lydgate," she said, looking up in the sky. Then she looked at her husband. "What did you need to speak on?"

Lares wasn't quite sure how to be tactful, so he simply came out with it. "Lydgate soldiers came into the village," he said. "They told my men that Lydgate has a plague and we are not to go there, but I am going to ride to the gatehouse and demand answers. I want to see my sons. I want to know what is happening. I dunna know how long it will take, so you and the children will plan on staying here for the night. I'll leave ye with my purse so ye'll have enough money for anything ye need, but I *must* go to Lydgate."

Mabel was listening seriously. "Sweet Mary," she muttered. "A plague? And we do not know what kind?"

Lares shook his head. "Nay," he said. "But ye can understand that I dunna want ye and the children going there."

"Of course," Mabel said. "But they may need help. If there are a good deal of sick, I can help."

He held up a hand to stop her. "Let me find out what has happened first," he said. "I'll return as soon as I can."

Mabel nodded quickly. "Aye, you must find out if our sons are safe," she said, trying not to worry. "We've not seen them for over a year and now…"

She trailed off, unable to continue. Lares could see in her eyes that she was fearing the worst, and he put a hand to her shoulder to comfort her.

"We'll see them very soon," he assured her softly. "Now, go back inside and eat with the youngers. I'll return as soon as I know something, I promise."

Mabel nodded, her throat tight with fear as Lares kissed her on the cheek and continued across the street, where his men had a fresh horse saddled for him. There were five of them, all ready to ride with him to Lydgate, and he mounted up quickly before spurring the horse onward, charging down the road that led to Lydgate.

All Mabel could do was stand there and pray.

☙

HE'D SIMPLY STOPPED breathing.

Valery was still coming to grips with the fact that her father had just stopped breathing. His lips and his face had been blue, and no amount of shaking or shouting could force him to take another breath. Adams de Leybourne, Earl of Wolsingham, had died while his daughter pounded on his chest and begged him to breathe.

But he didn't.

It had happened that morning, and several hours later, Valery was faced with her father's empty side of the bed because Aurelius and Maxwell had taken him away, down to the vault, where he would be stored until they decided when to bury him. Lady Wolsingham's illness had worsened, leaving her unable to truly react to her husband's death, while Valery had sobbed.

Her father was dead.

She simply couldn't believe it.

The disease, whatever it was, seemed to be progressing quickly on some and not on others. The Earl of Carlisle seemed to be feeling much better, while Rhori de Wolfe seemed worse. Carlisle and Northwood remained camped around Lydgate, outside of the walls and far enough from the castle.

Watching… waiting for the disease to grow worse or stabilize.

But word had spread that the Earl of Wolsingham had died, which sent a jolt of terror through Lydgate. He'd died shockingly fast, and when the physic from Willington finally arrived, he took one look at Lady Wolsingham and declared that the blue death was indeed upon the castle.

But the physic had come to fight.

At least, they'd thought so.

He was an older man by the name of Lydon who made a point of telling Aurelius and Valery that he had lived in Rome, among other places. He'd only returned to Willington because he'd married a woman who was born there, but Lydon knew of the blue death and was prepared to combat it, he said. Although it was too late for Lord Wolsingham, it wasn't too late for Lady Wolsingham. He promised a distraught Valery that he would do his best.

Unfortunately, she didn't know what that meant until it was too late.

As the afternoon progressed and most of the sick had been moved into the hall, Valery made the mistake of leaving the physic alone with her mother. She was struggling with her grief over her father's death, splitting her time between the dun Tarh brothers, who were holding their own, and men in the hall with the help of Lady St. John. By the time Valery returned to her mother, she was mortified to realize that Lydon was bleeding the woman. Entering the chamber, she could see that Lydon had drained far too much of her mother's blood into a small bowl and Lady Wolsingham was barely conscious. That brought screams from Valery, and those screams brought Aurelius and Maxwell running.

Weeping hysterically as she tried to rouse her mother, Aurelius nearly threw Lydon down the stairs. The physic swore that bleeding the poison was the only cure for what Lady Wolsingham had and insisted that every patient needed to be bled for that very reason. But Aurelius thought the man was mad. He'd seen enough illness and injury, especially in France, to know that bloodletting wasn't the answer. At least, he didn't believe in it. He'd seen it do far more harm than good. He tossed Lydon out into the bailey, where Maxwell finished the job for him and purged the man right through the gatehouse.

Lydon was sent on his way, which left Lydgate with no physic and hundreds ill. As Aurelius and Maxwell stood at the gatehouse, watching Lydon ride off on his small pony, Aurelius caught sight of incoming riders. Thinking that it was perhaps the second physic, he remained in the gatehouse, watching curiously as the party drew closer. Then he realized that one of the riders was very familiar to him.

His father had arrived.

Struck with shock, Aurelius couldn't believe it. He suddenly felt like a five-year-old boy again, and he wanted to dash to his father and feel that big, fatherly hug. He'd had to be the father, for all intents and purposes, when he was in France with his younger brothers, and although he was clearly capable, the fact was that he had a father whom he adored. A man who made the decisions and gave comfort. He'd missed him dreadfully.

It was all he could do to keep from running to the man.

"Da," he muttered, heading toward the first of the double portcullises with Maxwell trailing after him. "Do ye see him? It's my father."

Maxwell had only met Lares dun Tarh once, so he wasn't sure which man, out of the group of Scots wearing long tunics and leather boots, was Aurelius' father.

"He's here?" he said incredulously. "But I sent out riders to prevent guests from arriving. Did he not receive the message?"

Aurelius was at the portcullis, which was down, and the soldiers were securing the man-sized gate that the physic had just passed through.

He began to shout.

"Da!" he cried. "Da, dunna come any closer! Please!"

Lares heard his son's voice, and he was so overcome by the sound that he nearly fell off his horse as he dismounted it.

"Aurelius?" he called. "*Bear!* Ye're alive!"

"Of course I'm alive," Aurelius said. "What made ye think I wouldna be?"

Lares took several steps in the direction of the portcullis. "Because I was told that Lydgate was in the grip of a plague," he said. "Men are dying here, and I thought… I hoped it wasna ye or yer brothers. Where are they?"

"In the keep," Aurelius said, gesturing for the soldiers to unlock the man-sized gate. "They're ill, but they're alive. Where's Mam?"

"I left her back at a village to the north," Lares said. "It had a pig on the sign. I dunna know the name."

"At least she's not here," Aurelius said. "Thank God for

that.”

With that, the gate finally opened and he came through it, about thirty feet from his father. Lares took one look at his eldest son, tall and strong and proud, and put his hand over his heart. The man looked as if he wanted to cry.

“My son,” he whispered tightly. “Ye look fine, lad. So very fine.”

Aurelius had to admit that he had a lump in his throat too. “’Tis good to see ye, Da,” he said. “I’ve missed ye. How’s Mam?”

“Well,” Lares said. “Very well. I left her in a village to the north of here with the younger bairns while I came to discover what is happening here. What can ye tell me?”

The warmth on Aurelius’ face faded. “It started a few days ago,” he said. “Some servants were ill with a stomach ailment, only no one told the lady of Lydgate. Sick servants were forced to work in the kitchens, spreading their disease to the people who came for the celebration. Last night and this morning, many have come down with the illness. The physic says it is the blue death.”

Lares gasped. He couldn’t help it. “My God,” he muttered. “And ye say yer brothers have it?”

Aurelius nodded. “Estevan, Caelus, and Kal have it, but they are not terribly sick,” he said. “But Darien… He’s not well, Da. Not at all.”

“And ye?”

“I’m well, so far.”

Lares was clearly distressed. He looked at the keep soaring over the wall, knowing his sons were in there. They were ill. It was bad enough that he’d been separated from them for a year. Now, he was so close that it hurt his heart to realize he wasn’t going to see them. But thinking of them passing without seeing him, without a parent by their side, didn't sit well with him. He knew what he had to do.

He turned to the men behind him.

"Tell Lady Torridon that I will stay here with my sons," he said. "Four of the five are ill, and I must be with them. Tell her to stay at the tavern and I'll send her word as they improve. But tell her that under no circumstances is she to come to Lydgate. Do ye understand?"

The old soldier who had originally told him about the plague at Lydgate was the one who was receiving the orders. The man didn't seem too keen to return to Lady Torridon with that message, but he understood. Reluctantly, he nodded his head as Lares turned for the gate. He came closer and closer until Aurelius, who didn't know of his father's intentions, put out his hands to stop him.

"Da," he said. "Come no closer. Do ye hear me? Come no—"

Too late. Lares walked right into Aurelius and put his arms around the man, hugging him fiercely. Aurelius resisted for a split second before wrapping his father up in his big arms, returning the hug. After a year of not having seen one another, a year of battles and death and major life changes, it was one of the most satisfying hugs either one of them had ever experienced. It was joy personified.

Aurelius finally loosened his grip.

"Why did ye do that, ye crazy old man?" he demanded affectionately. "I told ye not to come any closer."

"Shut yer yap," Lares said, still holding on to his son. "I would be a poor father indeed if I dinna come to my sons when they needed me. Take me to them."

Aurelius didn't have much choice. His father had him by the arm, pulling him through the man-sized gate in the portcullis. When Lares wanted something, he got it, so Aurelius simply went with him. They continued through the gatehouse and out into the enormous outer bailey that seemed oddly uncrowded. For a castle this size, there should have been a hundred men in the bailey at any given time. Lares could have counted the number of men he saw on both hands.

The castle was barren.

"Before we continue, I should tell ye everything," Aurelius said. "Lord Wolsingham died this morning, and Lady Wolsingham is not doing very well. We may lose her, too, before the day is out."

Lares slowed his pace, glancing at his son. "Forgive me for not asking about anyone else," he said. "I was only concerned with my lads. And yer lady? Valery? How is she?"

"Well," Aurelius said, coming to a halt just shy of the entry to the inner bailey. "I've sent for a priest so we can be married. I dunna want to wait, Da. She's my wife in my heart and in my soul, and I want to make her my wife in the eyes of God. She's a remarkable woman."

Lares peered at him strangely. "Is she?" he said. "Ye… ye care for her, then?"

Aurelius smiled at his father's surprise. "Ye'll be happy to know I willna kill ye because ye brokered a betrothal behind my back," he said. "I more than care for Valery, Da. I love her, with everything I am."

Lares was shocked. "Truly?"

"Truly."

That had Lares bursting into loud, happy laughter. "Praise the saints!" he declared. "I thought for certain we were going to have a go-around about the betrothal, but it seems not. Do ye *really* love her, lad?"

Aurelius laughed softly. "I really do, I swear," he said. "I am going to prove it by marrying her as soon as the priest arrives."

Lares was beside himself with joy. He patted his son on the cheek. "Then I wish ye well," he said. "I wish ye all the happiness in the world."

"Thank ye, Da," Aurelius said, softening at the sight of his overjoyed father. "This is yer doing. I'll forever be grateful."

Lares clapped him on the shoulder. "Ye can thank me by introducing me to her," he said. "Where is she?"

Aurelius sobered dramatically. "With her mother," he said. "We had a physic that tried to bleed the woman, and she's already weak. It's truly a tragedy because she's a wonderful woman. Lady Wolsingham has been my ally since I first came to Lydgate. I dunna know what I would have done without her."

Lares was sympathetic. "That's good to hear," he said. "I'm glad she was kind to ye. I've known Adams for years, but I've never met his wife."

Aurelius gestured toward the keep and started walking again. "I hope ye will," he said. "Her family is from Mount Pleasant, which isn't far from Ashkirk. Mayhap ye know the family—de Gilsland?"

Lares was walking with his son, but he suddenly came to an unsteady halt. He was looking at Aurelius rather strangely. "De Gilsland?" he repeated. "From Mount Pleasant?"

"Aye," Aurelius said. "Do ye know them?"

Lares nodded hesitantly. "I… I do. At least, I did."

"I thought ye might."

"What is Lady Wolsingham's name? Her first name?"

"Davina."

Aurelius thought his father's eyeballs might actually pop from his skull. Lares stared at his son with his mouth hanging open, and Aurelius had no idea why. He looked at his father curiously.

"What's wrong with ye?" he asked.

Lares couldn't seem to speak. He started to, then stopped, then started again, then stopped. He put up a hand as if to beg for patience while he composed himself, but that hand came down on Aurelius' shoulder and he hung his head, looking at his feet.

"Da?" Aurelius said, concerned. "What's wrong? Do ye know her?"

Lares lifted his head. "Did she know ye were my son?" he asked in an oddly hoarse voice.

"She knows. Of course she knows."

"And she never mentioned… me?"

Aurelius shook his head. "Nay," he said. "Why?"

Lares seemed surprised by that answer, but he merely shook his head. "It doesna matter," he said, gesturing to the keep. "I… It doesna matter at all. Take me to yer brothers now, and let's get on with this."

But Aurelius didn't move. "Why did you ask about Lady Wolsingham?" he said. "Why did ye look so strange when I told ye her name? Ye did know her, didn't ye?"

Lares looked at him with an expression Aurelius had never seen before. So… uncertain. There was turmoil there, which was completely unlike his father. The mood between them, which had been full of concern and love, now turned oddly tense as Lares struggled to answer.

It was clear that he wasn't sure how.

"If she's not said anything, I'm not sure I should," he finally said. "Let's leave it at that."

Aurelius dug in. "I will *not* leave it at that," he said firmly.

"I'm not moving until ye tell me how ye know the woman, so ye might as well confess."

Lares wasn't prepared for this. He shuffled and coughed, trying to think of a way to begin the story, but there wasn't any other way *but* the beginning. It was something he'd not thought of in many years, ever since he married Mabel. Frankly, there was no reason for him to think of Davina after he married Mabel, because he loved her. He loved his wife and he wasn't in the habit of betraying her, even by thinking of a past love, so thoughts of Davina de Gilsland had long been pushed out of his mind. He'd never even asked after her to find out if she had married. He assumed she had, given that her father wanted a suitable husband for her, and he evidently found one in Adams de Leybourne. An ally of de Wolfe, who was allied with the dun Tarh clan. That was how they had become allies.

Allies with Davina's husband.

The irony was unfathomable.

"Ye're not to repeat what I tell ye," he finally said, his voice low. "Do ye understand me?"

Aurelius' brow furrowed. "Of course I do," he said. "But why?"

"Because yer mother doesna know," Lares said. "I never told her."

"Told her what?"

"That Davina de Gilsland and I were madly in love, once," he said. "We were so in love that we wanted to be married, but her father denied me, so we fled to Carlisle with the hope of finding a priest who would marry us."

Now it was Aurelius' turn to look shocked. His eyes widened. "Lady Wolsingham?" he said, astonished. "Before my mother?"

"Well before."

"Ye tried to *force* Lady Wolsingham into marriage?"

Lares waved him off. "It wasna like that," he said. "Davina wanted to marry me and I wanted to marry her, but the priests at Carlisle wouldna perform the mass. God… The memories are those I've not entertained in years. Not in many, many years. The love I had for Davina was something I thought I'd never feel again. It was scorching, like the surface of the sun."

The new information was startling to Aurelius, and simply by the expression on his father's face, he could see that it was true. The man's entire face was taut with the strength of a love he'd once known.

It had been something powerful.

"Astonishing," Aurelius finally muttered. "I never knew. Ye never spoke of any woman other than my mother."

Lares lifted his eyebrows. "I'd be a terrible man if I did," he said. "But there *was* a woman before yer mother, one that I loved so much that I was willing to defy her father. I took her to Carlisle Cathedral, and the priests refused to marry us. I knew we would be pursued, so time was critical. Therefore, I did something I shouldna have done."

"What?"

Lares appeared sheepish. "I tried to scare them into compliance by pretending to summon the devil," he said. "That's when yer grandfather and Davina's father found us. Ye wondered where the legend of Lucifer came from? That is where it started. Davina's father spread the rumor about it because of what he saw. He tried to turn men against me, and my father broke the alliance between Ashkirk and Mount Pleasant because of it."

Aurelius' mouth was hanging open in shock. "Are ye serious?" he said. "*That* is how it all came about?"

Lares nodded. "Aye," he said. "I was sent to Camerton Abbey and worked like a horse for two years until I met yer mother, quite by accident. By then, yer grandfather had passed on and I was the new Earl of Torridon. I married yer mother, and I've been happy ever since. There was really no reason to mention Davina de Gilsland, but now…"

Aurelius understood. "Now, Mam is going to meet her," he said. "Hopefully she survives, but if she does, Mam is going to meet her."

"Exactly," Lares said. "And I'm telling ye so ye know the story—that I did know Lady Wolsingham and I loved her. I wanted to marry her. But it was not to be."

Aurelius was a little stunned, to be truthful. He scratched his head, trying to digest everything he'd been told.

"I dunna see any reason for Lady Wolsingham to bring up that she knew ye," he said. "She never even told me that she knew ye, so she may not mention it at all. Mayhap she's forgotten."

Lares shook his head. "Ye dunna forget a man ye were in love with," he said. "Ye dunna forget being dragged out of a church, screaming. Ye dunna forget a love so powerful that ye breathe it and taste it every single day, when even the smallest separation is torture. Nay, she's not forgotten. But the fact she hasn't told ye tells me that she may harbor ill will toward me. Mayhap she grew to hate me."

Aurelius shook his head. "She's a kind woman," he said. "I canna see her hating anyone. Mayhap she simply didn't see any need to tell me. I wonder if Valery knows."

Lares shrugged. "Ye can always ask her."

Aurelius looked up at the keep, knowing the life-and-death struggle going on there, and eventually shook his head. "Nay," he said. "If she knew and wanted to tell me, she would have. We'll let it lie."

"'Tis probably for the best."

"But thank ye for telling me. It explains a good deal."

He was starting to walk again, heading toward the keep entry, and Lares followed. Faustus, the great tree with the great branches, enveloped them in its shadows as the keep entry loomed head.

"Explains what?" Lares wanted to know.

Aurelius' eyes glimmered with mirth. "Why they call ye Lucifer," he said. "Did ye really summon the devil in the middle of a cathedral?"

Lares shrugged. "If ye were denied permission to marry Lady Valery, what would ye do?"

"Anything I had to."

"And that's exactly what I did—*anything*."

Somehow, Aurelius' already-massive respect for his father grew in that moment. A man who was so in love that he had risked his entire life for a woman—two months ago, Aurelius wouldn't have believed it. He wouldn't have related to it. But he did now.

He completely understood.

And he loved him for it.

CHAPTER TWENTY-ONE

"THAT'S WHAT HE told me, Lady Torridon," the old soldier said. "The lads are ill and he is going to stay with them. He said to tell ye to stay away and he'll send word when he can."

Mabel was standing in the entry of the pig-sign tavern, mulling over the old soldier's words. Not that she didn't believe him, because she did, but she was trying to grasp the larger picture. Her older sons were ill and Lares was going to stay with them.

Nay, she didn't like that at all.

"What happened at Lydgate?" she asked. "Do we know more?"

The old soldier nodded. "We know that it had been a servants' disease for a few days," he said. "But those same servants prepared the feast for the celebration and the guests were made ill. The physic thinks it's the blue death."

Mabel knew what that was, and her stomach lurched at the mere thought. "I see," she said fearfully. "And now Lares is exposed to it."

"He wouldna leave his sons, m'lady."

Mabel understood. She simply wished that she had been the

one to go to Lydgate and not her husband. Behind her, in the tavern common room, Zora and Cruz were playing a game that Cruz was winning because Zora was unhappy about it. She could hear her daughter complaining. But it reminded Mabel that her place was here, with her younger children. Lares could do what he could for the older boys.

But her heart was aching for them.

"Very well," she said. "I have a feeling we may be here for some time. Get the men settled in the field next to the livery yard. I will speak to the tavernkeep about long-term accommodations."

"Aye, m'lady."

With her thoughts lingering heavily on her ill sons, Mabel made her way back into the tavern, hunting for the tavernkeep. They were baking bread back in the kitchens, filling the entire tavern with the sharp smell of fresh bread. She finally found the tavernkeeper in a storage room, opening up another barrel of ale, but he stopped hammering when he saw her at the door.

"M'lady?" he asked, wiping the sweat on his forehead with the back of his hand. "Do you need something?"

Mabel nodded. "I have just been informed that we will be remaining here for some time," she said. "Since I have four children with me, it might be better if we were to move to a cottage. A tavern is no place for children to live. Do you know whom I can speak to about finding appropriate housing?"

The tavernkeep cocked his head thoughtfully. "A cottage, you say?" he said, wiping his hands on his apron. "How large?"

Mabel shrugged. "Large enough for me and my four children."

The tavernkeep threw a thumb in the direction of the yard behind the tavern. "I have a cottage myself back there," he said.

"'Tis just me and my daughter, but we can move into the tavern and you and your offspring can take the cottage."

"That is very kind of you," Mabel said. "However, I do not wish to uproot you and your daughter. Is there anything else you might know of?"

The tavernkeep shook his shaggy head. "Nay," he said. "Not in this village. My cottage has four rooms. It was big enough for me and my wife and my four children, but just my daughter and I are left. It would not be any trouble to let it to you."

"You're certain?"

"Verily."

Mabel wasn't going to argue with him because it sounded like an excellent arrangement. "I would also need lodging for my husband's men," she said. "If they could remain encamped in the field next to the livery, I would be grateful."

The tavernkeep nodded. "They can camp there," he said. "The cottage would be a pence a day."

"I will gladly pay it."

"How long will you need it?"

Mabel shook her head. "I do not know," she said honestly. "At least a week or two."

"Then I'll have my daughter sweep it clean and you can stay there tonight."

Mabel thanked the man and paid him for a week in advance. Lares had given her his entire purse when he went to Lydgate, so she had plenty of money. And now, she had a cottage for the children to stay in. She was settled. But God only knew for how long.

All she could do now was wait.

Wait for her sons to live…

Or wait for them to die.

Time would tell.

☙

VALERY HEARD THE soft rapping on the chamber door.

She'd been sitting next to her mother, watching the woman sleep, and daydreaming herself. She kept seeing her father lying on his side of the bed. She kept imagining that she was hearing his voice, but then she'd look around only to be met with silence. Adams had only been there this morning, alive and speaking.

Now, he was lying cold in a vault.

It didn't seem possible.

The rapping on the door had jolted her out of her daze, and she turned to see Lady St. John poking her head into the chamber. When Valery saw who it was, she waved the woman in.

"Come," she said softly. "She is sleeping now."

Lady St. John tiptoed in, peering at Davina as she slept like the dead. An expression of sorrow crossed her features as her gaze fell upon her friend of many years.

"How is she?" she asked.

Valery's gaze moved to her mother. "She seems to be stable," she said. "But she has not drunk anything since last night. She refuses whenever I try."

"Would you like for me to sit with her so that you may rest?" Lady St. John asked, turning her focus to the very tired young woman at her mother's bedside. "I will try to get her to drink when she awakens."

Valery knew the woman meant well, but she shook her head. "Nay," she said. "But thank you. I will stay here in case she needs anything. I've even brought a book to read to her—

The Golden Ass—because, if nothing else, reading that book will rouse her from sheer anger. She very much disapproved of it."

She was smiling weakly as she said it, but being unable to read and having no concept of the story, Cedrica St. John wasn't in on the joke. It didn't matter, however. Cedrica was truly a kind woman, quiet and gentle—in sharp contrast to her husband, who hadn't been either of those things. But their marriage had been a solid one in spite of their differences.

She put a soft hand on Valery's shoulder.

"Then read her the book if it will help at all," she whispered. "If you need me, I will be in the hall."

Valery stood up as the woman moved to quit the chamber and followed her out onto the landing. Quietly, she closed the door behind her and turned to Cedrica.

"I wanted to ask about the situation in the hall," she said, her voice low. "How is Gaspard?"

Cedrica smiled. "He seems to be doing much better," she said. "I think he has only had a brush with this terrible illness. He is able to drink broth and ale without it coming out of him in unsubtle ways."

"That is good," Valery said. "What about the Earl of Carlisle? Or Rhori de Wolfe? Are they better?"

That brought Cedrica some pause. "The earl seems to be doing well," she said. "Rhori is another matter. He cannot take any broth or ale without it coming back up again. He sleeps a great deal."

Valery was saddened to hear it. "Mayhap tomorrow will see a better day for him," she said. "We can hope, anyway. Did the physic from Durham arrive?"

Cedrica nodded. "He did, indeed," she said. "And a priest is here from Durham, also. He is tending to the sick alongside the physic, who commended you on preparing the broth and gruel and ale. He has also brought something with him, something quite foul-smelling, that he is giving to the sick. An ancient recipe, he says, called rotten brew. He claims it helps with almost any illness."

Valery eyed her dubiously. "After the last physic, I am disinclined to let another try something radical on the sick," she said. "Mayhap I should send Aurelius to speak with him."

"There is no need to bother Aurelius," Cedrica said. "But I can assure you that the physic has been giving it to Carlisle, among others, and I do believe they are improving."

Valery still wasn't convinced, but Cedrica seemed to be. In fact, she hadn't seen the woman so engaged or interested in anything since the death of Sterling. It seemed that tending the sick of Lydgate gave her a distraction from her mourning. Valery was glad of it, not only because she had hoped Cedrica's grief would improve, but also because they needed the help. With her own mother down, quality help for the ill was limited. Moreover, Valery was spending her time going back and forth between her mother and Aurelius' brothers, although she hadn't visited the brothers in a few hours because of her mother's deteriorating condition.

"Would you please send the physic up to visit my mother?" she said. "Mayhap she needs some of the brew he's giving the others."

Cedrica nodded. "Of course I shall," she said. "I shall do it right away. Is there anything else you need?"

"Food."

The reply came from the stairwell, and they turned to see Aurelius coming up the stairs. He'd heard Cedrica's question and answered on Valery's behalf. He could see her in the weak light of the landing, that beautiful, spirited woman he'd fallen in love with. She was still beautiful and spirited, but she looked so very tired. She'd lost one parent and was on the precipice of losing another. Aurelius was determined to take care of her even though she was taking care of others. He only knew he couldn't bear it if she became ill also.

"Greetings, Aurelius," Cedrica said politely. "I was just coming to see if Valery needed any assistance."

Aurelius smiled weakly. "You are kind," he said. "I know you have more than your share of work in the great hall, so thank you for taking the time to think of Valery and her mother. I think Valery could use some food, however. I do not know when she has last eaten."

He looked at Valery, who merely shrugged. "Nor do I," she said. "And you? When have *you* last eaten?"

Frankly, Aurelius couldn't answer either. He smiled at her, as exhausted as she was, and reached out to take her hand in a comforting gesture. Meanwhile, Cedrica was looking between the pair, seeing the affection, the concern, and even the sorrow. It was touching to see.

"These are dark and sorrowful days," Cedrica said quietly. "We must all take care of each other now."

"That is true," Aurelius said, squeezing Valery's hand as he turned his attention to Cedrica. "How is Gaspard?"

"I was just telling Valery that he seems much better."

"Praise Christ and his saints. And the others?"

"Most are holding their own or feeling a little better," Cedrica said. But she didn't linger, knowing that Aurelius more than likely wanted to be alone with Valery, so she excused herself. "In fact, I have been gone overlong and I must return. I will send the physic up to see to your mother, Valery."

With that, she scurried back down the darkened stairwell, leaving Valery leaning wearily against the wall as Aurelius lifted her hand and kissed it gently.

"And ye, *leannan*?" he asked softly. "How do ye feel?"

Valery was so tired and grief-stricken that his sweet question had her breaking down into quiet tears. "She only sleeps," she sobbed softly. "She will not eat. She will not speak to me. All she does is sleep, and I do not know what more I can do for her."

Aurelius grunted softly, with great sorrow, and pulled her into his tight embrace. "Ye have been so very brave, lass," he murmured into her hair. "Ye must continue to be brave. Yer mother needs ye. We all need ye."

Valery was overwrought with sorrow and fatigue. "She cannot hear me," she wept. "I do not know if I am doing any good simply sitting with her."

She was collapsing against him, overcome and exhausted, so he swooped down and picked her up, cradling her against his broad chest.

"I'll sit with yer mother," he murmured. "Ye need to rest for a little while or you'll be no good to anyone."

"But I don't want to rest!"

"Ye must."

"I don't want to, and you cannot make me!"

He smiled as she argued with him but made no move to actually push herself from his arms. All she did was wrap her arms around his neck and sob as he carried her down to her bedchamber on the floor below, putting her in her bed and removing her shoes. She continued to protest until he pushed her over onto her side and tucked the coverlet around her tightly. As he did so, he heard soft grunting, and suddenly, he was faced with two geese as they poked their heads over the edge of the mattress. Evidently, they'd been under the bed. Those nosy, intrusive little beasts.

Aurelius never thought he'd be glad to see that pair.

"Look," he told her. "Yer friends are here. They'll stay with ye while ye rest. I'll go sit with yer mother while ye do."

The fat geese were jumping on the bed already. They didn't seem hostile toward Aurelius, simply more interested in lying down next to Valery. One of them plopped down in her face and she had to pull back a little, putting her arm around the big, solid bird. But the appearance of them seemed to calm her down, as Aurelius had hoped, and he was grateful.

"What about your brothers?" Valery asked, no longer weeping but sniffling now. "Someone needs to tend them."

Aurelius knew that if he told her about his father's appearance, she'd want to meet him, so he refrained from telling her. "Not to worry," he told her. "Someone is with them."

"Who?"

"I told ye not to worry," he said, going for the door. "Rest, *leannan*. Close your eyes. I'll come for ye in a while."

She didn't argue. When all was said and done, she was too tired to. The last sighting Aurelius had of Valery was of her closing her eyes as her geese lay on either side of her. Relieved, he shut the door softly and headed back up the stairs to Lady Wolsingham's chamber.

The chamber was dim because the sun was beginning to set, and he found a flint and stone, lighting the taper next to her bed. When he glanced at Lady Wolsingham, he was surprised to see her eyes open. She was looking at him, but her eyes weren't moving. She was just staring into space.

Curiously, he moved closer to the bed.

"Lady Wolsingham?" he said softly. "Can ye hear me?"

She blinked. "I can," she said, so faint he could barely hear her. "I can see you, also. What are you doing here?"

Aurelius pulled up the three-legged stool that Valery had been sitting on, perching his bulk on it. "I forced yer daughter to rest," he said. "She's been awake since last night, and it is starting to wear on her, so I told her I would watch over ye. If ye'd rather have Lady St. John, I can fetch her for ye."

Davina shook her head with as much strength as she could muster. "Nay," she said hoarsely. "You'll do."

He grinned. "I'm glad."

"Aurelius?"

"Aye, m'lady?"

"How are your brothers?"

His smile faded. "The younger three are doing well enough," he said. "Darien is having a more difficult time of it."

Her features tightened. "I am sorry to hear that," she rasped. "You must go to him, then. I will not keep you here."

"He already has someone to sit with him."

"Who?"

Aurelius hesitated, but only briefly. Knowing what he knew about his father and Lady Wolsingham, perhaps it was better if he didn't keep it from her. He honestly saw no reason to. She knew he was Lares dun Tarh's son, yet she'd never said a word about his father. Perhaps he didn't want to let on that he knew what she knew by pretending his father's presence wasn't a secret.

He supposed she'd find out soon enough anyway.

"My father," he said quietly. "He arrived today. He's come to tend my brothers."

Davina didn't react at first, but as his words sank in, her

muddled mind began to realize just what he was saying. She blinked as if startled. Then he saw her breathing quicken.

"Your… your father is here?" she said. "At Lydgate?"

"Aye, m'lady."

"Are your brothers in the keep?"

"They are, in the rooms near the solar."

"Then your father is downstairs."

"He is."

Her breathing was still quick, perhaps a little unsteady now. Aurelius watched her, wondering if she was going to continue the ruse that she didn't know Lares or if she was going to finally admit it. According to his father, he and Davina had shared a deep and abiding love. They had wanted to be married.

Ye dunna forget a love so powerful that ye breathe it and taste it every single day.

Would she admit it? Aurelius found himself hoping she would, hoping she would acknowledge a love his father seemed to think was something special. But perhaps the years had softened her memory of it. Perhaps it had even erased it completely. Aurelius felt as if he was holding back some great and overwhelming secret, but he wasn't going to say anything if she didn't.

Are ye going to tell me that ye knew him? he thought. But all she did was lie there and breathe.

"Does your father know that Adams has passed away?" she finally asked.

"He does," Aurelius said. "He also knows that ye are ill."

"You told him about me?"

"I told him about Davina de Gilsland. He said he knew ye in his youth."

Aurelius didn't know why he had said that. It just came

spilling out. God, he hoped it wouldn't upset her or drive her into a frenzy, or worse. He bit his lip, averting his gaze, as she lay there on the bed and stared at the ceiling. When she finally spoke, it was hardly a whisper.

"Did he tell you everything?" she asked.

"He did, m'lady."

Davina blinked, and tears trickled down her temples. "He remembered," she murmured.

There was pain in those words, like an old and rusty dagger that had been plunged in deep but long forgotten. It didn't hurt as long as no one touched it. But Aurelius had touched it.

He remembered.

Such painful words.

Aurelius reached out, taking her cold and paper-thin hand in his big mitt. "He remembers ye most fondly, m'lady," he said, trying to assure her that there was no animosity. "He told me the story. I wondered why ye dinna tell me ye knew him when you found out I was Lares dun Tarh's son."

There was no strength in her hand as she squeezed his. "What could I say?" she said as more tears ran down her temples. "I suppose I am glad that you know, glad that the secret is out. When I first met you, you looked so much like him that even if you hadn't told me he was your father, I would have known. How could I tell you that your father and I loved one another madly and wanted to be married those many years ago? That would have been a terrible thing to say to a man I had only just met. But those days are in the past, and that is where they belong."

Aurelius put his free hand over hers as he held it. "I under-stand," he said gently. "I suppose it would have been strange to confess something like that to someone you had just met. But my father told me about the priests at Carlisle who wouldna marry ye. He told me about conjuring Lucifer."

"And he paid the price," Davina said hoarsely. "His father took him away, and that was the last I ever saw of him. My last memory of your father was of him being dragged away by his father and his men. He was reaching out for me, calling to me, and there was nothing I could do to help him. My own father had me, taking me home, where he locked me up for following my heart. Truth be told, I never followed it again."

Those were brutal words for Aurelius to hear. He genuinely adored Lady Wolsingham, and to hear her confess that was difficult for him.

"I am sorry ye were separated," he said. "I canna imagine being separated from Valery. I'd rather die than live without her."

Davina turned her head, slowly, to look at him. When their eyes met, he smiled, trying to be of some comfort, and she weakly squeezed his hand again.

"You and Valery are fortunate," she murmured. "Your fathers are not keeping you apart. You are free to marry and live your life and have as many children as God will bless you with. But in seeing the two of you together, I know that my separation from Lares was for a purpose. *This* purpose. It was so you and Valery could be together, so you could go on to do great things together. The truth is that I am honored to sacrifice my happiness so that my daughter can know love—*true* love. That is what you are to her, Aurelius. You are her true love. Had your father and I married, this would have never happened."

Aurelius thought that was about the saddest thing he'd ever heard. A mother so glad to sacrifice her own happiness for the sake of her child. He lifted her hand and kissed it gently, smiling at a woman who seemed to be growing weaker by the moment.

"Then I owe ye everything," he said softly. "I've known many great men in my life, Lady Wolsingham. Great men who accomplished great deeds. But this is the first time I've ever met a hero. You *are* heroic in my eyes, lady."

He was rewarded by a very weak smile. "You are kind," she said. "Ridiculous, but kind. Any parent will tell you what I just did—of a willingness to sacrifice everything for your children. And now… now, I am coming to the end of my life. But I am where I was all those years ago, with Lares in the same building with me. We are about to be separated again."

Aurelius cocked his head curiously. "Separated again?"

Her eyes took on a faint glimmer. "By death," she murmured. "This time, by death. You see, your father was my one true love. Adams was kind, and as my husband, I was fond of him, but Lares was the only man I ever loved. Still, we were never meant to be together. I know that now. But he took my love those years ago and he never gave it back. He has it even now. But I am happy to give it to him because I hope it helped him find a new love with your mother. I hope my love made him eager to receive love again, having experienced it once before."

Aurelius had to admit that he had a lump in his throat. "My mother is a wonderful woman," he said. "I hope you can meet her for yourself. She will want to know you."

Davina closed her eyes and turned her head away. "I wish her all the joy in the world," she whispered. "I love her because she loved Lares. Because she made him happy. But I shall not meet her. Not now."

Aurelius stood up from the stool, leaning over her. "Are you feeling worse, m'lady?" he asked. "Shall I fetch Valery?"

"Nay," she said, her eyes still closed. "Let her rest. When I die, I would die alone. I do not want her here."

When I die, I would die alone.

Those were horrible words, but she stopped talking and drifted off into what Aurelius assumed to be sleep. But perhaps she'd lost consciousness. He didn't really know. But he didn't want a great lady like Lady Wolsingham to die alone. That was the worst thing he could think of.

He had an idea.

❧

"WHAT DO YE mean ye want me to go to her?" Lares said, bewildered. "Go to whom?"

"Lady Wolsingham."

"That's what I thought ye said."

Aurelius was standing just outside the chamber where Darien was sleeping. He'd just come down from Davina's chamber and rapped softly on the door because he knew his father was inside. After several long and impatient moments, at least on Aurelius' behalf, Lares finally opened the panel. Aurelius' hand had shot out and he pulled the man out into the corridor, relaying his request for Lady Wolsingham.

But the request to sit with a dying woman had Lares confused.

"She's upstairs," Aurelius said with quiet urgency. "Will ye not go to her, Da? She's ill. She may be dying. She has no one by her side with Adams gone. Will ye sit with her, at least?"

"Why?"

"Because ye loved her once."

Lares' expression twisted into disbelief. "Nay, I'll not go," he said. "How could ye ask me such a thing? I've not seen the woman in thirty-five years!"

Aurelius took a deep breath, trying to still his sense of urgency because it was clearly upsetting his father. "I just spoke with her," he said. "Da, the things she said… She sounded like ye when ye told me about her. She remembers ye. She said ye took her heart with her, and she hoped it gave ye the strength to love another."

Lares was still frowning. "It was so long ago," he said. "Another lifetime ago."

"Was it truly?"

"Of course it was!"

"She says ye're the only man she's ever loved."

Aurelius had said that on purpose, hoping it would force his father to start thinking more compassionately. But all it did was increase Lares' sense of angst and confusion.

The angst was winning out.

"Well, she's not the only woman *I* ever loved," he said, agitated. "She was the first, I'll admit it. But yer mother was the last."

"I know, but if ye could only come and talk to her," Aurelius said, trying not to plead. "I know it would give her comfort."

Lares looked at him in disbelief. "Ye want me to sit at the bedside of a dying woman?" he said. "Ye want me to betray yer mother like that?"

Aurelius frowned. "That is not what I'm asking at all," he said, pointing to the ceiling where, two floors above, Davina lay. "I'm simply asking ye to show some mercy and sit with a woman ye used to love. To give her some comfort in her last hours."

"I willna do it!"

"She's dying alone!"

Aurelius nearly shouted the words. He'd never shouted at his father in his life, so he had to step back and compose himself. When he spoke again, it was with measured calm.

"I'm not asking ye to sit with her and tell her ye love her," he said. "But I would remind ye that Lady Wolsingham has always been my ally. She is a fine, gentle, kind woman, and I know she wouldna expect ye to be disloyal to my mother. But if ye have even a tiny bit of compassion, if ye even have the smallest bit of fondness for the memory of Davina de Gilsland, then I'm asking ye to go sit with Valery's mother and give her some comfort in the last hours of her life. She remembers ye fondly. I canna believe ye'd disappoint her in her last moments."

Lares was increasingly indecisive as Aurelius tried to persuade him, but the last few words out of his son's mouth had his eyes narrowing.

"Did she ask ye to fetch me?" he demanded.

Aurelius rolled his eyes. "Of course not," he snapped. "The lady can hardly speak as it is. This is my idea."

"And it's a terrible one," Lares said. "Nay, I'll not go. I willna betray yer mother by sitting with another woman. I canna believe ye would ask this of me."

With that, he went back into Darien's chamber and shut the door, leaving Aurelius in the corridor, wondering if he had really asked such an awful thing of his father. Was he really asking the man to betray his mother? Was there really a sense of deception that he wasn't aware of? He thought he was being kind and compassionate by asking his father to be the same to a woman he had loved, long ago. He wanted to do it for Valery as well as for Lady Wolsingham, but evidently, he'd overstepped himself. Or perhaps he hadn't.

But he knew someone who would know.

CHAPTER TWENTY-TWO

THERE WAS KNOCKING on the cottage door. Nay, not knocking.

Pounding.

Someone was pounding on the door.

Clad in her sleeping shift and robe, Mabel left the chamber she'd been sleeping in, taper in hand, and crossed the darkened front room of the cottage to the door. There were windows, but they were shuttered for the night, and she didn't want to open the shutters to see who was out there.

"Mam!" came a voice. "Mam, it's Aurelius! Open the door!"

With a shriek, Mabel flew to the door and unbolted it, throwing it open to see her eldest son standing in the darkness several feet away.

It was like a dream.

"Aurelius!" she gasped. "My dearest boy, is it really you?"

Aurelius was nearly moved to tears by the sight of his beloved mother. He'd just ridden hard from Lydgate, beneath a cloudy sky, with hardly anything more than torches to light the way. He'd brought a few Lydgate soldiers with him, at least those who were well enough, and they'd held the torches up against the dark of night, illuminating the road as the horses headed for the small village that was, in fact, called Castleside. Aurelius had learned that. His father had told him that his mother and siblings were staying in the only tavern in town with a pig above the door, but the tavernkeep told him that his mother was in the cottage behind the tavern.

And that was where he found her.

"Aye, 'tis me," he said, his eyes glistening with unshed tears. "Mam… if I could hug ye, I would, but I dunna dare get any closer. Ye know there's illness at Lydgate."

Mabel wasn't so adept at hiding her feelings. She wiped at the happy tears. "I know," she said. "Your father told me. Why are you here? Please do not tell me something has happened to one of my sons."

Aurelius shook his head. "Nay," he said. "Estevan and Caelus and Kal are doing much better. Darien is, too, I think. Da is with him. He'll take good care of him. But I must speak to ye. I'm sorry to drag ye out of bed."

Knowing that her sons and husband weren't on the edge of death calmed Mabel down tremendously. Stepping out into the darkened yard, she shut the door behind her as she faced her eldest son.

"It must be important," she said. "Please tell me what it is."

Aurelius looked at her. She didn't look any older since the last time he saw her, the first woman he had ever loved. She had instilled so much in him that he valued—a sense of compassion, of empathy, and of humor. His mother had a good deal of humor. She was the rock of their family because no one could do without her. He truly wished he could give her a hug, but that was out of the question.

He was here on a mission.

"I'm going to tell ye something that I shouldna, but I think it's important," he said. "I'm going to tell ye something about Da that he's never told ye."

That had her attention. "And what is that?"

Aurelius knew this was not what his father wanted, but he had a purpose. That purpose was the woman he loved with all his heart and the woman's mother, who would probably not survive the night. He wanted to do something to give Lady Wolsingham some comfort, to give Valery some comfort, but he was doing it at his father's expense.

He only hoped his father would forgive him.

"Many years ago, before Da met you, he… he was in love with another woman," he said. "He wanted to marry her, but her father denied them. He tried to run away with her, but they were caught and Da was sent to an abbey. That's where ye met him."

"Ah… *that*," Mabel said, nodding her head. "You mean his first love."

That wasn't the reaction that Aurelius had expected. In fact, she said it so casually that it completely flummoxed him. "*First love?*" he said in shock. "What do ye mean, his first love?"

Mabel shrugged. "Isn't that what you were referring to?" she said. "The woman he ran off to Carlisle with?"

Aurelius' jaw dropped. "He said ye dinna know!"

Mabel chuckled. "He does not remember that he told me," she said. "He became quite drunk one night, right after we were married, and told me the entire sordid tale. I heard about the devil worship and the lady he loved with all his heart but could not marry. I know about it."

Aurelius clapped a disbelieving hand on his forehead. "God's Bones," he muttered. "Ye seem not to be bothered by it,

I must say."

Mabel pulled her robe more tightly around her body against the icy evening. "It used to bother me, I will admit it," she said. "I was haunted by a faceless lady whom my husband had once loved, but that was so long ago, Aurelius. I have not thought of her in thirty years, and, quite honestly, your father and I have had a wonderful marriage. I doubt he would have had a better marriage with her, and I'm quite certain if she were to return for him tomorrow, he would not go with her. Sometimes I wish he would, but alas, he is devoted to me."

She was jesting with her last sentence, conveying a complete lack of concern where Lares' first love was concerned, but Aurelius wondered if that would hold up after what he had to say.

He took a deep breath.

"Mam, I dunna know how to tell ye all of this, so I'll just come out with it," he said. "Lady Wolsingham is Valery's mother. She contracted the illness that has swept Lydgate, and I believe she is dying. I want ye to know that when I first came to Lydgate to meet Valery, Lady Wolsingham was kind and considerate to me. She was my ally from the start, and I have great admiration for her. Valery is heartbroken to see her mother so ill. Ye know that Lord Wolsingham died this morning, do ye not?"

Mabel was listening with great sympathy. "Nay, I did not know," she said. "Oh, Aurelius... I am so sorry to hear this. Your lady has been through so much."

Aurelius nodded. "I know," he said. "So what I am about to ask ye is for her. I am doing it for my Valery. Mam, Lady Wolsingham *is* Da's first love. We've only found it out by accident. Her name used to be Davina de Gilsland. But with her husband dead, the woman is lying in her bed, dying alone, and that is something she doesna deserve. I've asked Da to sit with her to give her some comfort, as any man of reason and compassion would do, but he refuses. He says he willna betray ye so. But I dunna believe it is betrayal to be kind to a woman he used to love as she lies dying. I believe it is showing a great kindness. If ye think I've asked too much of him, then I beg yer forgiveness. But if ye dunna think I've asked too much, mayhap ye'll send Da a missive and encourage him to sit with her. It seems like so little to ask."

By the time he was finished, Mabel was listening to him with a grim expression on her face. She didn't say anything for a moment, and Aurelius was starting to think that he had, indeed, overstepped himself. It was difficult to tell by the expression on her face, but he knew he didn't like it. He opened his mouth to apologize, but his mother suddenly turned for the cottage door.

"Wait here," she said.

With that, she was gone, and Aurelius was left with the horrible feeling that he'd upset her. He hadn't intended to, but he evidently had his answer to the question of overstepping. Clearly, he was guilty, and now his mother was upset with him.

That had not been his intention.

Since she told him to wait, he knew he'd be in more trouble if he moved, so he stood there in the damp darkness, alone because the men who had ridden escort with him were inside the tavern. He waited patiently, or not so patiently, wondering if she was inside writing a missive to Lares that would accuse Aurelius of terrible suggestions. Of trying to upset their marriage. The latter fear was a foolish one, he knew, but he couldn't help it. He'd upset his mother, and that was the last thing he wanted to do. Just when the wait became excessive, the cottage door opened and Mabel appeared.

She was fully dressed.

Leandro, the eldest of the younger children, was standing in the doorway, grinning at his brother. Aurelius was glad to see the lad, and he waved to him, but he was more distracted by the fact that his mother was completely dressed in a traveling ensemble and cloak.

He looked at her warily.

"Where are ye going?" he asked.

Mabel was pulling on her fine leather gloves. "With you," she said. "I am going back to Lydgate. If you tell me not to come, I will go anyway, so it is best if you simply escort me there."

Aurelius stood there, gaping. "But there is sickness there," he said. "Ye cannot go."

"I *am* going."

"And risk yerself?" Aurelius said in disbelief. "It was bad enough for Da to go, but now ye? Ye canna do it!"

"I can and I will."

She was set. Aurelius could see it. In desperation, he pointed to the cottage. "But what about the youngers?" he said. "Ye canna simply leave them. What will they do without their mother?"

Mabel glanced at Leandro. "Your brother knows what to do," she said. "He is responsible and competent. He knows not to let Zora get out of hand."

Aurelius looked at Leandro, who grinned. "If ye come back and find me tied up with a fire at my feet, then ye know Zora did it," he said. "It's all yer fault, Aurelius."

The young man didn't seem upset by his mother leaving to go into a disease-ridden castle. Aurelius was going to point that out, but there was no reason to. Leandro didn't control their mother any more than he did. Therefore, he simply sighed in exasperation.

There was nothing more he could do.

"I'm sure it is my fault," he said, rolling his eyes. "Everything is, I'm coming to think."

Mabel finished with her gloves. "*Now*, Aurelius," she said. "Take me to Lydgate immediately."

Aurelius didn't argue with her. Much like when Valery gave an order, he didn't question it. He knew when to move.

Beneath a cloudy night sky, they headed to Lydgate.

CHAPTER TWENTY-THREE

D ARIEN SEEMED BETTER.

Lares had given his son salty broth, in small portions, and it seemed to be staying down. Nothing was coming out of the bottom end, either. Darien was sleeping soundly, as were the other lads in the next room. All four of his sons were peaceful, which did Lares' heart good. He had just settled down himself to get a few minutes of sleep when the door to the chamber opened and Aurelius appeared.

"Da," he whispered. "Da, wake up."

Lares had nearly been asleep, but his eyes flew open and he sat up. "What is it?"

Aurelius simply motioned to him. Yawning, Lares staggered out of the bed and out into the corridor beyond. As Aurelius shut the door, he turned to his son to question him again, but as he did so, he caught sight of a figure a few feet away.

Mabel lowered the hood of her cloak.

"Mae!" Lares said. "What are ye doing here?"

Mabel's features were hard as she faced him. "Never mind that," she said. "What is this I hear? You will not give Lady Wolsingham comfort as she lies dying?"

Lares' eyes widened and he looked accusingly at Aurelius, but Mabel clapped her hands softly to get his attention.

"You will not be angry with Aurelius," she snapped quietly. "You will answer me. Why will you not sit with Lady Wolsingham?"

Lares wasn't sure what to say. He was so bloody furious with Aurelius that he wanted to throttle the man, but Aurelius turned away and headed up the stairs, leaving his parents alone in the darkened entry of Lydgate's keep. As Lares watched his son walk away, having no idea what he'd told his mother, Mabel went to her husband and grasped his chin between her thumb and forefinger. She forced him to look at her.

"Listen to me and listen well, Lares dun Tarh," she said in a low voice. "I have come of my own volition. Aurelius is only my escort, so remove all thoughts of anger toward him from your mind. You and I have something to discuss."

Lares looked into those lovely eyes, into the face of a woman who was stronger than the mountains of Scotland. All of them combined. She was an immovable rock, the one constant in his life, the one thing he could not do without. She was demanding answers, and Lares had a suspicion as to the subject.

"Aurelius told ye, did he?" he finally said.

Mabel's eyes narrowed. "He did," he said. "But only of Lady Wolsingham's failing condition. If you think he told me about the fact that she was your first love, that was something you yourself told me in a drunken fit many years ago. I knew you loved someone before me. I knew it was someone you wanted desperately to marry. This was not news to me. Do you understand?"

Lares tried not to appear too stricken by her revelation. "*I told ye?*"

Mabel nodded. "You did," she said. "I know you do not remember and, to be truthful, it was not something I felt the need to bring up. You did not live the life of a priest before I met you, Lares. I would have been worried if you had."

Lares held her eyes a moment longer before averting his gaze, unable to look at her. "I… I'm sorry, Mae," he said remorsefully. "I dinna know. If I told ye, I dunna remember any of it. I'm ashamed."

"Why?" Mabel said. "Because you loved a woman? Did you think you were the only man *I* had ever loved before we met?"

He looked at her sharply. "I wasn't?"

"Bodily, you were," she said. "But I gave my heart to another long ago. Fortunately, he did not take all of it. I had some left to give to you."

He frowned. "Then… ye dinna love me with all yer heart? Ye said ye did."

She snorted softly. "Of course I do, you old goat," she said. "I do not still love the man I fell in love with when I had seen but fourteen summers. That was very long ago. But if I were to see him now and he were in need of me, I would help him. I have nothing more than a fond memory of him. But you… I am concerned why you are so adamant to not see Lady Wolsingham. Is it possible there is still something left for her in your heart and you do not wish to face it?"

He looked at her, wounded. "Of course not," he said softly. "I dinna want to see her because I felt it would be disrespectful to ye. Ye're the only woman in my heart, Mae. What Davina and I shared was youthful passion. What I share with you is deeper than the ocean."

Mabel believed him. Truthfully, she never believed there was any lingering feelings for Lady Wolsingham, but she had to make him reflect upon it, too. He had to look inside himself and figure out why he was so resistant to seeing an old love. Mabel went to him, putting her hands on his broad shoulders.

"Lady Wolsingham taught you how to love," she said quietly. "I will always be grateful to her for that. Aurelius says she is a kind and generous woman. She has lost her husband, and she now lies alone, dying. Because I understand the love she had for you, and because I love you very much, I insist that you go to her, Lares. I want you to go to her and hold her hand and tell her that you remember your love for her. Tell her that it is something you have always cherished. Tell her that you hope she found love, too, and that until she sees her love again, you will stay with her."

Lares was looking at her with sorrow in his eyes. "Ye truly want me to?"

Mabel nodded firmly, forcing a smile. "What you say to her does not matter," she said. "If you see her again and find that the love for her never left you, then I hope you are honest with her. I hope you are honest with yourself. My love for you does not end because of it. My love for you is unconditional."

He shook his head with wonder, cupping her face as he gazed into her eyes. "Ye're a remarkable woman, Lady Torridon," he said. "That ye'd do this for a woman ye've never met is astonishing."

Mabel's smile turned soft. "Keep your time with her private if you wish," she said. "I will not ask you what you said to her or what you were feeling. But I hope you will do the love you once felt for her justice. For the brief and shining hours she remains on this earth, I give you permission to give her all of you, because I think, deep down, that you want to. That does not mean that you love me any less. It only means that you are willing to revisit something that was important to you, once, and I am willing to relinquish your heart for this brief time. Meanwhile, I will be here, tending our sons in your stead, until you are ready to return to me."

Lares simply stared at her. The depths of her compassion and understanding were beyond his comprehension. He was still holding her face when he pulled her to him, kissing her deeply, the way he used to when they were young and full of passion. It was a passion that had calmed over the years, but at this moment, he'd never loved her more.

A woman who was willing to make the ultimate sacrifice.

Without another word, he headed up the stairs.

CB

"WHERE DID YOU go?" Valery asked. "When I came to my mother's room a short time ago, Sela was here with her. She said you had left."

Aurelius entered Lady Wolsingham's vast chamber, going to Valery and kissing her on the top of her head.

"My mother is staying nearby," he said. "I went to see her."

Valery had been prepared to be irritated with him because he'd promised to watch over her mother while she slept, but she couldn't become annoyed with him after hearing why he'd left.

"Is your mother well?" she asked.

He nodded as he went to a nearby table, looking it over for signs of solid food but seeing nothing.

"She is," he said. "Have ye eaten anything? All I see is broth."

Valery shook her head. "Nay," she said. "I'm not hungry."

He looked at her. "I'm going to bring ye food myself," he said. "Ye need to keep up yer strength, and ye canna do that if ye starve yerself."

"I'm not starving," she insisted weakly, leaning forward to wipe her sleeping mother's brow. "You needn't worry over me."

That brought some frustration from him. "Of course I'm going to worry over ye," he said. "Would ye not worry over me if I wasna sleeping or eating?"

She glanced at him sheepishly. "Of course I would, but—"

"No more refusals," he snapped quietly, cutting her off. "I'll bring ye food myself, and ye're going to eat every bite of it."

She frowned. "You cannot force me."

He cocked an eyebrow. "Do ye want to wager money on that?"

For lack of a better response, she stuck her tongue out at him. Fighting off a grin, he pretended to storm over to her and then grabbed her by the head, trying to kiss her mouth and that tongue she'd so recently displayed. Valery resisted him, giggling, trying to pull away from him, but he had her by the face. She was trying desperately to stay quiet because of her mother's condition, but Aurelius ended up picking her up and swinging her across the chamber, all the while kissing her face, head, neck, and anything else he could come into contact with. They were over by the hearth when they heard a soft knock on the chamber door. Still up in Aurelius' arms, Valery put her hand over his face to stop his kisses so she could answer.

"Come," she said.

Aurelius was in the process of setting her on her feet, grinning, when the panel opened. His smile vanished when he saw his father in the doorway.

Immediately, he was concerned.

"Da?" he said. "What's amiss?"

Lares shook his head. "Nothing," he assured him, but his

gaze was on Valery. "But I hope this is yer betrothed. I'd hate to think ye'd kiss another woman with that manner of passion that ye weren't pledged to."

Aurelius' grin was back. "Aye, this is Valery," he said. Taking her by the hand, he led her over in his father's direction. "This is my father, Val. This is Lares dun Tarh."

Valery found herself looking at a man who resembled her future husband very much. Lares was a little shorter, perhaps not so big, but the resemblance was unmistakable. She could see, quite clearly, what her mother saw in him those years ago.

Faintly, she smiled.

"It is an honor to meet you, my lord," she said. "Aurelius has spoken of you so much that I feel as if I already know you."

Lares returned her smile, taking the hand of a truly beautiful young woman. He could see Davina in her face, around the eyes and the shape of her nose. In truth, he could see a young Davina in Valery, and all of that resistance he had about seeing her mother again fled. In Valery, he could see the humanity of what he was about to face.

He could see everything.

"Even if I knew nothing about ye, lass, I would know simply by looking at ye that ye're Davina's daughter," he said quietly. "Yer mother was a beautiful and spirited lass those years ago."

Valery's smile grew. "I know you knew her in your youth," she said. "She told me everything. I... I'm very glad you came."

Lares nodded, vaguely, as his gaze trailed over to the bed where an ashen-faced woman was flat on her back, buried in coverlets.

"Would it be acceptable if I sat with yer mother for a while?" he finally said, looking back to Valery. "She's an old friend, and... and I would be sad if she were to be alone at a time like this. What I mean to say is that I know ye're a great comfort to her, but I'd like to sit with an old friend. If ye'll let me."

That brought Valery to tears. "Of course," she whispered. "She has been asleep for many hours, and, to be truthful, I am not sure she will ever awaken, but if you were to sit with her and talk to her, mayhap it would be enough to rouse her."

Lares felt her burden of sorrow. It was written all over her face, a young woman who had lost one parent this day and faced losing another. Kissing her cheek, he left her by the door as he went over to the bed, gazing down at a woman he once knew very well.

Davina.

It was a poignant moment.

The last time he saw her, she was being taken away by her father. He would never forget that moment as Ralph de Gilsland and a soldier dragged Davina out of the cathedral by both arms. Memories he'd tried so hard to forget swamped him, and he remembered begging his father to bring her back to him. But Julius hadn't been forgiving. He'd been shamed by his son, doubly shamed to catch his son worshipping the devil in the midst of Carlisle Cathedral.

It wasn't a great memory.

But now, before him, lay the very woman who had been taken away from him all those years ago. She looked so small and pale on the bed, swathed in linens that were the same color as her skin. But the truth was that he wasn't exactly sure how he felt now that he was standing over her. Did he feel sad over something that never happened? Over a marriage that never was? Or did he only remember the good things between them, the love and the laughter? Those last moments he'd spent with her came back to him, and he looked around for something to sit on, spying the stool near the bed. Pulling it up, she sat down, his focus never leaving Davina's face.

"Davi?" he said softly. "'Tis me, lass. Lares. Yer daughter has given me permission to sit with ye, if ye'll allow it also. I thought we could speak of the things we both knew from our youth. Of Mount Pleasant and Ashkirk. There aren't many who remember them as they were. It's been a long time since we last spoke, but I hope ye dunna mind."

Davina didn't move. Lares knew it was foolish that he should be disappointed about it, but there was a small part of him that had been hoping she might hear his voice and awaken. He looked over his shoulder, at Valery and Aurelius, both of them standing anxiously, waiting and watching for Davina to open her eyes.

"I'll sit with her a while if ye want to rest," he murmured to Valery. "Yer mother and I have old times to talk over. I'll watch out for her."

Valery sensed he wanted to be alone with her mother. She looked at Aurelius, who nodded his approval. With some reluctance, she headed out of the chamber with Aurelius on her heels. When they were gone, and the door softly shut, Lares returned his attention to Davina.

"They're gone," he said. "I assume they wanted to make sure I wasna going to ravage ye. Considering I've not even ravaged my wife in a few years, I think their fears are unfounded. But I understand. They want to see if ye'll awaken when ye hear my voice. Do ye hear it, lass? Can ye hear me?"

Davina remained still, her breathing shallow but steady. Struggling not to feel defeated, Lares reached out and took her small, cold hand in his.

"My wife told me to come to ye," he said. "Mabel's a fine lady, Davi. I know ye would like her if ye knew her. We've been married many years now, and we've ten children, but ye probably already know that. Aurelius is the eldest. What a fine lad he turned out to be. Yer daughter could not find a finer man anywhere in the world. I'll fight anyone who says otherwise. Ye know who would say otherwise? Yer father. Ralph de Gilsland was a contrary man if I ever knew one. Do ye know how I know this? Because he turned down my suit for ye, and I was going to be an earl. A bloody earl! He told me he wanted someone finer for ye, and now I find out ye married an earl anyway? How can I not be angry with Ralph?"

Lares was on a roll. He went on about Davina's father, the man's sense of honor, and other things that had bothered him. Things he'd not thought about in years. He spoke of his own father, or "the big charlatan," as he called him. Not that Julius had ever really done anything to earn that title, but he had committed his son to an abbey in the middle of nowhere because he thought he'd tried to summon the devil. Lares found that a difficult thing to dispute, given what Julius had seen, but he was disappointed his father hadn't believed his story.

And then came the story of Camerton Abbey.

For that, he had to stand up because his voice was growing louder and his movements more animated. Even though he knew that his father had committed him to Camerton to mostly keep him from Ralph de Gilsland's reach should the man decide to press charges for stealing his daughter, the truth was that Camerton Abbey had been a horrific experience. It had been a place where the priests beat a man for no reason at all. Well, perhaps they *did* have a reason—in Lares' case, because he disputed them or told them what terrible men they were—but still, Lares felt that they were cruel masters when it came to the treatment of those serving the abbey. He told the story of a young pledge who had dropped his bowl of gruel and was punished by not being given a meal for three days in a row. Lares had smuggled the child some bread, and, when he was discovered, one of the priests tried to whip him. But Lares wouldn't stand for the punishment, snatched the whip from the priest, and beat him instead. That had earned him about a month in solitary confinement.

Camerton was a hellish place, indeed.

About two hours into his vigil, Davina had yet to awaken, and Lares stopped talking. He had exhausted every subject he could think of, but he'd long stopped hoping she would open her eyes for him. He'd paced around the chamber, telling his stories as only he could, until he finally stoked the fire and came back to the little stool next to the bed. He sat, watching Davina's face, feeling sorry that they hadn't been able to have a conversation. Perhaps he really had hoped for that, to speak to the woman whom he hoped didn't think he'd failed her those years ago.

"I heard what happened to yer husband," he said quietly. "I knew Adams. He was a good man, a decent man. I saw him at gatherings over the years, never imagining that he was yer husband. The only thing I knew about yer husband was what my father told me—that ye'd been given over to a man who had a home in the south. Yer father wanted ye away from the turmoil of the north… and away from me. I suppose I dunna blame him. No one wants their daughter married to a man who summons the devil."

An ironic smile creased his lips, and he looked away, thinking of Ralph and how resolute the man had been. Given that

Lares had two daughters, he understood Ralph's decision. He understood it the first time Lilliana's suitor came to him to ask for her hand.

"I have two daughters myself," he muttered. Then he chuckled ironically. "My eldest, Lilli, is a sweet lass, but she's got her mother in her. Like steel encased in silk. She married a few years ago. I have grandchildren now. Can ye believe that? And my youngest daughter is also my youngest child. Zora is her name. God help the man that marries her. He's in for a tempest."

"Congratulations."

He barely heard the murmur, but it was unmistakable. His head shot up, and he looked to the bed to see Davina's eyes slowly opening.

"Davina?" he said in surprise, standing up so he could look her in the eye. "It's Lares. Can ye hear me, lass?"

Davina turned her head slightly, and her muddled eyes beheld Lares as he stood next to her bed. He seemed rather anxious to see her. Her gaze drifted over him. He was completely recognizable to her. He simply looked like an older version of himself. A few gray hairs, a few lines, but it was him.

Her eyes took on a glimmer.

"I heard you'd come to Lydgate," she said weakly. "I hoped I would see you. I'm only sorry that it was under these circumstances."

Lares smiled. A truly delighted smile. "Why would ye say that?" he said. "Ye look as he did thirty-five years ago. Still that lovely lass from Mount Pleasant."

That drew a smile from her. "Still that silver-tongued Highlander," she said, watching him laugh. "Has it been so many years?"

He nodded, reaching out to take her hand as he sat on the edge of her bed. "I'm sorry to say that it has," he said. "Things have changed, but not so terribly."

Her hand was so cold in his big, warm mitt, but she squeezed him feebly. "I fear they have indeed changed," she said. "But we meet again in a surprising but joyful way, I should like to think. Our children are getting married."

Lares nodded, caressing her hand as friends sometimes warmly did. "Aurelius is a most fortunate man," he said. "He loves Valery. I can see it in everything about him. He'll be good to her, I promise."

Davina reached up with her other hand, so very weak, and he took it, holding both of her hands between his own. "And she will be good to him," she said. "I will assure you of that. Valery is a good lass, Lares. You needn't worry."

"If she's your daughter, I'll not worry one bit. They are meant for one another."

A ripple of a smile moved across Davina's lips. "And that is why you and I could not marry."

"What do ye mean?"

"I mean that if we had, there would be no Valery and no Aurelius," she said. "Do you remember the day we fled to Carlisle? And we stayed in that terrible inn that smelled of rot?"

He smirked. "And the minstrel who played the terrible song?" he said, remembering that dark day without the sorrow he'd felt in the past. "Ye sang it the next day, over and over."

She came as close to a laugh as she could. "I gave my heart to her," she muttered, repeating the words. "It was never mine to give again. For the love of her, I staked my claim, to be her shadow, evermore."

"That's the one. Ye remember it."

"Because it reminds me of the time when I had hope for the future," she said. "At the time, I hoped the song was about us. But it was not."

He sobered, realizing she remembered the song fondly when he thought it had been stupid. "If I could have sang it to ye, I would have," he said. "And if I did, it would have been meaningly."

Davina nodded faintly. "I know," she said. "But thinking of that song now, mayhap it was about our children. They have a greater purpose than we did, Lares. They are meant to be together, and they are meant to be happy. Their children will go on to do great deeds, mayhap forge great nations. This was always God's will. I see that now."

His eyes, which had been glowing so warmly at her, began to fade. "Do ye?" he asked. "Because I was never certain why God dinna let us marry. I will admit that I cursed him. When I was at Camerton Abbey, I cursed him more. Then I met my Mabel and I began to realize that had been His will all along. I was meant for Mabel. And ye were meant for Adams."

"Nay," Davina said, closing her eyes as a single tear popped from the right one. "Adams and I were not a love match. He was not my heart. But he was a good man, and we had a daughter together, a lass who will carry on the dun Tarh name as I never could. It was her destiny to be a Highlander's wife, not mine. But it was my destiny—nay, my privilege—to know you, Lares. I will always remember you as my one and only love."

Lares squeezed her hands carefully. "What an honor it is," he said, with the warmth back in his eyes. "A true honor that I'd be remembered so. I loved ye once, Davi. I truly did. But my Mabel said something to me that makes a good deal of sense."

"What did she say?"

"She said that she will always be grateful to ye for teaching me how to love," he said. "She's the one who told me to come and sit with ye. To be at your side while ye were ill so you wouldna be alone. She dinna want ye to be alone."

As he watched, Davina's eyes filled with tears that spilled over. "Your Mabel sounds like a most kind and considerate woman," she said. "But I am not alone, truly. I have great memories of you, Lares. That is something I keep with me, always. The truth is that I feel the life draining from me, but I am not afraid. I am not afraid because I know that Valery will be well taken care of, by Aurelius and by you and Mabel. She will have the family that I never had, the dun Tarh name that was denied me. That gives me more comfort than you can ever know."

"I'm glad."

"But I must ask you one thing."

"Anything, Davi."

"In the years to come… mayhap you will tell our grandchildren about me," she whispered. "Tell them about a fiery English lass who believed love could move mountains, because I truly did. Mayhap those mountains did not move for me, but they moved for you. And they will move for Valery and Aurelius."

Lares smiled a brave smile. He could see the woman that Aurelius had spoken of, the one who had been his ally since the beginning. This wasn't like the Davina he'd known those years ago. That Davina hadn't matured yet, but the one before him had, in so many ways.

It was both heartbreaking and wonderful to see.

"I will tell them," he said, his throat tight with emotion. "I will make sure they know ye."

"Adams, too."

"Indeed, I will."

Davina smiled, taking a deep breath, or as deep as she could, before her smile soon faded. "Then I am content," she whispered. "And you will tell Mabel something for me."

"What is that?"

"Although I do not know her, tell her that I love her for sharing you with me when it mattered most," she said. "What a great woman you have married, Lares. I wish I could have known her."

Tears filled Lares' eyes. "I'm a fortunate man, Davi," he said. "I've known two great ladies in my life. I couldna want for more."

Davina's lips curved with a smile, but she didn't have the energy for it. Lares could feel her hands weakening as her strength drained away. Her lips were blue and her breathing was becoming labored. The tears in his eyes spilled over as he realized death was upon the lovely English lass he used to know. Finally, it had come.

"Davi?" he murmured.

"Aye?"

"Would ye like me to hold yer hand until the end?"

"I would."

With tears streaming down his face, Lares leaned over Davina and kissed her on the forehead. It was a final goodbye to the first woman he ever loved, and as he promised, he held her hand, tightly and warmly.

Until the very end.

EPILOGUE

Year of Our Lord 1380
Castle Hydra, Scotland
The Highlands

"WE BURIED DAVINA alongside Adams at the cathedral in Durham," Lares said. "But that was the last death at Lydgate, at least from the disease. Everyone else recovered. Gaspard came to serve with Maxwell at Lydgate, but ye know that because ye've seen them every day since ye were born, as ye've been raised there. The Earl of Carlisle survived and went home, and so did Rhori de Wolfe. Yer Uncle Darien obviously survived. Even Lady St. John went on to marry a widower later in life, and she was very happy with him. And ye know what became of yer mother and father—they were married the same day we buried Davina and Adams."

Gabriela was sitting next to him, sobbing into her kerchief. "Oh, Nonno," she said, sniffing. "That's such a tragic story."

"Aye, it is," he said quietly, putting his arm around her. "But when ye think about it, it was a beautiful story, too."

Gabriela wiped at her eyes. "You always told me what a fine lady Davi was," she said. "You and Mama told us how much she would have loved us. I always felt as if I knew her, but now I know why. You promised her that you would tell us."

"I did, indeed," he said. "And Adams, too."

Gabriela nodded. "Both of them," she said. "Grandparents I never met, but I *know* them. Because of you, I know them. But Mamie… What she did for Davi. That is the most selfless thing I've ever heard."

"Yer Mamie is an extraordinary woman."

"More than I realized."

Lares gave her a squeeze, kissing the top of her head as she wept after that particularly emotional story. It was something he'd never spoken of, not to any of his children or his grandchildren. Mabel knew, and he knew, and Aurelius and Valery knew to a certain extent, but they didn't know everything. No one but him and Davina and Mabel knew what was said inside Davina's bedchamber as she lay dying.

But now, Gabriela knew.

"The point of my story was to tell ye that there are many forms of true love," he said. "A man and his wife, a mother or a father to their children. Even friend to friend, or grandfather to granddaughter. Mamie loved Davi because she had been important to me, once. Davi gave me an experience and a perspective that canna be taught. Davi loved Mamie because she'd been good to me. And I loved them all for different reasons, but the love was strong and true. As ye grow older, ye'll come to understand that true love is different for everyone."

Gabriela wiped away the last of her tears. "Thank you for telling me," she said. "I'm honored that you trusted me enough to tell me the story."

He smiled at his pale-eyed granddaughter. "'Tis our secret."

Gabriela smiled, nodded, and kissed him on the cheek.

Sliding off the seat, she headed off to find her new husband as Lares watched her go. He was so caught up in watching his granddaughter that he failed to see Aurelius coming up beside him. He only realized it when there was a cup of wine shoved in his face and he looked up to see his son offering it.

"Ye're a thousand miles away," Aurelius said. "Ye should be having some of this fine food and drink ye helped pay for. Look at the tables over there—beef and venison and chicken."

Lares took the wine. "But no roast goose," he said. "Ye never let me have any roast goose."

Aurelius waggled his brows. "Ye know Valery willna allow it," he said. "Sunny and Moonie have been dead and gone for many years, but every time she sees a roast goose, she bursts into tears."

Even Lares remembered those geese from years ago, pets that lived well into the first several years of Aurelius and Valery's marriage. But that didn't stop an old man from pouting.

"I miss the taste of goose," he said. "I hope she'll allow it someday."

"Is that what ye were thinking of?"

"What do ye mean?"

"When I walked up, ye were a thousand miles away. What were ye thinking?"

Lares took a sip of his of his wine. It wasn't hot like the other wine he'd drained, but it was good enough. "I was thinking of Lydgate back in the day when ye first met Valery."

Aurelius looked at him curiously. "What brought that about?"

"Because Gabby was telling me what she knew of true love, but I told her what true love really is."

Aurelius wasn't sure what he meant. "What did ye tell her?"

"About the last time I saw Davina."

Now, Aurelius knew. "I've not thought of that in many years," he said quietly. "Gabriela's middle name is Davina, ye know."

"I know."

"She's also wearing Davina's wedding dress today, the one she married Adams in."

"She looks lovely in it."

Aurelius turned to watch his daughter, so young and pretty. He couldn't have been prouder of the woman she'd become, and the truth was that he wasn't even sure, when Valery had been pregnant with her, that Gabriela would know life at all. It had been a difficult pregnancy and a difficult delivery, easily one of the most terrifying times of Aurelius' life. But since they'd been speaking of Davina, the reflection on Gabriela's birth brought about another memory he'd almost forgotten.

"I dunna know if I ever told ye," he said, "but when Val was laboring to bring Gabriela forth, she swore she saw her mother standing at the end of the bed. Val knew just by seeing her that everything would be well. Gabby was born a few moments later."

Lares smiled faintly. "Nay, ye never told me that," he said. "But I can promise ye that Davina *was* there. She was watching over her daughter and granddaughter, like a guardian angel."

Aurelius lifted his cup to his lips, taking a drink. "That is what Val says," he said. "She also said that her mother sang a song to her. Something about 'to be her shadow, evermore.' Keep in mind that the physic had given Val something for the pain at that point, so she was seeing butterflies and rainbows, too. Of course she would see her dead mother. But it gave her comfort to think so."

Those words rang a bell in Lares' head. Off in the distance, he could see Mabel, who had been pulled into a dance by two of her sons. He watched his wife, enjoying herself as the music played, and it occurred to him that he'd heard that phrase—*to be her shadow, evermore*—before. A very long time ago.

At that terrible inn in Carlisle.

A surprising sense of wonder filled him.

"Bear," he said to his son. "Fetch your wife for me, please."

Aurelius wandered off without question. Valery was across the hall, talking to a few of the guests, but Aurelius took her by the hand and led her back over to his father, who was still sitting in the window seat. Resplendent in a yellow silk gown, her blonde hair attractively arranged, Valery smiled when she saw Lares in the window.

"Why are you here?" she said, pointing to the dancing floor. "Your wife is having an enormously good time. You should be with her."

Lares chuckled softly. "She'll have more fun without me," he said. "I've got two left feet, and both of them are clumsy."

Valery extended a hand to him. "Will you dance with me, then?"

Lares took her hand, but only to pull her onto the seat next to him. "Later," he told her. "I want to speak to ye."

"What about?"

Lares pointed in the direction of Gabriela, who had found her exceedingly tall husband and was pulling him into the middle of the room with the rest of the dancers. "Gabriela," he said. "Aurelius tells me that ye believed ye saw yer mother when ye were giving birth to her."

Valery cocked her head, curious at the odd change in subject. "I did," she said. "Why do you ask?"

"He said she sang a song to ye."

Valery nodded. "She did," she said. "At least, I think she did. I had taken a potion for the pain, but I remember hearing pieces of a song. Something about 'to be her shadow, evermore.' Why?"

Lares had to smile. It was an ironic sort of smile, but one he was feeling from the heart. "Did it go something like, 'I gave my heart to her. It was never mine to give again. For the love of her, I staked my claim, to be her shadow, evermore'?"

Valery still wasn't clear. "I am not certain," she said, shrugging. "It was a long time ago. Eighteen years ago. I've never heard that song before."

Lares chuckled. "I have," he said. "The night before Davi and I were separated in Carlisle, we were forced to stay at an inn. It was a slovenly place, full of thieves and half-wits, but there was a minstrel and that was the only song he knew. He played it over and over again. I wouldna have believed that Davi's ghost appeared to ye had ye not mentioned that song, but those words… they mean something to her."

Valery was looking at him with some shock. "They *do*?" she said with awe. "Are you certain?"

"Quite certain, lass."

Valery was speechless for a moment as she processed what he was saying. "Lares, you cannot be serious," she said in a quiet tone, almost like a scolding. "Are you telling me that she really *did* appear to me?"

Lares shrugged. "It's possible," he said. "I thought it was an awful song, but she didn't. She told me the song meant hope to her. She'd hoped it would be a song just for us, but as it happens, she later believed it was a song for ye and Aurelius. A promise for the future, I suppose. Gabriela *is* our future… Isn't she?"

Valery looked to her daughter being twirled around by her husband. Gabriela bore her mother's name, and there were times she looked, and behaved, like Davina. She was even wearing Davina's wedding dress because she wanted to honor a woman she'd never met.

"*To be her shadow, evermore,*" Valery whispered. "Gabby was her first granddaughter. Mayhap she was telling me that she would always be Gabby's shadow."

"Her guardian angel?" Lares asked.

Valery nodded. "Mayhap that is my mother's legacy after all."

"'Tis a nice thought, *leannan,*" Aurelius said, putting a hand on her shoulder. "Lady Wolsingham would have liked that."

Valery smiled at him, but it was tremulous. "I was not emotional about Gabriela in my mother's dress until this moment," she said. "Now, I feel her everywhere. I did not before, but I do now. How proud she must be seeing me and you, and our children, and Lares and Mabel. We're happy. I know that must make her very happy, indeed."

Aurelius kissed her before gently pulling her with him, heading toward the people dancing, including Gabriela as her husband lifted her up above everyone. The crowd cheered as Gabriela shrieked, being frightened of heights. Given she'd married an extremely tall man, there was some irony there. Her brothers began to good-naturedly tease her about it until her husband set her on her feet and turned to the brothers, who understandably fled.

That set everyone to laughing.

Including Lares.

As he watched his older grandsons flee the groom, who was stalking them with good-natured malice, he realized what a rich life he'd had. Seeing Mabel break up the groom's pursuit filled his heart with more joy and love for her than he could possibly have imagined.

He'd been blessed when it came to love.

Perhaps he hadn't married the first woman he'd ever loved, but he'd certainly married the final woman he'd loved, and they'd had a marvelous life together. A woman who had shown him the true meaning of love and sacrifice, an example he'd been proud to pass on to his children and grandchildren. Of course, there was the little promise he'd made Davina those years ago. It was a promise he'd always kept.

Tell them about a fiery English lass who believed love could move mountains.

He had.

And he was a richer man for it.

C03 THE END 80

Aurelius and Valery's children

Alvarez "Al" b. 1350

Benedict "Ben" b. 1353

Cristopher b. 1355

Dominguez "Dom" b. 1358

Eduard b. 1360

Frederic b. 1361

Gabriela b. 1362

Hernando "Nando" b. 1367

Isabel b. 1370

Author's Afterword

I sincerely hope you enjoyed Aurelius and Valery's story, but it turned out to be almost an equal measure of Lares and Davina/Mabel's story, too. I love it when we see generational love stories. It gives the characters and families so much more depth!

So—what is the blue death? Simple—it's cholera. Cholera and dysentery, among other diseases, were very common in Medieval times, and they could spread like wildfire. While dysentery was caused by bacteria in water, cholera was spread by human feces—by unwashed hands and bad sanitation, among others.

Because it caused terrible diarrhea and—not to get too graphic—it was difficult to sanitize against those bodily fluids properly, it could really get around. It made for a terrible combination with a big gathering of people because it had a fairly short incubation period. Cholera outbreaks were very feared, and it was called the blue death because people tended to turn bluish when they were extremely dehydrated. If you've ever seen *Downton Abbey*, the dowager countess commented once about a ball held in Paris where Cholera broke out. As she said, "Half the guests were dead before they left."

Also, as you noticed, "rotten brew" or "rotten tea" once again made it into a book. That really was a "thing"—surgeons and physics in the Middle East had figured out its healing properties and used it for wounds and illnesses. Basically, it was an antibiotic, made from the blue mold on bread—and other things—so that was definitely something in use during Medieval times. How often, or by whom, or how they really brewed it, is a mystery, but the knowledge was there. Treatment for cholera is, in fact, antibiotics.

Lastly—and this is a fun fact—you've heard the story *The Golden Ass* mentioned a couple of times in this book. It is by a Roman author named Apuelius, and it really is a tale of a man named Lucius who is turned into an ass by an evil witch. The tale itself is full of adultery and scandal and—dare I say it—bestiality, when a maiden falls in love with the ass (not knowing it's really a man) and seduces the animal. The Romans has some truly *ahem* unusual and wild pieces of literature. And yes, you can buy *The Golden Ass* on Amazon. No kidding!

I hope this is a great kick-off for the dun Tarh family—with so many more stories to come.

Thank you for reading!

Kathryn Le Veque Novels

Medieval Romance:

De Wolfe Pack Series:
Warwolfe
The Wolfe
Nighthawk
ShadowWolfe
DarkWolfe
A Joyous de Wolfe Christmas
BlackWolfe
Serpent
A Wolfe Among Dragons
Scorpion
StormWolfe
Dark Destroyer
The Lion of the North
Walls of Babylon
The Best Is Yet To Be
BattleWolfe
Castle of Bones

De Wolfe Pack Generations:
WolfeHeart
WolfeStrike
WolfeSword
WolfeBlade
WolfeLord
WolfeShield
Nevermore
WolfeAx
WolfeBorn

The Executioner Knights:
By the Unholy Hand
The Mountain Dark
Starless
A Time of End
Winter of Solace
Lord of the Sky
The Splendid Hour
The Whispering Night
Netherworld
Lord of the Shadows
Of Mortal Fury
'Twas the Executioner Knight
Before Christmas
Crimson Shield

The de Russe Legacy:
The Falls of Erith
Lord of War: Black Angel
The Iron Knight
Beast
The Dark One: Dark Knight
The White Lord of Wellesbourne
Dark Moon
Dark Steel
A de Russe Christmas Miracle
Dark Warrior

The de Lohr Dynasty:
While Angels Slept
Rise of the Defender
Steelheart
Shadowmoor
Silversword
Spectre of the Sword

Unending Love
Archangel
A Blessed de Lohr Christmas
Lion of Twilight
Lion of War
Lion of Hearts

The Brothers de Lohr:
The Earl in Winter

Lords of East Anglia:
While Angels Slept
Godspeed
Age of Gods and Mortals

Great Lords of le Bec:
Great Protector

House of de Royans:
Lord of Winter
To the Lady Born
The Centurion

Lords of Eire:
Echoes of Ancient Dreams
Lord of Black Castle
The Darkland

Ancient Kings of Anglecynn:
The Whispering Night
Netherworld

Battle Lords of de Velt:
The Dark Lord
Devil's Dominion
Bay of Fear
The Dark Lord's First Christmas
The Dark Spawn
The Dark Conqueror
The Dark Angel

Reign of the House of de Winter:
Lespada
Swords and Shields

De Reyne Domination:
Guardian of Darkness
The Black Storm
A Cold Wynter's Knight
With Dreams
Master of the Dawn

House of d'Vant:
Tender is the Knight (House of d'Vant)
The Red Fury (House of d'Vant)

The Dragonblade Series:
Fragments of Grace
Dragonblade
Island of Glass
The Savage Curtain
The Fallen One
The Phantom Bride

Great Marcher Lords of de Lara
Dragonblade

House of St. Hever
Fragments of Grace
Island of Glass
Queen of Lost Stars

Lords of Pembury:
The Savage Curtain

Lords of Thunder: The de Shera Brotherhood Trilogy
The Thunder Lord
The Thunder Warrior
The Thunder Knight

The Great Knights of de Moray:
Shield of Kronos
The Gorgon

The House of De Nerra:
The Promise
The Falls of Erith
Vestiges of Valor
Realm of Angels

Highland Legion:
Highland Born

Highland Warriors of Munro:
The Red Lion
Deep Into Darkness

The House of de Garr:
Lord of Light
Realm of Angels

Saxon Lords of Hage:
The Crusader
Kingdom Come

High Warriors of Rohan:
High Warrior
High King

The House of Ashbourne:
Upon a Midnight Dream

The House of D'Aurilliac:
Valiant Chaos

The House of De Dere:
Of Love and Legend

St. John and de Gare Clans:
The Warrior Poet

The House of de Bretagne:

The Questing

The House of Summerlin:
The Legend

The Kingdom of Hendocia:
Kingdom by the Sea

The BlackChurch Guild: Shadow Knights:
The Leviathan
The Protector

Regency Historical Romance:
Sin Like Flynn: A Regency
Historical Romance Duet
The Sin Commandments
Georgina and the Red Charger

Gothic Regency Romance:
Emma

Contemporary Romance:

Kathlyn Trent/Marcus Burton Series:
Valley of the Shadow
The Eden Factor
Canyon of the Sphinx

The American Heroes Anthology Series:
The Lucius Robe
Fires of Autumn
Evenshade
Sea of Dreams
Purgatory

Other non-connected Contemporary Romance:
Lady of Heaven
Darkling, I Listen

In the Dreaming Hour
River's End
The Fountain

Sons of Poseidon:
The Immortal Sea

Pirates of Britannia Series (with

Eliza Knight):
Savage of the Sea by Eliza Knight
Leader of Titans by Kathryn Le Veque
The Sea Devil by Eliza Knight
Sea Wolfe by Kathryn Le Veque

Note: All Kathryn's novels are designed to be read as stand-alones, although many have cross-over characters or cross-over family groups. Novels that are grouped together have related characters or family groups. You will notice that some series have the same books; that is because they are cross-overs. A hero in one book may be the secondary character in another.

There is NO reading order except by chronology, but even in that case, you can still read the books as stand-alones. No novel is connected to another by a cliff hanger, and every book has an HEA.

Series are clearly marked. All series contain the same characters or family groups except the American Heroes Series, which is an anthology with unrelated characters.

For more information, find it in **A Reader's Guide to the Medieval World of Le Veque.**

ABOUT KATHRYN LE VEQUE

Bringing the Medieval to Romance

KATHRYN LE VEQUE is a critically acclaimed, multiple USA TODAY Bestselling author, an Indie Reader bestseller, a charter Amazon All-Star author, and a #1 bestselling, award-winning, multi-published author in Medieval Historical Romance with over 100 published novels.

Kathryn is a multiple award nominee and winner, including the winner of Uncaged Book Reviews Magazine 2017 and 2018 "Raven Award" for Favorite Medieval Romance. Kathryn is also a multiple RONE nominee (InD'Tale Magazine), holding a record for the number of nominations. In 2018, her novel WARWOLFE was the winner in the Romance category of the Book Excellence Award and in 2019, her novel A WOLFE AMONG DRAGONS won the prestigious RONE award for best pre-16th century romance.

Kathryn is considered one of the top Indie authors in the world with over 2M copies in circulation, and her novels have been translated into several languages. Kathryn recently signed with Sourcebooks Casablanca for a Medieval Fight Club series, first published in 2020.

In addition to her own published works, Kathryn is also the President/CEO of Dragonblade Publishing, a boutique publishing house specializing in Historical Romance. Dragonblade's success has seen it rise in the ranks to become Amazon's #1 e-book publisher of Historical Romance (K-Lytics report July 2020).

Kathryn loves to hear from her readers. Please find Kathryn on Facebook at Kathryn Le Veque, Author, or join her on Twitter @kathrynleveque. Sign up for Kathryn's blog at www.kathrynleveque.com for the latest news and sales.

9 781961 275799